Twinkies & Beefcake

I0700565

T. H. FOREST

HP Copyright © 2023 by Holdorf Press, LLC
www.fountainoffiction.com

Cover illustration: Sigrid Silberman

Paperback ISBN: 979-8-9870330-0-5
Hardcover ISBN: 979-8-9870330-1-2
eBook ISBN: 979-8-9870330-2-9

This is a work of fiction. It is not an actual autobiography. Unless otherwise indicated, all the names, characters, businesses, places, events and incidents in this book are either the product of the author's imagination or used in a fictitious manner. Any resemblance to persons living or dead is purely coincidental. The (often egregious) opinions expressed are those of the characters and should not be confused with the author's.

All rights reserved. No part of this publication may be reproduced or transmitted in any form or by any means, electronic or mechanical, including photocopy, recording, or any information storage and retrieval systems, without permission in writing from the copyright holder.

Printed in the United States of America.

For my late cousin, Tom Holdorf,
the mega-talented photographer
mentioned in the book.

I miss you every day,
nearly thirty years on.

CONTENTS

Contents

PART TWO

CHRYSALIS

Contents

PART THREE

BUTTERFLY

PROLOGUE

IF YOU'VE COME TO HEAR an original story, something unique and other-worldly, something gripping and far-fetched, then let me tell you to walk away now, save us both the disappointment. I mean, who hasn't been convinced as a teenager, by their much older boyfriend, to do porn? To call him daddy as he plowed you a hundred different ways on camera? Who hasn't put up with physical and emotional abuse for years, off-camera usually, and love, nearly, every minute of it? Who hasn't loved someone so wicked, given every bit of themselves to that person, only to be dumped like a used condom for a skinnier, shorter, more submissive twink?

Honestly, it's more likely that you'll walk away because you've heard me tell it already. After Vasyl (that fucker), dumped me, I told anyone who would listen about my pain. My therapist, my sponsor, my friends, my fans (oh I had such glorious fans, the best fans), and everyone else I would encounter, on The Tube, at the drug treatment centers, my fellow AA compadres, and the bartenders, please, we can't forget the bartenders. Bartenders are the unsung heroes of the mental health industry, and there's not one in the whole of the UK that didn't cringe when they saw me coming. I was pathetic. He ruined me, for years, his reach into my life extending far greater than you could imagine, or maybe you can, since I *clearly* can't stop thinking of him, here I am boring you about him all over again, nearly twenty years on.

Everyone listened so sympathetically at first, my best friend Dee especially. She would cradle my head in her soft, ample lap and brush the hair from my face as I sobbed, day after day, and then eventually just on weekends, until finally, after nearly a year, bless her heart, she cut me loose like a boat from a mooring, and off I drifted. She tried everything with me, taking me out, encouraging me, coming to open AA meetings with me, and things would be okay for a day or a week, and then I'd accidentally come across a hot-off-the-press video Vas made with his new twink (and by accidently I mean I would actively seek it out like picking a scab), and I would cry hot tears, my chest burning, as though Satan himself had reached into my ribcage with his fiery hand. My mum, my glorious, beautiful, perfect mum, would be there to pick up the pieces each time. She rubbed my back, did my laundry, paid my bills, but I digress, if you've made it this far I should really stay on topic so I don't lose you too.

I heard just the other month that Vassy died recently. I curled up in a ball, like a discarded wrapper, for nearly a week at that news. How could he have died without me feeling it like losing a limb? I missed his death, missed his funeral, missed my closure. My husband, the *saint*, tried everything he could to get me out of my funk, but I just needed time. He's the one who suggested I write my story down. Perhaps he hoped that by doing so, it would release me from Vas's grip, and I hoped so too. That by making my story a physical entity, and not just something I sang to the wind and to whatever ear would listen, I could shed him like an over coat or a hair shirt. My only fear, is that people might get the wrong idea, and maybe see me as the villain, but please, remember, I was a child.

Twink [twingk] *noun slang.* A young, attractive gay man with a slim, boyish appearance. (dictionary.com)

PART ONE

CATERPILLAR

1

Snatch'ed

"Let's go to Westfield's after school today," Dee said loudly over the din of the cafeteria as she finished her second biscuit. "I want to get my ears pierced," she said and fingered her earlobes.

"Okay," I said, looking past her round face and over her shoulder at Liam Dougherty, our school's star footballer sitting at the athlete table, and sighed quietly. His blonde hair shone so much brighter than my own, his blue eyes bright like sapphires compared to my washed-out grey ones. I fantasized about him regularly, not always sexually, but usually. Sometimes I liked to imagine just sitting with him, and listening to his beautiful voice complimenting me (naturally). Other times, I imagined him giving me his football shirt, stripping it off in the changing room after a game, his chest all sweaty and muscled.

"You looking at Liam?" Dee interrupted in a teasing tone following my eye.

"No," I scoffed, feeling myself blush, and straightened on the table bench, as my eyes drifted to Liam's girlfriend, Iris, the ice queen who ruled the school. "I was looking at Iris, god she's a beauty. I could never have a girl like that. Liam's so lucky," I said, my voice still an octave higher than every other boy in school, and patted my hair before stopping myself from doing something so obviously feminine.

Dee made a sound in her throat and narrowed her eyes at me. "Whatever, meet me at my locker at the bell, we'll take The Tube," she stood and grabbed her tray of empty containers and walked self-consciously to the return counter. Her uniform pants were tight over her wide bottom and her shirt was shapeless and bloused over the belt, making her look more like a prison matron from behind than a fifteen-year old girl. She had struggled with her weight for as long as I had known her. I crumpled the wrapper of my meal replacement bar and grabbed my water bottle and followed her, keeping my eyes forward so as not to invite any of the usual comments I got.

"Jack Sprat could eat no fat, his wife could eat no lean," someone said, followed by a round of laughter from the table in the middle of the room.

I gritted my teeth, that one was getting old. Fucking assholes, I hated secondary, couldn't wait to get through and get the fuck out of this town. Problem was I still had two more years, I hadn't even started my A-levels, and time was marching so slowly I felt as though my life was slogging through molasses. I would have given anything to be broader of chest, have a deeper voice, be less gay, not that I admitted it to anyone, though slews suspected it. But, how could I really be anything when I hadn't even been kissed by anyone, yet anyway, I slid my eyes across the rugby players to Liam. I wondered what it would be like to kiss Liam. He had thin lips, but I had more than enough so maybe we'd balance each other out. I sighed and went to class, tuning out the noise, one of the few things that I was really good at.

After class I found Dee waiting at my locker, impatient as always, and she took my arm after I stuffed my backpack with books and led me to The Tube. Her chatter filled my ears the whole ride, as she talked about her latest, unrequited, crush, the stack of homework she had, and what her slag of a sister had to say about her weight over dinner the night before.

"Darling, you're beautiful," I said to her as I put my arm around her, meaning it. Her face was stunning, like a rounder, teenage Brigit Bardot, and I loved her body as much as she, and every fat-shamer on the planet, hated it. I loved hugging her. She was pure, nurturing comfort, and someday, when we got out of this god-forsaken school and city, she and the world would realize it and embrace it.

I waited in Claire's, looking at the jewelry, imagining myself in dangly earrings, while she picked out the studs she wanted. She cried nervously for me to come hold her hand while the shop clerk prepped the ear-piercing gun.

"You're going to be fine Dee, you're the strongest girl I know, nothing fazes you," I squeezed her hand and looked out the glass wall into the shopping center, my eye drawn to a tall man outside, walking with two other men. He wore his short black hair in a buzzcut fade, and had what looked like a neck tattoo peeking up above his collar. He was wearing a black button-down shirt open at the throat and black pants that hugged his muscled body almost scandalously, or maybe I just thought it was scandalous because of how my body was reacting. Jesus Christ, my cock went ping in my pants and I had to look away, straightening my school blazer to cover myself. I turned to face Dee and then jumped when she shrieked with pain as the gun made a hole in her lobe with the gold stud, her voice echoing out the open doors of the shop. I looked back outside and met the man's eyes, her cry drawing his attention. He stopped briefly to look at me, his friends continuing on oblivious. Something in his look bent my shoulder and snatched my breath. I saw the faintest of a twitch to his mouth and eye, almost as if he were going to smile at me but didn't, and I looked away hurriedly.

"I don't think I can do the other," Dee was saying urgently.

"Ice might help," the shop clerk said. "You could run next door and get some."

"I'll be back in a flash," I said, squeezing Dee's hand before letting go, looking at her pale face and hoping she didn't faint.

I ran two stores down to the coffee shop and waited in the short line to ask for a cup of ice, a muffin, and a packet of crisps, paying with a twenty-pound note. I turned and found myself face to face with the dark-haired man, or rather face to neck. My stomach reacted like Simone Biles herself was inside me as I looked up at him. He was fucking beautiful up close, though some might say his chin was a little weak, but that would be the only thing they could say, well, that and that one of his hands was heavily tattooed like an ex-con. He looked Eastern European and smelled delicious.

"'Ello," he said in a cockney-sounding accent, "your girlfriend gonna live?" Again, his mouth twitched and his eye narrowed but this time he followed through and gave me a half smile, so full of sin it almost knocked me over.

I swallowed to free my voice. "She's not my girlfriend." I smoothed my hair nervously.

His eyes followed my hand and his eyebrow flicked at my answer, or maybe at my voice.

I looked past him to the entrance, suddenly feeling claustrophobic and in desperate need of air. "I've got to bring this to her," I walked past him and felt his eyes on my back.

Later on, I would think of all the witty things I wished I had said to him, wished that I was wearing something better than my school uniform, which made me look like a twelve-year old bean pole in a coat and tie. The wankers at school sometimes told me I looked like an anorexic girl, and that I'd never get my period if I didn't eat a sandwich.

I wished I'd met him some place more romantic like the river bank, or the pub. He could pick me a flower, or buy me a pint and offer me a smoke, and I would smoke it so expertly, though I had never had a cigarette in my short life, never actually wanted one before, but something about that man made me want to do bad things. It was absurd really, because everything that passed between us was fully in my head. He said one thing to me, five words actually, yes, I counted, and I made it an entire conversation.

Dee looked at me when I came back and pulled a face. "Why are you all red?"

"What?" I asked. "Oh, I made a Freudian slip when I ordered your crisps, it was so embarrassing."

"What did you say?" Dee asked with a grin, putting the ice in the napkin I handed her and holding it to her bare ear, the other earlobe flaming red.

"I asked for a packet of tits," I lied smoothly. "Her bosom was massive."

Dee laughed, an infectious raucous sound that always made me feel warm inside. "Robin Trumball you're a muppet."

"I didn't mean it, that's why it's called a Freudian slip. It's not like I asked if her muffin was any good."

Dee rewarded me with another belly laugh, I smiled, pleased.

We rode The Tube home, my eyes scanning the shops as we left the centre, hoping for a glimpse of the man in black. I giggled slightly to myself thinking he was nothing like Johnny Cash.

"What's so funny?" Dee asked, following my aimless eyes.

"Nothing, was just thinking again of what I said to that busty lady."

Dee made a sound and touched one of her red ears.

"You better use rubbing alcohol on those and turn them frequently, Felicity's got infected and she had to take them out and go back and do it all over again," I said. "But she's an idiot, you're not." I put my arm around her shoulder above her backpack and squeezed.

I left her at the corner and walked four blocks to the brick townhouse at the end of the row on a quiet street in Kensington where I lived with my parents, two younger brothers and my older sister, the idiot. It was a big house with windows on three sides, but not the biggest by far on the street or in the neighborhood, and we only had a medium-sized garden in back, big enough for a patio, flowers, and kicking a ball around, which my brothers did a lot. My dad made a slew of money doing something in high tech, I could never remember, only that his boss was occasionally a wanker, and his secretary was borderline incompetent, though it was his fourth one in as many years, so maybe it wasn't their incompetence that was to blame.

My mother was a housewife, though nowadays there's probably some more politically correct term, like domestic manager, or some shite, but she couldn't be anything otherwise with four kids at home to manage. She loved me best, though she never said, and was careful to dote on us all, but I knew the truth. I know most kids my age complain about their parents, are rude, and rebel, but not me, I loved my mum. She did everything for me, rubbed my back when we watched telly, laughed at my stupid jokes, and soothed my feelings when I came home sad, which I did on more than one occasion.

"Hallo," I called letting myself in with the key I wore on a long chain under my button-down.

"In the kitchen darling," my mother called.

I dropped my heavy bag at the bottom of the stairs and followed the fragrant smells into the kitchen. "Something smells amazing," I kissed my mum's waiting cheek, so soft and smooth, and ruffled my youngest brother, George's, hair as he sat at the kitchen table doing his homework.

"Where'd you go after school?" She asked, smiling at me.

"Dee and I went shopping, she got her ears pierced, finally," I said. "She's been talking about doing it for like three years now. She was such a baby, I had to get her ice," I laughed.

I saw my mum look at my ears, "I'm glad you didn't want to get yours pierced," she said with a weird smile.

"God no Mum, I don't need to give the wankers at school any more reason to harass me."

"Language, Robin," she looked pointedly at George.

"Sorry," I said, hating the way I lisped when I said it, and made a mental note to keep doing those mouth and tongue exercises. The ones that made Dee roll on the floor with laughter, saying it looked like I was practicing giving oral. That thought made me think of the man from the shops and I felt a twinge in my pants. "I'm just gonna study for a bit, call me when dinner's ready."

I grabbed my bag and took the stairs two at a time looking at my watch, and saw I had about twenty minutes before dinner. I hurriedly undressed, changing into track pants and a hoodie and laid on my bed, wishing that my cock was bigger, thinking of that man, his tattooed hand stroking me, his hand over mine, my hand over his, and came quickly, the thrill of it all and the urgency of not getting caught. I mopped myself with a tissue while I thought about him. He was nothing like Liam or the other ballers at school, and probably twice my age. I didn't know what it was about him. He could very easily have been a mobster, or criminal, no, not your average criminal for sure, more like a high-ranking Russian gangster. One with wads of cash in his pockets and women fawning over him, pressing their bare breasts against that neck tattoo of his, while he looked at me across the room and smiled that sinful smile.

2

I'm Coming Out

I FINALLY GAVE the man a name, given how much time I spent thinking about him. I named him Boris, after Boris the Blade from my favorite Guy Ritchie movie, the one where Brad Pitt absolutely *nailed* the tinker accent. Not because he looked like him, god no, but because it was the most Russian name I could think of, and I loved that bloody movie. I watched it again, for Brad of course, that man was beautiful, and marveled at Guy Ritchie's gift for movie making. He was hot too, or used to be, so I may or may not have wanked to him as well, guiltily of course. He broke my queen Madonna's heart, and he should never be forgiven for that, no matter how handsome he once was.

Halfway through the term, I had forgotten about Boris, well, forgotten is the wrong word, more like I shelved him, temporarily, for my renewed interest in Liam, someone who I could stare at daily, surreptitiously of course, didn't need any more fuel for the teasing. Dee kept watching me, wondering, and I worried she would declare it before me. I knew by then that I was most definitely 'team penis,' and not 'team vagina,' and I wanted to be the one to acknowledge it, not have someone else point it out to me, as if I needed help with my identity.

"You want to come over after school? Watch a movie?" I asked her, ready to spill the beans with some glitter and eye shadow if necessary.

"Of course," Dee said, ever the steadfast friend.

I smiled. "See you at my locker," I threw away my wrapper and left the cafeteria, careful to walk like a man, *whatever that meant*, I scoffed to myself. I am a man, why the bloody hell I couldn't walk however the fuck I wanted, really got under my skin to be honest.

"Watch those hands gay-boy. I don't want to lose an eye," some asshole of a baller said as he pushed past me.

"Sod off," I muttered.

The jock turned and stared at me. He was one of Marcus Willoughby's friends, and Marcus was the rugby star who went after me relentlessly. "What was that?"

"I said sorry," I shrugged, my testicles crawling up inside my body like the cowards they were.

He glared at me and kept walking, like a lion ignoring a mosquito. Well macho man, mosquitos carry malaria, and I spent Latin class fantasizing about him dying a horrible death.

I made popcorn and cuddled next to Dee on the couch in the basement, turning on *Rent*, thinking it'd be good but found myself dozing midway through.

Dee elbowed me awake. "Come on, this was an amazing musical, and was a huge hit in America."

"Sorry," I shrugged, thinking it was the over-hyped musical of the millennium (this was before *Hamilton* swooped in and stole that title). "I know the guy died."

Dee scoffed. "You have no taste."

"I beg your pardon," I chafed, "I am an expert on musicals, that one was overwrought, and pointless. No fucking thank you, I'll take Cole Porter or Gershwin any day over that shite. Even Sondheim, though at times he was tedious as well."

"You take that back!" Dee cried. "He is a musical genius."

I shrugged, holding my ground. I was fifteen, would be sixteen in three months and chock full of egregious opinions, though I stand by these, (especially about *Hamilton*, sorry, not sorry).

Dee turned the movie off. "Fine, should we watch something else, or paint our toenails?"

"Did you bring polish?"

"I always have polish," Dee grinned and I followed her up the stairs.

Once in my room, I peeled off my socks, running to the bathroom to get my sister's polish remover, q-tips, and clippers. I closed the door behind me and looked at Dee, rummaging through her bag, pulling out three different bottles of nail polish.

"I'm gay," I said and bit my lip, leaning back against the door. "I think," I remembered adding.

Dee stopped what she was doing and stared at me for a few beats. "No shit," she said like I had just said the sun was hot and went back to fishing through her bag, finding a fourth bottle and standing up straight.

"Well, that's not fair," I frowned. "There are plenty of guys who are like me and straight. It's not an open shut case."

Dee's face softened. "Of course not, I'm sorry," she said. "It's just that, I would have been more surprised if you said you were straight," she shrugged. "Either way, I love you, you're my best friend, and I don't care." I saw a mischievous look pass over her face. "That being said, how much do you lust after Liam Dougherty?"

I laughed with relief. "A lot, but so do you, and half the school," I stopped, and wondered about telling her about Boris.

"To be honest, Marcus is the one everyone lusts over, but he's such a bully to you I would never," she said and then shook the bottles in her hands.

Marcus was beautiful, and I felt like a weirdo thinking that about my bully. "Thank you, I promise to never lust over any of your bullies either."

She looked at me and laughed. "That's because you're gay! Now, which color do you want?" She asked, changing the subject.

3

Tongue Twisters

IT WAS HOT, for April, and I loosened my tie as I went straight from school to grab an ice cream alone. Dee had to go with her family to her cousins' for the weekend in Kent so we said goodbye in front of my locker.

I walked the two blocks to the ice cream shop that had only just opened for the season, my backpack feeling like it was full of bricks.

"Mint chip on a cone please," I ordered from the pretty girl behind the counter, careful not to lisp my 's.'

I handed her a quid and turned to leave, licking my ice cream happily. I pulled up short, nearly dropping the cone mid-lick as I found myself face to neck with Boris. He was wearing jeans and a blue sweatshirt with the sleeves pushed up, and I saw that he had another large tattoo on the same forearm as his hand ones. His eyes were locked on my ice cream covered tongue which I quickly drew into my mouth and swallowed. I saw his mouth move ever so slightly, and held my breath waiting for the half smile. He looked past me, to the girl behind the counter who was looking at him, appraisingly, that slag.

"I'll have a mint chip, in a cup," he ordered in a medium-deep voice, his accent sounding more Northern than straight cockney, but he hadn't said enough yet for me to discern.

I didn't know whether to stay or leave. My cock wanted me to stay, but my brain told me I was being an idiot, standing there like I didn't know where I was or what I was doing. I turned reluctantly back to the door and took a step.

"You got a hot date?" He asked my back.

I turned. "I'm sorry?" I lisped in my nervousness.

His mouth twitched, and he paid for his ice cream. He crossed the small space to stand next to me and ate a spoonful, his even white teeth visible for a split second. "You better lick that," he said in a soft voice, nodding with his head at my ice cream which was beginning to drip down the cone.

I snapped out of my daze and licked, turning the cone and running my tongue across the surface, catching the legs of ice cream before they touched my fingers. The way he was watching me, my tongue, made me feel like swooning. I felt like Elio seeing Oliver for the first time, and yes, I know I had an unhealthy obsession with the book *Call Me by Your Name*, but I promise I never tried to fuck a peach. I laughed nervously and made for the door, both wanting him to follow, and hoping that he wouldn't because I was certain I would say something dumb.

"Sit with me," Boris commanded and gestured to the café table outside the shop.

I looked around nervously and then shrugged, taking my backpack off and nearly groaning with relief as the weight was lifted and I sat down.

"Why the hell do you have so many books in that thing?" Boris asked, saying thing like 'fing,' and dropping his 'h's' because of his accent.

"I have a lot of homework," I shrugged and licked my ice cream, Boris' eyes locking again on my tongue as he took another bite of his.

"What's your name?" He asked, turning his spoon upside down and licking the ice cream.

"Robin, but my friends call me Robby, or Rob," I answered. "What's yours?" I held my breath, willing him to say Boris.

"Vasyl," he replied, "my friends call me Vas," he added, giving me a version of his half smile.

"Are you Russian?"

Vasyl laughed. "No, Ukrainian, though the Russians like to think of us as theirs," he added in a flinty tone.

"What are those tattoos?" I asked, feeling bold, nodding at his hand, not sure I wanted to know, or if he would tell me the truth. I prayed they weren't prison tattoos indicating just how many people he killed with his bare hands or a shiv.

Vas looked at the blue-green ink on his knuckles and then his arm, turning it under the sunlight. "This one," he pointed to a conch shell, which he had on his thumb and first two fingers, "is the Buddhist symbol for battles won, and these two are my initials in Ukrainian," he pointed to his ring finger and pinky. "The design up my arm is something my cousin drew," he raised his sleeve so I could see the full tattoo of two tigers locked in battle, one tail wrapped around his wrist and the other around his elbow.

I looked at his forearm briefly, having no idea then just how intimately I would become acquainted with it, and his other tattoos, in the coming years. "Why aren't the tigers orange and black?"

He just looked at me, and then away. I felt so stupid in that moment, I wanted the earth to swallow me up as I felt my face flame. I cursed my fair complexion and smoothed my hair to busy my free hand. He caught the movement in his peripheral and turned his gaze back to me, lifting one side of his mouth as he looked at my red face.

"You play any sports?" He asked. I watched him take another bite, the spoon disappearing into his beautiful mouth.

"Tennis, and squash, but not on a team," I answered, wishing in that moment I played something more impressive like football or rugby, I bet he played rugby. No, probably not, he still had all his teeth, it was more likely that he spent a lot of time in the gym, he certainly looked more than fit.

"What do you do for fun?" He asked.

"I like video games, movies, hanging out with friends," I shrugged and licked my ice cream with the tip of my tongue, feeling that the flat of my tongue winding around the mound of ice cream was too suggestive. It looked like he thought otherwise, his gaze was even more focused on the point of my tongue, and I tucked it back into my mouth quickly.

"How old are you?" He asked in a forced casual tone.

"I'm sixteen," I lied, "but my birthday is coming up," I added, wondering about the tension I heard in his tone. He seemed so sophisticated and confident I hated pointing out how young I was, but didn't dare try to pass for any older.

The little half-smile returned. "When's your birthday?"

"June Fourteenth. How old are you?" I countered.

"Twenty-seven," he said holding my gaze and shifting in his seat. "You must think I'm ancient."

"No, definitely not," I said and licked my ice cream before it could drip down my hand, I really wanted to throw it away, it made me feel like little kid, why didn't I get it in a cup?

"What video games do you play?" He asked after a moment.

"League, Halo, Call of Duty, Sometimes Pokémon with my friend Dee. Do you play?"

"No," he answered and looked around again. "Haven't got the time."

"What do you do for fun?" I asked, licking my ice cream while his eyes were averted.

"Go to the gym, hang out with friends, go to the pub," he looked back at me. "I love football, though I watch more than I play."

"You look really fit," I said, and then blushed a deep red.

I got a full smile from him for that, and felt the effects of it all the way down to my toes, his features softened as they folded into laugh lines. He looked as though he was about to say something but my phone buzzed in my pocket, interrupting us. I fumbled getting it out, this pair of pants tighter than my other ones, and I looked at the screen. It was my mum reminding me I had to look after George today so she could get her hair done. I cursed silently to myself, not wanting to leave without finding out why Vas was here sitting and talking with me.

"I've gotta run," I stood and picked up my backpack, slinging it over my shoulder.

Vas stood. "What's your number?" He asked quietly, putting down his ice cream and taking out his phone.

"You want my phone number?" I asked, unable to keep the incredulous tone out of my voice, as my knees went weak.

"Yeah," he said simply, his mouth transforming into a wicked smile.

I blew out a breath. "But I don't know you."

"You worried about stranger danger?" He asked in a mocking voice. "You have an Instagram?"

Holy shit, that would be so much worse if he turned out to be a serial murderer. Photos of my family and friends, my house, no I wasn't going to give him my Instagram, yet. I shifted on my feet as I chanted, 'should I? Shouldn't I?' in my head. I don't know why I hesitated. This hot-as-fuck man, with a smile full of sin and promises, wanted my phone number and I was shifting back and forth like I had to pee, what the fuck was there to consider? I rattled off my number in a rush and fled.

4

Ghosted

"LET'S EAT OUTSIDE on the wall," I suggested to Dee at lunch on Monday, "it's so nice out."

"Sure," Dee grabbed her lunch bag and followed me out to the wall that separated the school from the cricket field.

Dee unwrapped her sandwich after sitting and took a bite, washing it down with a sip of her diet coke. I watched her, the sun bright overhead, making her blonde hair shine. I was desperate to tell her about Vasyl, his muscles, his beautiful face, his tattoos, and at the same time hesitant to. Christ, I was making something out of nothing. He asked me for my number and then didn't call or text all weekend, I was certain of this because I checked my phone every five minutes, even when I was gaming. I checked my filters and my spam folder, while also marveling about people in the olden days who had to sit by the phone waiting for a call, no texting or voicemail, how did those people live or go to the bathroom? I shuddered and looked at Dee.

"I met the most beautiful man on Friday after school," I said, my words tumbling over each other like Cirque du Soleil performers. "He asked me for my number." Desperation overrode hesitancy, apparently.

Dee put her sandwich down and stared at me with an open mouth. "What?" She shook her head. "You've been gay for like five minutes, well *admittedly* gay anyway, and all of a sudden you're out meeting guys? Men?"

I smiled happily at her excited expression. "He's beautiful, so fit. Ukrainian, tan skin, gorgeous brown eyes, jet black hair and his bloody body, so muscly." I was working myself up just thinking about him. I must've come a dozen times over the weekend fantasizing about him and here I was on the verge of popping another boner just talking about him.

"Bloody hell, he sounds amazing!" Dee said taking a bite of her sandwich. "Where does he go to school? Is he at university?"

"No, he's a bit older. I didn't get a chance to find out more, my mum texted me mid-ice cream, but if he calls, I'll get you more intel," I grinned and drank my water.

"How much older?"

I looked away, suddenly worried that Dee would burst my bubble. She was so fun but so pragmatic sometimes. "Twenty-seven."

Dee put her sandwich down again. "What? He's like a fucking adult," I watched her eyes shift away and when she looked back it was with her old woman eyes. Oh god, how I hated those eyes. "Where'd you meet him?"

"Carly's."

"He just started talking to you?" Dee puzzled.

"I think he remembered me from Westfield's, I saw him when you were getting your ears pierced, he spoke to me in the coffee shop."

"You saw him at Westfield's, and again in Notting Hill?" Dee frowned in a way that made me defensive.

"Yeah, so what? They're practically the same neighborhood and I bump into people all the time all over London, of course I usually dread it, because the last two times it was Marcus and his gang of thugs." I shuddered dramatically.

Dee made a skeptical sound. "Okay, so he just started talking to you, what'd he say?" She picked up her sandwich and took another bite.

I smiled, thrilled to speak about him out loud, ignoring the judgement in Dee's voice, the judgement that made me doubt (fuck's sake, a hot man was interested in me, focus on the important part of the story).

"He just asked about school, sports, gaming. He's so confident and *gorgeous*, I could barely speak. I asked him about his tattoos," I smiled remembering how sexy his muscled forearm looked under that tattoo of tigers killing each other.

Dee put her sandwich down for the third time, and looked at me. "Tattoos?" She drew out the plural like she was a bloody bumblebee. "Were they prison tattoos?"

"No," I said my voice trilling. I'll admit it wasn't a very convincing denial, as I didn't have a fucking clue that they weren't.

"A twenty-seven-year-old, tattooed, Ukrainian, muscle man starts talking to you over ice cream," she shook her head worriedly. "Robby, you're fifteen, sounds quite pedo to me."

"You're so racist! There's nothing wrong with Ukrainians, and I'll be sixteen in two months, that's old enough for consent," I said with a pout, leaving out that I had lied to him about my age. I had spent all weekend fantasizing about Vas, I didn't need Dee to dump cold water on me with her pedo talk.

"Yeah but you look *really* young Robby, especially lately. You've bitched about that to me endlessly, and here's this guy you've bumped into twice now, in two different neighborhoods, sounds creepy," she shook her head. "Was he wearing a trench coat? Christ, he could be a *sex* trader, you're gonna get kidnapped and sold into *sex* slavery. I'll have to do interviews on the telly," Dee sighed and fluffed her hair as she looked away.

"Sod off," I pushed her harder than I usually would, angry at her for spoiling my fun, my fantasy. Maybe he was a stalker pedo, maybe he was a recruiter for a sex ring, maybe I would end up in a million pieces under someone's stoop. I smoothed my hair. "He didn't give off a creepy vibe. He was so sexy, and plain, like no weird stuff at all," I said emphatically, eager to assuage her fears and doubts as much as my own.

"Robby, you're so naïve I just worry. I want to be happy for you, because on the one hand it's so thrilling, but on the other, what the fuck does he want a fifteen-year old's number for?" She shook her head. "What twenty-seven-year-old wants to hang out with someone in secondary? If this were me, you would have the same concerns. I mean really," she said emphatically. "People like us are exactly who predators prey on."

I thought of the tigers again and shuddered slightly. "I know, but he's not," I shook my head, "and anyway, he hasn't called, and if he does, I'll just meet him somewhere public."

"Ok, or maybe I should come too, I could sit at another table like a chaperone," she smiled. "I'll bring my pepper spray in case he tries anything."

"Don't be ridiculous," I looked at the time on my phone. "Come on, lunch's over."

5

Fast Times at Westfield ~~High~~ Mall

IT HAD BEEN TWO WEEKS since I gave Vas my number, and I heard nothing from him. I checked my phone obsessively, checked and rechecked my settings to be sure I didn't have anything that would prevent his call from getting through. Every time it buzzed my heart would go into my throat and I'd rush to look, only to feel crushing disappointment. After the first week I began to worry that he transcribed it wrong, and that I'd never hear from him. I went to Carly's every day after school the second week, sometimes with Dee, sometimes alone. Sitting at the outside table that he and I had shared, like it was some sort of shrine, doing my homework until I'd pack everything up and head home, my feet dragging.

By Sunday I was certain I would never hear from him. It was pathetic really, that I had such expectations from someone I'd spent twenty minutes with, that I let myself get so worked up. He probably had to report to prison, or got arrested, or maybe he had to go on the lam, a rival gangster on his tail. I imagined he was in a safe house in Amsterdam or some place, unable to use his phone for fear of it being traced. Just the type of person I had no business knowing or being around, or for Christ's sake being obsessed with.

I rolled out of bed and made myself a bowl of cereal before going back to my room to lose myself in League, quickly shouting myself hoarse at the number of wankers who didn't know how to check the map. I checked my phone at the end of the game and saw that I had missed a text, because of all the yelling, from a number, not a name. My stomach bottomed out as I sat up and swiped into my phone.

You free?

That's all it said. My heart was beating so loudly I heard it in my ears. It could be Vas, but it could be a wrong number, of course something told me it wasn't.

When?

I pressed send, wondering if I should say more, or confirm it was him. The minutes dragged by, I turned off my computer and paced the room. I texted again, unable to bear the silence.

Where?

Westfield's 1 hour

I looked at the time on my phone and saw that would be one o'clock. I didn't have anything to do until Sunday dinner with my grandparents.

Kk

I hurried to the bathroom with the best shower and saw the door was closed. "Hurry up Felicity!" I knocked on the door with irritation.

"Sod off! I'll take as long as I want to," she called angrily. "Use the other bathroom."

My fucking sister, always slowing me down, hogging the good bathroom, leaving her shit everywhere. She was a goddamn princess and my father spoiled her. She was the only girl and he gave her whatever she wanted, he was completely wrapped around her stupid finger.

"I've got to meet friends soon and you know that's the best shower," I said, my irritation and impatience growing.

"Ha, that's a laugh, you mean friend, and Dee can wait, she always waits for you."

"Fuck you Feliss, I'm meeting a new friend."

The door opened and Felicity stared at me skeptically, one blue eye made up and the other waiting for mascara and eyeliner. Her strawberry blonde hair was piled on her head and her robe was tied tightly around her tiny waist. "You made a new friend?"

I put my chin in the air, *fuck her*. "Yes, and I have other friends, not just Dee."

Felicity laughed and made a face. "Online friends don't count you loser."

I wanted to smack the smirk off her face but didn't dare. The last time I did that, when she was twelve and I was ten, Dad paddled my bottom raw and I couldn't sit for days. "I just want to shower, I'll be quick. Put your make-up on in your room."

Her eyes scanned my skinny body as I stood there in my shorts. "Oh, you're finally getting some chest hair, maybe you are actually a boy."

I clenched my fists, she had been teasing me that I was girl for years, I don't know why she was such a bitch to me, I was so glad she went to a different school, I didn't need her joining in with Marcus and them. "Just finish painting your hag face or get out of the way. If anyone ever saw you without make-up they'd scream and cross the street."

"Ha, you wish, you're just jealous I'm prettier than you," she slammed the door in my face.

I called her all kinds of choice words in my head and waited, looking again at the texts from Vas.

Finally, the twat got out of my way after ten long minutes, and I took a shower. I washed thoroughly, and styled my hair, frustrated with the waves that wouldn't lay still. I tried on ten different outfits: two were just trying too hard, four were too casual, one was too girlie, one was too baggy until finally I settled on jeans (boring) and a peach colored Nike hoodie (perfectly genderless) with a white, anime-printed t-shirt underneath. I slipped on my fancy Duke + Dexter trainers, the ones I'd never even worn because I never had an occasion special enough, and I wasn't so stupid as to wear them to school.

I rode The Tube from Notting Hill Gate to Shepherd's Bush for Westfield's and stopped outside the mall. Christ, he didn't say where in the shopping centre to meet him, and I sure as shit didn't want to be the twat who asked. I smoothed my wavy hair and walked through the mall to the coffee shop. He was standing outside, not like a nervous teen, not like a criminal, but like a man waiting for the director to yell cut, someone so at ease with eyes on him, that he didn't give a shit about *anyone's* eyes on him.

He saw me coming, his eyes swept over me like searchlights laying me bare. I swallowed, my mouth and throat suddenly dry and sticky. I smoothed my hair again self-consciously, sweeping my bangs a bit to the side as I ran my eyes over him. He was in American jeans, trainers, and some designer t-shirt that fit him like a second skin, outlining his muscular man-breasts, and exposed his, literally, bulging biceps. I felt like swooning. He looked like he had just come from the gym so pronounced his muscles were, and suddenly all I could think of was how Marcus and them would kill to look that buff, and how Liam wished he looked that beautiful. Just this week Liam had his hair cut in a style similar to Vas' fade (and I promise you it did not make them look anything alike).

He smiled at me, something halfway between the mouth twitch and sinful half-smile. "You look different out of your uniform," he said, "and your hair looks different too."

"It's too long, I've been meaning to get it cut," I said self-consciously and smiled. *What did he mean by different? Better or worse?*

"You look good," he said quietly, reading my mind.

"So do you," I blushed.

He turned and started walking, I immediately followed and we began our circumnavigation of the mall. We shopped, upstairs and downstairs, ducking into quite a few stores, including a gaming store where I browsed games and headsets, with my mind on my birthday and what I was going to ask for from my parents. I watched him as well, his body and face like magnets for my eyes, and later, after my birthday, for my hands.

We chatted most of the time, he asked me a lot of questions about my life, my family, where I've traveled. I asked him similar questions, so curious I was about him, but the biggest question of all I didn't dare ask, in case he'd question it himself.

"Were you born here?" I asked as he rifled through the girls' racks at Hollister. He pulled out a pair of short pink denim shorts, and a grey, baby t-shirt that said 'Los Angeles' on it.

"Try these on for me, you and my sister are about the same size, and I want to see if this would fit her."

I raised my eyebrows. "You want me to try on girls' clothes? What if someone sees me?" I looked left and right, certain that Marcus was going to pop up from inside a clothing rack.

"You're doing it for my sister, and no one is going to say anything, I'll go in with you," he looked at me with something behind his eyes.

"No," I laughed nervously at the thought of being alone in a changing room with him, him seeing my scrawny naked chest. "I'll be alright."

"Ok, but I want you to come out when you're changed, so I can see, I'll sit on a bench in there so you don't have to come back out into the store if you don't want," he smiled and headed for the changing rooms. He grabbed a pair of short pajama shorts that cinched on the sides, "try these too."

I went alone, thankfully, into the changing room and put on the shorts and baby tee, the shorts were snug but fit and the t-shirt was a crop-top that exposed my bare stomach and the faint line of hair around my bellybutton. I wavered about letting him see me in the outfit. God my skin was so pale, and I was so skinny, my legs looked like they went on for miles. I suppose if I was a girl in this outfit, I would be quite pleased with my appearance. I looked kinda hot to be honest, especially my ass. I took a deep breath and opened the door, looking both ways to be sure no other people were around and stepped out. I stood self-consciously in front of him, crossing my hands over my junk as if I were standing naked.

His eyes ran slowly down my body and back up. "Move your hands," he commanded quietly.

I moved them, but they felt like birds, fluttering around, not knowing where to go or what to do. I finally let them hang by my sides.

"Turn around."

I pivoted quickly and looked back at him. He nodded. "Good, try on the sleep shorts."

I did as I was told, swapping the shorts for the even more revealing pajama bottoms. They were tight over my round ass, and I stepped out again, feeling even more exposed, and, something else. I heard Vas blow out a breath. He gestured with his finger for me to turn around, as though he was incapable of speech, which made me giggle to assume that my skinny, glow-in-the-dark body was turning this man on. Right, I scoffed to myself as I turned, more slowly this time.

"How old is your sister?" I asked and went back into the dressing room.

"Sixteen, but she looks twelve," He answered through the door.

I changed quickly and stepped out, handing the clothes to Vas. "Do you want to buy these?"

"Yes," he answered simply and gestured for me to walk in front of him.

I waited as he paid, looking at the jewelry, wondering what it would be like to have pierced ears. I thought of Dee and how hers had healed so nicely and she was nearly ready for the big hoops that she bought the last time we were here at the mall.

"You want pizza?" Vas asked, suddenly next to my shoulder.

His voice gave me goosebumps and I nodded. We walked out, side by side, in silence. The mall was crowded, and I had to step close to him, our knuckles touching as a group of loud girls walked past, oblivious of how much disruption they were causing to the foot traffic around them. He took my hand for the briefest of moments, so quickly it was gone that I wondered later if I had only imagined it, but I felt the thrill of his touch all the way into every nook and cranny of my body, particularly the one between my legs. I looked at him and he flashed a smile without looking at me, giving me a small wink.

We were seated in a booth and made small talk until our pizza came. I took a bite of my slice and sipped my soda, while I stared at Vas, particularly his neck tattoo, which looked like a wing or no, a winged person.

"What's your neck tattoo?" I asked as I watched him fold his slice in half and take a big bite.

"The archangel Michael," he answered around his bite. "He keeps watch, and evil at bay."

I nodded, vaguely familiar with the story of Michael and Lucifer. "Where in London do you live? And do you still live at home?" I asked taking a small bite of my pizza crust.

"I don't live in London, and no, I don't live at home."

"Where do you live?" I put my soda down.

"Manchester."

"Whoa," I was shocked, Manchester was so far away, like practically Scotland. "What do you do for work?"

"I'm in construction, carpentry mostly, though I have a working knowledge of most trades," he shrugged.

"Do you work here, in London?" I asked, my voice going up an octave. "How long is that commute?"

He shook his head, a twitch to his mouth. "I work and live in Manchester, it's less than three hours by train from here."

"What were you doing in London then?"

"Visiting my cousin and his blokes." He took another slice of pizza. "Have another slice, you're an 'air too thin," he added.

I looked at the pizza without seeing it, my mind was spinning with thoughts like a wheel on a game show. "Where does your cousin live?"

"East London."

"Oh." That was an area I never dared venture near. "Was that your cousin then that I saw you with, here when I was with Dee?"

"When Dee were getting murdered you mean?" He grinned. "Yeah, my cousin and one of his flatmates. His bird works in one of the stores here, and we came to visit her," he preempted my next question.

"What were you doing in Notting Hill?" I puzzled.

"Looking for you," he answered holding my gaze prisoner.

"Looking for me?" I think I said, but it could have just been an exhale. I swallowed, or rather tried to, and picked up my glass, breaking free of his eye contact. Now my mind was really reeling and my cock was at full mast, not that anyone could possibly see something so insignificant. The look he gave me, the tone of his voice, his knee brushing mine under the table, all scalded me inside and out. "How?"

He gave me his lopsided smile. "Your uniform."

Oh, Christ, he *was* going to murder me after all.

"You've never found someone so attractive that you thought about them and wanted to see them again?"

Wait, did he just say he found me attractive? My eyes focused on his mouth, and watched as it twitched into that sinful smile.

"You can't be serious," I said, my voice trailing off, and my stomach clenching, as the more likely alternative just occurred to me, sobering me up like a smack to the face. "Someone put you up to this," I pushed my chair back, my erection gone, my face flaming, tears in my throat, certain that Marcus and them were having a laugh somewhere behind a potted plant. "It's not funny," I stood, willing the earth to swallow me up. Christ he probably took pictures of me in that ridiculous outfit and was going to post them online for my classmates, shit, the entire world to see.

He reached out quick as a flash and grabbed my arm. "Jesus Robby, no one put me up to this, I'm being serious," he frowned at me. "No one's ever said that to you before?"

I shook my head and looked at my feet and then at his hand on my arm, squeezing me.

"I swear to god, I'm telling the truth," he eased his grip. "I saw you in Claire's, your hair shining, face like an angel, comforting your friend, and wanted to talk to you, hear your voice. I'm so glad you had your uniform on or I would never have been able to find you again, and I couldn't stop thinking about you."

His eyes went around the restaurant, and I was glad there was no one near us to overhear. "Sit back down," he ordered. "Have another slice," he waved to the waitress and ordered a pint. "You want one?"

"I can't, it's a school night," I answered, sounding like a prim nerd, while willing my heart to stop racing.

He smiled. "You're a good student, aren't you?"

"I do okay."

"You want to go to university?"

"Of course," and then I blushed thinking that he probably hadn't. "My father would never allow me not to. He wants me to do something in high-tech like he does, or at least be a solicitor or something."

"Your dad's in high-tech?" He took a long swallow of beer as I nodded. "Where do you live?"

"Kensington, near Notting Hill," I smoothed my hair nervously, suddenly hating my address at the flicker in his eye.

"You have siblings?"

"I have two younger brothers and an older sister, who's a total pain in the ass," I answered, taking a small bite of pizza. I really disliked most food to be honest, but my weakness was pizza and I didn't want to look like a pig in front of Vas, so I ate daintily.

"Do you have siblings, other than your sister?" I asked him.

"I had an older brother, he died," Vasyl said with an inscrutable expression. "The idiot went back to the homeland and got himself killed when the Russians invaded last year," he shook his head, dropping his 'h's' even more with the emotion. "Fuck patriotism," he looked at me.

"Oh, Vas, I'm so sorry, that's awful." As much as I hated my sister I would never want her to die.

He nodded and let out a sigh. He looked at his watch and then at me. "I've gotta go soon."

I made an involuntary sound of disappointment. After his promise that he wasn't pulling a prank, and especially after his admission that he thought I had the face of an angel I never wanted him to leave. I looked at my phone and saw that it was nearly five. "Oh shite! I have to go too, it's Sunday dinner with my grandparents." I reached into my pocket for my wallet, the one I bought on holiday with my family in Florence last year.

"No, I got this," Vas held his hand up and pulled out his wallet. "I asked you out," he said with his half smile. I watched him and wanted to kiss that mouth, feel what it felt like against my own lips, guessing it would feel like perfection, rainbows and unicorns, and I giggled lightly.

Vas looked up from counting cash, his face sharp. "What?"

I blushed and looked at his mouth before looking away. "Nothing."

Next time I looked at him, he was watching me intently. "The fourteenth of June feels like a lifetime away," he said in a voice full of meaning.

I blushed then, in an entirely different way than I ever had before. I felt like my whole body was red and not from embarrassment.

Vas put his wallet away after leaving bills on the check. "Do you need to use the bathroom?" He asked.

His voice sounded expectant, so I said yes and followed him to the bathroom. He checked to make sure we were alone before turning to me. "I want to kiss you."

The air left my body as though god himself had squeezed my lungs. I nodded, incapable of speech. He stepped forward and kissed me gently, the feeling of his lips on mine so foreign and arousing. His lips were thin, but soft and his tongue came briefly across the divide between our mouths to touch mine. His kiss made me feel like a complete amateur, which I was by most accounts, and I couldn't believe how good it felt. My arms came up around his neck and it was as though I were the ingénue in some rom-com, who goes through a dramatic transformation and ends up a whore (I'm looking at you Sandy Olsson). I panted against his mouth, kissing him sloppily and urgently as he devoured my full lips. He squeezed my ass and pull me up against him with a tiny moan. The hardness I felt against my hip stunned me, and I nearly collapsed as my asshole tingled with the thought of it inside me.

He pulled back, his face intent and full of promise, "Jesus Robby," he whispered as he looked down at me, his eyes lingering on my mouth, "I can't wait to see you again, but it feels weird that you're not eighteen."

I smiled feeling so powerful in that moment, and then frowned, "Consent is sixteen in the UK."

"And how do you know that?"

"I looked it up after we had ice cream," I said quietly with a shrug.

He gave me a smoldering look and kissed me again. "I'll still feel better after the fourteenth," he said in a husky voice and put distance between us, picking up his shopping bag. "Let's say good bye here, I don't want to watch you leave."

I exhaled and kissed him again, sweeping my tongue through his mouth, pressing my humble erection against his.

He undid my arms and stepped back. "I'm serious Robby, you need to go. I'll text you."

I groaned loudly and said goodbye, willing my erection to go away once I passed through the door and then out of the restaurant. All I wanted to do was let him do whatever he wanted to me, and since that couldn't be a reality, the next thing I wanted was some serious alone time. I had all new material for my wanking session. His mouth, his tongue, his hands, holy shit, the way he tasted, what he said to me? I thought I might even have enough to fantasize about to last me six weeks until my birthday. *Fucking hell, six weeks?!* I wished for a time machine as I hoofed it to The Tube.

$$6$$

Kiss and Tell

"AND THEN HE KISSED ME," I finished telling Dee on the way home from school on Wednesday. She was sick Monday and I had to babysit Tuesday so that was the first chance I had to tell her all about my Ukrainian boyfriend (okay, I know he wasn't my boyfriend, but a *newly* gay boy can dream and fantasize about things as if they were real). It's not like I had picked out china patterns, or baby names, yet anyway.

"Holy shit Robby! You got your first kiss!" She shrieked and wrapped her arms around me on the sidewalk. "Was it amazing? What does it feel like?"

I jumped up and down slightly on feet that had no rhythm, feeling as though I was walking around on a cloud. "Oh my god, it were amazing. His lips are perfect, like," I rubbed my lips together remembering, "thin but soft, and not at all slobbery like that kiss Angie told us about with Bart and his fish lips."

We laughed thinking about how disgusting we thought kissing someone sounded after hearing about her sister and the boy up the street.

"Vas' kiss, his tongue, oh I swear to god I could have kissed him until today, so long as no one walked in that is," I laughed. "There were fireworks."

Dee made a jealous sound. "Cor, you're so lucky. And he's not a weirdo? You swear?"

I shook my head emphatically. "No, he's normal, a builder, so that's different, but not bad."

"No, I guess not, but it's not ideal. You and I swore we'd marry filthy rich," she grinned mischievously, "and titled."

"He's young, he could have ambition, want to own his own company, he said he knows a lot about all the trades."

"When am I gonna get to meet him?" She asked stopping in front of her house.

"I don't know, I'll ask him, next time I see him, when I'm *of age*," I said dramatically, feeling the thrill of it in my marrow. Vas had made it very clear that he was waiting for me to turn seventeen before seeing me, so that he could do more of what he did to me in the bathroom at Franco Manca's. I couldn't wait to feel his hands on my bare skin.

"You've a really pervy expression on your face right now Robin, it's gross," Dee wrinkled her nose and made a face.

"Sorry," I blushed lightly, "he's really fucking fit."

"And he's gay? I mean no offense, I love you, you know that, but it's that he's so much older, and he's interested in a *boy*."

"Oh please, older men have been interested in girls, and boys, since the dawn of time, and always will be. Don't get me wrong, I don't think I'm anything special, and I have no idea how or why I caught his eye, but it doesn't matter. All that matters is that he is interested in me, he wants me, and he's not some pedo who wants me when I'm underage, he's the one who wants to wait, I'm the one begging for it."

"Oh my god, you mean you're going to have, sex?" Dee looked around to be sure no one heard us.

"I fucking hope so," I said making a sound in my throat. "It's different for men, we don't have the bullshit patriarchy rules that you do," I stopped and thought for a minute. Dee and I told each other everything, mostly, but I'm not sure I was ready to talk about sex, especially gay sex, with her.

"Won't it hurt?"

I looked away thinking. "Judging by the size of what I felt on my hip, yes," I said salaciously, "he's a grown man, and while I expect pain, I couldn't say no, my body demands it."

"Oh my," Dee shook her head. "I honestly think you should wait, get to know him, really be sure he's not a weirdo."

"I can't make any promises," I shrugged, remembering how out-of-body it felt to be with him in that bathroom. Anyone could have walked in at any moment and I felt as though I would have let him strip me naked and fuck me raw. "I swear, Sunday morning I woke up normal, and Sunday night I went to bed a sex maniac."

"Yeah, one without a filter," Dee shook her head and looked again at her house. "My parents would most definitely not approve of this line of discourse. I'll see you tomorrow."

$$7$$

Not So Fast, Sexy Boy

I SPENT EVEN MORE TIME alone in my room, using every minute of privacy I could to fuck my hand, or hands rather, because I had taken to putting a finger in my butt, ever since it tingled under Vas' hands. Holy shit that felt good, especially in the tub, when I used my sister's bath oils. I had to remind myself to do my homework, and to continue to study for my GCSEs. I wasn't kidding when I told Dee I went to bed a sex maniac. If I had thought I was overly obsessed with my cock before, then I was an idiot, because now I couldn't keep my hands or thoughts off it. The only time I held it together was at school, and that was because I didn't want to get beaten to death without having seen Vas naked, let him fuck me with his, seemingly giant and gorgeous, cock, the one I felt against my hip in that pizza restaurant bathroom. Oh yes, I went back to that bathroom, and took a picture, first of the spot where we had kissed, and then a selfie against the door. I know it was ridiculous, but I missed him, and on impulse I sent them to him, with no explanation.

I heard nothing from him, not then and not from the other texts I sent. I'm not gonna lie, it fucking hurt. I imagined him laughing at me, the doubt and self-loathing welling up. As the weeks passed, I questioned everything. I imagined a secret look behind his eyes when he said he wasn't hired to torment me, imagined his fingers crossed behind his back, a smile in his throat as he kissed me. Someone that beautiful, that confident, that straight seeming, would never be interested in *me.* I was certain I made things out to be more than they were, as usual. He pulled my arms off him in disgust, not unbridled passion. He didn't push me away because he didn't trust himself not to ravage me, he pushed me away because I was a little femboy who took him too seriously. I cried a few nights, all that confidence he gave me was like smoke and mirrors, and I was left with the real me, the one who deserved to be mocked, by my sister, by the entire school, by the population at large. I needed reassurance and wasn't getting it from Vas.

Marcus and them harassed me, Marcus somehow always sensing my weakness, or maybe he was just bored. He and his gang of thugs would taunt me, call me names, until they broke apart and went their separate ways, except for Marcus, who followed me relentlessly, once his guys were gone. I detoured through the park on those days, or sometime through a different neighborhood, cutting through alleys to my destination. Always arriving home late and breathless.

After one such afternoon, I studied myself in the mirror on the back of my closet door. I was pale, and skinny, all elbows and bony shoulders. I smoothed my hair, the unruly mop of dull-to-me blonde waves, that popped back up instantly, that didn't shine like Vas claimed, that was more wheat than gold, and poofy. I deserved to be teased, sometimes I wonder if I encouraged it with Marcus, swishing my hips before walking as straight and narrow as possible. Nobody beat me up anymore, but that was probably because there were stricter consequences for hate crimes.

I sat up and called the hair salon (well, barber shop really), and made an appointment for the Friday before my birthday. I went down for dinner in a sullen mood.

My mother watched me, I could feel her eyes on me as I helped David with his homework, bickered with Felicity, and encouraged George with his recorder practice, everyone else groaning and covering their ears. I secretly loved it, I loved that they all loved me, needed me, came to me for help or hugs, except Felicity, she thought she was above all that, which is why Mum always asked me to babysit, and help with my brothers. Felicity would burn the house down or lose one of them, she was so untrustworthy, so irresponsible, so self-absorbed.

My dad came home and ruffled everyone's hair but mine, kissing Felicity's cheek like she was a ballerina, and not a bitch on wheels. He rummaged through the fridge for a beer and left the kitchen to change after kissing Mum. I loved that they loved each other, but I couldn't help but wonder why she loved him. He was handsome, and successful, but old and nonchalant, and seemed as though sometimes he wished he were somewhere else when he was home. She was beautiful, my mum, and witty, and smart, and a great cook, even though I didn't like her food. I ate it, oh god, I'm not an ogre, I ate it with a smile, but always a small portion, so I could finish, and everyone knew I was weird about my weight.

I helped set the table and plate the food as Dad came back and sat down, asking everyone how school was, and what we learned and what our plans were for finishing the term strong. I watched him, looking at us all, knowing he was proud of what his seed had created, but also knowing he had already dismissed me. He was 'woke,' he voted labor (sometimes, okay rarely, but more than most Tories), he had no problem with gay people, but I know as his first-born son he looked at me with disappointment. Christ, I was thankful for my little brothers, because if I had been my father's only son, I'm not sure he would have felt so embracing of the 'alternative lifestyle,' as he was so wont to say.

I felt my mother's eyes again and finished my food, desperate to get away from the look she was giving me. Unfortunately, all my siblings and my father fled the kitchen once dinner was done, leaving me to help my mother clean up and put everything away.

"How's school going Robin?" My mum asked as she washed the pots.

"Fine, I've got top marks."

"I know, you always have top marks, you're so clever," she smiled at me and put the last pot on the drying rack, turned the water off and dried her hands. "You seem distracted though, you have a special someone?" She asked meaningfully.

I blushed. "No," I scoffed, thinking I most assuredly didn't.

"But there was someone wasn't there?" She faced me. "Was it a boy from school?"

"What Mum?" I gasped, feeling exposed.

"You're gay, aren't you?" She said gently. "It's okay, I don't care, I love you, you know that."

I looked around the room feeling short of oxygen. I put down the drying towel and fled. Jesus Christ, I was wholly unprepared for my mum saying that to me. I know, especially according to Dee, I always gave off a gay vibe, but to have had my mum say it out loud, confirm it in our house, presumably tell my father later, made me want to throw up.

There was a knock on my door a short while later.

"Come in."

My mum came through and closed the door behind her. She crossed the room and sat next to me on my bed. "Robin, I love you, Dad loves you, I don't care. I only asked because I want to be a part of your life, and let you know that whatever path is yours I will support you," she looked at her hands nervously. "I don't care if you're gay."

I looked away, this was so much different from telling Dee, there was so much more at stake.

"Mum, I am," I whispered. "But Dad," I trailed off.

"Dad loves you, and he doesn't care either, we just want you to be safe and happy." She hugged me tightly. "Is there someone?" She prodded.

I shook my head. "No, just unrequited attraction," I said, my tone harsher than I meant, feeling morose again about Vas' neglect. "I should have told you, but the secret felt too big to share."

"Oh, Robby. You can tell me anything," my mum soothed. "This changes nothing, and Dad and I love you to the moon and back," she kissed my forehead.

I nodded and squeezed her hand. "I love you too Mum," I stood and walked to my desk. "Now, I have homework to finish."

My mum stood and hugged me tightly. "I'm so proud of you."

I smiled as she left and then my face fell as reality caught my eye on the back of my closet door to mock me.

8

Please Don't Let Me Hit the Ground

I FELT WEIRD the next day or so, exposed I suppose you could say, my secret laid bare to my parents. After a few awkward encounters, I realized that I was making more of it than it was. They had accepted me, and I should do the same, and once I shed that, I was able to eat again.

Thursday my phone buzzed. My stomach somersaulted and I swiped into the message from Vas.

Let's have lunch Sunday

I smiled, my face nearly splitting in two, while stifling irritation at having been ignored for so long.

Okay. Where?

It's your bday u decide

I typed quickly.

Franco Manca

I loved that restaurant now, and maybe we would even do more than just kiss in the bathroom.

See u at 1

* * *

The hairdresser cut my hair short, shorter than I wanted and I obsessed about it all weekend. I tried on every single hat in my closet and decided I would wear a beanie, like a skater boy, on Sunday. I had asked for a Caesar that was longer on top than she ended up giving me, and the sides were nearly bald, it was a fade like Vas' and I worried that it looked like I was copying him.

My mum made me breakfast in bed for my birthday on Sunday. "We're having dinner with Gram and Grandfather tonight, what do you and Dee have planned this afternoon?" My mum asked.

"I think we're just going to go to the mall, grab a bite, maybe hang at her house. I'll be home in time," I assured her, uncertain of what Vas had planned for us other than eating, and took a small bite of toast with blackberry jam, my favorite.

"After you eat, come down to open your presents," my Mum kissed my forehead and left the room.

I got everything I asked for and then some, including a new graphics card, a new gaming mouse for my computer, and cash. I hugged my parents, and hurried off with my bounty to get the good shower before Felicity cut in. I used my new shampoo and cologne, which smelled a bit more like perfume, just like I liked it, and hoped Vas would too. I combed and styled my hair, willing it to grow before covering it with a Commando beanie, sliding it back on my head, making sure my bangs peeked out.

I hollered goodbye as I skipped out the front door, my heart happy, I felt like breaking into song, (but didn't). I walked quickly to the Notting Hill Gate Tube stop, my step faltering as I saw Marcus walking ahead of me, shit, fuck, damn. I ducked behind a building and watched to see which way he was going. He went into the convenience mart and I hurried past, desperate to make it down the stairs to The Tube and disappear before he could see me.

"Where are you prancing off to princess?" Gareth, Marcus' lead henchman, said in a chiding voice. I looked behind me and saw his large face sneering at me. "I saw you duck behind the building, you're right to be scared."

"I'm just off, I don't want any trouble," I mumbled, more fearful of Gareth than I was Marcus, who somehow kept his goons in line. I went from wanting to avoid him, to willing him to come back outside and call off his dog. I kept walking and suddenly felt the beanie snatched from my head. "Hey! Give that back," I cried, smoothing my hair reflexively.

Marcus emerged from the store with a drink in his hand, and looked between us. "Hey Gareth," he smiled and opened his bottle. He took a sip and looked at me. "Where are you off to?" He asked me, his green eyes sweeping over my new outfit, the jeans and an Adidas t-shirt with my Duke + Dexter trainers. I saw him sniff the air. "Are you wearing perfume?"

Shit, why did I put on cologne? "It's my birthday, I'm going to the mall," I looked at Gareth. "I just want my beanie back."

Marcus nodded his head at Gareth and held out his hand. I prayed that Marcus would do the right thing and give it back to me. He was handsome in a straight way, appealing to the masses of girls who followed him around, or he would be if he weren't such a bully, because when he was being cruel he was not attractive. He put the beanie on his head.

"How's it look?" He asked Gareth.

"Suits you," Gareth shrugged. "You of course make it look hetero. This one makes everything look gay," Gareth nodded at me derisively with his chin.

"Please Marcus," I pleaded with my eyes, not feeling very hopeful.

"It's your birthday today?" He asked, ignoring my pleas.

I nodded.

He looked at Gareth. "Why don't you go inside and get the little princess here some champagne."

Gareth snickered and went inside.

"Marcus, I'm late, I just want my hat," I shifted on my feet, uncertain of his mood.

"Late for the mall?" Marcus scoffed and shook his head. "I've got something for you for your birthday," he said in a low menacing sounding tone.

"I'm meeting my boyfriend," I said in a rush, not knowing why I blabbed.

Something passed over Marcus' features and settled behind his eyes. "You've got a boyfriend?" he laughed meanly. "What does your fag-hag think about that?" He stepped closer to me.

He looked angry, not just playfully mean and I turned and fled before he could grab me, running as fast as I could down the stairs and away hurrying through the stiles, my eyes searching for any uniform I could find to hide behind. I shouldn't have said anything about a boyfriend.

It took the whole Tube ride to stop shaking and I walked the short distance down the sidewalk and into the mall, stopping in the bathroom to check my hair one last time.

Vas was sitting at our table, and there was a big bag with handles sitting on the table in front of him, he was halfway through a pint when he stood as I came in. I hugged him impulsively as I saw the bag was filled with wrapped gifts, smelling his neck as he smelled mine. He looked beautiful in a white button-down with grey geometric patterns and a pair of tight-fitting black pants.

"You cut your hair," he said looking at me.

I smoothed my hand over it. "She went shorter than I wanted."

"I like it," Vas smiled.

"Are those for me?" I asked, my voice high and girly, looking away from his heated glance.

"No, they're for the other birthday boy I'm meeting later," he grinned and shook his head. "Happy birthday Robin."

I smiled shyly and looked in the bag. "Do you want me to open these now, or later, somewhere else?" I trailed off, so hopeful.

His eyes flicked to my mouth briefly. "Sadly, there is nowhere else, today anyway, so open them now. I ordered pizza."

There were several gifts inside the bag and I looked at Vas with shock. "These are all for me? There's too many," I shook my head and blushed.

"Just open them."

The first one was a pink gaming headset with kitty ears and I nearly squealed. They were the ones I was fawning over at the game store weeks ago. Dee was going to die when she saw them. The next box had the shirt, shorts, and pajama bottom shorts that he had me try on the last time we were here. I looked at him with bewilderment.

"I don't have a sister," he grinned. "But if I did, I would never give her something that looked so spectacular on someone else," he added with a shrug and his sinful smile.

I blushed, remembering how he looked at me in the outfit. I put the clothes aside and pulled out another package. This one contained a Gillette razor and expensive looking shaving cream.

"You're seventeen now, I'm sure you have hair you have to shave," he said meaningfully, again dropping his 'h's.' Something I came to realize he did, like a tell, when he was feeling emotional.

I blushed an even deeper red as the waitress came with our pizza and my soda, which I drank, suddenly thirsty. I opened the last gift which was a bottle of Nair. I looked up at him as he chewed with a hooded expression.

"For the spots you don't want a blade near or can't reach," he said quietly.

"You're serious?"

He nodded and finished his beer. "And, I'm certain you will love it, I know I will."

And cue the erection. It was really straining this time, and that made me wonder about his. I wished I could look. Maybe I could drop my napkin. I took a bite of pizza and watched him watching me.

"What have you been up to for the past six weeks?" I asked hoping my voice was full of enough nonchalance to cover the petulant undertone.

"Finishing a big project for some rich wanker, wanted his house done yesterday but with all imported materials, and too stupid to understand production and shipping delays," he scoffed. "I love the creative aspect of my job, and the guys I work with, but most of the customers are pure shite."

I thought of the neighbors to the left of us who were always complaining about how slow their remodel was going, and now I wondered what the other side of the story was. "Must be frustrating, I never thought about it of course," I said taking another small bite. "Is your dad in construction? What made you go into it?"

"My Da is a machinist, a damn good one, and I like working with engines, but prefer carpentry, and he saw that, so he recommended me to a friend of his who has his own company when I got out of prison."

Wait, did he just say prison? (I heard him, did you?) "What were you in prison for?"

He threw his head back and laughed. "I fucking knew it," he said and looked at me. "I've never been to prison, I've never been to jail, and yet you're so fucking sheltered you think because I have tattoos, that because my cousin lives in East London, that we're all criminals," he said it with a laugh but there was an undercurrent. "You're so posh, I really can't wait to see you naked."

My eyes went wide, and my stomach nearly tumbled its way out of my body. We went from a, not-so-innocent, kiss to seeing me naked in the space of six weeks and a breath. I put my pizza down. Whatever game I thought we were playing, him lulling me into a sense of security by assuring me there was no stranger danger, just proved to me how far out of my league I really was. I caught my breath, and tried to backpedal my judgement. "I didn't think you were a criminal. You said it, not me."

"Ah, but you didn't question it, and you're as transparent as a window pane. I saw you judging my tattoos, your wince when I said where my cousin lived, and your frown when I said I worked construction," he shook his head, more with amusement than bitterness. "You ever come out of your ivory tower?"

I looked away, hating how he was making me feel. "I can't help where I was born, I don't judge you Vas. You're putting words in my mouth, and misreading my expressions," I looked around the restaurant. "I like your tattoos, I think they're quite sexy," I bit my lip, my voice high. I saw him smile. "I think you're the one judging me."

"Sorry, you *are* young and sheltered, but perhaps I can fix that," he said, something behind his eyes, and smiled at the waitress as she brought him another pint. "Have a sip," he pushed the glass to me.

I held his gaze and took the glass in two hands like a toddler, and sipped lightly, letting the foam coat my upper lip. I swallowed and licked my bottom lip before using just the tip of my tongue to lick my top. I put the glass down, feeling a thrill in my belly at his expression. He reached under the table and grabbed my knees, squeezing tightly before sitting back in the booth and looking down at his lap. Oh Christ, you'd have to be an imbecile to miss his meaning, and I would have dived under the table in a heartbeat if I hadn't heard my name being called. I exhaled to cool myself and looked to my left.

"Happy birthday Robby!" Dee cried as she came toward us. Oh, that sneak, I told her I was using her as cover and apparently, gave her too many details about my plans.

I stood and hugged her, as she stared at Vas. "You little sneak, payback's a bitch," I whispered in her ear.

She beamed, her beautiful face alight with mischief.

"Vasyl, this is my *former* best friend, Dee," I said pointedly, squeezing her waist good naturedly, "Dee this is Vas."

Vas stood and turned his smile on her, shaking her hand. "Wonderful to meet you Dee."

I saw and felt Dee's knees go weak, I felt like crowing 'I told you so!' from the top of my lungs.

"I don't mean to interrupt," she said, meaning exactly that as she looked at the bag of gifts and the half-eaten pizza on the table.

Vas moved the bag to his side of the booth smoothly and gestured for her to sit next to me. God, he was winning me over even more with his patience with her. I loved Dee, but she talked a mile a minute and dominated every conversation she was a part of, it's why we worked so well together, because I loved that shit, and she listened to me as much as she talked.

I gave her the piece of pizza I wasn't going to eat, and pushed my soda in front of her.

"Is it diet?" She asked, taking a bite.

"No, but don't worry, it's only half a glass," I said with a smile and looked at Vas who was watching us.

She took a sip, and wiped her mouth on my napkin, looking at Vas. "So, are you like a gangster, or a model or something?" She gestured at his tattoos and then his face.

"Sorry Vas, she has even less of a filter than me," I shrugged.

To his credit, Vas laughed, and as I watched him I imagined that he had had a raging hard-on for me, but had to extinguish it for Dee, just like I had. I wondered when we would ever be alone, and where. Couldn't be at my house, and he said his cousin had at least one flatmate. His place was a million miles away, and he never said if he lived with someone or not. Oh Christ, what if he lived with a lover, and that's why I never heard from him. I was vaguely aware of them talking. I looked between them and tried to see Vas from Dee's perspective. Was he a creep? He gave me women's clothing, teen girl's clothing actually, and implements to remove my body hair, that was weird right? I felt the air leave my body as I thought about how hot he was, and I really didn't care if anyone thought his gifts were weird. I couldn't wait to strip the hair from my body and dress in that outfit for him. I imagined dancing for him, maybe to Troye Sivan, or One Direction.

Dee elbowed me with a look of disgust. "Robin, pervy look," she hissed.

I shook my head and looked at Vas who was giving me that half-smile I felt in my gonads. "Sorry, did you ask me something?" I looked at Dee.

She narrowed her eyes and looked at her phone. "I know for a fact you have to be home in an hour to get ready to go to dinner with your grandparents in Knightsbridge. Do you want me to come?"

"No, Dee. But thank you. My grandparents love you but it's a school night, you and I can go another time," I smiled at her, and then looked at Vas who was sitting back in the booth and drinking. I wondered what he was thinking, and hoped he wasn't regretting being here, buying me the gifts he bought me. I looked at Dee, and then at my phone, seeing two missed texts from my Mum. Impulsively I stood. "I have to go to the loo, I'll be right back." I stood willing Vas to follow me.

I waited inside the door, making sure no one else was in there with me and pounced on Vas as he came through, he didn't know what hit him, only that it was tongue, and hands, and horny teen. His arms came around my body and hugged me, squeezing the breath from me while melding my body to his. I kissed him, and licked his neck, nibbling his ear lobe as he panted heavily, as though he'd run a road race.

"Jesus, Robby, I want you so badly, but not here," he shook his head as he kissed my lips, and my neck. "Next weekend, I'll get a hotel, can you get away for the night? Would Dee cover for you and not turn up unannounced?" he asked pointedly, a smile in his voice.

I nodded, knowing I would come up with something, anything to have this man to myself. "Yes, I'll make sure of it." I ran my hands over his muscled chest, he really was fit, and I couldn't wait to see him naked either.

He groaned and ran his hands over my bottom and squeezed, pulling me in tight against his groin so I could feel the effect I was having on him. I sighed against his mouth and stood on my tiptoes, my hands gripping the back of his neck as I rubbed myself against him. He ran his fingertips up the seam of pants while keeping my body clutched against his with his other hand and I nearly came in my pants. He pushed me away suddenly, with a shake of his head, his eyelids fluttered like butterflies breathing, and he gasped lightly.

"Robby," he breathed. "Next weekend, promise me," he said urgently.

"I promise," I nodded and licked my bottom lip as I looked at the bulge in his pants.

"Go," he said in a strangled voice "Dee is wondering, and like last time, here is where we'll say goodbye. Take your bag and go, I'll pay the bill."

I nodded and kissed him one last time, swirling my tongue around his before flouncing out the door.

I grabbed Dee, and my bag, and threw two twenty-pound notes on the table, he could punish me later for paying.

We rode The Tube to Queensway, I didn't want to run into Marcus, and Queensway was closer to Dee's anyway.

"Cor, he's hot, just like you said," Dee marveled. "What did you two do in the bathroom? You came out all hot and bothered."

I smiled and wrinkled my nose happily. "God he's so hot Dee, and such a good kisser. I know we're going to have sex soon. I can't wait," I shook my head. "I don't mean to be gross, or overshare, but Christ I almost came in my pants kissing him."

Dee blushed as her eyes went wide. "Really? Like that could happen? Not just in a book or a movie? You got so turned on you almost came?"

"Yes Dee, I almost did, it was so hot," I took a deep breath. "Oh god, I hope you find someone who makes you feel like this. I can't be the only one, I know I'm not the only one," I corrected, "I felt Vas on the verge too, he pushed me away, god his boner was huge."

Dee giggled uncontrollably. "He had a boner? Sounds gross."

"It's not, I promise," I said salaciously with a grin before kissing her at the corner of her street and continued home on cloud nine, knowing that I would be seeing Vas next weekend and it was going to be overnight. I couldn't wait to be alone with myself and felt impatient at the thought of sitting through dinner with my grandparents.

I pulled up short at the sight of my stolen beanie on the stone post at the entrance to my house. It had been cut into strips and the word 'fag' had been written in sharpie on the biggest bit. I looked around worriedly as I grabbed the hat so no one else would see. I knew Marcus wasn't done with me.

9

Man With a Plan

DEE AND I LOOKED at each other with secret smiles whenever we passed in the hall and pressed our heads together at lunch the next day. We talked about Vas and the upcoming weekend, and what I should do or wear. I hadn't told her about the Nair or the outfit, letting her think he just got me the headset and a razor as a little joke that now I was a 'man.' I had thought a lot about those things last night after dinner, reading the instructions on the bottle and giving the contents a sniff. It smelled awful and I wondered how I was going to use it without stinking up the whole house, guessing the bathroom in the basement was my best bet.

I was so happy, I was able to ignore Marcus and his goons, managing to avoid them for three full days, though Monday, in particular, I felt him watching me at lunch and worried he was plotting something. Monday night, once I was certain everyone was in bed, I tried on the outfit again, and took pictures of myself in the mirror, posing and turning to find the best angle before sending one to Vas and receiving a response right away.

> God you're so hot. I got us a room
> at the Blue Sapphire, I'll send u the
> address and see u there Sat afternoon.
> Bring the outfit I gave u

I smiled.

Can't wait

* * *

Wednesday was a normal day, usual classes, Dee and I were joined at lunch by our friend Sandra and we talked about TV programmes and plans for the weekend. I kept my mouth shut, not wanting to discuss Vas with anyone other than Dee. After school Dee had a dentist appointment so I walked home alone, past Carly's which wasn't on my way but I did love looking at 'our' table. I was about two blocks from home when Marcus popped out from behind a hedge.

"Took you long enough," he said in a rough voice. "You have a date with your boyfriend?" He sneered.

"Jesus Marcus," I cried, "you scared me." I collected myself, my heart was racing like a fucking train. I looked around for his goons who were conspicuously absent, and then at him warily. I did not like the look on his face, and began walking quickly away, searching for any adult to race toward.

"I asked you a fucking question," he said, grabbing my arm painfully. "You have a date with your boyfriend?"

"I don't have a boyfriend," I stammered, "I only said that so you would leave me alone, and give me my beanie back."

He narrowed his eyes. "I returned your stupid hat." He squeezed my arm, and looked away thinking. "Let's cut through the park."

Marcus followed me home and watched me go inside. I wasn't sure why, he never had before. I knew now that rugby season was over, I would be seeing more of him and his friends, and thought about hiring a car to take me to and from school for the remainder of the term. I couldn't wait for school to be over, for so many reasons, not the least of which was our holiday in Spain, where my parents had a house. It was a big house with a proper yard, and a pool, and trees and views of the ocean. I hoped that this year I could stay there by myself, maybe invite Vas, but then told myself to slow down, to see how this weekend went before planning vacations with the man. He was still a stranger, though we had spoken on the phone last night, laughing and getting to know each other better, both of us talking in hushed tones and innuendos.

I let myself in with the key around my neck and closed the door without a word. The house felt empty, and I went to my room to change out of my uniform. I put it in the hamper with a few other dirty things and took them to the wash-room, not wanting to have my mum do my laundry. I brought the bottle of Nair with me and went into the bathroom while the wash was running. I spread the goop around my balls and between my legs, careful not to get it on the tip of my cock, that shit smelled like it would sting. I waited the prescribed amount of time and then stepped into the shower. My asshole tingled as I rinsed and I watched the cream and the hair go down the drain, I hoped, belatedly, that it wouldn't clog. I soaped and tried not to breathe the fumes too deeply, the smell of sulfur in my nose. I turned on the vent fan when I got out and toweled off, taking the bottle of Nair with me when I went back upstairs.

I admired my handiwork in my closet mirror, using the flashlight on my phone to see my undercarriage, which looked as pink and smooth as a baby's bottom. That was unnerving, but I was guessing Vas was going to love it. I wasn't such a numpty to not know that part of my appeal to him was how young I looked, and it didn't bother me one bit. I used to hate looking so young, but now that I caught a god's eye, I was going to milk it for everything I could. I laughed out loud, 'milk it,' fuck, I couldn't wait to milk him.

I got dressed and sat at my desk to do homework, working my tongue as I did.

10

The Grand Blew-You-Best Hotel

"I'M GOING TO DEE'S for the night, there's a Pokémon match and she wants my help," I said to my Mum after breakfast on Saturday.

"Okay, do you want a ride?" She put the cereal box away and took George's bowl to the sink.

"No, I'm gonna meet her for ice cream first and then we're hunkering down."

"Have fun," she smiled and returned my hug.

I packed a small bag, figuring I didn't need much more than what he told me to bring and left the house at two, knowing I had to change Tube lines and it would take me about a half an hour to get there. I sent him a quick text.

> I've just changed trains, should
> b there in less than 10

Vas responded immediately that he would meet me out front and my heart ka-thunked in my chest, I looked around the full train with a big smile and then went back to surfing Instagram.

Vas greeted me with a hug and ushered me inside, taking my bag and putting his arm on my shoulder.

I suppose you think you're entitled to hear about what happened once we stepped through the hotel room door, that you expect to hear the description of the room (clean and sparsely modern), demand to know what Vas was wearing (jeans and a sinfully tight t-shirt), and what it was that he said to me (something about my appearance) but I'll tell you nothing other than it was over quickly, and hurt, a lot. He tried to go slow, oh we both had such youthful ambition, and he tried to be gentle, truly, but he was massive and no amount of lube or slow pace could have helped our first time be anything less than lip-biting, nails in the flesh, agony. And I loved every minute of it.

"I'm sorry Robby," he breathed in my ear, still panting with passion and exertion, "I promise to take my time next time. You just felt so fucking good."

And he did take his time, we both did. His tongue soothing my pain, my mouth devouring him, my heart and stomach fluttering at the sounds of delight he was making between my legs. We did everything, I'm pretty sure we hit every position in the Kama Sutra, and it wasn't even dawn. Vas went out for pizza at some point, we ate crossed legged on the bed before cuddling again, which turned to kissing, and petting, and then of course, sex. I marveled at being in a bed with him, with anyone really, especially doing what we just did, without worry of anyone happening upon us. The mattress was soft, the sheets white and virginal and I fought the urge to look for blood.

He didn't laugh at my small penis, in fact he stroked it happily enough, though awkwardly, so we could come together, (which we did, a lot). I thought it was because he hadn't handled anything quite so small since maybe he was ten, fondling his own undeveloped cock, but then he told me why.

"I have something to confess," he said as he trailed his fingers over my white bicep. "I've never had sex with a man before," he said.

I propped myself up on my elbow in shock. "What?"

He grinned. "I've done it with plenty of women, in fact, I have a girlfriend," he looked askance at me, "but I was always curious, and then I saw you, like you had a spotlight on you," he shook his head. "And now, well," he blew out a breath.

My body went cold, and frankly, I kind of stopped listening after the mention of him having a girlfriend. I felt stupid for having slept with him so quickly, and not at least insisting that we be boyfriend-boyfriend first, or at least agree to be exclusive, but I suppose that was naïve and passé of me. Did people even do that anymore? I didn't know but I couldn't let the comment go. "You have a girlfriend?"

"Yes, but Robby, I'm breaking up with her tomorrow," he sat up as I pulled away. "This was magical, I don't know how else to describe it," he raised his eyebrows and kissed my shoulder. "You don't have a boyfriend?"

I didn't know how to respond, so I just told the truth. "No, of course I don't," I scoffed. "God, the only people who want to be seen with me are girls who think I will be their perfect gay best friend, and Dee, who loves me for who I am," I winced. "No boy at school would dare be caught dead with me, and while I'm not the only femboy there, we're not interested in each other," I shuddered.

"Okay, I get it," Vas put his hand up defensively. "But I look at you and think who wouldn't want you? You have the face, and the body of an angel," his eyes scanned me heatedly. "I love that you shaved. Your body is so smooth, so white," his touch was like fire on my skin. He leaned forward and kissed my nipple, and put his hand between my legs.

* * *

I woke early and rolled out of Vas' arms to look at him. He looked younger, but still a man, and I felt a tiny thrill. His body was as dreamy as you could imagine, and he shaved too, though not between his legs. His chest was perfect and smooth, he told me he worked out at the gym every day, usually after work, because he was up early to be at the job site. He had a bunch of gym friends and they would encourage each other to be better and look better, some of them competed professionally but Vas said he wasn't into that, he just wanted to look good. I assured him that he looked spectacular, and while he loved hearing that, he especially loved me telling him how big his cock was which I did emphatically. I wasn't lying, it was the biggest thing I'd ever seen, aside from my dad's, which I thankfully never saw hard. Gross, that was a disgusting thought I put out of my head immediately and decidedly by lifting the sheet and looking at Vas' morning wood.

I reached for my phone and took a few selfies of me with Vas, not to share, but to have, god he was so beautiful. I put my phone down as I felt him stir, and pretended to be asleep. He kissed my shoulder, and then my neck, and then my shoulder again, as he ran his hand lightly down my side and over my hip, raising goosebumps on my flesh. He kissed my ear and nibbled my lobe, I raised my shoulder and giggled reflexively. He reached between my legs as he pressed his hardness against my ass and I came alive.

"There's breakfast," he said as he rolled out of bed to take a shower. "Put on the outfit I gave you and let's go eat."

"You want me to wear that in public?" I asked, not keeping the surprise out of my voice.

"Yes," he grinned his wicked grin and disappeared into the small bathroom.

We went down to breakfast, the dining room thankfully small and not overly populated though I felt eyes on me, and on Vas, and on us together. He winked at me and walked through the buffet line, heaping his plate with eggs and food, more food than I had ever seen a human eat in one sitting. I put some bread in the toaster and looked for a decent jam from the selection of pods.

"You're eating more than toast," he raised his eyebrows. "You're too skinny, you could stand about four kilos, but no more," his mouth twitched.

I took some bacon and a waffle, but skipped the eggs.

I wrinkled my nose as I sat down across from him and his plate that was heaped with eggs, giving the judgey lady next to us the side eye. "You know what an egg is right?" I asked him.

Vas just looked at me and put a heaping forkful of food in his mouth. "It comes from a chicken and it tastes delicious. It is used in a billion different recipes, including cake, and not a day goes by that I don't eat them."

"A chicken poops them out, it's ovulation, and mucus, it's disgusting," I scoffed.

"You know too much. I just want to enjoy my food," Vas said eventually and kept eating.

I smoothed my hair and began eating, taking small bites and looking around the dining room. I knew we were getting looks, him with his tattoos and me with my bare midriff and short shorts. But Vas didn't give a shit, and so neither did I, though it was hard to be nonchalant, I could only imagine what they thought, as I was really playing up the young angle, the response I got from Vas was invigorating.

I put my elbows on the table and shook my shoulders back and forth slightly. "When do we have to check out?"

Vas looked at his watch, a plain watch, maybe a Casio, maybe a Timex, I didn't know because no one I knew wore a watch, except for old people, like my parents, and my dad wore a Rolex. One thing I knew for sure, it wasn't a Rolex on Vas' wrist.

"We have another two hours," he raised his eyebrows at me, and his mouth turned up in that delicious, sinful half-smile.

I took another bite and pushed my plate away with a challenging expression.

Vas tilted his head inquisitively before finishing his food. He stood and nodded to the door.

We did it in the shower, with extra lube because I was so sore I felt like crying. I eventually made him stop and I took him in my mouth, he groaned at that, ass-to-mouth. I didn't even think about it, I just wanted the pain to stop but not at the expense of Vas' pleasure. I definitely wouldn't tell Dee that little detail, though it became a big feature in our porn, so I suppose she and anyone who was interested could look it up and see it within two clicks of a mouse.

***

We kissed, Vas worshipping my mouth like it was his last drop of water before venturing into the Sahara, and left the hotel, him headed north and me headed west. I went straight to Dee's, not wanting to speak of what happened the night before at a place like school where we could be overheard. She let me in and we scurried to her room like fugitives. I flopped down on her unmade bed and sighed.

"Christ I could absolutely go to sleep right this minute."

"Did you sleep at all last night?" Dee asked with a laugh.

"Not really no," I said suggestively and got out my phone.

"Oh Jesus, did you film yourselves?" Dee asked in horror. "I don't want to see it!"

"No, god no," I laughed as I swiped to the picture I took of Vas in his boxer briefs. I held it up to her and she gasped.

"Holy mother of god, he is beautiful," she covered her mouth and then peered at the screen. "Does he shave or is his hair so faint you can't see it?"

"He said he waxes, it's a gym thing, and oh my god, his skin was so smooth."

"What was it like? Did it hurt like, for a woman?"

"It still does, I think it might hurt more, but of course I have nothing to compare it to. He was massive so that was one reason, and the fact that we did it like seven or eight times was the other."

"No way! You exaggerate," she shook her head with a laugh. "How is that even possible?"

"Youth, desire, and time, are the three magic ingredients," I grinned, wishing that we had had more of the latter, though my asshole definitely needed a break. I told her a few more details, particularly the breakfast stares, and the fact that I was Vas' first.

"He was straight?" She frowned. "I could have met him first?" She sighed. "Wait, you were your both firsts. How romantic!"

I smiled and looked away. "He has a girlfriend," I said with a pout, "but he swears he's breaking up with her, said I was 'magical.'"

"Oh, how romantic, and I hope he does, and that he's not one of those cheaters who never leaves his main bitch," she looked at my bare legs sticking out of my generic sports shorts and turned her head. "Did you shave your legs?"

I pressed my lips together and exhaled an amused sound. "Maybe," I shrugged. "He wanted me to."

"Why?" she furrowed her brow.

"I didn't ask, but I'm guessing because he's mostly straight and wanted me to be more feminine," I replied thinking of the girl's clothes and him calling my ass a pussy. Again, I didn't say a word of this to Dee. "I liked it, a lot. Everything is very smooth," I smiled secretly, "and his smooth chest against mine felt like heaven," I looked around her room. "Do you have any laxatives? Or Metamucil?"

She went to her desk drawer and pulled out a sheet of pills, half of them were missing. "You can have them, they don't work for weight loss," she pulled a face.

"Thanks, I just need them till I'm no longer sore," I laughed. "And it better be before next weekend, because I am dying to see him again. Dee, he smells and tastes so good, and sleeping in his arms was like a dream. Thank you for covering for me, I said we were playing Pokémon so if my mum ever asks when you're over, just make something up about the match."

"Of course, so am I going to be your cover for next weekend too?" She asked. "What does he do again? Can he just afford swanky hotels every weekend?"

"He's a builder, and the hotel was very nice, clean and modern but apparently not that expensive, and I could certainly offer to pay."

"Wouldn't your parents notice the charges?" Dee scoffed.

"I'd give him the cash and he could put it on his card. I have a slew of money in the bank from birthdays and Christmas."

We talked some more until I yawned, exhausted, thinking about the mountain of homework I still had to do. I hugged her and told her I'd see her tomorrow.

My mum was in the garden when I got home. I kissed her hello and made up some story about the night before begging off with a glass of water to go study. I fell asleep at my desk, halfway through calculus and woke to David's knock and bellow that dinner was ready. I looked at my phone and saw two missed messages from Vas.

I opened them excitedly.

> God this train ride is long, thank god
> I have some spectacular memories to
> tide me over

> R u napping sleepyhead?

I laughed as I typed.

> Yes, as a matter of fact I completely fell
> asleep on my math homework. I've dinner
> now and I've got to keep the shit-eating
> grin off my face so no one suspects that
> I was anywhere other than Dee's

I'm home now, and wondering already
if u can come next weekend, for the
whole weekend, my flatmate is going
on holiday with his girlfriend

I'll have to think of something,
but I hope so

He sent back a smiley face with a peach and an eggplant.
I sent him a smile and a heart.

11

Chased by the Wolves of Willoughby

MONDAY WAS BUSY with schoolwork, in fact the whole week was and I was focused on classes, homework and Vas. I was so busy daydreaming about what I was going to tell my parents that I didn't notice Marcus and them fall in behind me on my way home Wednesday. My backpack felt like it was filled with bricks as usual, and I walked slowly, counting the white cars that were parked and drove by, one of the little games I played when I was walking home. I was on thirteen when I heard my name. My bowels clenched at the sound of Gareth's voice, asking me what I did with his hat, and saying that he wanted it back. I didn't dare look over my shoulder, but I was praying that Marcus was there, because I felt a beating coming, so I sneaked a peek.

I saw Gareth, Frank, and Hector, all rugby mates of Marcus', and then Marcus himself, standing at the back, his handsome face glaring at me. I puzzled over his intense expression before turning my head and continuing on my way, wondering if I should detour through the park in hopes of losing them, or whether I should make a beeline for home.

"What's your hurry fag?" Gareth called. "You got a hot date with your boyfriend, can't wait to suck his dick?"

I ignored him, I learned long ago to never engage, respond, or try to defend myself, only focus on trying to find a sympathetic adult, or a store to duck into, or better yet, the safety of home, like in a game of tag. This year their teasing had felt like a game but today it felt sinister, and I didn't know why.

"Gareth's talking to you femboy," one of the other guys called, I couldn't tell Frank and Hector apart, they looked alike, thick necks, brutish and dark though one was skinnier than the other. Even their voices were the same, and their mouths frozen permanently in a sneering expression of degradation. My stomach went cold with fear, and I willed Marcus to say something. I wondered if I detoured myself through the park whether Marcus would shoo them away. He loved to cajole me, and call me names but he never hurt me. This felt feral and I wished they had rugby practice to get their excess fucking testosterone out.

Someone shoved me and the weight of my backpack propelled me forward, I couldn't catch my feet and went flying on my face, the skin of my palms torn open on the sidewalk, my chin scraping before I was able to lift my neck to avoid further damage. I cried out involuntarily feeling tears behind my eyes from the pain and humiliation. First one, then another and another kicked me while I was down, knocking the wind from me so that I gasped like a fish out of water, before Marcus came to stand over me. He looked down at me with something dark in his eyes before kicking me hardest of all.

They filed away laughing while tears streamed from my eyes, and I finally regained my breath. My heart felt cold in a way that it hadn't since the last time I was beaten like this. I remember that time so well. It was thugs from my old school, when I was year nine, and they were beating me near the park after school, and Marcus had called a stop to it, happening upon it as one of the guys held my arms and another punched my skinny frame. One word from him and they released me. They didn't know who he was, just that he was older, and bigger and he had that way about him. As a result, when I transferred to his school and saw him, I showed him respect, sometimes nonchalantly and other times openly. He and I were like the lion and the mouse, I occasionally helped him with his homework (and by helped him I mean I did it for him), and in return he would make sure no one physically harassed me anymore, until then.

I pushed myself to my feet, noticing a tear in the left knee of my pants that I would have to sew, and dusted myself off, picking the gravel from my palms, thinking I would deal with my chin later.

I snuck quietly into the house, tucking my key back under my shirt and headed for the stairs. Felicity came out of her room on her way to her afterschool job and pulled up short. "Jesus Robby, your chin is bleeding all over your shirt," she frowned and then scanned my body, noticing the rip in my pants.

I held her gaze defiantly. "I tripped," my voice breathless because it hurt to breathe.

She narrowed her eyes. "Did you get jumped?"

"No," I scoffed. "Oh, you fucking care? Mind your business," I turned and slammed the door to my room.

I dropped my bag and peeled my uniform off, noticing the blood on my shirt, and the bruising on my side, where it felt as though they had broken a rib, no, that bastard Marcus had broken a rib. I knew there was nothing that could be done for a cracked rib, and I certainly wasn't going to tell my parents about it, so I ignored that and focused on changing so I could go to the bathroom and wash my hands and chin. I waited to be sure Felicity had left for her shift and crossed the hallway to the bathroom, scraping the gravel out of my hands and chin carefully, knowing it would scab and I wouldn't be able to hide it at school, or at the dinner table. I wondered if my mum would let me miss the next two days. I touched my side gingerly and wondered if I should cancel this weekend with Vas. I felt fresh tears at that thought. I was already missing his beautiful body, that flat muscle expanse around his perfect bellybutton, his perfect square man boobs, excuse me, pecs, he very firmly corrected me when I called them man boobs.

I went back to my room for my phone. I opened my messages.

> I'm not sure if I can come this wknd.
> I had a little accident on the way
> home from school today, my bag
> was too heavy

It was early so I didn't expect a response, I knew he was still at the gym. About forty minutes later I got a text.

> R u okay? I can come to London,
> I want to c u

I smiled and wondered about telling him the truth. I didn't want to say anything over text so I told him never mind I would be fine, and then would think of a story once I got to Manchester.

$$12$$

Man, Oh Manchester

MARCUS AND THEM avoided me for the next two days, as they rightly should. I made a big show of wincing with pain in my side whenever I saw Marcus, and my chin spoke for itself, I was lucky I hadn't chipped a tooth. I was especially angry at Marcus, not that I could say anything to him about it, Christ that would earn me a punch to the face or worse. Instead I focused on the weekend in Manchester with Vas.

I told my parents I was meeting friends that Dee and I knew from gaming, and that I'd be gone until Sunday. My mother expressed concern because of my chin and hands, and because she noticed I was favoring my side. She let me go thinking I would be well taken care of at Dee's.

I only came home Friday to change out of my uniform and grab my packed bag, running down to the laundry to get the shorts and belly shirt Vas had given me. I searched through the baskets, and the dryer and couldn't find them. *Fuck*, I knew I washed them with my other clothes, but they were missing. I was worried about missing my train as I came up the stairs to search my room. Felicity was coming out of her room all dolled up for a Friday afternoon out with friends, wearing the shorts that Vas had given me. I guessed the belly shirt was under her cute sweatshirt and my blood began to boil.

"Those are my shorts Feliss, take them off," I said angrily.

Felicity pulled a face at me. "These are girl's shorts you perv, they're not yours."

"I mean it Feliss," I said in my deepest, angriest tone. "Those are mine and I want them back. Go change, or I swear to god you will regret it."

She studied me for a moment, sussing out my sincerity. "Fine," she relented.

"The shirt too, you slag. I know you've got it on."

She narrowed her eyes and looked at my chin before slamming her door behind her. I waited as she came back out, in a new outfit and handed me my crumpled clothing.

"You're such a freak. No wonder people bully you at school," she sneered.

I grimaced slightly at that comment, but refused to let her wear me down, instead focusing on Vas and how good he was going to make me feel in about three point two hours. I packed the clothes in my bag, hating that they smelled like Felicity now, and headed to the train station, ever wary of Marcus and his goons, though I doubted he would try anything again.

Vas met me at the train station in a BMW that looked to be about ten years old but was in mint condition. He kissed me across the console, pressing his tongue into my mouth before pulling back with a smile that quickly fell.

"What the fuck happened to your chin?" He frowned.

"I told you, I fell, it's okay," I shook my head. "Do you live far from here? I can't wait to be alone with you," I said in a high voice. I smiled inside at his reaction and watched him put the car in gear, pulling away from the curb with a chirp.

I knew Vas was a horndog for me, knew he couldn't wait to see me naked any more than I could wait to see him, but once inside, when we started undressing in his small bedroom he stopped and stared at my hands, and then at the ugly bruise on my side which was a reddish purple. He looked at my face with an angry expression, one that frightened me, one that was just a glimpse of what was to come.

"Who the fuck did this to you?"

I swallowed and looked away, not wanting to give Marcus up, but loving, and not questioning, Vas' concern. "No one Vassy, please, kiss me," I begged softly, and kissed him, slipping my hand into his underwear.

He let me kiss him, met my tongue with his before pushing me gently away with a frown. "I mean it Robby. Who did this to you? And if you tell me you fell I will lose my shit, don't ever lie to me."

"Oh please, you're surprised I get bullied? I told you," I pulled out of his arms and stepped away. "You don't have to feel sorry for me, you just have to take care, I'm pretty sure I have a broken rib."

Vas' hands went instantly to his head before clenching by his sides. "Some rich, poncy fucker broke your rib and you want me to ignore it? Who was it?" He asked in a cold voice.

"I don't know their names, they're all upper sixth."

"Bullshit!" Vas cried. "Don't fucking lie to me."

"What are you going to do? Beat them up for me? They're just rugby bullies," I said, a small part of me was thrilled with the idea of Vas taking them on. "You can't come after a classmate, I'll handle it."

"I can scare the shit out of them," he looked at me. "Please Robby, I can't stand the thought of someone hurting you."

"No," I breathed and turned back, my cock as hard as a rock with his bravado. "Just fuck me, my legs in the air, I do so love the view."

He looked as though he wanted to say something more but grabbed me gently around the waist and kissed me deeply.

* * *

Our time together passed in a blur, Vas loving me from every angle, telling me stories and jokes, showing me first around his tiny flat, and then around the bigger neighborhood. He didn't seem bothered about running into people he knew with me, introducing me as his friend. I kept my lisp in check so no one would speculate, standing quietly to the side as he chatted, admiring his smooth confident way of being. I wondered about him in his previous life, pre-me. Watched how women looked at him, how he flirted so easily with them.

I asked him about his girlfriend when we got back to his flat on Saturday after brunch.

"I broke it off with her," he looked at me. "I did it on Sunday when I got back. We weren't serious but at any rate, being with you was, is, what I want, not her."

I smiled and kissed him, feeling thrilled to my toes with his declaration. Of *course he wanted me and not some slag.*

"You said you've never had a boyfriend, but is there someone you liked, or have a crush on?" Vas asked me as we laid in bed Saturday afternoon.

I blushed. "I used to think our star footballer was cute, but then I met you, and now when I look at him I can't imagine what I was thinking."

Vas smiled and rolled on top of me, holding himself off my rib. "You are the beautiful one," he kissed me, little feathering kisses that smacked gently and audibly.

He pressed me about my injuries but I remained firm in my silence. "It doesn't matter, they won't try it again. I promise," I soothed him. "Tell me about your flatmate."

"Olek? What do you want to know?" Vas asked with a hint of amusement and stood from the bed. "I'm hungry," he left the room and I followed, pulling on the little pajama shorts.

"I don't know, how long have you known him? What does he do for work? Where are he and girlfriend this weekend?"

"He and I work together, he's an electrician, and I've known him since I was around twenty," Vas went to the kitchen and got two sodas and a bag of crisps, handing me one and following me to the couch. He opened the bag and began eating, his teeth crunching loudly. "They went to Paris I think."

I looked around the simple room, taking in the mismatched furniture and large coffee table with a couple of bodybuilding and car magazines. There was an Xbox under the oversized TV with several controllers. I looked back at him. "Does he know about me?"

"No," Vas said simply. "Does anyone other than Dee know about me?" He countered.

"No," I pursed my lips thinking. "We're secret lovers then. It's fine with me," I lisped and shifted my shoulders back and forth absentmindedly. I felt Vas' eyes on me as I looked away and smiled to myself.

I couldn't keep my hands off him, hands that looked so small and pale on his impossibly muscular body, hands that made him sigh and moan. I especially loved his neck, the stubble of hair above St. Michael's head and wings under my fingers as I gripped him and pulled his mouth to mine. The sense of being in a movie, like this was happening to someone else, was ever-present, incredibly sexy, and at times dizzying. I wondered if he felt the same. I wondered if he liked the look of his dark hands on me, one tattooed, both of them nearly spanning my waist as he lifted me easily into his lap. I also wondered, for the hundredth time, why me?

13

Introducing Ronald, Later Known as Ronnie

WE SPENT EVERY WEEKEND together between my birthday and August, with the exception of two, passing the time in much the same way, just in different locations, usually hotels. We had taken to renting interior, windowless rooms which were cheaper, because we were far more interested in the view inside anyway. When we were out and about people couldn't help but look at us. I knew we were an odd couple to say the least, and our attraction to each other was undeniable, kinetic. I loved holding his hand when we walked from the pub back to the hotel after a few pints, and loved that he let me. I would run my fingers over his tattoos, imagining that I could feel them like braille, and each time I did, they told me a different story.

The first weekend after Manchester, he took my ID from my hand after the waiter handed it back to me.

"Hey," I said feebly.

Vas perused my fake ID, the one that said I was eighteen, and looked at me with raised eyebrows.

"What? It's only a little fake," I said, nearly telling the truth.

"This is professional. Where'd you get it Ronald?" Calling me by the name on the ID and handed it back to me.

"The internet," another half-truth.

He made a sound of agreement. "You can find anything on the internet," he said with his sinful half-smile.

I looked at him and didn't have to think too hard about what he was implying, and weeks later it came up again, as I wondered aloud, finally, about what drew him to me.

"I always had an interest, but thought everyone did," he grinned sitting crossed-legged opposite me on the bed eating pizza, our preferred between-sex meal. "I started with threesome porn, two guys and a girl, but the guys were too hairy, and I'm not into flip-fucking," he looked at me. "I happened upon twink porn somehow, so hairless and unreal the boys were. Like women but without all the distracting, fake moaning," he laughed. "I was turned on by the idea of men who look like women, but not trannies," he clarified quickly, "I don't like chicks with dicks, or long hair, I mean they're clearly men, but lean and smooth," he looked at me and then grew serious. "And then I saw you, and you looked at me like you knew, so I followed you to the coffee shop."

I put my pizza crust back into the box and looked at him. "I couldn't believe you noticed me, and then our first kiss," I gave him my coy smile, the one I had been perfecting in the mirror since we first met, "was magic Vassy. I'm the luckiest boy."

Vas pushed the pizza box aside and met me on his knees.

14

Summer Lovin'

SCHOOL ENDED MID-JULY and my parents declared we were leaving for Spain the last week of the month and staying until the third week of August. I chafed at being away from Vas that long and begged to stay home for the first week, saying I had some study sessions set up for my A-levels. My father praised my initiative, my mother looked worriedly at me as though I couldn't manage on my own for a few days, while Felicity looked at me suspiciously. I ignored her, knowing she wouldn't press the issue because she had done the same thing at Christmas, joining us two days after we left so she could have sex with her boyfriend. I narrowed my eyes at her when it looked as though she were going to suggest staying home too, just as Mum said they'd be fine without me for a week since Feliss would be there to help with George and David. I fought to keep the triumph off my face and succeeded, for the most part.

I called Vas from bed, wearing the pajama shorts he gave me, the sides cinched up and no shirt, the hair on my chest growing in stubbly.

"Hi sexy," I said when he answered. "What are you doing the last week of July?"

"Hey doll. I have to work, why?"

"Because I'll have the house to myself, before I leave for Spain," I replied and held my breath.

Vas was quiet, thinking maybe, plotting perhaps. "The whole week?"

"Yes," I said quietly.

"I can't take the whole week off, but I could work Wednesday and Thursday, only being gone Wednesday night," he answered, sounding out the idea.

"That's perfect," I said beaming, letting my happiness shine down the phoneline to him. "I'll have you the rest of the time, and that's all that matters."

"I'll have to work this weekend, in order to pull it off, but send me your address and I'll come, and then we'll both come," he said suggestively.

"Oh, I love that idea, but hate not seeing you this weekend," I pouted.

"Me too Robby, but I'll call you Saturday night and we can pretend."

I felt a twinge at the thought. We'd had phone sex for the first time last week, and after a minute of awkwardness we fell into it like we'd been doing it all along, kind of like the porn later.

* * *

I kissed my parents goodbye the following Saturday morning, and had Vas through the door an hour after their flight left.

"Jesus, you live here?" Vas said as he walked into the large marble foyer carrying a small duffle bag. "It's massive."

I looked around self-consciously. The modern art, and décor were noticeably expensive and well-kept, as my dad had high standards, and my mum was a neat freak. I knew we lived a posh life, but so did everyone I knew, except maybe Dee, whose house was big but not as grand. I didn't know what to say, because obviously I did live there, so I just showed him in, pointing briefly at the rooms as we passed. I took him to my room, which I had cleaned from top to bottom all week, doing it in little bits so as not to be obvious to my mum. I had changed the sheets on the double bed the minute they left the house and ran the hoover.

Vas stepped through the door and looked around. He put his bag in my desk chair and turned to look at me, his eyes amused. He waved a hand at my anime and Pokémon and teeny bopper posters, and the stuffed animals on the bed. "It looks like a twelve-year-old lives here."

I walked closer to him and undid his zipper. "Does that turn you on?" I asked in my youngest, huskiest voice.

He tilted his head. "You turn me on," he kissed me as I did things to him with my hand. "I like how young and smooth you look, so feminine, but I wouldn't be interested in you if you were *actually* underage. I've no interest in going to prison," he pressed me back onto the bed. "I can't wait to fuck you surrounded by all your stuffed animals," he grinned.

I know, there's a lot of sex in this story, but first, I told you there was porn, so don't be shocked now, and second, I was sixteen, and horny *all* the time. He was twenty-seven and beautiful, and horny for me, so we did it, a lot. We did it in the kitchen, in the living room, and even outside in the garden. We talked a lot too, learning about each other, sharing secrets, dreams, plans. I heard about his girlfriends, and was really fascinated by the idea that this hetero man suddenly switched teams for me, because of me.

"You've really never been with a man before?" I asked over breakfast on Monday. I had made eggs (disgusting I know), but don't be surprised, I can cook, I just don't like to eat. My mum made me learn to cook the things my younger siblings liked. I watched Vas finish his omelet.

"I fooled around in secondary with a couple of guys, let one of them suck my cock, but we never had the opportunity to have sex, and I wouldn't dare risk it in the park or somewhere," he looked at me.

I looked away, a little deflated at the thought that I wasn't his actual first, but I shouldn't have been surprised, I'm certain members of both sexes threw themselves at him, I saw how people looked at him when we were out, before they noticed me of course. "When did you know you were gay? Did you ever tell any of your girlfriends?"

"I've always known I was attracted to guys, or bi, but I never felt comfortable admitting that to anyone, I would never tell my girlfriends but I always asked for anal, so they might have wondered," he shrugged.

"Did any of them let you?"

"One or two, it wasn't like fucking you though," he pushed his empty plate away and reached for my hand. "Your ass is so tight and so beautiful, and tastes so good," he licked his bottom lip. "Come here," and he bent me over the table, lifting my leg up and knelt down.

He would do *that*, but he wouldn't ever suck my cock. He licked it, but never took it all the way in his mouth. I mean, he loved making me come, watching my face intently when I did, insisting that I let him know when I was about to, because he loved coming with me, but he never did it with his mouth. It was ages before I ever felt a mouth on my cock, and when I did, holy shit, I would never go willingly without it again. If a guy wouldn't take me in his mouth that was a deal breaker, and unfortunately, for more than a few tops, doing it was a deal breaker for them too.

* * *

Vas was looking at the family pictures in the big living room, picking one up and then putting it down to pick up another one, when I came up from the laundry room.

"Who's who?" He asked, looking over his shoulder as he heard me come in.

"Mum and Dad, obviously," I pointed, "my older sister Felicity, she's a bitch, that's David," I pointed at the brown-haired boy next to me, "and that's George."

"How old are they? He looks really young," he pointed at George.

"Oh god, you're not already looking to move on, are you?" I half-teased.

"No, don't be gross," Vas elbowed me.

"Feliss is eighteen, David is twelve, and George is eight," I rattled off.

"Oh, are you two Irish twins?" He asked looking at Felicity's picture.

"She's gonna be nineteen," I mentally kicked myself for not catching that before I said it, in fact Felicity had her birthday just before me. Eventually this lie was going to catch up with me and I hoped Vas wouldn't be too mad.

"Nice looking family, your mum's pretty, she looks a lot younger than your dad."

"She is, by ten years," I twisted my mouth. "I often wonder what she sees in him, I mean he's nice looking, but he's pretty strict with us, and kind of a douche to people."

Vas put the picture down and looked around the room, and then gestured with his hand. "I think it's fairly apparent what she sees in him."

I chuckled slightly. "She's the one with the money, he used to work at a company my grandfather owned, that's how they met, he married the boss' daughter."

"Oh, is that right?" Vas made a thoughtful sound.

"Yup, until recently anyway, now he makes a boatload doing something in high-tech, don't ask because I have no bloody idea," I laughed and turned. "I'm running to the market for some milk and soda, do you want anything?"

"Bananas, if they have 'em," Vas said and kissed me.

I left the house, the afternoon sun baking the back of my neck as I made my way to Sainsbury's with an empty shopping bag in my hand. I shopped for what I needed with purpose, not wanting to be away from Vas for too long. I bought some chocolate-filled croissants for breakfast in addition to the bananas and paid, bagging my items and walking out into the sun. It was a perfect day really, not too hot, sun shining brightly, traffic was light since most Londoners were on vacation, and I felt like singing, in fact I did sing, to myself of course, I'm not a complete nut job.

"Buenos tardes, Robby. Aren't you supposed to be in Spain?" I heard a voice say to me from my left. I felt my bowels churn and winced, increasing my pace.

"I'm talking to you Robby," Marcus called again. "What's your hurry? You have a date with your *boyfriend*?"

I glanced at him, his bare legs and arms tan. He looked beautiful in a bad guy way, in a way I never would. "No, I have to pack. My parents are waiting for me," I said in a quiet voice, and kept walking, willing him to have an errand so he would leave me alone.

He grabbed the bag out of my hand and looked inside. He took a soda and handed the bag back to me. "Why did you run to the market for all this then? I'm pretty sure your family left already Robby, you lying to me, again?" He opened the soda and took a long swallow, looking at me from the side of his eye.

"Marcus, I don't want any trouble, I thought you understood my position," I said meaningfully.

Marcus stopped. "You threatening me?" He narrowed his eyes and I began walking again, he grabbed for my pocket and I dashed out of reach, breaking into a run.

He tackled me in the park. I landed hard on my knees, my bag went flying, the contents mostly staying inside. "What hotel you meeting him at today? Or is he at your house, waiting for you?"

I swallowed nervously, wondering how Marcus knew, what had he seen? "Nowhere. No. Why do you care?"

He shrugged as he pinned me to the ground. "I hate it when people lie to me. Just tell me the truth and I'll let you go."

I eventually got away from him and made it home, late, sans croissants and a banana short, but home in one piece. I was drinking my soda as I came through the front door and nearly bumped into Vas.

"Where the hell have you been?" He asked me, looking into my soul it felt like. "I was just about to come looking for you."

I took another sip of soda to clear my throat. "I walked through the park, I love looking at Princess Di's memorial, and I fed the birds," I shrugged. "Did we have plans?" I added nonchalantly with my coy smile, and brushed past him. The last thing I need was him going on some sort of beat down spree, seeking out Marcus for harassing me and stealing my croissants.

"I texted you, and then called," Vas continued with a frown, taking the bag from me and following me into the house.

"Sorry," I pulled my phone out and saw three missed texts and a missed call from him. "I always keep my phone on silent and didn't feel the buzz."

Vas put the bag on the counter and took out the milk, soda, and bananas. He put the milk and soda in the fridge and looked back at me. "You making dinner or should we get take away?" His eyes scanned my body and stopped on my knees. "Did you stop to pray at her statue?"

"Always, she was a goddess, and taken from us far too soon. My mum knew her."

"Seriously?" Vas asked almost reverently.

"Yes, my mother's family knows hers, they weren't the same age of course, but Diana loved my mum, she loved all little kids, she was an *angel*."

Vas nodded in agreement. "Dinner in or out?" He asked again.

"I can make shrimp scampi over angel hair, or we can order in," I answered.

"You can't make that," he said doubtfully, his eyes skimming my body.

"Yes, I absolutely fucking can, it's my parents' favorite meal and I make it for them on special occasions, and I actually love it too."

"Aren't you a picky eater?"

"It's not so much being picky for the sake of being picky, I just don't like certain textures, and flavors," I looked at him as I pulled the shrimp out of the freezer. "But, please don't worry about it, I can always find something to eat, or not, I don't have a huge appetite. It bugs my dad, please don't let it bug you," I said and got out the butter and garlic from the fridge.

"I won't," Vas said and grabbed me around the waist. I kissed his neck, dropped to my knees and unzipped his fly.

* * *

Wednesday, when Vas was away, felt empty and I stupidly slept with the lights on. I hated being alone in the house, it was so big and creaky, and while I knew we had a security system, which I armed, with cameras that I unplugged while Vas was there (I'm not an imbecile), I still slept fitfully without Vas' large body next to mine. I didn't leave the house, just played my computer the whole time, stopping only to eat and use the bathroom. Thursday evening finally came, along with Vas' knock on the front door. We had two more nights together before I had to fly to Spain.

Friday night, after dinner and a tub, Vas watched me as we toweled off in my room. He looked at the desk and then at the bed. "I'm gonna miss you while you're in Spain, for what, the whole month of August?"

I stopped drying myself. "You could come visit."

Vas laughed. "And stay with you and your family? I couldn't afford such a big trip otherwise," he looked away. "No, we'll just have to text and talk, but I would really love a video of us, *together*, to tide me over," he said meaningfully.

I furrowed my brow. "Like a sex video? Shit, no, that could get hacked and end up online somewhere."

"No, I wouldn't let that happen, it would just be for you and me, I could airdrop it to you right here after we make it. It would be so hot," he took me in his arms and kissed me, pressing his hardness against my hip. "I'm hot just thinking about it. And if it's shite, we can delete it."

So, Vas propped his iPhone up on my desk and pressed record, and that was the video that prompted the beginning of our porn career. He paused it midway through, after my first orgasm, and then held it in his hand for the rest of the time. For an amateur video, one with a complete noob, me, and an alleged noob, Vas, it was pretty fucking hot. I came just watching the phone screen, the sight of him pounding in and out of me, with such an intense look on his face as he watched my head craned to the desk, was too much for my libido. The second part I watched later, his finger and then cock penetrating my tiny hole, all pink and hairless, was the hottest thing I'd ever seen and I envied Vas and his view. Honestly, the best part of it all wasn't me (though I was hot), it was Vas, his heavy breathing and his occasional moan, caught in perfect audio for the viewer, that was so ball-blowing.

We watched it on the couch later, drinking beers that Vas ran out for. Part critic, part voyeur, we decided that we looked really hot fucking each other.

"Send that to me and I promise my hand is going to develop callouses in Spain," I said with a grin.

"I told you, you're fucking hot. I'm gonna miss you," he said and kissed me, putting his phone down.

15

The Cat Peeks its Head From the Bag

SPAIN WAS GORGEOUS, as always, and completely boring and painful. I struggled through and then felt like a completely privileged shithead for it. We went to the beach, spent time in the pool, ate amazing food. Spanish food always pleased my taste buds, I think it was the association of relaxation and the fact that no one ever bullied me in Barcelona, even Felicity was tolerable there, as she had her friends and admirers to keep her occupied and her focus off me.

Vas and I texted, I knew he was working around the clock, because he told me so. He said he was doing it for two reasons, one to fill the time and distract himself from me, and the other for the extra money he earned. He couldn't decide whether he wanted his own place, or if he wanted money for hotel rooms.

"It's just until uni for you next year, we could get a place together then," he said one night on the phone. "Have you considered schools up here in Manchester?"

"Uh, Vas, I'm old for my grade," I lied quickly, "I still have two more years."

There was silence. "Jesus, Robby, you're not even lower sixth? I'll have a boy-friend who's in secondary for two more years because he ain't even started his A-levels?"

I nodded, and then realizing he couldn't see me, whispered yes. "But, maybe I could finish my A-levels somewhere else, and we could get a flat together."

Vas made a sound on his end of the phone and said he had to go.

I wondered and worried about that for over a week. The only distraction for that time was taking David into Barcelona-proper, and spending the day looking around with some spending money Dad had given us. David spent his on churros and candy, and I bought a few things for Vas and an extendable selfie stick.

"Who's that t-shirt for? That's way too big for you," David asked.

"Someone I like," I answered coyly.

"Marcus Willoughby?"

I stopped walking. "No, don't be ridiculous, I don't like Marcus."

"I see you guys talking quite a bit, when I cut through the park," David said and ate his last churro.

"He bullies me, it's not fun, he's not my friend," I strode off, leaving David to try and catch up.

"Did he do that to your chin, a while back?" David asked, his legs nearly long enough to keep up with mine without running.

"Yeah," I answered brusquely.

"Well then you should be happy he's off to uni this fall then, his sister said he's going to Trinity, he must be pretty smart."

"He is, I just wish he'd use his brains to leave me alone," I said, feeling peculiar at the thought of Marcus gone for good, the freedom that implied.

* * *

I had a few texts from Vas, mostly brusque and distracted which both irritated and frightened me. I watched our video almost obsessively, trying to regain the intimacy of us but failing. I decided to make a video of me in the tub, using the selfie stick I bought, it was only a few minutes long, because I had the other video in my head while touching myself, rolling over at the end so he could see my fingers going in and out of my hole as I moaned quietly.

I sent it to him, watching as it loaded and then registered as delivered.

Ten minutes later I got a breathless phone call from him. "Jesus Robby, when do you get home?"

16

Meet the Roommate

MY REUNION WITH VAS was as passionate as you'd expect, especially after the video I sent him, though he was a little distant and I could only imagine it was because of my school disclosure, and not because of anything I had done. I couldn't help my age, and while he thought I was a year older, he presumed I had a year left anyway, so what difference did a second year really make? I just prayed he wouldn't break up with me, or dig further.

He had me come to Manchester for the weekend, even though his flatmate came home Saturday. It was weird meeting Olek; he looked me up and down and then at Vas with his eyebrows raised and said something in Ukrainian. Vas stared back at him with a blank, but challenging expression. He was slimmer than Vas, and even more Eastern European looking. His face was angular, and he was covered in tattoos, seemingly everywhere but his face. Both arms had full sleeves, and what I could see of his legs were tattooed as well.

I worried about being alone with Vas when Olek was there, thinking he would be reserved or maybe not want sex at all but he didn't even try to keep it down when we were in his room so neither did I.

"How old are you?" Olek asked me Sunday morning when he caught me alone, dropping his 'h's' just like Vas.

"Seventeen," I said in as deep a voice I could manage, keeping my tongue behind my teeth as I said it.

His eyes swept my body, I was wearing the cinch-legged sleep shorts Vas insisted that I wear when I had to have clothes on in the flat, and no shirt. I smoothed my hair self-consciously under his scrutiny and went to the fridge for water. I felt his eyes on my hairless body and round ass.

I straightened and held his gaze defiantly, lifting the veil so to speak.

"What year are you? God you look like you're thirteen, there's no way you're seventeen."

"I'm lower sixth because I started late, I've a summer birthday," I looked out the small kitchen window at the concrete building next door. "You've a problem with my youth, or my gender?" I brought my eyes back to his with a challenge Vas had yet to see. I was timid by nature, on most accounts, but there were certain people I could read, like a book, and Olek was one of them. He was one of those people I could speak to without fear. I knew he would tell Vas what I said, but he was also one of those people that Vas would only half-believe at best.

Olek stood up from his chair. "Both, I suppose. It's kind of weird when someone you've known for nearly a decade, who has dated the hottest woman in any room, turns up with a jailbait boyfriend," he shrugged. "I can only imagine it's a phase because he had a rough winter with Andriy's death, so please, don't get too attached, for your own sake."

I looked at him, I mean really looked at him, and smiled my boldest, most royal smile. "Thanks for the advice. I hope you don't mind the moaning and screaming as Vas realizes that the only reason he's been out of sorts before meeting me is because he's been playing in the sandbox, and now he's discovered the beach," I took my bottle of water and walked confidently out of the kitchen, feeling Olek's wide eyes on me.

Believe me when I tell you I ravaged Vas after that, making sure he was as vocal as he'd ever been, letting him do whatever he wanted to me. In my short life, I knew a few things with great certainty, and one of them was my place in the world. Certain people could never get under my skin, because of my upbringing, and my influencers. God, my mum was wicked when she wanted to be, and my dad was just a prick most of the time to everyone. You might think I didn't have a bevy of friends because no one wanted to be my friend, but you'd be wrong. And that's all I'm going to say about that.

* * *

I don't know, or care, what happened between Vas and Olek after I left, I just knew Vas was mine as much as I was his. I went back to London focused on school and catching up with Dee, who had been on her own holiday in America, visiting cousins. She raved as usual, people loving her accent and accepting her for her body and all, I was guessing that she was supermodel slim compared to Americans. I smiled and listened happily, sitting on the floor of her bedroom, I felt like her champion, and I would die for her happiness.

"We went to Cape Cod for a week, it was beautiful, all sand and weathered shingles," she handed me her phone and I swiped through the pictures. It was beautiful, and nothing like the America I had seen on my one trip to Disney, when I was twelve, and felt surrounded by super-sized people eating super-sized portions.

"Wow, this is pretty," I handed her phone back after I had been through all the pictures, having seen many of them on Instagram. "So nice. I had no idea."

"Oh, Robby, America is beautiful. I mean, I've only seen the east coast where my cousins live and it's perfect. New York City is amazing, so much to do and see, and it really never sleeps!" She said emphatically. "Jory and I went out dancing, and it was after two when we went back to the hotel and the sidewalks were full, stores open, it were amazing. I can't wait to go back." She flopped back on her bed.

"Well, it sounds a lot better than the America I experienced, so some day, I'll have to go with you," I smiled.

"Yes!" She exclaimed and swiped into her camera. "Let's take some pictures, I love your hair."

17

The Tigers Get Out of the Bag

THE AUTUMN PASSED in a blur of school, meeting Vas every few weekends, either in a hotel or up in Manchester, studying hard, and babysitting my siblings. Things were peaceful at home without Felicity around. She had left for Cambridge with a superior smile and a carload of her shit. I hugged her tightly, happy to see her go, while my parents came home teary-eyed after dropping her off, and moped around the house for a few days until they remembered that they still had three other children at home.

One weekend when I was in Manchester, on a whim, probably October, maybe early November, I grabbed a glass of water, turned on the Xbox and started playing Call of Duty with the headphones that were next to the console. Vas was still fast asleep, because I wore the shit out of him, and I didn't want to wake him or Olek. Thirty minutes later, deep in the mission, I saw Olek emerge from his bedroom. He was in a pair of shorts and a baggy t-shirt, his hair all bedhead. He'd have been sexy if he wasn't such a douche, and covered in tattoos. I nodded hello and continued playing. He disappeared into the kitchen and came back a few minutes later with a cup of coffee. He stood in the doorway watching me play, and I kept my expression carefully blank, focused on the mission. I don't mean to brag, but I fucking kicked ass at COD, and all the other games I played, to be honest. He finished his coffee and sat on the floor next to me, picking up the other controller.

"Mind if I join?" he asked with nonchalance.

"Sure," I said, keeping my grin to myself. "Let me log out."

An hour later we were both shouting at the screen and high-fiving each other as we kicked ass and didn't take names.

"Shit Robby, you're fucking good at this," he said looking at my K/D (that's kill death ratio for you non-gamers).

"I was raised on this shit," I smiled at him. "You like Halo?"

"I fucking love Halo, which one?" He asked, looking me over in my pajama leggings and pink belly shirt.

"Halo 2 is the best one in my opinion, but they're all good," I kept my euphoria to myself.

Vas came out then, looking glorious in just his underwear and pulled up at the sight of us sitting side-by-side in the living room, fully engrossed in our video game and raised his eyebrows in surprise. Olek didn't even look up, but I was good enough at the game that I could spare a glance and smiled at him triumphantly.

After that Olek wasn't so hard on me. He asked me for my gamer tag and we played all the time together online. He wasn't in love with the idea of Vas and me, but he let go of his hang-ups about Vas not being straight anymore. I didn't lisp around him, but I didn't stop being what Vas wanted either, so I got really good at riding the line.

Vas seemed so much more relaxed after seeing Olek and me with some common ground, an unspoken comradery that made things easier for Vas to have me over, and all I wanted was for things to be easier for me and Vas, so he could have me over, and under him. God, we fucked so much that autumn. I learned exactly what he liked, and we both learned exactly what I liked.

I truly felt as though I was living in a dream. I realized that I had fallen head over heels in love with Vas. I knew nothing about love then, only that Vas was so good to me, so gentle, so funny and we spent so much time just laughing and telling stories, I really missed those days later. One night, must've been a Saturday night, I was laying in Vas' arms, tracing his tattoos with my fingertips, the bared teeth of the tigers almost cutting me, when I took a breath and held it.

"I love you," I whispered, and as soon as the words were out of my mouth, I wished I could evaporate or be swallowed up by his mattress, so uncertain I was about his true feelings for me.

"I love you too Robin," he said, his voice a deep rumble in his chest under my ear. I remember closing my eyes as warmth flooded my body, that moment frozen in my memory forever, though in hindsight, there was a forced feel to the words that my juvenile brain didn't, or couldn't, comprehend.

I immediately rolled on top of him and lavished kisses on his lips, the tips of his wings, his nipples and then his glorious cock. I don't mean to sound like a broken record, but that gorgeous man, wanted me, *loved* me, and I couldn't keep my hands or lips off him. It was in that moment that I knew I would do anything for him.

*** *** ***

My phone buzzed on a crisp winter day on my way home from school in early December. I was walking leisurely, taking my time, thinking about Vas, as usual, not worried about Marcus and his goons anymore because they had all graduated, and thankful that no other wankers had picked up his slack.

> I've got a room at the Sapphire
> for Saturday

I smiled and felt my heart skip a beat. I sent back two thumbs up, a heart emoji, and an eggplant with a peach, and kept walking. I cut through the park, taking the long way home, thinking and looking around at the mostly empty benches, and the thick bushes that lined the paths. I thought about my trip to the mall Monday shopping for Vas' upcoming birthday. I bought him more of the cologne he wears that makes him smell like heaven, a silver chain that was neither thick nor thin, and a new shirt, but those items weren't the ones that occupied my mind the most. What was dominating most of the space in my brain was the lingerie I bought to wear for him. The shop assistant was sweet, mistaking my blush for embarrassment about buying my girlfriend lingerie when I was really buying the thongs and a see-through nightie for myself. My cock went *ping* in my pants as I smiled, thinking about Vas' reaction on Saturday.

I let myself into the house using the key around my neck and called hello.

"Robby, come here for a minute," my mum called.

I dropped my bag at the foot of the stairs and wandered into her home office which doubled as a sitting room. My mum had great taste and the room was done in white with colorful accents, perfectly sparse and cozy at the same time.

"Hi, how was your day?" I asked stopping in the doorway.

"Busy," she smiled at me, "and how was school?"

"Fine. Dee invited me again for Saturday, I hope that's okay," I shrugged one shoulder and smiled.

My mum sat back in her chair and stared at me. "Funny you should mention that. I bumped into her mum at Whole Foods, I didn't know she shopped there," she said off-handedly as my stomach tightened nervously. Oh shit, I could see what was coming by the look on her face, the language of her body. "She said you hadn't been over at all, really," Mum's eyebrows went up. "So where have you been Robin? I can't believe you, of all my children, would lie to me."

My mind raced as my bowels loosened, and I tightened my sphincter. "Well, I have been over to her house, but I've also not been."

"And whose house have you been going to? Jesus Christ Robin! I felt like a complete idiot standing there, her judging me for your lies," she spat.

I'd never seen my mum this angry, well, not with me, anyway. "I'm seeing someone," I whispered.

"What? Speak up."

"I said, I'm seeing someone," I repeated, louder, the words sounding peculiar, saying them to her.

My mother's mouth dropped open. "Seeing someone, implies dinner dates and going to the movies, you're spending the entire night out, weekends even. Do his parents let you stay in his room?"

I just nodded my head and made a small sound.

"Who is it? Do I know him, or his family?" She stood out of her chair. "Christ, Robby, this is a bloody bombshell you're dropping on me."

"No, he doesn't go to my school," I swallowed, my mouth dry. Fuck, if she kept pressing I didn't know what I'd say, I was desperate for an excuse to leave. "I have to go to the loo."

"No Robby, we're not done talking," she said in her firm, don't-you-dare-walk-away-from-me voice. "Where does he go to school? How did you meet him? Please don't say online."

"No, Mum," I laughed nervously, "I met him at the mall, with Dee, she knows and likes him, he's very nice."

"Oh, okay," she looked around the room. "What's his name?"

"Vasyl."

She looked at me. "That's an unusual name. Is he British?"

"Yes, he was born here."

She narrowed her eyes at me. "Where's his family from?"

"Manchester."

"Before that?" She asked pointedly.

Shit, she was on to me. "Ukraine."

Her eyes went wide.

"What?" I frowned. "You're not a bigot or racist, are you?"

I saw her flinch, exactly the response I wanted. She considered herself to be quite the liberal, more so than my father, who most definitely wasn't a liberal, but anyone was a liberal compared to him.

"No, of course not," she scoffed. "Where in London do they live?"

I so wanted to say East London and watch her faint, but I didn't want her to even know that anyone he was related to lived there.

"That's the thing Mum, he still lives in Manchester, that's why I have to spend the night. He was visiting his cousins when he was at the shopping centre, and we'd already decided we liked each other when I found out how far away he lived."

"Manchester! That's practically Scotland."

"Mum, don't be ridiculous, it's nowhere near Scotland," I scoffed.

"It's closer to Scotland than we are," she pursed her lips. "How long you been seeing him?"

"Since my birthday," I answered, definitely ready to end the conversation.

"And you were planning on going to Manchester this weekend? To spend the night?"

I nodded and made that sound again.

"Well, you'd better call him and tell him you can't, because you're grounded for lying to me, and your father will be furious as well," she shook her head. "And Robin, you're only sixteen, I don't care if his parents are okay with it, I'm not."

"But Mum!" I cried, my anger bubbling up at being denied Vassy. "I'm sorry, but I didn't know how to tell you, and I've already promised, and bought my ticket," I lied.

"You can get a refund on the train ticket, you're staying in London, and that's final."

I thought quickly. "Fine, I'll stay in London, but it's not fair." I flounced out of the room and took my backpack upstairs. I texted Vas the minute I closed the door.

> My mum found out I was lying
> about going to Dee's, and now I'm
> grounded. I can prob still come to
> the hotel but I def can't spend the night

My phone buzzed a moment later.

"Hi Vas, I'm sorry," I said quickly.

"What happened?"

"She bumped into Dee's mum at the shop and found out I lied. Then she asked me all about you, but I didn't say hardly anything. She knows you live in Manchester, and your name, but that's it. I let her think you're my age."

"Shit. It's only a matter of time, she's gonna keep asking," I heard him blow out a breath. "I really wanted to see you this weekend."

"I know, me too. I want to celebrate your birthday, so please still come. I'll sneak away, just have to be home before eleven or so and then can come right back in the morning."

"No Robby, if you get caught then they'll never let us see each other," Vas said firmly.

"I'd fucking run away if they tried to do that," I said vehemently.

"Robby, stop it. You're not running away. She grounded you for lying, is that it? Or for having a boyfriend?" Vas asked.

"For lying."

"Well, then it's probably only for a week, and then I'll come next weekend, and you'll tell them you're coming to see me, no more lies."

I sighed and looked at my dejected reflection in the mirror. "But I'll miss you," I pouted.

"Just keep your grades perfect and don't give them any other reason to punish you, so I can touch every part of your beautiful body next weekend," Vas said quietly.

"Okay Vassy, but I'll talk to you before then. I love you," I blew a kiss and listened as he returned it to me.

"I love you too."

My dad really ripped me a new one when he came home. Just ranting about lies, exaggerating everything as usual, and then he called me a little slut. That hurt. I stood up then, and stared him down.

"If I were straight you'd be congratulating me right now," I said tears in my eyes and throat. "I hate you!"

I ran from the room, nearly bumping into George, who just stared at me.

I skipped dinner, and cried myself to sleep, for the first time in my life wishing I weren't gay, thinking my dad really wouldn't have had a problem with it if I were straight. It never really bothered me before, being gay, I had always thought the male form was far superior to the female one, and with the exception of my mum and my gram, and Dee, I never really found women attractive. I liked them well enough, had more than a few female friends, but couldn't understand wanting to be a gay woman, or a straight man; honestly the only thing grosser than the thought of one vagina was two. No, I had always felt fine with who I was, and now my dad had me feeling really bad about myself, as if I were some anomaly, that didn't deserve to love or be loved.

18

Shawshank Kensington

I LEFT FOR SCHOOL without eating breakfast, scowling at my mother who tried everything she could to engage with me, but I wasn't having it. I wanted to skip school, but I made a promise to Vas about doing well, and behaving myself so we could be together, so I paid extra attention in class and on my homework. Dee and I had lunch at a table in the corner where I told her about her mum and mine and about what my dad had said, tearing up a bit as I said the awful part.

"Oh, Robby, darling," she hugged me, her soft chest full of comfort for me, making me wish I had run to her house last night when I felt so down. "That's just awful, he's a troll for saying such things to you. I will be better about covering for you, I had no idea they would ever cross paths," she took a bite of her sandwich after we pulled apart. "When do you think you can see Vas again?"

"He's coming next weekend, and he said I should be honest and tell them, since they grounded me for lying, not for having a boyfriend," I shrugged.

"What if they want to meet him?" She asked, her eyes round.

"Oh god, I don't know," I looked away. "I'll just put it off, plenty of people date without introducing their partner to their parents, right?"

"I wouldn't know," Dee said with a bit of chagrin.

I looked at her and smiled. "You are beautiful, and I know there are boys here who stare at you when you're not looking, I'm just not sure if any of them are worthy," I kissed her forehead. "You are a treasure."

She beamed at me and then looked away. "But Robby, you're not objective, you're my best friend, you have to say these things to me."

"Bullshit," I said emphatically. "If I were straight I'd be down on one knee begging for you to marry me. You are perfect," and I meant every word. She was the best of the best, and I was a selfish cad.

She wrinkled her nose and punched my shoulder lightly. "I love you too Robby."

I had to watch George after school, David had a doctor's appointment that Mum had to take him to. I made him snacks, thinking of how nice it was that Felicity was off at uni, and then scowled about missing Vas, feeling empty at the thought of not seeing him until the following weekend. I had such things planned for him, for us at the hotel, I was even going to suggest filming me in my new lingerie.

"Why do you hate Daddy?" George asked me, his eyes wide as he waited for my answer.

Oh, the innocence that radiated off him, I remember thinking our dad walked on water when I was his age too, and it made me sad.

"Nothing bud, I didn't mean it. Don't worry, Dad's a *great* guy," I lied through my teeth, my tone dripping with sarcasm that I knew he wouldn't get. "Get your homework out and stop worrying."

"I don't have any, I want to go to the park and play football," George said, his mouth full of fruit.

"Don't talk with your mouth full," I scolded and looked out the window at the cold sunshine and thought about the openness of the park. I wanted some freedom, I mean, I wasn't in jail, but something psychological about being grounded weighed heavily on me.

"Okay, call a friend," I said putting the dishes in the dishwasher. I ran my hands through my hair, trying to tame the waves and curls, and looked at myself in the mirror before grabbing my phone and my coat and following him out the door.

George brought his football and we stopped at his friend Phineas' house so he could join us. I sat on the bench two down from a giant rhododendron bush and kept an eye on them. I got my phone out and sent a few Snapchats to Vas, pouting and preening for him with different filters. He responded after a while, I knew he was busy with work, though he said he was missing me. He sent some snaps back, of him in his work gear, looking dirty and so fit. I got a semi looking at him and then thinking about him. I smiled and put the kitty filter on sending him another picture with a giggle. I looked at George and Phineas and then back at my phone.

God, I shouldn't have been so focused on myself because a moment later my phone was snatched from my hand and Marcus was standing in my sun.

"Who you snapping?" He asked with a smirk.

"Give that back!" I shouted indignantly and stood grabbing for my phone. God he was such an asshole, and if he saw Vassy I would die.

Marcus pushed me back down on the bench and held my phone out of reach, looking at my contacts. "Who's Vassy with two hearts?" He sneered. "Maybe I should I snap him, because of course a fag like you wouldn't heart a girl, unless it was Faddee," he held the camera and took a picture of the top of my head as I ducked it, and typed something before pressing send.

I grabbed the phone from his hand, my heart in my throat. "What the fuck Marcus? Why are you even here?" I looked at the field, seeing George watching me with a worried expression.

"It's my dad's birthday," he shrugged. "Believe me, I don't want to be here, university is amazing, I haven't got time for little boys and girls," his eyes skimmed my body derisively.

My phone buzzed insistently in my hand, I pocketed it with a nervous swallow. "Well, happy birthday to your dad. I hope you have a nice weekend at home," I turned to call to George.

Marcus touched my arm, grabbed it really, and held my gaze, before looking away and around in that way he always did. "Where you running off to? *Vassy* waiting for you?" He said, something behind his eyes.

"No, I'm babysitting and I have to get home, I'm grounded," I added, not sure why.

"Bullshit," Marcus laughed. "Perfect Robin Trumball doesn't get grounded. What'd you do, say dammit? Get an A minus?"

"I lied about where I was all night," I said defiantly and then regretted it from the look on Marcus' face. I knew he was going to tease me about it.

"Where were you? Did you lock yourself in the library?"

"No," I turned and called to George. "Five minutes George."

I felt Marcus' eyes on me, and wished I had a *Star Trek* transporter that would beam me away from that gaze.

He pushed my shoulder, catching me off-balance as my phone buzzed again in my pocket. "Faggot," he said in a harsh voice before turning away.

I didn't dare answer my phone, I didn't know what I would say, and so just hustled George and Phineas home.

My mum was home when we let ourselves in and George took off to greet her. I ran upstairs to be alone and look at my phone. There were three missed calls from Vas and no texts. I paced my room wondering what to do. I couldn't avoid him forever so I took a breath and called him.

"Who the fuck snapped me?" He asked, the first words out of his mouth.

"Oh, that was nobody, someone from school last year," I answered nonchalantly. "Why? What did he say?"

"You gave him your phone, you tell me," Vas said, a harsh note in his voice.

Oh fuck, Marcus said something awful and if I say he stole my phone then Vas would want to know where he lived, and if I said I gave him my phone then Vas would think I was an asshole.

"He took my phone off the bench, I couldn't see what he wrote, but he gave it back, and he's just a dumb jock, goes to uni in Dublin now, nothing to worry about."

Vas was quiet, and as the silence stretched I grew more nervous. "You fucking around on me?" he asked finally.

"God no," I exclaimed in a panic, wondering what Marcus had written. "That was one of the stud boys in school, he had hundreds of girlfriends. Whatever he wrote was just to be a wanker."

"You better not be cheating on me," Vas said.

"I'm not, I swear," I said vehemently.

"Okay. If he just did it to be a wanker, fine. If he's one of the bullies though, and I ever see him, he's going to feel my fist."

I smiled with relief. "He's just a dickhead, he razzed me plenty, but never beat me up," I lied.

19

Application DENIED, No Chance of Parole

"HOW LONG AM I GROUNDED FOR?" I asked my mum on Tuesday, unable to keep the harsh note out of my voice.

"Why?" She countered.

"Because I'd like to see Vassy this coming weekend, and I think ten days is long enough for lying."

My mum turned her head slightly as she considered my words. If she narrowed her eyes, I was in trouble. Shit, she narrowed her eyes.

"I'll be the judge of how long a punishment should last. Christ Robby, it was a pretty big lie, for six months, and you're only sixteen, sneaking around, sleeping," she winced at that, "with another boy. I wouldn't condone it with Felicity, and I just can't condone it with you," she shook her head. She held her hand up at my protests. "You can see him, you just can't spend the night."

"But Mum!" I shouted. "He lives in Manchester, it's too far to just have dinner or go to a movie," I railed. My world felt as though it were crumbling around me (dramatic I know), at the thought of not being able to see Vas, to sleep in his arms, to be naked with him. I legitimately felt my extremities go numb. I wanted to fall on the floor like a toddler, and had to lock my knees to be sure I didn't.

"I'm sorry for that," she shrugged. "Maybe you should find someone closer to home."

"Mum!" I frowned and stomped my foot (childish I know). "I don't want anyone else, I love him!"

"Love?" Her eyes went wide and she looked away briefly. "If this is serious your father and I are going to have to meet him."

Shit! "No Mum, that's mortifying, and I was going there not him coming here," I lied.

"You're not going there unless I meet or speak with his parents, to be sure they're home and aware of what's going on," she said firmly.

"Mum!" I was getting sick of shouting that. My stomach fell. "This isn't the 1900s! It's the twenty-first century and nobody does that anymore."

"In our house we do," she frowned.

"You don't make Felicity bring her boyfriends' parents around," I scoffed.

"Felicity wasn't sleeping over at her boyfriends' houses."

I made a sound of frustration. "I can't ask him for that, it's so embarrassing, and if we can't see each other then he's gonna find someone else. He's so beautiful and you should see how people stare at him," I felt the tears spring to my eyes. "He's so cool, so confident, I could never find someone like that again. I mean look at me!" I gestured down my scrawny body, sobbed, and ran from the room.

"Robby!" She called after me.

She knocked on my door a moment later.

"Go away," I called, my voice muffled by my pillow. I really was worried that Vas would find someone else. There was no way he would want to meet my parents, and his *parents*? I hadn't even met them. Christ, everything felt like sand slipping through my fingers. Vas would realize I was too young, too much trouble, our meetings too infrequent and he would dump me for someone more available. He could have anyone, and he had the freedom to go find another lover. My throat swelled hotly and I felt a fresh round of tears flood out of my eyes. I heard the door open.

"Robby," my mum said softly, standing over me. "I'm sorry, I know things seem so dramatic at your age, but if he loves you too, he won't run out and find someone new. And he'll want to meet us to make us happy," she placated.

"No Mum, you don't understand, I can't make you understand," I said, rolling over to look at her. She winced at my tear-stained face. "I just really want to see him this weekend and I think you're making unfair demands."

She sighed. "I'll have to ask your father, but darling, you broke our trust, and I can't tell you how disappointed that made me, that *makes* me," she corrected herself.

"I didn't mean to Mum," I sat up. "I'm so sorry, I will never lie to you again," I lied, but vehemently and hopefully convincingly.

"It's not going to be that easy Robby," she shook her head. "And certainly not with your dad. He was really cross."

I laid back with a harrumph on my pillow and rolled away from her. "Fine, but if he dumps me because I can't see him anymore, I will never forgive you," I said my voice hitching. "Please leave me alone."

She rubbed my back and I closed my eyes against the soothing feeling of it, shrugging my shoulder away like a spoiled little bitch, and I was definitely (albeit justifiably), being a spoiled little bitch. Yes, I lied, I sneaked around, I was fucking a much older man, so they had every right to be mad at me, but I was of age and felt slighted and wronged and denied my true love.

I skipped dinner again. It was easy to because my dad made hamburgers on the grill, which he did on purpose, knowing I hated the smell and taste of red meat. I decided to take a bath and tune everyone out, ignoring David pounding on the door after dinner. "Go use one of the other bathrooms or Mum and Dad's," I called over Taylor Swift's beautiful voice.

"Robby, you've been in there for ages, and my toothbrush is in there," David whined. "Hurry up."

I looked at my water-wrinkled fingers and sighed. "Fine," I said, putting as much annoyance in my voice as possible. "I'll be out in ten."

Vas called as I was getting dressed. I answered and flopped onto my bed.

"I can't wait to see you in three days," he said huskily.

A tingle pulsed through my body at the tenor of his voice. I flexed my toes and sighed unhappily. "I don't think I can see you this weekend," I felt tears again. "My parents are still mad, and my mum said she had to ask my dad, but the bastard made burgers for dinner so I'm guessing his answer is no."

"What? Didn't you tell them that you'd be seeing me, in full transparency?" Vas asked, I could hear the frown in his voice and a pit of worry formed in my belly.

"I did, and my mum said she wanted to meet you, or meet your parents," I pouted. "I'm sorry Vas," I added hurriedly, "I wish I was eighteen."

The silence stretched with my nerves.

"If they met me, they'd let you date me?" He asked.

"Well, she didn't say that exactly," I said, thinking of how disastrous that meeting would be. "You can't possibly be considering it?"

"Why not?" Vas asked, a weird note in his voice.

"You're just so much older," I said quickly. "They won't let me date you."

"Are you sure it's that? And not, say, my tattoos, or my job," he said quietly. "You ashamed of me?"

"Christ no!" I exclaimed, maybe a little too shrilly, because of course it was all three of those things if I was being honest with myself. My dad would take one look at him and call the police, and then lock me away in a monastery somewhere.

"Find out," he commanded. "And if that's all it is, then I will meet them Saturday." The line went dead.

I swallowed and looked at the blank screen. Oh shit.

My dad barreled in without knocking as I was studying. "Robin, what's this nonsense about going to Manchester this weekend?"

I flared my nostrils, suppressing the anger I felt, as best I could. "I asked Mum if I could go see Vas, I don't think it's an unreasonable request. I am very sorry about lying to you, and it won't happen again," I said taking a breath. "I'm being honest now, I only lied before because I didn't know how to tell you. You scare me," I added, swallowing roughly for the effect.

My dad straightened, as I guessed he would, at that. "Robin, you shouldn't be frightened of me, that's absurd."

"Are you telling me my feelings are absurd?" I quavered my voice.

"No, dammit," I saw him clench his fists in frustration. "I'm just saying there's no reason to be afraid of me, for god's sake, you're a man you should act like one."

"I'm trying to, but you and Mum are treating me like a child," I countered.

I watched him look away, caught in his own conundrum. "Robin, we can't allow for you to spend the night at some stranger's house, even if his parents are home. We need to meet him, or them, or preferably both, and maybe then we can see."

I turned in my chair. "You're saying, if you meet him, you will let me see him? And I don't mean for dinner, or something because I'm not riding six hours on the train just to see him for two hours. That's not fair," I said calmly. "You were my age once, please, remember," I said with my most imploring look.

He looked at me and then out the window. "I'll meet him, and then let you know," he closed the door behind him.

> **They want to meet u. R u sure?**

I waited ten minutes for his response.

> **I'll c u at your house at noon.**
> **They will love me**

I doubted that very much but responded with a thumbs up and a heart emoji.

20

Covered Tigers,
Hidden Angel

 I threw up my oatmeal. I started to call Vas about a million times, wanting to tell him not to come, tell him that it was fun while it lasted, tell him the truth, about everything, but I didn't. I tried on forty different outfits and packed a small bag I knew I wouldn't need.

Dee texted me, wishing me luck, asking for me to remember every detail so I could tell her at school on Monday, as if I weren't going to tell her about the train wreck that was certain to happen immediately after it occurred, later that day.

The doorbell rang, and I cursed Vas for not texting me a warning that he was here. I flew down the stairs, nearly slipping midway and falling on my ass before catching myself on the railing. My mum beat me to the door and was holding it open, gesturing for Vas to come in. I nearly fainted at the sight of him. He was wearing jeans and a light blue Nike hoodie that covered Michael's face and wings. He had fancy trainers, black frame glasses that made him look like a nerd, and, shockingly, a temporary cast on his left hand, hiding his tattoos. Clever bastard. I nearly laughed. He looked all of twenty-two and so handsomely studious I felt a twinge in my pants, or I would have if I weren't so fucking nervous.

My mum was clearly floored by his age, I mean he looked younger than his *actual* age, but he definitely didn't look my age, and I hadn't prepared her because I didn't want to get yelled at. Fortunately, I knew she was too one-degree-of-separation from the monarchy to cause a scene in front of him, but I was definitely going to hear all about it later. Vas was shaking her hand politely and smiling his gorgeous smile, his teeth even and white as he looked up at me and continued smiling.

"Pleasure to meet you Mrs. Trumball," he was saying, his Mancunian accent nearly undetectable. Don't get me wrong, he didn't sound like Prince William or anything, but he didn't sound Scally either.

"Likewise, Vasyl. Please come in," she swept her hand and closed the door behind him as he stepped onto the marble.

"Hi Vas," I said as I reached the bottom of the stairs. I wanted to hug him, but took his outstretched hand instead, our palms lingering together ever so briefly as he held my gaze.

"Hello Robby," he said, pronouncing the 'h' and giving me his half-smile.

I smoothed my hair nervously as I heard my dad coming from his study. Vas turned as my dad appeared, his step faltering nearly imperceptibly as his eyes swept Vas' body.

"Mr. Trumball sir, Vasyl Boiko. Pleasure to meet you," he held out his hand.

My father took it and squeezed. He gave Vas his thin-lipped smile, the one he used when he was forced to commune with people he didn't want to know, like at school functions and church.

"Nice to meet you Vasyl," he said letting go of his hand. "What kind of name is that? Russian?"

Vasyl's eyes flickered. "Ukrainian sir. It means king," he said, quirking his eyebrow ever so slightly.

My father's body shifted and he made a thoughtful sound. I wondered what a body language expert would have made of the four of us standing there in our marble foyer. My mother looking Vas over appraisingly, my father posturing possessively, Vas responding accordingly and me, watching it all whilst trying not to shit my pants.

"Well, come in, have a seat," my father gestured to the living room. "Are you joining us for lunch?"

Oh god please say no. Was my dad insane?

Vas looked at me and then at my mother who nodded, "I've got sandwiches and crisps."

"Thank you," he said, which wasn't quite an affirmative, but my parents took it as such.

My dad gestured to one of the white couches and took his seat in the Barcelona chair next to him. I didn't know where the hell to sit. Should I sit next to Vas, in solidarity, or would that make my dad think of us *together*? Should I sit opposite or would that make Vas feel like he was at an interrogation? I ended up on the couch with him but sitting with a cushion between us. Vas sat back so he could see us both, while my mum fetched drinks for us all.

"So," my father began, once we were all settled and waiting for our waters, "how old are you Vasyl, you are clearly out of secondary."

"I'm twenty-two," he lied smoothly. "Just had my birthday."

That part was true, though he turned twenty-eight.

My dad made a judgey sound and looked at me, something behind his eyes. "How did you two meet?" He looked back at Vas.

"At Westfields, in the coffee shop," Vas replied looking at me with a smile.

"You live in London?" My dad asked.

I was getting annoyed with my dad's questions. He knew all the answers, was he trying to catch us in a lie? Because if so, I was sure he eventually would. I had to get Vas out of there.

"No sir, Manchester," his accent slipped.

"You at university there?"

My mum appeared with a tray of ice waters and handed them around, putting out coasters for the coffee table.

"No sir, I work. I'm a carpenter," he replied, preempting my father's next question and holding his gaze almost challengingly.

My dad pursed his lips and looked at my mother before looking back at Vas and then at his hand. "You hurt your arm at work?"

I saw that Vas had wrapped the part of his hand that extended beyond the brace so that the tattoos above his knuckles didn't show. He nodded. "I injured it on a job and then made it worse at the gym," he shrugged sheepishly, looking very young.

"Mummy," I heard George calling, his voice getting closer. He appeared in the doorway. "I'm hungry," he stopped short, looking at Vas with wide eyes. His mouth slammed shut and he looked at my mum who stood.

"George, this is Robby's friend Vasyl," she said. "Let's have lunch, everything is ready."

Vas followed me through the archway into the dining room as if he'd never been in the house before and we somehow made it through lunch without anything catastrophic happening. David joined us, and managed to dominate the conversation so the attention wasn't focused on Vas, who looked as relieved as I felt. George stared at Vas from time to time, seemingly intimidated by his presence, and too afraid to address him directly. Vas was impressive. He managed to be the perfect mix of polite and youthful, goofing with David while calling my dad 'sir,' as though he came from one of the finest families on the island.

I snuck a peek at my phone and saw it was just past one. I cleared my plate and Vas' and went through the butler's pantry to meet my mum in the kitchen.

"Is it okay if we go?" I asked quietly.

She looked at me and then over my shoulder at the doorway where we could just see my dad at the head of the table. "He's a lot older than you let us think Robin," she said crisply. "Your father is very upset about that."

"Mum," I said urgently, "he's not *that* much older, I mean Jesus, Dad's ten years older than you. And sixteen is old enough in the UK, I checked."

My mum's eyes flickered, I know she wanted to tell me it was different for them, but it wasn't really.

"Besides his age, you like him, don't you?" I asked earnestly. "He's really nice, and polite, and funny," I added as I heard laughter from dining room.

"Yes Robby, he's all those things," she said and closed the dishwasher. "But he doesn't live at home, does he? So, you have been," she frowned, unable to say the words. "Christ, are you being safe?"

I blushed so hard I was certain I turned purple. "Mum!" Oh god, the thought of my mum thinking about me having sex, was worse than the thought of her having sex with my dad. "It's not like that," I said, my voice shrill, because honestly it was even worse. I had gone from inexperienced teen, to whore with thongs in less than six months, with nary a condom in sight. I looked into the dining room at Vas who was talking to David but looking at me with his eyebrows raised. I looked back at my mum. "Can we please just go, I'll be back tomorrow in time for dinner with Gram and Grandfather." I felt her hesitate. "Mum, you promised, if you met him I could go. Please," I pleaded and gave her my most endearing eyes.

"You'll have to ask your father," she deferred.

"Can't you just tell him you said I could. You have every right to make the decision yourself, this is the twenty-first century," I added.

She sighed. "Robby, it's a big thing, I should at least speak with your father. I wouldn't want him making this decision without me," she caught my dad's eye and nodded slightly at the door to the hallway.

Dad stood and excused himself, walking into the kitchen and past us without looking at me. My mum followed him out of the room and I stood awkwardly for a moment, praying fervently under my breath that he would say yes.

Vas appeared at my side. "Well?" He asked softly, his eyes roving over my body. I saw the tip of his tongue and my pulse accelerated.

"If they say no, I'm leaving anyway," I said staring at his mouth. "Especially with you looking at me like that." He gave me a half-smile. "They like you, but unsurprisingly, they're not happy about your age," I looked at his outfit and grinned. "I like the get up. Hides your tattoos."

"This isn't my first rodeo with parents," Vas answered with a small shrug. "Sorry," he added at my expression. "Honestly, age is just a number, and I hope they can see past that, especially with their age difference."

"Robin," my mum called from the other room.

My stomach tightened at that tone. "I'll be right back."

Vas squeezed my hand and nodded.

"Yeah Mum," I said as I came around the corner and through the doorway into my dad's home office. I hardly ever went into that room. It was all brown leather and wood and masculinity and he hated any of us being in there touching his shit. They were standing in the middle of the room, on the large Persian carpet that my father bought in Iran before he and my mum were married.

"Robin," my father said, finally looking at me, "you lied about where you were going, and you lied about his age. Christ he's a man," my dad made a face. "I'm not feeling as though I need to make any concessions to you."

"But dad, you promised," I wheedled. "He's barely over twenty, and he's really nice, you saw."

"I don't care how nice he is. He's a grown man, and what does a grown man want with a sixteen-year-old boy?" My father narrowed his eyes. "The same thing he would want with a sixteen-year-old girl. Nothing good," he spat.

"Dad!" I blushed. "It's not like that," I looked at my mum. "We play video games and go to the mall, the movies, and hang out with his friends and Dee."

His eyes went wide. "He's introduced you to his friends? What in the bloody hell does he say?"

Technically it was just the one friend, Olek, that I had met, but he held my hand around town, so I don't think he would be embarrassed to introduce me.

"That I'm his boyfriend," I said putting my chin up slightly. "It's the twenty-first century. You're the only one who has an issue with me being gay."

"Oh no Robby, your sexuality is not what I'm taking issue with here," he shook his head.

"Yeah, but if I were a pretty sixteen-year-old girl, you think he and his friends would be high-fiving each other, but that because I'm a boy I should feel embarrassed? He should feel embarrassed?" I furrowed my brow indignantly. "Do you know how your words cut me?"

My father blanched, I had successfully turned the tables on him and I fought hard to keep the triumph off my face.

"Robin," he said in a contrite voice.

"No Dad," I straightened, "I get to be happy. I'm responsible, even more responsible than Felicity. Who do you guys trust more with David and George?" I shook my head, looking between them. "I lied. I'm sorry. I honestly didn't know how to tell you, and if he lived in London, this wouldn't even be an issue. He's a great guy, and he's so nice to me. I'm really lucky. Age is just a number, please look past that and accept him," I summoned tears, and felt my eyes shine.

My parents gave in. I don't know which of my maneuvers worked, but something did and Vas and I were off, my overnight bag and his bag of gifts over his shoulder as we headed to The Tube.

"How'd it go? What did your dad say?" Vas asked, putting his arm around my shoulder after taking off the arm brace and glasses. They were fake, of course, his eyesight was as perfect as the rest of him.

"Fine, it was fine, they like you," I smiled up at him.

He kissed my forehead and laughed. "You're a terrible liar, but I'm just glad they let you go. I know your dad doesna like me. He's a snob, innee?"

Yes, he was a colossal snob but I didn't want to give Vas a complex. I wrapped my arms around his waist as we walked. "No, he just takes time to warm up to people, *all* people," I said and looked up as we continued down the sidewalk. My heart froze and my stomach plummeted as I saw Marcus coming toward us with Gareth, staring at me with pure hostility. He sneered and said something to Gareth.

"Let's cross," I said stepping out from under Vas' arm. I looked both ways and made to step off the curb.

"Robby, The Tube is just up there, why are you crossing?' He asked bewilderedly. "Stop."

I froze, and looked at him, I guess my face was white, or panicked, or just stupid because he frowned and looked around as he stopped. His eyes lighted on Marcus and Gareth and narrowed. "Robby," he said quietly and handed me the bags before taking my hand, "come, we're walking."

I took his hand, feeling safe, but bloody exposed. I looked anywhere but at the two of them as Vas led me down the middle of the sidewalk, straight for a confrontation. It happened so fast, I wished later that I had recorded it so I could slow it down and understand it as Vas grabbed Marcus, and propelled him into the side of the building to our left. He looked over his shoulder at Gareth as he pressed his unleashed tigers under Marcus' windpipe. "You fucking stay where you are," he said calmly, something in his tone freezing Gareth, before looking back at Marcus who was immobilized with fear. I could see it in his eyes like it had weight and substance. Gareth stood as helplessly as I did as everything unfolded and was finished in less than a minute.

"I'm guessing you're the tosser who broke Robby's rib. And if you're the asshole who snapped me," He paused with a humorless laugh, glaring at Marcus' white face, "I'm gonna *snap* you." He punched Marcus then, right in the side, just under the ribcage, and I swear I heard his tigers snarl against Marcus' neck, or it could have been the breath leaving Marcus' body with an audible groan.

Vas stepped back and turned away as Marcus doubled over and collapsed. He took my hand again and called over his shoulder. "You ever come near Robby again, and the last thing you'll see is my fist coming straight for your face."

I didn't dare look back. I didn't dare ever go home again, to be honest. There's no way I could ever face Marcus again without fear or apprehension. Vas was valiant but he couldn't be with me everywhere.

"Robby, he won't bother you ever again," Vas said, slightly winded with adrenaline, sensing my worry. "Trust me, guys like him, they only bully if they think they can get away with it. He knows I mean it. You're mine, and I will crush anyone who dares fuck with you," he squeezed my hand and took the bags from me.

I got so hard, my cock would have sprung forward and bulged (modestly of course) if it weren't constrained by the thong I had on. The thong I couldn't wait for Vas to strip me down to.

Later, in the windowless hotel room, lying naked in Vas' arms, contented to my core, my fingers tracing his snarling tigers, Vas buried his nose in my hair and breathed in slowly.

"You ever gonna give me the straight story about that guy?"

"I don't know what you mean," I said carefully.

"How long has he been harassing ya?"

"It's no big deal Vas. He never did anything really bad. In fact, he usually kept his gang of goons at bay. I never dared get caught by them without him."

"I didn't like the way he looked at you," Vas said in a tight voice. "You tell me if he or any of them ever bother you again Robin, I mean that."

I decided we had discussed Marcus enough. He was supposed to be in Dublin and I have no idea why I kept bumping into him, but I decided to put him out of my mind entirely and went into the bathroom where I had left my overnight bag.

Vas was sitting up against the pillows scrolling through his phone when I walked back into the room. I giggled to myself as I watched him do a double take, his eyes raking my body, and going wide at the tight, pink lace nightie I had on.

"Bloody hell," he whispered, putting his phone down.

I propped my phone up on the small dresser and pressed record.

21

Guess Who's Coming to Dinner

MY PARENTS HAD GIVEN UP trying to discourage me from seeing Vas and finally accepted him, not quite with open arms, but he was invited to come and stay over for Boxing Day. He arrived in the damp cold with a small bag, carrying a large bouquet of flowers and a shopping bag with a bottle of Lagavulin for my dad, a bottle of my mum's favorite white wine, and chocolate for my siblings. He was wearing the new turtleneck jumper I had given him, his fake glasses, and his arm brace, which invited my mother's concern.

"Have you been to the doctor for that?" She asked as she passed him a small glass of homemade eggnog with rum.

Vas nodded. "She said I should be getting it off soon, just a torn tendon or something. Thank you for your concern," he smiled. He was so smooth, it made my heart flutter and my cock go ping in my pants.

She returned his smile with the one I loved seeing on her face. She liked him more than she admitted, and I knew she found him attractive, I mean who didn't? You should have seen Felicity's face when he came into the dining room, god I wished I had my camera out. That slag was gaga for him, and kept shooting me looks of disbelief which I met with smug satisfaction.

David was thrilled to see Vas too and kept drawing his attention with talk of football and which team was the best (Manchester United) and which was the worst (Liverpool). Vas was in his element talking football, as he was a raging United fan, and was more than happy to expound upon their extensive virtues with David.

George finally worked up the courage to talk to him as well, I didn't listen too closely to that as I was still keeping an eye on my dad. He was no longer giving Vas the thin-lipped smile, but he wasn't slapping him on the back heartily either. I could tell he was really pleased about the scotch from his body language and seemingly casual smile when he thanked Vas. I had snuck into my dad's study and took pictures of his bar cart for Vas as he requested, and done the same for my mum's wine in the fridge door. He wanted to get something for Felicity but I told him to just do chocolate for everyone, no need to single her out and make her feel special, people had been doing that her whole life, so fuck her.

I helped with dinner, making shrimp scampi, which reminded me of when Vas and I were here for nearly a week, playing house. I blushed lightly thinking of him fucking me on the counter where I was now standing, mincing the garlic. Mum made a beef wellington, which I would only eat the outside of, and noodles and veggies, to go with the shrimp.

I knew what it took for Vas to eat with decorum, we had rehearsed at the pub not too long ago, me making sure he knew which fork went with what, how to pass food, and where to place your knife when you weren't using it, etc. These were all things my mum, and her mum, hammered into us, and I wanted to be sure Vas' table manners were above reproach. He sat next to me, and brushed his leg against mine from time to time, never looking at me when he did, but there would be the barest hint of a smile around his mouth. He asked my dad about work, and I tuned it out, sorry, I found my dad's line of work to be exceptionally boring. I loved technology, I knew quite a bit about it, but what my dad did was management, and not at all interesting to me. Vas seemed fascinated though, and was nodding encouragingly as my dad talked about their latest merger and the subsequent personnel decisions that needed to be made.

I looked at George who seemed to be having trouble cutting his beef and turned his plate so I could cut it for him. "Let me do it big guy, that way they're all the right size for your mouth."

"Thanks Robby," he said and patted my arm. "Will you play Pokémon with me later?"

"Maybe tomorrow, I've got company and it would be rude," I said quietly, turning the plate back to George.

"Does he play Pokémon?" George peered around me to look at Vas.

I chuckled at the thought. "No."

"I used to," Vas said tuning into our conversation. "I never had a Switch though. I wouldn't know how to play," he added, his accent slipping briefly.

"You could use David's, I could teach you how," George said earnestly.

Vas shrugged. "Okay," he raised his eyebrows at me.

I looked away to keep myself from hugging him. George was my favorite, and I think Vas remembered that. Boy was he being slick. I finished my four shrimp and the pastry from my mum's piece of wellington and watched Vas take another bite of his thick cut of beef. His eyes closed briefly as he chewed, I loved watching him eat something he found delicious. I looked across the table at Felicity and met her gaze before she shifted it back to Vas.

"So, Vasyl," she said his name carefully, "where did you grow up? You have the most unusual accent."

"Manchester, but I work all over the north, and have family scattered around," he answered with a polite smile.

I wasn't sure where she was going with this, but she sounded snobby.

"Do you speak Ukrainian or Russian?"

"Ukrainian. My parents speak both but forbade me and my brother from speaking Russian, and I wouldn't speak it for all the money in the world," he said and looked at my dad.

"Have you ever been to the Ukraine?" Felicity asked, picking up her wine glass.

"It's just 'Ukraine,'" Vas corrected gently, "and yes, but not since before the war."

"Do you still have family there?" My mum asked.

"Yes, my father came from a very large family, and many are still there," Vas took a sip of his wine.

"Are any of them involved in the conflict?" My dad asked, drawing Vas's eye again.

I felt Vas tense, and wondered if I should interrupt and change the subject. I was just about to open my mouth when he answered.

"Yes, nearly all my male relatives have served in some capacity in the war. My brother died fighting last year," Vas said quietly.

I put my hand on his arm and squeezed gently.

"Oh my god, I'm so sorry Vasyl," my mother exclaimed. "That's just awful."

"I'm sorry for your loss, and I'm sorry for bringing it up," my dad apologized.

Vas nodded with a wry smile. "It's okay. I miss him every day but he was the gung-ho patriot who just had to go, against my parents' wishes."

My mum looked at me then, but with sympathy, and perhaps not just a little relief knowing that I would never join any armed service. She glanced at David and then George and then at my dad.

"What war?" David asked Vas, suddenly interested in the conversation.

"In Ukraine, and Crimea, with Russia. It's complicated, as most wars are," Vas answered diplomatically.

"How far is that?" David asked. "Is it close to us?"

"No darling," my mum said gently. "Th-" she caught herself, "*Ukraine* is on the other side of the EU from us. Don't worry."

Vas rubbed his knee against mine and smiled across the table at David. "Your mum's right duck, you've got nothing to worry about," he looked at my mum. "This wellington is the most delicious thing I've ever eaten."

My mum smiled, pleased on so many levels. "Thank you, it's Gordon Ramsey's recipe."

"I don't think even he could make it taste this good," Vas smiled and raised his glass at her.

Everyone looked at Vas differently after that dinner, especially Felicity and I knew she wanted his attention. She seemed different after her first term at university, maybe slightly more mature, but I knew underneath it all she was still a pain in the arse. She was practicing all her feminine wiles on Vas, and he flirted politely with her, so as not to seem unfriendly. She had on a short skirt over tights and mid-calf boots that accentuated her willowy frame. I'm not such a jealous knob that I couldn't admit how pretty she was, with her perfect wavy hair and big blue eyes. She looked like a younger version of my mum, which is probably why my dad loved her so, but I could only see her as Felicity the bitch, and she was nothing like my perfect mum.

Felicity, David and I helped Mum clear the plates while George showed Vas the basics of Switch at the kitchen table. My mum cried out suddenly and I turned to look at her at the sink. I saw a jet of water coming from where the spray nozzle used to be before it disappeared down the hole in the countertop.

Vas stood immediately. "Turn off the water," he called on his way across the kitchen.

My dad came in from his study. "What's happened?" He asked.

"The nozzle just came off in my hand!" My mum cried, the front of her shirt wet.

My dad looked in the sink and then down the hole where the nozzle used to be. He opened the cabinet below and stepped back from the water dripping out. "Oh shite. Don't suppose we can get a plumber to come on Boxing Day," he said with a frown.

"I can fix it," Vas said confidently and turned to me, taking his glasses off. "There's a small flashlight in the outside pocket of my bag, can you get it for me?"

"Of course," I said, already headed to the foyer.

Vas then proceeded to wow everyone by laying on his back half in the cabinet, flashlight in his mouth feeding the hose up through the hole so my dad could hold it while he replaced the fastener that had come loose underneath. His jumper rode up and exposed his flat stomach and the thin line of dark hair that disappeared into his pants. He used to wax that too, until I begged him to leave it, like a pathway to heaven. I looked away and my eyes lighted on Felicity sitting at the kitchen island, her eyes locked on that very same goody trail. Vas backed out of the cabinet and stood, straightening his jumper with one hand and taking the flashlight out of his mouth with the other.

"That's done," he said with a smile at my dad. "I just need to fix the couplin' here and screw the nozzle back on." He took the hose from my dad as he stepped away.

One minute later Vas was testing the water and the squeezing the spray nozzle to make sure everything worked. My mum came back in wearing a new shirt and marveled over the quick fix.

"Thank you, Vas!" she exclaimed.

"My pleasure, it was nothing really, the couplin' came loose is all," he said humbly, his accent slipping again, and dried his hands on the kitchen towel my dad handed him. Vas looked at me and I beamed back at him happily.

"Can I pour you a scotch as a thank you?" My dad said. I nearly fell over at his tone. Christ, he sounded like he almost liked Vas in that moment.

"I would love one," Vas smiled and followed my dad to his study.

Oh shit. This could go well, or Vas could slip and reveal his age, or my dad could slip and mention my age. All of a sudden, I felt panicked, because I hadn't been invited, and I certainly couldn't follow them, that was just not done in the Trumball household. I looked at my mum.

She smiled at me. "He's very handy."

"That's nothing Mum. He's quite talented," I said proudly pulling out my phone and swiping to the photos he sent me of the cabinets and detail work he had done at his latest job. My mum made sounds of delight and praise as she looked at them.

"What's he doing with you then?" Felicity interrupted.

"Fuck you Feliss," I said angrily, not caring that Mum was standing right there, or that David and George were nearby.

"Felicity, Robin!" My mum said sternly. "Enough with the language and the insults."

"What? There must be something glaringly wrong with him if he's interested in a boy who looks like a thirteen-year-old girl," Felicity scoffed. "Are we just going to ignore the elephant in the room?"

"Oh, your jealousy is seething right now you slag," I gasped turning red with anger. "You wish you had someone half as beautiful and amazing as Vas, interested in you."

Felicity snorted. "Does he make you dress like a teenage girl or was that your idea?"

My stomach fell and I blushed an even deeper red. Oh, she was going to pay for that. I snuck a glance at my mother and wished I didn't.

"What?" She asked her face full of concern, looking between Felicity and me.

"Nothing Mum," I held up my hands. "I bought some cute shorts and a shirt, ages ago when I was out with Dee, she told me I looked good."

Felicity rolled her eyes.

"Seriously Mum, call her. Feliss is just trying to stir up trouble because she's jealous. I have no idea why she thinks her shit doesn't stink," I said meaningfully, looking at Felicity and narrowing my eyes.

Felicity looked away then. Oh, she knew only half the shit I knew about her, and just that half should have crumpled her womb. She stood and exhaled, swiping her hair haughtily. "Whatever, I just think it's weird," she said and left the room.

"You wouldn't think it was weird at all if it were you he was interested in," I called after her. I looked back at my mum who was looking between the doorway and me.

"Robin, what is she talking about?" She held my gaze.

"Nothing Mum, I swear," I said earnestly. "I found some cute shorts at Hollister. It really bugs me that men's clothes are so square and sporty and not me at all," I stepped forward. "I'm not trying to be a girl, and Vas is not weird like that. I like clothes that flatter, you know I'm not into shiny gym shorts that come to my knees."

My mum relaxed and began nodding. "I know. Men's fashion for your age is sorely lacking. But darling, I really don't want you dressing like a girl, or dressing in clothes that don't make you feel comfortable at someone else's behest," she said carefully.

"I would never Mum, I promise," I said truthfully.

She relaxed visibly and nodded. "I know you wouldn't Robin," she smiled at me and cupped my chin. "You are so precious, and so self-assured, despite what people might think of you, I know there's a heart of steel under there."

She didn't know quite how right she was about that, but I let my eyes shine happily as though I didn't believe her.

Vas and my dad came back then, my dad smiling happily and Vas nodding in agreement with whatever he was saying. Vas looked at me and winked, holding his nearly empty glass of scotch up to me in salute. I really wished Felicity had stayed for that look. I hated that she made our love sound sordid, in a way that I didn't feel even when I told Dee. Looking at him, I felt everything wash away, like it was just the two of us in the room, and I stepped forward, drawn to him like the tide to the shore, and bit my lip as I took his hand. I saw his eyes dart between my parents as he took a small step back.

"We can watch a movie downstairs," I suggested and then looked at my parents. "We're just going to watch the new Spiderman, if that's alright?"

"Of course," my mum smiled.

I looked at Vas. "Do you want a beer?" I looked at my dad. "Can he have a beer?"

My dad shrugged, "Sure Robby."

"Does Vas know where the guest room is?" My mother asked pointedly.

I got Vas a beer and straightened. "No, but I'll show him after the movie," I smiled at her.

Vas sat on the sectional while I found the remotes and queued up the movie. I turned to find his eyes on me and smiled as I sat next to him. "What?" I asked coyly.

"You are so bloody sexy I could barely keep my hands off you," he said and reached for me.

Our hands were everywhere and his tongue met mine with the same unmeasured passion. I rolled into his lap and straddled his glorious body as he ran his hands under my shirt and then down the back of my pants.

"Oh god Robby," he panted against my mouth as he felt my bare ass cheeks. He ran his fingertips along the V of my thong and moaned.

I pressed myself down against his hardness and arched my back. My body wanted his and was completely unwilling to take no for an answer, until I heard footsteps on the stairs that is. I jolted out of his lap as though I had been poked with a cattle prod and pressed my lips together angrily as we both caught our breath. David appeared with a can of soda in his hand.

"Mum said you're watching the new Spiderman," he said with the obliviousness of a twelve-year-old and sat on the other end of the couch.

I looked at Vas and shrugged my shoulders and pressed play. Vas pulled me back to the couch next to him, putting his arm around me. I looked worriedly at David and Vas nudged me.

"Don't make it weird," he said quietly. "There's nothing wrong with me sitting here with my arm around you."

I blew out a breath, wishing I had a modicum of his adult confidence, and relaxed into my spot under his arm.

Twenty minutes into the movie Felicity came down with her glass of wine. I scoffed at her still in her boots and full make-up, as though she were at a club and Vas would be interested in her. I fought hard to keep the smug expression off my face as she came around the sectional and saw Vas' arm around me (but sorry, wasn't able to). I watched as she sat next to David and then ran my hand across Vas' flat stomach deliberately. He had his beer in his other hand next to his thigh and took a swig before nodding at her.

Felicity was beyond put out, and I loved every minute of it. She watched the movie with us, not commenting much on the action, her phone at her side, texting or snapping or whatever the fuck she was doing, I didn't care, because Vas was with me, not her. Yeah, he was a laborer, and she was being a snob about that, but he fixed the kitchen sink, was fucking beautiful, and had Dad's approval so I wasn't feeling bad at all.

David dozed after an hour, exhausted from the holiday and from waking up before dawn on Christmas. I nudged him awake and offered to take him to bed, but he looked at Vas and said he was fine, before disappearing from the room. I looked at Felicity, willing her to leave too but she looked at me with a bitchy expression and I knew she wouldn't leave us alone. I pursed my lips and gave her a look that said I couldn't wait to return the favor.

She hesitated then but decided whatever torment she had planned seemed worth it, so she stayed. "Vasyl," she said his name carefully again, "now that my parents aren't here, and no siblings under foot, what exactly is it you see in my little brother?"

My bowels churned slightly, panicked that she would divulge my true age.

Vas took his feet down from the ottoman and put his empty bottle on the side table. He sat forward and looked at her, holding her gaze. I'll never forget the intensity of his gaze in that moment as he said, "he's smart, and handsome, and funny, and I love being around him." He flashed his sinful smile at her. "Anyone ever said that about you? Or to you?" He asked holding his breath and raising his brows.

Oh my god, I wanted to get up and dance. I watched Felicity as she processed his words, and maybe if she were anyone else, I would have felt sympathy for her, but she was such a slag to me my whole life that I just reveled in her discomfort.

Vas shrugged at her silence and sat back, putting his arm around my shoulder. "You're a beauty to be sure, but it seems as though you think there is no beauty beyond yours, and that in itself, is not beautiful at all."

Holy shit, no one had ever spoken to her so frankly, I am quite sure, in her entire life. I saw so many emotions flash across her face before she stood. She looked around and then at me, as though her gaze were searchlights looking for purchase.

"Good night," she said and left the room with her empty wine glass.

We waited for her footsteps to disappear and the door at the top of the stairs to close before looking at each other.

"Vas, shit," I said and raised my eyebrows.

He smiled at me. "She needed to hear that," he said calmly. "She's not going to say anything, so come here and kiss me," he breathed against my mouth as he pulled me into his lap.

* * *

I woke satiated and smelling Vas on the pillow next to me, but his physical being nowhere in sight. He had snuck in for a few hours in the deep dark of night and I had slept like a rock after. I sighed and rolled out of bed, my morning erection deflating at his absence. I brushed my teeth and dressed in track pants and a hoodie before going downstairs to look for food. I heard voices coming from the direction of my mother's study. Vas was standing in the doorway, wearing a hoodie and his arm brace, with my dad's rechargeable drill, tightening the screws in the doorframe.

He looked over his shoulder at me with a smile as he stopped when the screw was tight. "Morning Robby," he smiled and then tested the door, which no longer stuck when it was closed.

My dad smiled happily and squeezed Vas' shoulder. "Thank you!" He exclaimed. "I thought the house was settling and that I'd have to get a structural engineer in here."

"No, sir," Vas smiled. "You have any issues you check with me first," he nodded. "Too many tradesmen come around this neighborhood and charge too much or make up problems."

"Will do, Vasyl," my dad said and looked at me before heading to the kitchen.

"Where's your toolbelt, stud?" I asked him with a cheeky grin once my dad was out of earshot.

"I think I left it in your bedroom," Vas said and waggled his eyebrows.

"I'm very disappointed that you didn't find my morning wood worthy of attention, Mr. Carpenter," I said making the most dramatic face I could. "You'd rather screw a door jamb than me?"

Vas chuckled low in his throat. "Robby, don't be ridiculous. I'm only down here doing this, so your parents will let me do this," he said and thrust his groin against my bottom.

I shifted my shoulders back and forth happily and kissed him quickly. "I love you. God you're so gorgeous," I said and teased my thumb and forefinger across my bottom lip.

Vas made an appreciative sound as he followed me into the kitchen.

22

Meet the Bat'kiv

I MET VAS' PARENTS after the new year, in February, and it was exactly as terrifying and nerve-wracking as you might imagine. His father said five, heavily-accented, words to me before leaving for his workroom and his mother spoke kindly but watched me suspiciously. Vas told me not to worry, they were quiet and private people and took time to warm up with everyone, but I sensed that was not entirely true. They seemed a lot older than they were, and I didn't know if that was from hard living or grief, or both probably. It made me feel so pampered and sheltered, and I felt like it made them uncomfortable. I tried my best to win them over, and it only took less than a year. I honestly couldn't tell if it was solely because their only remaining son was in a gay relationship or if they didn't like me because I was posh. His father had grimaced when he heard my accent. You might think it was my lisp, but you'd be wrong; I didn't lisp the first few times I spoke with them.

There were pictures of Vas' brother Andriy everywhere, and a literal shrine to him in the small living room that no one was allowed to touch. He was handsome, like Vas, and even bigger and more masculine. It was a shame he died, it was shame anyone died in war. I never understood that part of the male psyche, and certainly never identified with it. Vas caught me looking at the pictures and stood with me after the meal. He looked anywhere but at the photos and took my hand.

"When we were kids, he had the best sense of humor, and he were so fearless," Vas said looking at the ground, all his 'h's' gone with the emotion. "As he got older, he stopped laughing as much and became even more fearless, as though he had to choose between the two. I wish he had chosen mirth over death."

I didn't know what to say so I just hugged him. Christ that was heavy, too heavy for my bony shoulders.

We left, and when we got back to his flat we went to bed and I just held him.

We went to his parents for dinner after that about once a month, and then every other week, until finally, in our last year together, we were back to once a month. They had finally accepted me, and I guess it seemed as though we were together for the long haul, but that wasn't the case and I'm getting ahead of myself.

—————

23

—————

House Trumball Gains a Builder

VAS WENT ALL OUT for what he thought was my eighteenth birthday. We stayed at a more upscale hotel in town, and had dinner in Soho to celebrate. He made love to me slowly and remarkably, all the ways I liked it. The second time he fucked me, he had me wear the new lilac-colored lace nightie he'd given me for my birthday and filmed us. Then he woke me in the morning and filmed us having morning sex. It was really a turn-on to watch the footage after, except for the parts where my hair was standing up or the red pimple on my ass. I asked him to edit those parts if he could, or fix my hair for me, which he did the next time. Later, I got really good at instinctively smoothing my hair as he flopped me around, and using pimple cream on my ass so I wouldn't have break-outs from his hands gripping me. Everything else was just riding or laying back and enjoying myself.

* * *

He came for Sunday dinner at the house the following weekend, because my grand-parents had other plans. He knew he couldn't keep wearing the arm brace forever, or a turtleneck in the summer, so not long after Boxing Day we finally just came clean to my parents about his tattoos. My dad went back to thinning his lips, and my mum just got wide-eyed but they eventually got over it by my birthday, just like they had with his age. He did so much around the house, and his manners were impeccable, they really couldn't complain.

"How's that new development in north Manchester coming?" My dad asked between bites.

"Great, most of the houses are already sold, and more than half are occupied," Vas answered, letting his accent slip with familiarity, happy to talk about work. "We've got three left I'm bouncing between, doing a mix of supervising and building."

"Impressive," my dad nodded. "You're so young to be in charge, you must really be good."

I kept my eyes studiously elsewhere at that comment.

"Yes sir. I work hard, and people listen to me. I've been doing this nearly my whole life so," he shrugged, "I've got years of experience over some of the other guys even though they're older."

"You ever have time for a side job?"

"I will soon, what did you have in mind?"

My dad asked Vas to install shelves and a row of cabinets in my mum's study and he began in early July. It was a mixture of custom and store bought and looked better than the ones in my dad's study. My parents were blown away by his workmanship, and they were right to be, Vas was an incredible talent. He stayed with us for a few weekends, and weekdays finishing the project, me sneaking into the guest room after hours, horny from watching him work, using his table saw in the garden, swinging his hammer, smelling like sawdust until he showered.

He filmed us up there on the third floor too. We had to be super quiet, and when he posted that one later, he called it something dirty like, '*Step-brother Sneaks a Fuck, Cream Pie*,' or something disturbing to most. We usually laughed when we titled the videos, but we never laughed at the money we made, but I'm getting ahead of myself again.

Speaking of money, my dad paid Vas for his work, and the materials obviously, but not what the job was worth because Vas was adamant and didn't want to take any money for it at all. I should've known he was playing us all like an (amateur) chess master, giving up the little pieces for the payload.

* * *

After the shelves were finished, my parents invited Vas to Spain, to spend a week. There was work there and my dad insisted on paying Vas so he could justify taking the time off and paid for his travel. Having Vas there was heaven. He worked on the little projects, leaks, replacing some rot caused by the ocean air, installing new lighting and a few other things and then spent the rest of the time soaking up the sun by the pool, his tattoos on full display, along with his beautiful body which neither I, nor my mum, nor Felicity could keep our eyes off of, much to my father's chagrin. Dad picked up running again, which made my mum happy, and improved his mood, and toward the end of the week he joined Vas on some of his workouts. Vas was really good at finding ways to work out without gym equipment and showed my dad how he could do the same.

"You know your father has warmed up to him, I honestly never thought he would," my mum said to me at the farmer's market one morning while Vas was working, David acting as his apprentice.

"I'm really glad Mum. I know he's not anything or anyone you imagined for me, but, he makes me really happy, and he loves me as much as I love him," I smiled. "And he's making Dad look great," I chuckled.

"I know, I hope he keeps it up when we get home," my mum laughed and sniffed some fruit. "Have you started your application to Oxford?" She asked changing the subject.

"I haven't, because with things being serious between me and Vassy, I'm now considering Manchester."

"What? How's their computer science program?" She asked with concern.

"They're a top school, it's the oldest program in England I think, and certainly a great option, truly," I said defensively.

She sighed. "Robby, Oxford is the best, and Cambridge of course, and you've had your heart set on it. What if things don't work out between you and Vas, I don't mean to be pessimistic but young love is so fleeting. You wouldn't want to stay there, and it can be really difficult to transfer."

"It's more than four hours by train from Manchester to Oxford," I whined. "I'd never see him."

"Robby, you can't base your life on that, and this is your whole future we're talking about. If it's meant to be, he will wait for you, he will take that train happily," she patted my cheek. "You have legacy at Oxford, your father will be furious if you choose Manchester over it, and he may not pay," she added in a whisper.

"You have money, you could pay," I said pleadingly.

"But, I agree with your father," she shrugged.

"Mum," I cried. "Manchester is a great uni. You're not being fair."

"Robby," she looked around discreetly, "I don't want to have this conversation with you here, and it's far too soon to say anyway, you haven't applied yet to either," she squeezed my hand. "Come on, help me find some veggies for dinner." She walked away, effectively ending the conversation.

We got back to the house as Vas was finishing the doorframe around the slider. He looked at me with a smile, his eyes sweeping my body in that distinctive way of his that indicated he wanted sex.

"I'm gonna have a shower and then let's pop off to the beach," he said.

"Sounds great," I felt my little buddy stir in my pants. "I'll get my suit and my sunscreen."

Vas filmed me polishing his knob at the beach, in broad daylight. No one was around, but Vas kept careful watch, and then we went back later that night so he could film himself fucking me. I didn't think to ask why he was filming us so much, I was having fun, getting laid, and he was showering me with compliments and praise. I was seventeen and a complete muppet when it came to him, I honestly couldn't think straight around him, not the first two years anyway.

* * *

That whole summer was fun and exciting both back home, and on the continent. When I wasn't with Vas, or babysitting, I was working at my dad's company, like I had the previous summer, but more often because I was older. Last year I was making copies, and sorting the mail, but toward the end of the summer, I worked alongside some of the other programmers and discovered I had an aptitude for programming, so my dad arranged for me to work in that department again, running code, testing code, and writing code. I was really good at debugging programs, more so than writing them per se, but I was pretty good at that too. I felt a bit like Cypher from *The Matrix*, seeing 'blonde, brunette, redhead,' instead of ones and zeros as lines of code. I got along with the people who worked in that department, and in the IT department, a lot of them gamers like me, though much older. One of the guys in IT, Joel, he was twenty-something, took a shine to me, he's the one I got the fake ID from. I never asked him where he got it or if he was the one who made it, but I was very grateful, it saved me a lot down the road.

24

Good News (for Eighteen-Year-Olds)

SCHOOL RESUMED, and we were finally top of the food chain, not that Dee and I benefitted in any way from that, but there was a crop of new year nines who didn't know anything about us that we could briefly lord over. I hadn't seen hide nor hair of Marcus all summer, and certainly not since Vas threatened him, it was both freeing and weird, but I didn't dwell on it.

Dee and I sat at our new table in the cafeteria, not anything close to Marcus' old table in the middle which was solidly for the athletes, but not in the back corner anymore. I had grown an inch since the end of last term, and had to get all new uniform pants and shirts, as did Dee but because she had lost quite a bit of weight over the summer.

"How was America?" I asked Dee dramatically. "You look amazing, nice fucking tan."

"Thank you, it was incredible, I met a boy," she sighed and fake swooned.

"Stop it!" I cried. "No, wait, I already knew that, all of Instagram already knew that, thanks for nothing," I scowled.

"Robby! No, I'm sorry!" She grabbed my arm.

"I'm kidding, don't worry," I smiled. "I know if you had met him here I would have been the first to know. So, he's cute! Tell me all about him."

She filled me in on how they met (getting ice cream in Cape Cod), what his name was (Chad, oh god what an awful name), and where he was from (some place called Belmont, near Boston). She went on and on and I listened because I'm a good friend, and because she listened to me about Vas all the time.

I showed her the pictures of me and Vas that I didn't dare share on the internet and she marveled over him poolside.

"I can't believe your parents have embraced him and not only that, but had him join you on holiday," she shook her head. "They saw all those tattoos?" She gestured to my phone.

"Yes, kind of hard to hide by our pool. He won them over with his manners and his skill with fixing things. He's tightened every screw and replaced every broken thing in both houses, and not only that, but my dad was working out with him."

"Shut. Up!" She said dropping her mouth open. "Mr. Upper-Crust-Snob was working out with a Ukrainian laborer from Manchester? I can't believe it," she shook her head and sipped her water.

"I know. It's crazy. And then Vas still had time to do his workout with me," I said lasciviously.

"You're disgusting Robby," she laughed and threw her crumpled napkin at me.

"I gave him head on the beach in broad daylight," I said and bit my lip.

She widened her eyes and looked around. "Weren't you scared someone would see you?"

"Of course, I nearly pissed myself, but no one did, it's our secret forever, well, except now you know," I winked.

My phone buzzed in my pocket as I was walking home.

> I'm coming this weekend,
> we're staying at the Ritz

I stopped walking and read Vas' text four times before responding.

> Okaaaaay. What's the occasion?

> I have great news to share
> and want to celebrate u

I responded with two thumbs up and a peach and an eggplant, and then let my parents know over dinner that I would be seeing Vas Saturday.

"Is he coming here or are you going there?" My mum asked. "He's welcome to stay here you know."

"I know, but I'm going there, dinner with his parents or something," I lied smoothly. "I'll tell him to come here next weekend, if that's okay?"

"Of course," my mum smiled and looked at George. "Eat your veggies love."

"Robby doesn't have to," George wheedled.

"I had to when I was your age," I said to him. "When you get top marks and are as amazing as me, you won't have to," I shrugged and winked.

George looked at me thoughtfully and then ate his vegetables.

✳ ✳ ✳

I had been to the London Ritz before, not to brag but, more than once. Vas clearly hadn't and I loved him for it, he was like a kid pretending to be a grown up. He was dressed to the nines, and so handsome sitting at the bar. It was the first time I had seen him in a suit and he looked gorgeous. I wore my pink Burberry pants and cream-colored jumper with my hair styled short and neat like Vas liked. I put my mum's Gucci overnight bag in the chair next to Vas as he kissed me right there in the bar. The bartender nearly fainted, but fuck him. I sat next to Vas and ordered a soda.

"I've ordered champagne," he said with a smile.

I made a surprised face and sound. "Like gangster champagne, or Krug?"

Vas frowned briefly. "What's gangster champagne?"

"Cristal," I giggled, "Or Dom Perignon, depending on the vintage," I said thinking of what I heard my dad say.

"What vintage?"

I changed my sound to one of excitement to spare him. "Dom Perignon?! I love it, all vintages," I wrapped my arms around his neck and kissed his cheek. "Well, the two I've had in my short life."

Vas smiled, and his cheek bulged under my lips. "And I love you Robin," he turned his face and kissed me again as the bartender put down two glasses in front of us. I sat back in my chair and watched as he opened the bottle, not looking at me.

I thought then, that if I were him, and had these two people in front of me, or any two mismatched people in front of me, that I would make up a romantic, or suspenseful story about them in my head, while I served them. In our scenario I suppose I would say that the younger one (me, obviously) was an international spy-slash-playboy, who was seducing the older, possibly-Russian spy (Vas, obviously) and that the younger one would do whatever was necessary to get information from said Russian spy, even if that meant drinking gangster bubbly, and kissing his tattooed neck. I slipped into that role as if I were born for it. By the second glass, I almost suggested drinking the third from Vas' shoe, but I'm posh and, even drunk, I don't make a scene. I was, however, a lightweight (then anyway), and after pouring me a smidgen more, he finished the bottle, paid, and then led me to the elevator, carrying my very posh bag in his gloriously tattooed hand, with his other arm firmly around my shoulder. I pretended it was because he loved me so, and wanted the world to know, but it was probably more that I may or may not have been able to walk a straight line on my own.

He closed the hotel room door behind us and I pounced on him. He dropped my bag and brought his arms up around me. "Wait," he said softly and got out his phone.

I noticed a tripod next to the bed with a large circle on top. He put his phone into the holder in the middle and flicked on a switch and I saw that the circle was a ring of light. He pressed record on his phone and came back to me, guiding me into the camera's view, kissing me passionately. I held my, several, questions until later, because the buzz of alcohol in my blood made me crave everything that he was doing to me. He undressed me as I undressed him, and he pressed my shoulders until I was on my knees. He said things, I said things, he put me on the bed and spit into my asshole. Oh, was that too much information? (Sorry). I was drunk and truly it became so rote later, that it's best I told you now, so I never need to mention it again, that he did that all the time, he never used lube after our first time.

I waited until he shut off the camera, until after we had showered, to ask him what the fuck was going on.

He rubbed my body down with lotion and eased me between the sheets, his body warm next to mine. "I posted a video of us online, anonymously of course," he said in a rush, "and we got a flurry of interest. So, I created a profile, and I posted more," he held my gaze in the low-light. "Not only do we have interest, we have gained nearly ten thousand subscribers in under three months," he said and bit his lip as he looked at me. "I posted our videos on a whim and between multiple sites, subscription fees, and tips etc., we've made more than five thousand quid this month."

I felt so many emotions in that moment, and I was drunk, so ninety percent of them were euphoric, and the ten percent that were ringing madly like air-raid sirens, were squashed and beaten like little gay boys by rugby stars.

"Holy shit Vassy. You're joking," I looked at his beaming face.

He shook his head. "No Robby, I'm not. I hope you're not mad I did it, but honestly, I never thought anything would come of it. They fucking love you. I fucking love you," he kissed me and loved my body without asking for anything in return. I fell asleep on clouds.

In the morning there was room service and more filming, of course, and I was hesitant until he licked my asshole and promised that I was protected under a pseudonym. I was seventeen and really not much smarter than I had been four months ago when I was sixteen, and the man I was in love with was dancing on the moon because of something we had produced together, how could I not completely ignore the elephant in the room?

I learned that Vas had named me Ronnie in our videos, using my fake ID pseudonym, but kept his own name because I gasped it like every other breath in our first videos, so he couldn't be anyone but Vas or Vassy. Thank god, because I couldn't have changed it. Crying out 'oh god Vas' as I came was something I did even after we broke up, much to the chagrin of those first several men I was with, but in my defense, I was drunk or high or both when I did, so. . . .

25

Catch a Tiger
by the Tail

WE MADE SO MUCH MONEY from our videos, which we released on some sites partially, and other, paid sites, in full with the money shots included, that Vas encouraged me to apply only to Oxford, with the expectation that he could retire, or semi-retire and live with me, and we'd continuing filming whilst I went to university. It was win-win actually. I would go to the uni that my parents so desperately wanted me to attend, and would pay for, including my accommodations in town, and Vas could live with me and just pay the bills. He could do carpentry if he wanted to but didn't need to because the porn we were making would more than cover our living expenses.

Every weekend we were together after the Ritz was spent making videos. Initially, we could only make three or four at most, because Vas could only get hard so many times, until he got himself a prescription for Viagra, and we would film me until I came, and then he came, and then I came, and we would pause and I would come again, and then he came, never losing his erection between orgasms. I teased him off-camera, but as soon as he pressed record, I was right there with my moans and 'fuck me harder Daddy,' eager to please him.

Daddy porn is quite common, often bottoms just call their tops 'Daddy,' not because of any age difference, but because it's a 'thing.' In our case, it was undeniable that I was so much younger than Vas, so Vas instructed me to call him 'Daddy,' in a fetish way (those made more money), and it never really bothered me because we looked nothing alike, I certainly wasn't worried that anyone would think he was my actual father (disgusting). I alternated between Daddy and Vas, because how could I be expected to remember in the heat of the moment what to call him? Ultimately it didn't matter because our fans loved it, loved me slipping character, and we gained tens of thousands over the next year and a half, such that we were literally rolling in dough. We filmed one video of Vas fucking me surrounded by the queen's face, just to be cheeky. He fucked my feet, we did ass-to-mouth, and a few other things only the people who watched, Vas, and my therapist know.

* * *

Autumn was turning out to be even more spectacular than the summer had been. Vas was making so much money from our videos, and work, such that we (and by we, I mean he) were already looking at places to live in Oxford for when I got accepted, because for fuck's sake, I was legacy and a top student, why wouldn't I get in? We made new videos, sometimes spontaneously like our sex was, and sometimes at the behest of our fans.

I don't mean to get ahead of myself, but so much of our porn was real, especially at the beginning. I hate to draw attention to it, because the first few videos were illegal, child porn really, but as I said, it was authentic, him loving me, me eager to please. Later, as his mask slipped, it became rote, and angry, and very fan-driven, which was, at times, gross. I did porn for Christ's sake, so who was I to judge, but holy hell, some of our fans were truly demented, and I went to confession more than once after filming, and I wasn't even Catholic.

Everything was great and we were so happy until someone recognized Vas and texted him, and then it spread in his circle, like all bad news does. He raged over the phone, yelling at me for saying his name when we were fucking, which somehow forced him to use his real name on the sites. I didn't dare point out that he could have dubbed me, that he could have tricked me into saying something else in those early videos, and of course I didn't dare mention that his tattoos were pretty recogniz-able and, perhaps most importantly of all, maybe he shouldn't have posted any of them without my consent, but, bygones. 'If onlys' were as meaningless as 'should haves.' Christ, I'd be a billionaire if either if those things had any monetary value.

His parents found out, Olek found out, everyone he worked with found out, ex-girlfriends found out, and Vas holed himself up in his flat for two weeks. He wouldn't respond to me, and it seemed like he was trying to do damage control when he should have just said fuck you to everyone, like he usually did when he was seen in public with me, but he was so busy being greedy he got reckless, and I was the was easy target he took his frustration out on.

* * *

I took the train to Manchester the second weekend after hearing nothing from him. Olek glared at me and left after he let me in. Vas was coiled, and unlike I had ever seen. I can't recall if he said anything to me before he pushed me into the bathroom and told me to disrobe and make myself hard.

He opened the door as I stood there naked, in the dark, with my hand on my cock. He looked me over in the light that illuminated me from the open door and nodded derisively with his head. "Get in my room."

I walked past him, covering my junk like I was in one of those prison line-ups just before they looked up your orifices for contraband. When I stepped into his room I realized that I was one of those prisoners. There was a sheet on the wall and he had me stand there while he did things to me on camera. I hope that video was taken down, because he fucked me without spit till I bled, and the bruises he gave me were real.

"You ran and never looked back!" I heard the masses cry expectantly. But no. I stayed. I loved him. He gave me a pill that took away the pain and made me higher than I'd ever been.

The next day he was blah, blah, blah. Stop it! I loved him and I explained everything away, I don't need to hear shit from you, what did I already say about if onlys and should haves?

26

Bad News
(for Seventeen-Year-
Olds and the Men
Who Exploit Them)

VAS CALMED DOWN, we made more porn (of course we did), his parents could look at me again, Christmas came and went, I got into Oxford, early, and Vas and I celebrated at the Ritz again. All was great until mid-February, in the middle of class, I got a call from Felicity. I frowned as I sent the auto-reply that I couldn't talk.

> **Call me the minute you're
> out of class**

I suddenly worried that something had happened to one of our parents, or one of our brothers and willed the clock hands to move faster. When class ended I hurried to the quiet corner of the building outside the counseling office and swiped into my phone.

"You fucking dirty perv! You're doing porn?" Felicity screeched into my ear when she answered.

I almost shit myself, legitimately, I'm not exaggerating. "What?" I managed to squeak.

"Don't play dumb with me Robby. Christ! I'm mortified," she shouted. "It's bad enough that someone else told me about it, but then I saw one of your videos," she began sobbing.

God, she was such a drama queen, but at the same time I began sobbing myself.

"You're not even eighteen, it's child porn, and he's twenty-nine! I looked him up. You fucking lied to Mum and Dad, he's a goddamn *pedophile*." Every word she shouted at me cut me like axe blades. "He was at our house. He was in Spain! A full-fledged man, and you, on the beach," she stopped talking as if she was rendered speechless, and I wished it were a permanent state for her. "While we were at the house like five minutes away. You're disgusting!"

"Fuck you, Feliss!" I hissed, mindful of the people that could hear. "There's nothing wrong with porn and he loves me, I love him, you're the one with the hang up."

"ARE YOU FUCKING KIDDING ME?" She shouted so loudly I was worried the continent would hear her. "He knowingly posted videos of you two having sex and you're not eighteen. That's against the law."

I felt true panic then, if my identity came out it could be disastrous. "He thinks I'm eighteen."

"What?"

"I lied to him Feliss, I told him I was seventeen when we met. Come on, you've never lied about your age to someone you liked?"

"Of course I have, but none of the guys have filmed us having sex and then posted it for the world to see!" She cried. "Those sites go everywhere. Robby, you're a child, do you know what he's done?"

"You're exaggerating, please calm down. Please don't say anything to Mum and Dad," my heart was pounding so loud I could barely hear her response.

"You don't think they'll eventually find out?" Felicity asked with a voice full of incredulity. "Jesus Robby, Daddy works in high-tech, he's definitely going to find out."

"Please don't be the one to tell them," I whispered. "I'll figure something out, but please Feliss, I'm begging you."

There was a long pause. My stomach felt full of lead. "Fine, but that Pikey is still a pedophile," she said and the line went dead.

I immediately went in search of Dee, gesturing wildly to her from outside the window in the door of her classroom. I dragged her outside and sat her down, and immediately burst into tears.

"Oh my god, Robby, what is it?" She pulled my head to her bosom, which is really all I wanted.

I soaked her blouse with my tears before pulling back. "Please, listen, and don't judge, promise?" I said earnestly and raised my eyebrows.

"I promise, just tell me what's wrong," she said, her face full of concern.

"Sometimes, when Vassy and I had sex, he filmed us, *we* filmed us," I breathed, searching her face for judgement. "He posted a few online," I winced.

Her eyes went wide at that and then she reined them in. "What?"

"Felicity found out, and now she's threatening to tell Mum and Dad," I started crying again.

Dee hugged me, and I'm certain she was looking around flabbergasted and trying not to judge but was wholly unable to.

"Robby," she began quietly, her voice coming from her chest under my ear, "you're not eighteen, and I know you told me sixteen is consent for sex, but I'm pretty sure anything that goes out to the world has to be over eighteen." She squeezed my shoulders. "Does he know, did you ever tell him the truth?"

I shook my head and pulled back to look at her. "He thought I was eighteen, he never posted anything until this summer, after my birthday."

She pulled a face and shook her head. "He could get in real trouble for this."

"He posted us under my fake name, the ID that Joel made, from Dad's work. He did me a solid and created a whole background identity for me linked to that," I explained. "The only way Vas could get in trouble is if someone ratted on us, and the only people that know about us are people who wouldn't want us to get arrested, with the possible exception of Felicity, but I think even she wouldn't want to see me get in that kind of trouble."

Dee looked away thinking. "Okay," she looked back at me, "we should make a list of everyone who knows about you two, who has seen you together and knows your names. Then we can potentially block any rats."

"Good idea!" I kissed her cheek and pulled out my phone and swiped into the notes app. I started typing as she threw out names and watched over my shoulder.

"Wait, Marcus knows? And Gareth?" She looked at me with concern.

I stopped typing. "Yeah, they saw us together. I never told you?"

She shook her head.

"Oh, it was quite dramatic really. Vas knew from my reaction and the look on Marcus' face when he saw us walking arm in arm that he had been bullying me and he punched him," I looked away.

"Jesus. Wait, Robby, if Marcus finds out won't he run to the police? I mean Vas assaulted him, he'll want payback," she said, her voice full of concern.

I looked back at my phone. "He won't say a word."

"How can you be so sure?" She asked skeptically.

"He's off at uni, he can't be bothered with doing anything," I shrugged. "I'm sure he's bullying somebody else now, wouldn't take the time to think about me."

"Okay. So that's everyone then?" We both scanned the short list.

I nodded.

"Okay, Marcus and Gareth aside, the only other ones would be your parents, and they would only do something if they thought he had intentionally exposed you as a minor, but he didn't so, I think you're in the clear," she stopped. "Unless someone from school administration found out, like a teacher or something. They have a duty to report I think," she looked frightened.

My body went cold. "Fuck," I stood and put my phone away. "I need to call Vas. We have to take the videos down."

She stood with me. "You definitely should."

27

Sleeping
with the Enemy

IT TOOK ME seven tries to actually call Vas, my stomach was like lead and I'd already been to the bathroom making it just in time before shitting myself. I snuck two shots of vodka from my dad's bar cart and finally pressed send on the phone.

"Hey doll," Vas said happily when he answered.

I blew out a quiet breath. "Hey babe, I have something I have to tell you."

Vas was quiet, it was never good news when someone said those words.

"Felicity called me, she found out about the videos," I said quietly. "She yelled at me, a lot."

"Oh shit!" Vas said loudly. "She gonna say anything to your parents?"

"No, I made her promise, but that's not the really bad news," I paused. "I liked you so much and I didn't want you to leave when we first met, so I lied about my age. I'm only seventeen."

"WHAT?!" Vas exploded, after a long pause. Then he swore and went on a tirade in Ukrainian. I felt like throwing up.

"I'm sorry, I should have told you," I cried. "We can just delete the videos," I said when he stopped.

"Are you fucking daft?" He spat. "I've sold them. People have downloaded them they're fucking everywhere now. Of course I will delete them but for fuck's sake Rob, there's more to it. I gotta go."

The line went dead.

I cried myself to sleep that night, skipping dinner. I couldn't eat, I couldn't do my homework, I couldn't do anything but lay there and sob. I texted Vas that I was sorry, that I loved him, that I would accept full responsibility if anyone ever found out, and I heard nothing back, for days.

I checked the sites for our profiles and saw that Vas still had them active, but had taken down most of the videos, leaving the ones he filmed from his point of view that didn't have my face (those ones are quite popular) and a few that he had filmed of himself masturbating. Those were titled 'Daddy Thinking of Ronnie, edging. Cum Shot!' and 'Waiting for Ronnie's tight hole. Jets of Cum.' Not award-winning titles, but in porn they don't need to be, they just need to be searchable and to the point. I wish I had chosen a different name for my fake ID, one that wasn't so close to my real name, but I that's why I picked it. I only wanted something easy to remember so I could drink, not a cover identity for underage pornography.

* * *

I was terrified at the thought of seeing Vas again, but terrified not to. I missed him, my body craved him, so I bought a ticket to Manchester. I stopped for a vodka at the pub before going to his apartment.

Olek let me in and shook his head. "You got some nerve boy. I knew you wasn't eighteen."

"Is Vassy here?" I ignored him.

"No."

"I'll wait then," I took out my phone and texted Vas that I was at his place.

"I wouldn't recommend it. His temper is off the charts, with good fucking reason."

I felt a quiver of fear in my belly at that, joining the already quaking sensation that had been there since the train ride. But he hurt me before and I survived.

I didn't have to wait long. Vas came in and ordered Olek to leave. Olek left and Vas was on me. He smacked me hard across my face, I saw stars as my head whipped around.

"You fucking lying little cunt," he said, his voice nearly unrecognizable. He stalked me as I stumbled back, and grabbed the front of my shirt with his hand, holding me as he back-handed me with his conch shells. It felt like the conch shells were real, bruising my flesh, and my teeth rattled. I broke free and ran. "I could go to prison. Do you know what the penalty for production and distribution of child pornography is?" he snarled as he and his tigers chased me. "What they do to child rapists in prison?"

I won't say anything other than he pummeled and kicked me as I huddle in the corner of his room, and then later handed me a happy pill and put me to bed with some ice. I was only glad that he didn't make me leave, as much as I hated what he did to me, I told myself he did it from fear, I knew I couldn't face my parents looking the way I did and had no other choice but to stay.

I wasn't sure what kind of pill he gave me, it felt different from the other ones. I was so high I hallucinated that I was bird or a winged creature, caught in thunderstorm. Every so often a bolt of lightning would hit me and my wings wouldn't work, then the thunder would be so loud in my ears that I couldn't tell which way was up and I felt the real stomach-lurching sensation of falling, like on a rollercoaster. I would flap my wings and be fine until a final bolt of lightning did me in and everything went white. There was no sound, there was no air, or rather it was all air and nothing else. St. Michael, the archangel, came to me with his army of angels, his wings, one of which was crooked, were massive, his arms strong, as he picked me up and carried me to the edge of heaven and dumped me over the side into a vat of cold liquid. I had been expecting a lake of fire and was wholly unprepared for the chill that overcame me. I struggled to get out but there were too many angels holding me down, their wings fanning me their voices speaking angel tongue. It felt like one of them was sticking their cock down my throat and I tried to turn my head. The tip of it touched the back of my throat and I vomited before blacking out.

I woke up hours later to voices murmuring at the foot of Vas' bed.

"You nearly fucking killed him," a voice that sounded like Olek's said. "He should be in a hospital."

"You're the one who bought those pills, who the fuck did you get them from?" Vas said in an angry voice.

"The same guy I always do, he said they were a little stronger, you should only have given him half. Christ, he looks like he weighs fifty kilos." There was a pause. "What did you do to him? He's covered in bruises. You gonna send him home to his mummy looking like that?"

I moved then, and everything hurt, especially my back, which took most of the abuse.

Vas came to the bed as Olek left, closing the door. My eyes worked, but my mouth felt swollen. He touched me gingerly as he sat down. "Robby, I'm so sorry.

I love you. I," he paused. "I lost my head, I'm just so scared of getting caught, of losing you."

I sat up and hugged him, covering St. Michael's face with my arms. "I'm sorry I lied to you. I should've told you when you posted the videos but you were so happy, and making so much money," I said thickly, still feeling drugged in addition to swollen.

Vas feathered kisses over my face. "You need coffee, or a red bull or something. I'll be right back."

He took care of me the whole weekend, told me that I had a bad reaction to the pill he gave me (bullshit, he nearly killed me with an overdose, but I didn't contradict him) and he had to put me in an ice bath and stick his finger down my throat to get me to vomit. There was true panic on his face when he saw the blood in my urine. To be honest, he wasn't nearly as panicked as I was but I wasn't going to say a word, I was more focused on icing the bruises on my face, both of which weren't all that bad and I could easily hide with the make-up I sent Vas to the store for.

Saturday, after lunch I found Vas sitting on the couch staring at nothing. He looked up when I came to sit in his lap.

"Are you still mad at me?" I whispered.

He nodded with a sigh. "But, I love you Robin, and I've been through this over and over in my mind. I couldn't take everything down because I didn't want to raise suspicion. We have an even bigger fan base now, and before all this went down, I had been amassing fan clubs and made a Patreon account for us," he kissed my lips gently. "Thing is, we need to be making more videos, to keep up our momentum. I figured for the next four months we can do only POV, film without your face, and get creative with hats, maybe costumes, sunglasses. I've looked for ideas online and found a lot of different things we can do," he took my hand. "And then after your birthday, I can go back to fucking you proper."

I gave him a smile at that. I loved hearing him talk about our future, especially when I was so worried about him dumping me. I should have known that if not for the porn he would have dumped me on my ass. He beat the golden goose, but after coming close to killing it, he realized the error of his ways.

"You fancy a fuck now?" I said in a coy voice and shook my shoulders back and forth, ignoring the pain in my back. The twinge I felt under my butt cheek indicated the answer to that was a resounding yes.

He filmed solely from his perspective, and I kept my shirt on, the bruises visible from time to time, and my head in the pillow or with a cap on. That weekend was the first time we took a fan request for him fucking my feet. We kept having to pause the camera, because I couldn't stop laughing. It tickled and it was bloody ridiculous, but it made us a lot of money so I guess we laughed all the way to the bank. We filmed me giving Vas a blow job wearing a baseball hat, which shielded my face well, and made plans to get a go-pro that I could wear when doing it, and then he could wear it and free up both of his hands.

By Sunday, my face was better, and Vas and I were back on track, though once he lost his temper with me and saw that I forgave him for it, it gave him permission to do it going forward. He never beat me as badly again, but he smacked my around when we didn't hit our numbers, or if I didn't shower (often I was too high to remember to), or if I didn't moan enough.

I applied my make-up, quite expertly I thought, and kissed Vas goodbye at the train. I made sure to get home after dinner so I didn't have anyone's scrutiny on me for too long, and chatted with my mum briefly before taking a long bath with the Epsom salts Vas had given me. I took two paracetamols and said a silent prayer of thanks that the blood was almost gone from my pee.

28

The Oxford
Cummer

THE NEXT FOUR MONTHS were nerve-wracking. I kept jumping every time the door-bell rang or approached my parents on eggshells when they called for me, but my birthday came and we really celebrated, because it was also our second anniversary. Vas had bought a new camera, better resolution and audio, along with the go-pro and a few other accessories, and gave me a promise ring, not an engagement ring, but I was thrilled to my core. The other surprise he had for me was a brand-new tattoo over his heart of a tiny bird, a robin with a beautiful, reddish-brown chest, his first colored tattoo, and I loved it. I kissed it with my soft lips and he moaned. Then I got all dressed up in lingerie and he fucked me fully clothed, peeling aside the thong instead of taking it off, to the delight of our fans.

Felicity wouldn't even speak to me. She was disgusted that he hadn't taken all the videos down, and I told her she was disgusting for checking.

"You're the sick one. You like watching your brother have sex? You should have your head examined," I said to her one night when she came to my room.

"No, don't you dare turn this on to me," she hissed. "I only checked because I'm concerned about you, this is going to ruin your life. You will never be able to escape it. I know you don't realize that now, but believe me when I say, I'm very sorry to be speaking the truth," she shook her head.

"Oh Feliss, it's just porn, there's nothing wrong with porn," I said, repeating what Vas always said. "Billions of people watch it."

"That may be true, but not the kind of porn you're doing. Those titles, what you call him," she made a ghastly face. "If Mum ever saw that. Did you ever think about that? Her or your REAL daddy?" She slammed my door leaving me white-faced at the thought. I really never allowed myself to think about my parents seeing it. I looked at my watch and ran out to the store for a six pack of beer. I drank all of them and passed out on my bed, waking just before pissing myself. I fell back into a dreamless sleep and woke with a pounding headache.

* * *

Vas had quit his job because he was making so much money, and he spent his days promoting our videos on social media, dummy accounts he had created and monitored for both of us. We found a flat in Oxford near the campus of the college I would be attending and moved as soon as I graduated, though my mum was sad to have me move out so soon.

"Robby, this is the last summer before you really go off to be a man," she said hugging me tightly. "Won't you reconsider?"

"Mum, I'm already a man." In fact my voice had deepened, though I forced it higher because Vas and our fans liked it, and I was nearly Vas' height, at one hundred and eighty-three centimeters (that's six feet for you Americans) to his one eighty-four. I was still stick thin, as Vas preferred me to be (all the easier to drag me around the bed), and kept the waves of my hair short.

I kissed my mum and hugged her tightly as Vas waited in his new (used) BMW SUV which was packed to the roof with my things. We said our goodbyes, Vas shaking my dad's hand and hugging everyone until we got to Felicity.

Felicity hugged me. "I mean it Robby," was all she whispered in my ear, and then turned her back on Vas. He kept his face calm, but I knew he felt and resented the snub.

Vas carried me across the threshold of our new flat and those days were so happy. I loved decorating and playing house, and Dee came to visit quite a bit once school started because she was at Oxford too. She was still as bothered by the porn as Felicity was, but she didn't treat me so badly about it. She confessed to watching a snippet and feeling sick.

"No offense Robby, but it was awful," Dee winced. "How do you say those things?"

"Vas makes me, says it's for the fans. I didn't want you to ever see it, I'm sorry," I hugged her. "It makes us a fuck-ton of money though," I smiled. "Want a drink?"

"It's a school night," she laughed with a frown. "I've gotta run," she hugged me again and left.

I made myself a vodka with a splash of club soda and turned on the X-Box.

Vas kissed my neck an hour later when he came home. I took off my headphones with a smile. "Sorry I didn't hear you," I said turning the game off.

He smiled. "Did you do your homework?" He looked at his watch. "We're filming, I was hoping to catch the light and do two tonight because I'm popping up to Manchester tomorrow."

I stood and picked up my empty glass. "My homework won't take long, let's get started. I can't wait for you to fuck me," I kissed him.

"Have you showered?" He sniffed me.

"Doing it now," I called as I walked to the bedroom.

He smacked my ass. "I'll get the camera."

I brushed my teeth and then lathered myself slowly. I had a solid buzz and I couldn't wait for him to join me. I heard him setting up the tripod outside the shower door and felt a thrill. I loved shower sex.

I saw him press record and began my litany. "I can't wait to suck your cock in here Daddy," I lisped flirtatiously, smoothing my soapy hands down my body while looking at the camera. I skimmed my eyes down his beautiful naked body and noticed immediately from his *Vlad*, that he taken his Viagra, and was ready to impale me.

"Turn the temperature down, I don't want the lens to fog. You're hot enough to set the world on fire," he said huskily as he looked at me. He crossed into the camera frame and took my hips in his hands.

29

Welcome to Miami, Aye Papi

VAS HELD ME all night every night, and we still had sex off-camera back then. First term our routine was perfect, and I had always been someone who thrived on routine, predictability, so I was ecstatic. We would have morning sex on the three days I didn't have early meetings, and the two days that I did, I would rush home between lectures and pounce on Vas before he left for the gym. Sometimes we would film those sessions, then I would go back to campus, and a yoga class, which Vas encouraged for flexibility, and then home for dinner. After dinner I would work on papers and projects, while Vas went to the pub or out, I don't know where he went, but when he came home, I would hear him setting up the camera equipment and my dick would get hard like I was Pavlov's horn dog, and we'd film until bedtime.

He worked on editing and posting the videos, requesting my input on the titles when he felt stuck in a rut, and managing our social media, while I earned top grades, did all the cooking and laundry, and whatever else Vas wanted or demanded. That term, and the next were perfect, and I could have lived that way forever, I knew Vas felt the same because he excitedly began planning a vacation for us. I had a full month off between terms, so Vas did a massive amount of research and found the perfect place for us, and promised I would love it.

He packed our filming equipment and our bathing suits and we headed to Miami, which Vas assured me was nothing like Disney and that I would love it, and he was right. We hit South Beach and I was in heaven. The eye candy there was like nothing I had ever seen or imagined, there was so much beauty as far as the eye could see. I sat in the shade of an oversized umbrella, while Vas sunned and frolicked in the surf, ever the extrovert, drawing eyes and chatting with more than one hot guy. I had more than a few admirers of my own who would come and stand over me in their incredibly small speedos and flirt with me, or sit on the chaise next to me, in hopes of wooing me away from Vas. We were definitely recognized, I felt exposed and eye-raped while Vas loved every minute of it, giving out our websites and Twitter handle to anyone who'd listen.

He kept his arm around me everywhere we went, partly to mark his territory, and partly to keep me from getting any other ideas. He saw my eyes on the beach, he caught me talking to more than one buff body, and told me in no uncertain terms to knock it off. His jealousy was flattering to my immature brain, but in hindsight it was driven by a desire to protect his investment more than by a desire for me. It was irritating that he policed me so much when he himself had a wandering eye far worse than my own, but I didn't dare call him out on it, so I pushed those jealous feelings aside with the help of the little pills Vas had brought with him, and reveled in the resulting high.

Miami was bloody incredible, the food, the weather, the spas, I never wanted to leave. Vas spoiled me, and it truly was heaven, I felt like we were so solid, little did I know that it was more like the finale of an incredible fireworks show, where they pull out all the stops, and all that's left when it's over is noxious smoke and scattered bits of detritus everywhere.

* * *

We filmed every day in the hotel suite and a little bit outside. Outside we had no privacy so those bits were just make-out sessions on the beach that would transition to Vas filming me and my ass in my short swim trunks as I walked ahead into the building, and then going down on him in the elevator, and finally into the room, where he fucked me without Viagra, and I moaned at the top of my lungs.

We were there for two weeks and drove to Key West for a long weekend. If I thought Miami was beautiful nothing could prepare me for the beauty of the Keys. The drive was stunning, if not a bit terrifying at first as Vas sometimes forgot to stay on the American side of the road, especially when turning, but once we hit the highway it was a matter of following the cars in front of us and admiring the view. I saw my first alligator and nearly pissed myself. Vas wanted a picture with it but I told him he was daft and forbade it, thing was nearly as big as he was and I was not going to rescue him, I mean, just because I was blonde didn't mean I was Steve Irwin.

We stayed at a little boutique hotel and chartered a boat our second day there. I couldn't believe how blue and warm the water was. We went snorkeling, I wore a long-sleeve swim shirt to protect my skin while Vas just wore his usual tight trunks, his skin dark and beautiful. I sucked his cock on the diving platform while he filmed me, half in the water. Vas told the captain to stay in the front of the boat, but I'm certain he wouldn't have needed to ask. That man was so straight he would have gone blind if he watched us.

"Take your trunks off," Vas panted. I sat up and looked in the boat, the captain was way at the front with his back to us. I shrugged and slipped off my trunks and rode Vas reverse cowboy so he could continue to film. We both came, Vas on my ass and me in the water. I rubbed it in and then fell forward into the blue to wash off, Vas filming me with a laugh.

The captain barely looked at us on the way back to shore, but I didn't care, I was so happy I could have exploded. We snuggled on the bench in front, my barely golden skin in sharp contrast to Vas'.

"I love you," I said and kissed him. "This is the best vacation ever."

"I love you Robby," he swirled his tongue around mine. "The videos we're making here are going to be huge money makers for us. You're so bloody hot."

"You're so bloody hot," I kissed him again.

It was hard to leave the Keys, but I was thrilled to be going back to Miami. We went dancing our second to last night there. Vas gave me another pill, because I was too young to drink but he wanted me to have fun. I was in black sequin hot pants (I don't know why they're called hot *pants*, when they're actually super short-shorts), and a tight t-shirt that was striped with mesh so that my nipples and my belly-button were visible. I wore this outfit with black lace-up ankle boots and glitter on my face. Vas could barely keep his eyes off me, he wanted to film before we left, but I knew if we did that, I would never want to leave so I flounced saucily out of the suite.

The drugs kicked in once we were inside the eighteen-plus club and holy shit, I had never felt so high, so euphoric, I wanted to fuck everyone there, and couldn't stop touching Vas. He had to push my hands away from his zipper more than once. I felt so sexy, my little skin-tight outfit, the music thumping in my ears, the eyes that wouldn't leave me.

"Fuck's sake Vas, what'd you give me?"

He grinned at me, his eyes hooded, "Molly."

I rolled my head back on my neck and then did it again because it felt so amazing.

"Christ, Miley *loves* her, and no wonder," I shook my head and felt the air breeze across my face as though it wanted to fuck me too.

Vas laughed and handed me a drink which I sipped.

"Holy shit, this tastes amazing, what is it?" I drank again, deeply, savoring the bubbles that felt like they were fucking my mouth.

"Club soda, Robby," Vas laughed again and put his arm around my waist.

I pressed myself against him, wanting his body deep inside mine, wanting him to don my skin, claim my body as his own.

"God, Americans know how to make club soda right," I said and kissed his neck, as I writhed to the music against his body. "And their music," I breathed wondrously. "This is the most amazing music I have ever heard." I handed him my glass and lost myself in the pulsating beat. I closed my eyes and saw myself as a music note, bouncing along the turntables as the DJ played me. Vas danced with me and his body was like a pheromone filled with dopamine and I wanted him, on me, over me, under me, *inside* me. He kept up with me as I gyrated as if my life depended on it.

He left for a drink refill. "I'll be right back Robby, don't go anywhere," he said commandingly and I never defied a direct order so I continued to move my shoulders and shake my ass as though I were Madonna on my very own Blonde Ambition tour. I spun and saw Vas had returned, but I didn't recognize him right away because he had his shirt off. I put my hands on his shoulders and pressed against him as his arms came up around me. My brain looked at his muscular arms and wondered briefly how he managed to take his tattoos off too before kissing his waiting mouth.

"God you are so fucking hot," he said, his accent American. "You are on fire."

I laughed at him teasing me. "You've got me on fire."

He squeezed my ass. "How old are you?"

"Eighteen Vas, you know that," I kissed him, swirling my tongue around his as his hands were like fire on my body.

"Oh, thank god, I bet you got a tight little hole don't you," he licked my ear.

"I do, and it's your tight little hole Daddy, you love how it tastes, and I love when you taste it," I rolled my head back again, the music, the sounds, fueling my body, every nerve-ending was on fire, and I was having the best night of my life.

"Get your fucking hands off my boyfriend!" I heard Vas shout just before being wrenched out of Vas' arms.

I spun confused and saw Vas' angry face. It was the face I hated, and if I weren't so high, I would have been very, *very* afraid.

"Dude, he came onto me, he kissed me," the other Vas said, his hands up defensively after clothed Vas shoved him.

Looking between them, I realized that the shirtless Vas wasn't Vas at all, he was some gorgeous, buff American, but he definitely wasn't Vas and I frowned confused. "Vas, why aren't you wearing a shirt? And how come there's two of you?"

Shirtless Vas gave me one last heated glance and disappeared, swallowed up by the dancing masses. I looked back at my Vas and his face was a storm cloud.

I reached out for him. "There you are," I smiled and put my arms around his neck, the edges of my vision were fuzzy like a video where they want you see what's happening in the frame and not the background. He let me undulate against him as he finished his drink in three swallows. He dropped the plastic cup where we stood and wrapped his arms around my body, nearly squeezing the breath from me and ran his hands down my back to my ass. He spanked me, and then gripped both cheeks tightly. My cock was so hard there was no way he couldn't feel it through the thin material of my shorts.

"You are mine Robby. This," he squeezed roughly, "is mine and mine alone. You and I are going back to the hotel and I'm going to fuck the living shit out of you and you are going to apologize the whole time."

He took my wrist and led me out of the club. The night air was still warm but cool compared to the heat of the dance floor and my tiny outfit was no match for it. I shivered as we got into the taxi and rode back to the hotel in silence.

My body was still on fire. Molly was my favorite by far and she became a close friend of mine over the next couple of years. When we got to the hotel room, Vas turned on the camera and degraded me. He edited out the part where I threw up on his cock because he held my head, pressing my face against his stomach such that his cock was halfway down my throat and my nose was smothered. He cleaned up, wiped my face and pressed record. He fucked me in those little shorts, ripping them and the shirt from my body, leaving them in the trash can when we left.

You would think I would be upset about him destroying my cute outfit that made me look so hot, about him ignoring my tapping his leg furiously to get his cock out of my mouth, but I was so high I just wanted to come and make him come, and I didn't care. It wasn't until after, when I saw the video online, that the memories came back, and I thought, maybe that wasn't such a great thing that he did to me.

30

Start of the Breakdown

MY SECOND TERM, which started mid-January, was even more grueling than the first, and Vas gave me the space I needed to study. The routine was nearly as perfect as term one, which thrilled me as you can imagine, though we didn't get to have as much sex (only two times a day if I was lucky). It also happened to be the end of our off-camera sex, with a few exceptions. At first, it wasn't such a big deal, I mean, we had been filming ourselves having sex for nearly two years, albeit intermittently initially. But I couldn't help but feel as though all our intimacy was lost once it happened only on camera, and I wasn't wrong. Once sex became all camera angles, and what works best for the viewer, and not what works best for the pleasure of the people having the sex, then how is it not just work? Not to mention that having sex with someone wearing a GoPro isn't as hot as you might think.

Vas would close himself in the second bedroom, where we had a twin bed and a computer for social media and editing, while I was at school. We also used it as second filming location, swapping out furniture from elsewhere in the flat, and changing up the fabrics to make it look as though we were in different locations. It's amazing what you can do with camera angles, sheets and lighting. He was so focused on the videos, and the business side of things, the money, I really should've been paying more attention, but I was eighteen, and what the fuck did I know?

Finding the time to film was tricky because of my schedule and homework, but we always managed to fit in at least one session a day, and Molly often joined us, (which I loved). Vas was adamant about having new material for the fans, rotating through the sites, teasing some material on one, giving the paid fans the full-length stuff on another, and following up on fan requests because those always earned more money.

When Vas wasn't around, I would check the fan comments on all the sites, and read them with a big smile. Our fans, more women than men, were from all over the world, and so complimentary, especially of me. A few of the men were fellow creators of porn who wanted to fuck me, or fuck Vas, or fuck us both, which we always said no to. The fans told me how beautiful I was, and how perfect my voice was, and how much they loved how in love we were with each other. There was unfortunately the occasional troll who would come through, and make fun of my lisp, or tell me my lips were too puffy, or my shoulders were too bony. I also got a lot of derisive talk about being too tall to be a twink, or my ass wasn't round enough, it didn't ripple enough when Vas smacked it. I felt bad when I read those comments. I couldn't help my lips or my height, and I turned to booze, or my ever-faithful happy pills and Molly to feel better. Vas said to ignore them, because it was his ass, and his mouth, and he thought they were perfect, and you know what, it was his ass, and his mouth, and he could do whatever he wanted to them.

* * *

Vas loved going out, he loved having so much extra spending money, and wanted me to go out with him (not really, in hindsight) but I couldn't keep up my grades and do porn and go out at night, every night. We went out to dinner from time to time, because I wanted to keep a normal dating life, but Vas liked staying out and drinking after, and I liked to be home, so more often than not it would end in an argument. Olek came to stay with us a few times and they would stay out all night and sleep most of the day. As much as I hated having Olek there, because of the way he looked at me, at least Vas would have sex with me without the camera rolling, and I really savored those last few times, not knowing at the time of course, that they were the last.

Things began to feel different and it took me awhile to figure out why (maybe that was because when I wasn't at school I was usually high, I had to be, otherwise it was just denial). It was the sensation that he was pulling away and I didn't know how to keep him, because I didn't know why it was happening. When he would disappear to Manchester for the weekend, or longer, and leave me home to study, I would go to the pubs, sometimes meeting Dee, and sometimes alone just to chat with the bartenders. Then I'd go home to an empty flat, and take whatever pills I could find in Vas' stash, and pass out so I wouldn't focus on the fact that I was alone.

I knew something was up when Vas stopped holding me when we slept, which happened sometime after the end of term two and the beginning of term three. I tried so hard to hold everything together, but he slipped away like sand through my fingers. I tried talking to him about it, but he told me I was imagining things, that I was being too clingy, too needy and he just needed space. I gave him his space, but it wasn't enough.

"Let's go away this weekend, to Bath, or to Paris," I suggested as we ate dinner, I had made his favorite, prime rib in a cast iron skillet, medium rare (gagging from the smell while it cooked), and buttered noodles with roasted brussels sprouts. I ate everything but the meat, and watched him as he closed his eyes and chewed.

"I'm going to London to see my cousins," he shook his head and took a big bite of bloody meat. "This is delicious Robin, thank you," he flashed me a brief smile that didn't reach his eyes.

"I'm glad you like it," I smiled and shifted my shoulders back and forth happily. I saw something pass across his face like irritation. He used to love it when I did that shoulder-thing, and now it just annoyed him. I swallowed the lump in my throat, and reached for my drink.

"Let's go next weekend then. And we should look at places to go when my term ends, I'll have the whole summer, we could go to Greece, or Italy, or Bali. Film everywhere," I suggested, hating the note of desperation in my voice.

He shrugged and finished his steak. "Sure, that sounds fun," he answered noncommittally.

I left the rest of my plate untouched and clung to him later in bed, waking in the middle of the night to find that he had put me on my own side of the bed and was sleeping with his back to me.

31

Blue Monday,
Everyday

OUR NUMBERS STARTED DROPPING, he blamed me, he smacked me, he tried different drugs on me, and our views would go up briefly, but then dip. More than a few
videos were of him setting up scenarios where he would punish me for something,
telling me the fans wanted it, but he was always rough, with that mean gleam in his
eye, and the fear and confusion on my face in those videos were real. I hated the
way I was feeling, the way *he* was making me feel, and I found myself using more
and more, my days (and nights) spent in a constant, altered state. I passed out more
than once mid-fuck, and either woke to a smack, or an empty flat.

I thought our views dipped from a combination of us over-saturating our
market, and the simple fact that people were fickle, they got bored looking at the
same two people fucking. I didn't dare mention that perhaps it was because he no
longer performed like his heart was in it, and more than one fan commented that
he didn't say 'I love you' anymore (I was glad they did, because I was too scared to
mention it myself). People began calling for us to mix things up. Some wanted me
to fuck Vas (he said absolutely not), some wanted another top (he said absolutely
not) and some wanted another bottom (I said absolutely not). We were at an impasse.

"I don't want a third person, I think that's a disaster for relationships," I said one day when we were stuck in a loop (again). "And I don't want to fuck you, but you could go down on me," I suggested (very hopefully, believe me). I turned the water off and put the pot on the stove. I was making mashed potatoes and pork chops, another of Vas' favorites.

"No, I won't do that," he scoffed. "The people want to see us with someone else. I could find another twink," he said (very hopefully, believe me).

"No way Vas," I shook my head. "Any threesome porn is always two tops and a bottom, or flip-fucking. What the fuck would I do with another twink?"

"That's not true, there are plenty of videos with two bottoms. You just act like lesbians. It's simple, kissing, and stroking, and the like."

Did I just see a dreamy look pass through his eyes? I stopped peeling the potato in my hand. "If you think I'm going to dress like a girl and kiss another guy dressed like a girl, you're out of your bloody mind."

"I never said anything about dressing up, just fooling around, he could suck your dick while I fucked him," he added as a tease. I would like my cock sucked, but by Vas.

"If that's the scenario you want, then get someone other than a twink, and we'll both be happy," I challenged. "You could even fuck him while he fucked me."

Vas frowned. "I don't want you fucking anyone else."

"Well then I don't want you fucking anyone else," I put the lid on the pot of potatoes and peeked at the pork chops in the oven. I turned and Vas was right there, or rather his hand was.

He smacked me, hard. "Don't you dictate to me who we'd get, and what I can and can't do. I'm the one posting the videos, I'm the one checking out the competition, I'm the one reading the suggestions. People like seeing two twinks, and there are plenty of twink couples out there. I'm not going to fuck a guy," he said it as though I had suggested he have sex with a chicken, and stormed out of the kitchen. I heard the door of the flat a moment later.

"Vas!" I called futilely.

I saved dinner in the fridge with a note, and then threw it away in the morning, Vas didn't eat leftovers, I recently got three conch shells and a small sample of the Ukrainian alphabet across my face for suggesting that he should. He hadn't come home, and I didn't know where he went, he wasn't responding to my texts. I went to meet my professors, I had to stick to my routine, my reliable routine. He was at the flat when I returned and I ran to him for a hug. He let me go down on him and I realized mid-way through it was because he was filming me. I suppressed my sigh and continued doing what I loved to the man I loved.

* * *

I wanted to spend more time on us, I wanted to fix things, I tried to fix things, but I had school, I had an obligation to my parents, to my future, and I know he resented that. I tried to limit the time I had to be away from the flat, away from Vas, but my schedule was filled with meetings and going to the library to work on my projects and papers. I barely saw Dee anymore, though we still spoke or texted weekly.

One day, in mid-May I left the library early and hurried home, figuring Vas and I could film something entirely new based on a yoga position I had done, or maybe just have slow sex off-camera. As I turned the corner onto our street, I saw a short, very twinkie-looking guy sauntering down the sidewalk toward me. He passed me without looking and I thought nothing of it at the time. There were plenty of skinny young guys around Oxford, we called them nerds, though this one was too pretty and dumb-looking to be a nerd. I let myself into the flat and heard the shower running. I stripped off my bag and my clothes and opened the shower door and Vas turned with surprise.

I smiled at him and closed the door behind me, kneeling as I did. He let me take him in my mouth.

"I just filmed myself wanking, sorry," he shrugged and stepped back when nothing happened.

I stood and put my arms around him kissing the side of his mouth as he turned his head. "I wish you had waited."

"I wish you had let me know you were coming home early," he said and turned off the water.

32

Lost in Space

IT TOOK ME WEEKS, and another two sightings of that slag of a twink, to realize Vas was cheating on me. I had given up *everything*, except for school, for that man. I barely saw my family, I barely saw Dee, I barely slept so that I could divide my time between school and Vas. There were so many warning signs, all along, as to why I should never have been with him, that he was just using me, but hindsight is twenty-twenty and when you're young and in love you think you know everything (spoiler alert, you know nothing Jon Snow).

I drowned my sorrows at the pub, blathering to the bartender, and four vodkas later I made my way to Dee's. I was incoherent of course but that didn't matter, she let me in and soothed me. I spent the night, ignoring Vas' calls and texts. *Fuck him.*

I had school in the morning and met with one of my professors. My head was pounding and my mouth was fuzzy, and I wasn't sure how much sense I was making. He was sympathetic as I mumbled that I was going through some shit but I promised I'd have everything together by our next meeting.

I went back to the flat and Vas had the audacity to yell at me, smack my head and then push me down. "Where the fuck you been?"

I covered my ears and cowered. "I was at Dee's, where have you been?" I asked, my voice breaking. I swallowed and uncovered my ears, looking up at him as I felt the silence pressing down on me. He had his back to me, and when he turned as

I stood, my eyes went straight to the little robin on his chest, which looked as sad and on the verge of death as I was.

"Robby, you've been slacking. Your heart isn't in this and our fans can tell."

"It's not me, it's you," I spat. "They love me."

He backhanded my face then with his conch shells, and I tasted blood. He was mad because I was right, but pointing it out to him wasn't going to bring him back to me. "You're so high half the time, how would you know what the fans think?"

"You're the one giving me the drugs. That's like turning out the light and then complaining when you can't see," I cried defiantly (how dare he blame me), and then ducked as he swung at me.

He grabbed me as I straightened, and hit me with his other hand. "Don't put this on me," he scoffed. "I wanted you buzzed not incoherent, and Christ, a regular shower wouldn't kill you." He wrinkled his nose.

"I'm sorry," I shook my head, the tears coming to my eyes. "I'll try harder, I'll do more, I'll shower now. We can have another twink, please, Vas."

He just stared at me, and in that moment, in that look, I saw so much apathy and such a lack of desire, that I truly wanted to die. The previous three years flashed in front of my eyes like people say during a near death experience. I saw all our happiness, all my give and his take, and just at the edges, like a niggling of consciousness, was the smudge of dark stuff. I knew in that moment that he saw the same things flashing by, but all the darkness in sharp focus with the happiness as the smudge, the opposite of me, like the negative of a photograph.

"I'm going out," he said and grabbed a shirt from the chair and left the room. I heard his keys and then the door shut behind him.

I fell to the floor. I don't know how I made it to the other room, maybe I crawled, maybe I rolled, maybe I flew, but I found myself in the kitchen eventually, drinking whatever bottle of booze was the closest to the front of the cabinet, and passed out.

I was in bed when Vas came back the next morning. He had Olek with him and some other guy. They moved his shit out and I never left the bed. *What could I do?* I tried talking to him, I grabbed his hand when he came to get his things off the side table and he just looked at me, with that look. I let my hand drop, and the big part of my brain wailed, maybe my mouth did too, but the small part of my brain was silent, and watching.

PART TWO

CHRYSALIS

———

33

———

Not You Again

I FINISHED THE TERM, I have no fucking idea how I did, but it was in large part due to Dee, and her steadfast support, and the local bartenders. Dee knew I was drinking a fuck-ton, and she knew it was the only thing keeping the pain at bay, but it was also keeping it fresh because I couldn't stop blubbering about Vas once I got drunk. What she didn't know was that I was popping pills too. I had gone with Vas once to meet his supplier, and so, contacted him after Vas left (taking his stash with him). The dealer was more than happy to take my large order, and I spent the rest of the term working my way through it.

* * *

I was high as fuck. It was a week after the term ended, and I had planned on packing my shit, because I couldn't stay in that flat. Vas was everywhere I looked even though he wasn't anywhere I looked, but I couldn't find my things. The buzzer rang and I wasn't sure if it was the ringing in my head from the drugs, or from the telly, which I realized belatedly wasn't even there (Vas had taken it), or if it was actually the door so I just ignored it. It buzzed again, so I got up off the couch, no, I was on the floor (Vas had taken the couch too), and I went to the door, which wasn't

– 143 –

where I left it, so the buzzer rang one more time before I could locate the knob and I opened it. My mum was standing there with her twin.

"Hi," I said happy to see them. "What are you two doing here?"

They looked at each other and then back at me with matching frowns. The one on the left looked so concerned I think I saw tears, but I couldn't be sure, and the one on the right looked so angry that I stepped back and rubbed my eyes because I couldn't tell which one was my mum. I thought you were supposed to be able to tell twins apart *especially* when one was your mum, and I couldn't, so I felt a panic rise inside me, like I was a bad son, and a bad person. I turned away and made to close the door on that bad feeling.

"Robby, wait, what's the matter with you?" My mum asked, her voice wavery and shrill. "Are you high?"

"No," I scoffed and then laughed, because I was. I was so high I couldn't feel my limbs but was somehow itchy all over. "Thanks for coming," I smiled and made to close the door again but she pushed past me. I held the door waiting for her twin but there was no one there and the inside mum grabbed my arm, and her face crumpled. I fell then, my legs could no longer hold me up, but I felt better close to the ground, there was less stress down there. It took no effort at all to just lay there. I saw a bottle cap under the bookcase in my line of sight and smiled at it. It spoke to me.

"Robin, what are you doing on the floor?"

"The same thing you're doing," I replied to it with a giggle. "Only you're lucky, no can see you under there. How long you been there? Is there room for me under there?" I began inching my way to the bookcase.

I felt hands on my shoulder and startled, flailing wildly. I looked up and saw my mum. "Hi," I relaxed, happy to see her. "What are you doing here?"

Her face shifted and suddenly was under water, and she was making a weird keening sound. I rolled over and blinked, trying to clear her face, but the water kept coming and she turned away from me. I tried to get to my feet, but when I put my hands on the carpet, they disappeared and then I went in search of them but my head got lost.

Seemingly hours later, I saw my mum's face again, only this time there were strangers with her, and one of them had wings. They closed in all around me, there was a ripping sound and my arm was squeezed, hands were tugging at my clothes and I tried to push them away, with limbs like lead, begging them to just leave me be, but no one would listen, not even my mum who was all eyes and had something silver pressed to her face. It could have been her phone, but I was too busy keeping an eye on the angel standing there beside her with his giant wings unfolded. He stared at me, though I couldn't see his eyes, or his face, and I noticed, as the room went cold, that one of his wings was crooked. Dee appeared, blocking my view.

"Dee," I cried, flailing weakly for her, "hug me, St. Michael's come for me, again."

The silver thing fell from my mum's face and she rushed forward as everything went dark.

34

Boy Interrupted

I WOKE IN THE HOSPITAL, hooked up to every machine they had in the place. I saw my mum asleep in the chair in the corner and tried to speak but there was something in my throat and I suddenly felt like I was gagging and couldn't breathe. I tried to use my tongue and to cough to get it out but couldn't, and that's when I began to panic and thrash. My mum sprung awake and immediately pressed the call button screaming out the door for help. Everything happened in a blur, people came, someone pulled the tube from my throat and I vomited, but there was nothing to vomit so it was more like foam and air. My throat hurt like a motherfucker and I tried to make sense of what was happening as a nurse or a doctor or a fucking angel put a needle into the IV port in my arm and everything went smooth again.

The next time I woke my mum and dad were there, talking in hushed tones. I watched them, and thought they looked old and worried, and then I wondered if I was old. What day was it? What year was it? Where was Dee? Where was Vas? Oh *god*, *Vas*, and then the pain started again and my eyes flooded. I looked around futilely for my pills, or vodka and then I heard the worst sound I had ever heard in my entire life. My parents stood immediately and rushed over, and that was when I realized the sound was coming from me. My throat was raw from being intubated and I was wailing from the pain I felt in my heart, in my whole body, because of Vas, and the sound was inhuman. My dad ran to the door as my mum sobbed over me.

***

I was admitted into an inpatient drug treatment program and had a therapist assigned to me specifically. My parents had money to spare and my mum told my dad to spare no expense.

I spent six weeks getting sober, getting therapy, getting exercise. Had to spend my birthday in captivity, ate a shitty piece of cake, sat there like an imbecile while everyone sang happy birthday to me.

My mum came with David and George to get me when I was done. They cheered me up with mindless chatter on the drive home. My flat was gone, my parents had packed everything up for me, not that there was much after Vas cleaned the place out. I cringed thinking about all the things they found, what they saw, but the therapist said I had to let go of the shame, and that there was nothing to be ashamed of. Easier fucking said than done *Susan*, but whatever. I don't know if that was her name or not, I didn't care, I never spoke to her again after my release.

Everyone walked on eggshells around me, even my dad but he had something angry stuffed in his pocket that he kept from me, or tried to anyway. I knew my parents were tremendously disappointed with me, because I was tremendously disappointed with me, so I hid in my room.

Felicity came in after knocking. I was just laying on my bed, trying not to think of anything but not succeeding.

"How are you?" She asked tentatively.

"Fine," I lied.

"Were you trying to kill yourself?"

Apparently, I had taken four of whatever pills I got from that dealer (I think it was a mix of Molly and Oxy but I can't remember). What I do remember was taking one, and it not working fast enough, so I took a second, and I'm guessing that they both kicked in right around the same time and I loved the feeling so much, that I took two more. I knew it was four because that's all I had left in the bag, and I remembered thinking that four was a good number because that's how many corners were in a room, and being in a room felt safe.

I looked at her without turning my head. "Would it make you happy if I was?"

"Christ Robby, no!" She sat on the bed next to me. "You're a pain in the ass but I love you. Everyone's been so worried."

"Sorry."

"What happened?" She asked quietly.

"Vas left me," I closed my eyes. The pain was still there like the pea under a stack of mattresses.

"That fucking Chav bastard is not worth this Robby," she frowned. "I knew he was trouble the minute I laid eyes on him, and that porn," she shook her head.

I opened my eyes to look at her. "I loved him, I *love* him," I corrected myself.

She shook her head. "He fucked with your head, I can't believe he got you to do what you did."

I looked at the wall. There was another knock on the door and Dee peeked her head in, my eyes filled instantly and I sat up for a soothing hug. She rushed to me as Felicity left us alone.

"How are you?" She asked, her voice full of concern, her soft breast soothing like no other. "How was rehab?"

"I'm barely okay, and rehab was like a combination of tedium, bad food, and white privilege, but I have to say I loved the routine of it," I pulled back to look at her. "I've already got a schedule to follow." She followed my eyes to the bright orange paper with a list of daily activities that I had taped to the wall next to my computer. "And I have to leave for an AA meeting soon, and then go to yoga after."

"Were you trying to kill yourself?" She asked softly. "Robby, you looked awful surrounded by the EMTs. I was so scared when I saw the ambulance outside your flat, and your mum, she fainted when they said they lost your vitals," she shook her head, her eyes filling. "I thought she died too."

"I dunno," I whispered, touching my finger where the promise ring used to be. They took it away at rehab and my mum must have kept it. "I just wanted the pain to stop. When I had school as a focus, I could keep it at bay, mostly, but then," I trailed off. "How could he do that to me? I did everything for that man," I sobbed and hugged her again.

"He's awful, I hate him. He was just using you Rob. I wonder if he targeted you just like I worried when you first met him. I wonder if he's done this before."

I shook my head (the denial was still strong with me then). "I don't think so. It wasn't until after we started making all that money that he bought a proper camera and tripods and such. If he'd been doing it before he'd have had all that already," I looked at her, not knowing if what I said was true. "Speaking of equipment and things, did you pack my stuff or someone else?" I held my breath.

"There weren't much stuff, and your Mum started packing your room, but then called me to do it. I was glad she did. Robby, you went full perv," she shook her head with a laugh.

I chuckled with a blush and looked at my watch. "I need to head to my meeting and yoga," I grabbed a handful of tissues from my side table and stood wiping my face. I picked up my yoga mat from the shelf under the window. "Walk with me?"

"Of course," she followed me downstairs.

"Robby," my mum called as she came from the kitchen. "You need to eat something before you go."

"I did Mum," I lied and kissed her cheek, "I had a protein bar."

"You have to eat *real* food Robin," she admonished and then hugged Dee.

"There'll be food at the meeting, I'm sure." Not that I would touch it. "I'll be home after yoga."

I walked Dee to her house and then headed to the church basement where the meeting was to be held. I thought about rehab, and the people I met, many with real issues, and many like me who were paying the price for their poor decision making. I felt a little light-headed and pretended it was because I was high and not starving. They made me eat at the facility but I ate lightly or pushed my food around, and since I'd been home I hadn't eaten at all. Everyone was being really careful around me as I said, so I begged off dinner the first night, saying I had eaten before leaving rehab, and then yesterday, I flushed what Mum brought me down the toilet.

My weight, at my heaviest and my happiest with Vas, was fifty-seven kilograms (that's about one hundred twenty-five pounds for you Americans), and I had grown to one hundred and eighty-three centimeters. I was always skinny, I told you that (I was a twink and Vas liked it that way). When he left, I didn't have much of an appetite, and then of course the drugs killed whatever appetite I did have. In rehab, the weight really started falling off me. My life felt so out of control, everything inside me felt so chaotic and I couldn't self-medicate, so I did the next best thing. I exerted control over what I put into my mouth.

I had weighed myself when I got home and according to the scale, I dropped ten kilos. My ribs were standing out and my shoulders were like rectangles under my skin. I wore several layers to hide it from everyone, and sweated my ass off, but being hot distracted me from being hungry and more importantly, from being sad. Looking back, I was wasting away, and I *wanted* to. I sat quietly through the meeting thinking about how fucking hot I was in that stuffy room, and listened to the struggle all around me. My sponsor was there. He was a kind man about five years younger than my dad, and worked in some sort of academia, and he was my rock. I came to rely on him so much over the years, even after I moved to America with my husband. We chatted for a bit and I told him I would see him the following night.

I let myself in after yoga, after I knew everyone would be done eating and my stomach squeaked at the smell coming from the kitchen. My mum, the sneak, had made my favorite noodle dish for dinner, I could tell from the garlic and hint of curry. I didn't dare go into the kitchen so I headed for the stairs.

"Robin," my dad called from the living room, causing me to jump, "Mum saved a plate for you."

He was sitting facing the stairs, like he was waiting for me (because of course he was). The anger was there, hovering just around the edge of his voice, along with the concern, of course. He and I didn't see eye to eye, but he did love me.

"How was the meeting? And yoga?" He looked at my mat and my sweaty hair.

I stopped on the bottom step. "Good, it was a Big Book meeting," I shrugged with a friendly smile.

"What does that mean?"

"Apparently there are all different themes to the meetings, and this one they just talked about the AA handbook," I shrugged again. "It was interesting."

He made a sound like he didn't find that interesting at all and gave me a tight-lipped smile. "I'm glad you're going, at any rate, and getting your life back in order," he stood. "Come eat."

"I grabbed a sandwich at the shop next to the studio," I lied and held up the bottle of water which was the only thing I'd actually bought.

His eyes swept my body and he looked as though he were going to insist, so I took a deep breath and continued up the stairs.

"I stink, I need a shower. Good night." And I ran.

35

The Guy with the Dragon Tattoo

I PASSED OUT in yoga a few times over the next week or so, before the instructor finally called for an ambulance. When I started the classes there, I had let all the instructors know I didn't want to be touched (it was nobody's business that I was literally wasting away), and no one did, until the EMTs arrived and the instructor saw how fucking skinny I was when they lifted my clothes for vitals. I was just over forty-five kilos and probably ready for full-on organ failure. I cried when they said they had to take me to the hospital and tell my parents. I felt like such a fucking disaster. I couldn't live, I couldn't die, I couldn't stand to look at my parents, I couldn't stand to look at myself.

It had been nearly three months since Vas left and I was still a bloody mess, and I hadn't even looked up any of his new porn yet. I had stopped texting him weeks before, figuring he blocked me after the first few pathetic ones I sent, begging him to take me back. My parents found me a new therapist, one who specialized in self-harm, and substance abuse, and suicidal thoughts. Her name was Miranda, she was task master and a magician with a mental sleight of hand. I was constantly saying 'how the fuck'd you do that?' when she got me to admit something. Her treatment style was called Dialectical Behavior Therapy. Didn't know what the fuck that meant at the time, but it saved my life (though not right away, this isn't a bloody fairytale). I had to get a nutritionist too, because DBT doesn't work with anorexics, so I was on my way to having my own team of professionals like a movie star.

I had private sessions and lots of group therapy, and homework, and accountability which I both loved and hated. I put weight back on, slowly, and I started looking and feeling somewhat normal again. Dee had been right by my side through it all, a steadfast friend listening to a broken record. She came to tell me she was headed to America for her annual August holiday at the same time that we would be in Spain.

"I'm sorry to leave you," she said, her voice soothing but her eyes relieved to be leaving my depressing orbit, "but it's only for three weeks, and your mum said you guys are going to Spain, so that will be amazing," she smiled. "I think you need a change of scenery and a lot of vitamin D," she raised her eyebrows and looked at my pale skin.

My parents (and I, if we're being honest), were nervous about disrupting my new routine which was working wonderfully. My mum had broached the subject of Spain with me a few weeks prior, and said if I didn't want to go, she could send Dad and Felicity with the boys and she would stay home with me. I was selfish but not that selfish, I knew how much my mum loved going to Spain.

"We are," I nodded to Dee. "We leave on Friday and will be back around the same time as you. I have Miranda on-call, and I found AA meetings for English speakers, so it's obvious I'm not the only traveling drunk," I grinned. "I also have my sponsor who I can call twenty-four-seven, and my mum, so I'm in good shape."

"I'm glad you thought of everything and that you'll be in good hands," she hugged me. "I expect to see a tan on that body of yours when I return."

I kissed her and went to my closet to get my suitcase when she left.

* * *

It was hard, initially, being there again, after having been there last time with Vas. I kept expecting to see him by the pool in his swimsuit, his fit body soaking up all the sun and leaving none for the rest of us. The first few nights were the absolute worst and I ended up sitting through meetings in Spanish, because there were only four of the English ones and I had been to all those each day. On the third night there was a woman there who was kind enough to translate for me when I stood to speak, she blushed a few times (well, a lot), but no one threw stones at me so that was good.

You're not supposed to date or get sexually involved with anyone in your first year of sobriety. It's not a law or anything, but it makes a lot of sense, for people without the sex drive I had anyway. The only times I didn't want to have sex were right after Vas left, and when I was so hungry and hot, I couldn't think straight enough to feel horny. With therapy and weight came the return of my libido, and with a vengeance. There was a Spanish guy whose ears perked up at my translated story, and he was hot as fuck (and DTF, if you know what I mean). He came to speak with me after the meeting leader, 'the Chair,' asked the burning desire question which closed every meeting. His English was as good as my Spanish (which is to say not very), but we were both well-versed in the language of love and condoms.

I went back to his place and it was pretty, pretty, pretty, *pretty* good (to quote Larry David). I got my first blow-job, so *that* was incredible. I came like, right away, and then we fucked, and I came again. I left feeling so amazing (that dopamine can't be beat), that he and I hooked up several more times while I was there, but nothing more. It was so freeing to not have to explain my reasons for not wanting to get attached, and be with someone who felt the same way.

He came to hang by the pool a few times, marveling at the house (it was a pretty fucking amazing house, if I hadn't already said so), but saying very little because of the language barrier. I was up front with my parents about where I met him and what I was doing with him. I also promised that they would never see him again, and they never did. My dad *hated* him but begrudgingly understood my motivation, and my mum was happy to see me with my attention on (a sober) someone other than Vas so didn't say one negative word.

Having F. (it's Alcoholics ANONYMOUS, I can't tell you his name) over to the house was exactly what I needed. His presence erased Vas, well, near enough anyway, so that when I looked at the chaise I made him sit in, which was the one Vas had favored, I no longer saw Vas and his tattoos, I saw F. and his lean brown body. He had long hair that he wore in a man-bun (the opposite of Vas) and only one tattoo, of a dragon, with a long body that went down his thigh, whose open mouth was breathing fire on his cock. All you could see was the dragon's head on his stomach with the beginning of said flame disappearing into his tiny speedo, but there was no mistaking what it was doing and why. His cock was on fire, and I couldn't wait to ride it again. I took him to the beach and gave him head, to erase Vas' memory there too. I'm pretty sure F. would never forget *that* summer.

* * *

I was as reluctant to go home as I had been to go to Barcelona, but alas, all good things must come to an end, and I had to get back to Oxford. I was determined to find a new flat far away from the one I shared with Vas, good roommates (Dee already had her flat and roommates, with no room for little old me), and someone like F., who could help me erase the memories I had of Vas all over town.

We arrived back in London, me a nearly new man, ready to embark on his new life, *everything* mapped out. Well, I don't need to tell you what happens to the best laid plans.

36

Madonna, Rescue Me

DEE CAME OVER as soon as she got home and we settled right back into our routine of catching up and discussing pop culture, watching movies and avoiding the topic of Vas at all costs. I told her about F. and she told me about breaking up with Chad, the two-year summer fling ended because he was a dick to her, so she found another guy (thank god, because anyone named Chad just instantly sounded like a douche and this one was no exception apparently), and he was even hotter, and nicer. He worked at some fish market or something, which sounded smelly, but I didn't want to bring her down so I just nodded encouragingly as she told me about the lobster pots he and his co-workers had labeled 'hot tub number one' and 'hot tub number two.' My eyebrows desperately wanted to shoot up and off my face but I managed to keep them in check and chuckle along with her.

She left and I felt so good about everything (she was happy, I was happy), that I made a *terrible* decision. I looked up Vas on the famous (free) porn site where he loaded all our videos, the site that had links to all the other paid sites, and *oh my god*, there were nearly twenty videos and teasers uploaded already with his new slag. I watched a few (noticing that the first one he posted wasn't even a *week* after he left me), until I collapsed and felt my heart come undone, snapping free of its tethers like a giant inflatable at the New Year's Day parade. I turned everything off, grabbed my phone and ran for a meeting, calling my sponsor, T., and leaving him a message on the way.

I had every intention of making it to the meeting, but there was a pub, and its doors and windows were open to the summer night air. There was a game on and people were cheering. It sounded happy, and I needed happy, so I went in and then I don't know what happened. *Well, that's not true*, I know exactly what happened, I ordered like a zillion vodka drinks, poured my heart out to the bartender and then I guess I blacked out, so what I actually didn't remember was how T. found me. He told me later that the bartender had answered my phone when it rang insistently in front of me, the contact name alarming enough for him to ignore protocol and answer it for me when I was too incoherent to do so myself (I had him in my phone as 'EMERGENCY! ANSWER AT ONCE,' mostly to protect his privacy, but also as a reminder to myself that when he called it was for a good reason).

T. took me to the bathroom and stood calmly over me as I stuck my finger down my throat repeatedly, at his insistence, until I was dry heaving. I blubbered into his shoulder as he walked me home. He listened, making the appropriate sounds at the appropriate times. He didn't make me feel bad about fucking up, in fact he made it okay, and shared his own relapse story. I didn't feel like such a failure around him, and that's why I loved him for my whole life. He stressed the importance of calling my therapist in the morning, and spoke with my parents when we got home. He kept my confidence, not divulging why I relapsed, only that I was triggered and needed patience and understanding. He spoke to both of them, but aimed his words at my dad, who he sensed (correctly) was not someone who could tolerate weakness or failure.

My mum put me to bed and slept on top of the covers next to me. I woke with an awful headache and the worst cotton mouth of my life. She made me tea, and gave me B vitamins along with paracetamol, when what I really wanted was one of Vas' happy pills, and that craving made me get out of bed and head to a meeting. I had an appointment with Miranda who gave me tough love coated with under-standing and then a litany of tasks that I needed to do, partly because that was DBT and partly because she knew I needed something to do. She was very disappointed that I didn't follow the strategies we had in place, (easier said than done *Randy*, she hated when I called her that, said I was the randy one), and then asked me if I was at all serious about getting better. We did a chain analysis, analyzing my behaviors and making strategies for the future, should I ever run into him in person, and she instructed me to never look at his website again and I swore I wouldn't (with my fingers crossed behind my back).

Dee came over after lunch with a six pack of diet coke, a six pack of regular coke, and a DVD under her arm.

"Oh, is it the turn of the century then?" I asked eying the DVD and taking the soda from her.

"In a way, yes it fucking is," she said saucily, her face full of attitude. She held up the DVD and I shrieked. It was motherfucking *Truth or Dare*. Peak Madonna, and I nearly cried because Dee knew me so well. We raced to the basement and put it on the big screen and Christ, by the end of the movie I felt as bad-ass as my fucking queen was. Fuck Vas, and fuck that twink slag, I'm Madonna, bitch. I'm the best thing that ever happened to that low-class, mouth-breather, what the fuck was I doing sitting around feeling sorry for myself?

We danced, we went shopping, we got dinner, she came with me to an open meeting and then we parted ways. I went home, thinking about everything the entire way. Fuck Vas, and what he'd done to me. He deserved that little slag with the fucking accent that matched his. I took a moment to get inside his head (Vas', not that stupid cunt he was currently fucking), and I wondered, *what would really bug him?* He had clearly come undone at all the fan chatter that I had stayed on top of during rehab, sneaking on my phone after hours.

Not to sound like a broken record (which I am, I know), but I had the greatest fans. They loved us as a couple, but I was definitely the favorite, the one they wrote to more often and about. They liked Vas, I mean physically he was quite the specimen, but when Vas dumped me, they *ripped* him, and his new twink. I was secretly happy, because fuck them both. After a time though, the fans got a little out of hand and I wanted to speak up, but I was in rehab, and wasn't supposed to have my phone (whoopsie). Some of the things they wrote I saved as screenshots and would look at them to make myself feel better until finally deleting them because they really only made me feel worse by reminding me of it all.

The things they said weren't wrong, I mean, in addition to not being nearly as attractive as I was, *Zaisy* (what the fuck kind of porn name was that?), was even smaller and younger looking than I, (some might say he was 'fun-sized'), and he was a complete slag. He was using Vas, you could tell by the vacant expression he had on his face whenever he stared at the camera, and oh my god, he stared at the camera all the bloody time. *Who likes that?* Oh, right, the demented fans who felt like eye contact made them a part of the action. They were the ones I mentioned earlier with the weird, dirty fetishes that Vas would make me do. I do NOT miss them, Vas and Zaisy were welcome to those weirdos.

In addition to defending me vehemently online, my non-demented fans discussed us, a lot. There were conversations I was tagged in on my Finsta (that's fake

Instagram, if you didn't know), and chat rooms where people asked and answered each other about us. Did we break up? (gasp!). Why did we break up? They analyzed what we said, or didn't say, to each other during sex, trying to dissect when and where everything started to fall apart. One fan wrote that she was certain that in 'Daddy bends and breeds loud little slut over the couch, rimming,' that we didn't kiss as much as we used to and that was a sign of Vas pulling away (actually, Vas had a tuna sandwich for lunch that day and his breath stank). Another one thought it was 'Little slut takes THICK lumberjack cock in the woods, sexy orgasmic end!' She wrote that she saw tears in my eyes because Vas said something no one could hear and she was certain that he said 'I don't love you anymore,' (actually, there was a rock digging into my back, which left a mark for days, and Vas said 'I just love your tiny hole,' sometimes his accent was unintelligible even to me). They were like those people who spend hours dissecting movies, and books, and song lyrics, trying to find meaning and purpose behind everything. Part of me couldn't understand the fascination, but the other part loved the attention.

I knew Vas read everything, every comment, every hashtag, so I know after we split, he was torn apart by all the hate. He responded to a lot of them, trying to explain himself, but he came off as insincere, defensive, and heartless. My fans just doubled-down on their scourging of him and he eventually stopped trying. Oh well, shouldn't have been such an arsemonger.

I turned on my computer when I got home and saw that the vitriol had died down but was still going on between a few specific accounts, almost three months later, and that night I finally broke my silence. I urged them to back off, writing to them that I was happy for Vas and Zaisy and that I had moved onto a great place, and was at peace. I hadn't yet, but was hoping I would be soon. After I wrote that on my Finsta, I went into the porn site and typed in a name, smiling happily when I saw that Jem Foxxx, Mr. Midwest, was still the number one porn star on the site, with his nearly one hundred million views, and over two hundred thousand subscribers.

Earlier that year he had reached out to me, which had sent Vas into the stratosphere. He was just paying me, us, a compliment on our rapid rise up the amateur rankings, and said I had a 'beautiful bloom.' I didn't know how we caught his eye, but then again, I had no idea how the industry worked, and it didn't matter. I logged in and wrote to him as a delayed response, not an actual response, because Vas had deleted the message (not before I took a screenshot though, saving Jem's contact info). I told him that if he was ever in the UK, or on the Continent, that he should call me, because I was DTF. I asked if he wanted to make a video, and added that I just wanted him to 'top me so hard' and nothing else.

I went to bed listening to Madonna and feeling like a million bucks.

37

Come Here,
Big Daddy

JEM RESPONDED IN THE MORNING, and I danced around my room after I read it.

Hey Ronnie,

Thanks for reaching out. It just so happens that my husband
and I are going to be in the south of France in a week, and are
passing through London, to make the rounds. I'd love to top you
so hard. Here's where we're staying. Send me your number and
I'll call you when I land.

I paused over the mention of a husband. I couldn't imagine being married to someone who fucked as many guys as Jem did, and as well as he did, and not be a jealous hag. His husband must be the most secure person on the planet, and I wanted to be like him. Jem included his hotel info and a picture of himself naked. *Holy mother of god*, that man had the most beautiful body and his cock was like a woman's arm (and that's only a *slight* exaggeration). He was so big, that all the men he fucked had to use poppers (amyl nitrite, it relaxes your muscles but can give you one mother of migraine). I imagine he had to provide them to all his bottoms, like a doctor giving you a dressing gown before she examined you, but I made a mental note to order some, just in case, as I responded with my phone number and a video of me giving Vas the best blow-job in our collection.

He sent back the emoji with hearts for eyes and a thumbs-up.

* * *

I spent the rest of the week doing yoga, eating healthy and keeping my eyes focused on the prize. I watched his videos for research, and for their intended purpose, of course. The day before I was expecting to hear from him, I went to the spa and got my whole body and my asshole waxed. It hurt like a motherfucker but it was so worth it. I didn't dare let them do my balls, so I used Nair, and I was so smooth, and white, and pink, I couldn't wait to be naked in front of him.

I was at an AA meeting after dinner when my phone buzzed in my pocket and I nearly tripped running out of the room to answer the American number.

"Hello, this is Ronnie," I answered breathlessly.

"Hey Ronnie, its Jem," he said, and nothing on earth could have prepared me for the effect his deep voice had on my body as it rolled down the phone line like molasses. I felt star struck and weak-kneed. His accent was so sexy, I felt a twinge in my pants.

I searched for my voice, and then cringed when I heard it. "Hi Jem, so glad you made it safely," I sounded girly, and nervous, and my lisp was back.

He ignored it, or at least didn't comment on it, thankfully. "We landed yesterday, and I was thinking, tomorrow at eleven is good for me. Does that work?"

"If you mean in the morning, then yes, that works for me," I responded with a smile in my voice.

"Great, I'll see you then. Room 1424," he said and the line went dead.

I barely slept, I was so thrilled with the excitement of it all. I did everything to prepare, I showered, slathered my body with lotion, and put on a pink lace thong under Burberry shorts and an Armani t-shirt. I wanted to make a posh impression, and I succeeded. Jem's eyes swept over me like he was a diamond jeweler looking at the Great Star of Africa (okay, that might be laying it on a little thick but he was impressed). I was so nervous I could barely speak, he was larger than life and so beautiful, so charming. We spoke for like ten minutes, getting the business part of things out of the way. We looked over each other's negative test results and he asked to see my ID.

"You look like you're sixteen," he said in that deep voice of his as he handed me back the ID with my real name. "How long you been doing porn?"

"I only did it with my ex for like a year. I don't plan on continuing," I answered.

He paused at that. "What are you doing here then?"

"I think that should be quite obvious," I scanned my eyes over his body just as he had mine.

He smiled a heavenly smile at me, dimples on full display, and asked what I liked, asked me if I need poppers, and then told me to get undressed.

I think that was the weirdest part. It was like a few minutes of pleasantries, exchange of papers, and then straight to sex. It was a little off-putting, and I seriously doubted my decision, until he stripped his clothes off that is, and I saw him in all his glory. His body was like Adonis' and he had a raging hard-on thanks to Viagra, which of course was to be expected, a professional like him. I swallowed and stripped down to my thong. He made a sound like a growl that gave me goosebumps and the next thing I knew the camera was on and we were making out in front of the window. He was a passionate kisser and devoured me; he really knew how to make a bottom feel loved.

I won't go into too much detail, anyone who has seen any kind of porn knows the sequence of events, but I had a couple of observations. One, I knew he loved eating 'bussy,' as he called it (I told you I did my research), but nothing could have prepared me for how good he was at it. I nearly came, and told him as much, moaning for him to stop as I pulled away, which made him groan with pleasure. Two, his cock was so much bigger in real life than it looked on camera, and I thought the camera was supposed to work the *opposite* way. I had to sniff nearly the entire bottle of poppers just to accommodate him and then promptly came as he began fucking me because he felt so good I couldn't stop myself. I barely had time to say "I'm gonna come," before doing so. He came too, I felt it shooting inside me all warm and soothing. His hands squeezed my hips and he covered my back with his body. He kissed my neck, breathing heavy in my ear as though he'd been fucking me for hours and not two minutes.

"Holy shit Ronnie, I have never come that fast on film," he whispered so the camera couldn't hear. And then he straightened as if it never happened and kept fucking me, because, *Viagra.* "You are so sexy," he groaned.

It's very sensitive in there after you orgasm, so after a few minutes I pulled away and turned around so I could suck his cock, and I went to town, praising him profusely between mouthfuls. I was on cloud nine that I made this pro blow his nut in under five minutes, but I also remembered I was there to do a job, and that job was to make Vas insane with jealously. I wanted Vas to feel a modicum of what I felt when I watched him tell that new slag how hot he was, and how hot it felt fucking him, each of those words like a slap across my face and a cut to my heart. So, I moaned (but not too much, because that's just annoying), and told Jem how

I loved his big cock (I did love it), how he was such a man (he was the man) and on and on, which Jem ate up. I mean who doesn't love praise? The cream on top was that Jem was heaping me with praise too, telling me how sexy I was (I was pretty fucking sexy), moaning that my hole was so tight (I imagined any hole was tight to him), and panting about my perfect lips (they were soft and beautiful), all of which just fueled me and my inner Madonna.

I knew Vas would see this video, I was going to make sure of it. He used to follow Jem's profile, checking it every week or so for new content, because he wanted to be Jem, and I couldn't imagine that had changed. Vas didn't want to just be in the top ten (which we had been), or be among the top performers (which we were), he wanted to be the top performer. Well, he wasn't ever going to be, certainly not fucking the slag he dumped me for, and here I was riding number one, literally. I felt like I was on top of the world.

Jem fucked me for another hour and a half, moving me around, moving the camera around, holding it at times for shots from his point of view. He was sweaty and red and looked at me with such a stunned expression after his last orgasm, which he pulled out for (hello money shot), that I smiled seductively and reached up to pull him down for a kiss. He kissed me lingeringly and then glanced at the connecting door. I wondered if his husband was on the other side listening.

I took a quick shower without getting my hair wet while he watched silently.

"Thank you, that was mind-blowing," I said toweling off and getting dressed. "I've only been with a handful of men, but I don't need a lot of experience to know that you were the best, you are the best," I corrected with a coy smile and smoothed my hair briefly in the mirror before looking back at him. "I want named credit on the video, and I want it to be the featured one on all your sites. I'll direct my fans to it, but I don't want any money. I did this for me, and for revenge, and because I want to go out on the top, 'top.'" I smiled.

He looked away, thinking (perhaps of his great fortune), and then back at me with such a quintessentially American-pie smile, all dimples and full of charm, like straight up Rhett Butler. "I saw your ex had a new bottom. Believe me when I say he's nothing compared to you," he stepped forward and kissed me softly, no cameras rolling, but he glanced at the connecting door again. "Consider it done. I'm happy to oblige."

I nearly swooned, but gathered myself with a nod and left the room.

I was so out of practice that I could barely walk when I left. My leg muscles were like jelly from riding him and my ass was burning, but I left triumphant because little me had made the biggest gay porn star on the planet come three times, and not only that, I had stunned him. I headed straight to the pharmacy for some paracetamol and washed down three with a bottle of water. I treated myself to half a pizza and a fizzy soda because I was fucking ravenous after my marathon session with Jem. I wished I had remembered to ask when he would be posting the video, but knew it wouldn't be until he got back to LA, or wherever it was that he lived. I was guessing it would probably take someone like him at least a month to edit and post, if I was lucky.

* * *

As it turned out, I didn't have to wait long at all. He sent me a short note letting me know it was up, and also wrote that he would love to fuck me again, but I had no intention of ever making another video, so I responded with a big thank you and nothing else. The video was so hot, we both looked amazing, and it had thousands of views within the first few days. By the end of the week it was in the tens of thousands, and within a month it shot up to six-figures. The reviews were an astounding one hundred percent thumbs up. I shared the link on my Finsta, and the comments there and then on the video from my fans were more than I could ever have hoped for.

Less than two weeks later, the trolls arrived and the thumbs-up percentage dropped, but only to ninety-six, and while I knew it was Vas and *Zaisy* with fake accounts and probably their fans whom they prompted, it still hurt to read them, so I stopped. But not before my fans, my beautiful fans, chimed in and a war raged in the comments, which only drew more viewers, and more positive reviews, and turns out that video was Jem's highest rated, highest viewed, and biggest money maker he'd had ever had outside the studios. He sent me a case of champagne which I blended slowly into my parents' wine cellar, with the exception of one bottle, in case there was ever a day I could drink again.

38

It All Falls Apart (and Little Bitches Get What They Deserve)

UNFORTUNATELY, MY HAPPINESS WAS SHORT-LIVED. It was an impulsive decision that I ultimately regretted for three big reasons. One, I became obsessed with following Vas and *Zaisy* online, and felt so hollow and miserable as a result. Two, I began drinking again, smarter this time though. I bought vodka, transferred it to water bottles, and was careful not to get too blitzed, just drunk enough that I stopped caring about anything. And three, perhaps the biggest regret of all, was my parents found out about all of it. I blamed Vas for making me miserable, and Marcus for getting me caught.

* * *

Three weeks into my stealthy drinking ways, and two weeks before the start of school, I had blown off another meeting and was coming back from talking a bartender's ear off in Soho (and promoting my video with Jem) with a bottle of water (vodka) in my hand when I heard my name. Well, not my real name.

"Well, well, well, if it isn't Daddy's little slut, *Ronnie*."

It was dark, but there was no mistaking the voice. I was so caught off guard I looked over my shoulder (huge mistake). Marcus was crossing the street toward me, clearly on his way home from somewhere. He looked even more handsome, and older, but with something angry shining out of him. It had been more than two years since I'd seen him and he looked leaner, like he'd finally shed his teenage skin.

"I thought it might be you, but nearly didn't recognize you with all your clothes on."

That cut me, coming from him, from someone in my Kensington bubble. I felt it like a blow, and shifted my shoulder to absorb his words. I wondered how many people he told and felt exposed. I turned and kept walking.

"Hey little slut, I'm talking to you," Marcus sneered. "What, you think you're some big porn star now, can't stop for a little chat with an old chum?"

Ha, he was not my friend, and I wanted to say as much but I had learned to just let him say his piece, and get it out of his system. Each step was taking me closer to home and that's all I was focused on, getting home and continuing my drunk.

I felt his hand grip my bicep and he whirled me around. I saw that maybe he had been drinking too, and remembered the rugby match blaring over the bar.

"Where's your *daddy*? Oh wait, he got sick of you, or maybe the things you did were too disgusting, even for a scally like him," Marcus said in a derisive tone, his eyes scanning my body.

The tears fell then and I ran, horrified that I had let him see me break. He might have called after me, he might even have chased me, but I never heard his words and he never caught me. I ran into my house and straight up the stairs, dropping the water (vodka) bottle on the floor next to my bed as I sobbed into my pillow. I *was* disgusting, he *had* dumped me, and now everyone knew how unworthy I was. I felt things spinning into chaos again and left a barely coherent message for Miranda. I waited for my mum's regular check-in and then sat at my desk and drank straight from the bottle. I didn't care that it was warm or that it burned my throat, I just needed oblivion. I logged into my Finsta, and then into Vas' sites, thankful there was nothing new, but as I sat there I felt the urge to contact him again, I wanted to rail at him, to belittle him, *and* I wanted to beg him to take me back. I read some fan comments which made me feel better and kept me from doing something that stupid, because I noticed while I was searching, that the fucker still had *our* site active and had posted previously-unreleased videos of him and me, so he was still profiting off me. I kept drinking to suppress the pain, the hurt, and the anger, and eventually passed out in my chair.

And *that's* when the shit hit the fan. My dad came to check on me, because as he said later, my mum thought I seemed 'weird' when she checked earlier. My computer was on and unlocked, I guess I kept bumping the mouse, or had my head on the space bar or something, but my father saw *everything*. He clicked on all my open tabs, my whole secret life laid bare, and I slept through it all.

When I woke in the morning my mum was sitting on my bed crying. I thought someone had died (in my mouth to be honest, it tasted like shit), but she just looked toward the computer, which my dad, the high-tech genius he was, had turned off the sleep function of, so my porn was right there staring at me. It was frozen on Vas' cock dripping come into my mouth. I whipped my eyes back to hers and then launched myself out of bed, nearly falling over in pain from the resulting pounding in my head.

"It's too late Robby, we know everything," she said quietly and then sobbed. "How could you? Your father said there's over a hundred videos," she took a deep shuddering breath, "all as disgusting as that one," she nodded at the computer screen without actually looking at it.

I fell into my desk chair and just put my head in my hands. I shouldn't be expected to deal with this first thing in the morning, especially not with a bloody hangover that could kill a city block. "I'm sorry," I whispered. I wanted to blame Vas, and to be honest he was fully responsible for making this path for me, he used me, but I have to admit I liked pleasing him, I liked how happy he was with the monetary rewards. I could have said no, I could have left him (who the fuck am I kidding? I couldn't have done either of those things or anything else that would have potentially ended our relationship). "It just happened."

"What do you mean it just happened?" She shook her head incredulously. "Robby you're a good boy, you've always been such a good boy. Did he drug you? Is that why?" My mum asked, giving me a way out. "I knew he was bad news, I should've forbidden you from seeing him," she cried. "All those lies."

Felicity appeared in the doorway and looked from Mum on the bed, to me at my computer, to the computer screen, and then back at Mum.

"Not now Felicity," my mum panicked.

"Christ Robby, you didn't delete all those when you broke up?" She asked in a horrified tone. "And you're such a perv, close the browser," she scoffed pulling a face, "That's disgusting in front of Mum."

"You knew about this?" My mum asked horrified.

Felicity caught her mistake and was in full CYA mode. "A friend told me about it last year and I yelled at him for being with a pedophile, he told me he would get the videos taken down," she said in a rush.

My mum turned her eyes to me, and I sincerely wished my head would just explode already, for *all* the reasons. She looked back at Felicity. "Everything. Now," she demanded wiping her face.

Felicity snuck a glance at me as I shook my head, gently of course because of the pain but I urged her silence with my eyes.

"Fuck's sake Robby, why you still protecting him? He's ruined your life," she looked back at Mum. "Vasyl," she sneered, "is thirty, or maybe thirty-one by now, and he's the one who posted the videos, and he posted them when Robby was still underage, without his permission."

I winced, wishing I had never told her the rest of the story, but that's why you shouldn't drink folks.

Mum stood abruptly from the bed and with a look at me, she pushed past Felicity, and went, presumably, in search of Gerald the Enforcer.

"Why the fuck did you say anything?" I asked harshly and then rubbed my head.

She frowned at me. "Are you hungover?" She shook her head with her mouth hanging open. "Robin, you have to pull your shit together. You are a Trumball, a Wenham, you're going to let some Pikey, piece of shit from *the* Ukraine, bring you down?" She shook her head, looking so much like Dad in that moment it took my breath. "Straighten up, or I'll do it for you," she left the room.

I took several deep breaths and didn't feel any better, so I opened my desk drawer and found my stash of pills hidden in a tin of Altoids. (Oh, did I forget to mention that I had procured some really fantastic DMT along with the ever-faithful Oxy?) My dad had taken the nearly empty bottle of water (vodka) from my desk but I found an insulated bottle that had rolled under my bed with about two mouthfuls of cranberry juice and vodka left in it that helped me get that pill where it needed to be. I laid back down on the bed and waited for it to kick in.

Ten minutes later my dad (Gerald) came striding through the door, with my mum in tow. "Robin," he said looking at the floor next to the bed and not at me, "I want some answers, and I strongly encourage you to tell me the truth, or we are going to have a real problem," he paused, and I eventually realized that he was waiting for a response. Holy shit, the pill was tickling my senses quicker than I had anticipated.

"Okay," I shrugged.

"How old is Vasyl?"

I thought for a minute, calculating. "Almost thirty-one."

My dad closed his eyes and rolled his tongue through his mouth. "How old were you when he first filmed you?"

"Sixteen," I sat up as my dad's eyes flew open, "but he didn't post that one, he didn't post until I was seventeen," I said in a rush.

"You think somehow that makes it better?" He looked at my mum. "You were still a child," he spat and shook his head. "Boy you two really pulled the wool over our eyes, and I blame him."

"I lied about my age. He was a good guy, he loved me," my eyes filled as I laid back.

"Oh yeah?" My father shouted. "Where was he when you nearly died? Where the fuck is he now? Profiting off you *and* fucking some other child," he clenched his hands as my eyes glassed over, oh, what an unfortunate time for the drugs to kick in. "And who was that other man? How many others are there? I couldn't stand to keep looking."

"That was," my body was warm and tingly, and I just wanted them to leave so I could enjoy my high, "the number one porn star in America, probably the world, and he liked me," I giggled accidentally. "There is no one else," I trailed off and sighed as my body sunk into my bed and I disappeared. I slipped through the mattress and onto a cloud. I floated up above the room, looking to escape, but the ceiling stopped me. I floated to the window but that was locked, so I closed my eyes and wished myself away, and it worked.

If I thought I wanted to die before, now I really did, but even more drastic, like, I wish I'd never been born at all, me and Freddie Mercury.

The next thing I knew my forehead was pressed against the cool glass of my father's fancy Mercedes sedan, and I was marveling at the world rushing by, such a beautiful blur. I wondered what it would be like to join with that blur, that chaos that was all external and not internal. I fumbled for the door handle with one hand and my seatbelt with the other when hands pulled me away from the cool, from the intent, and I cried out.

"Robin!" Someone who sounded like my mum cried, but it was an angel on the seat next to me, its wings took up the space all around.

I felt my own wings threaten to unfurl and pulled away. "Did Michael send you?" I asked full of panic, I didn't want to see him again.

I saw the wings retract, and the angel retreated cautiously. "Who is Michael?" It asked in a soft voice. It sounded coy and full of trickery.

I narrowed my eyes and put my head back on the glass looking out, wanting blur and oblivion not conversation and deceit.

"Robin, I'm talking to you. Do you mean St. Michael? You did mention him before. Have you seen him?" The voice asked gently.

I looked back. The angel looked like my mum, but its face kept shifting, showing its true self. I figured if it was one of Michael's soldiers, I was pretty much already fucked. "Yes, he's tried to come for me twice, and you can tell him if he wants me, he can come for me himself. I won't go anywhere with you."

The angel looked around worriedly, *good*, I thought. I was done fucking around, and if that bastard wanted me, I was ready for him. He might have won in the heavens but this was earth.

"When did he come for you the first time?" The angel asked tentatively, as though it were questioning my honesty, my truthfulness.

"Last year, I swear," I said defensively. "I recorded him."

The angel looked frightened, and it was then that I realized we weren't alone, there was another angel with us, sitting with his back to me, and who knew how many more, so I shut down, and slumped over, surrendering to the safety of the high.

I became aware of melting faces, white hallways, doors that had to be swiped with a card to enter and I collapsed to my knees like a toddler. I fought them. Oh, *fuck no, not this again.* I prayed loudly then to St. Michael.

"Come for me, you crooked-winged bastard!" I cried. "I'd rather fight you and die, than be locked away again."

I'm sure it won't surprise you to know that he didn't come, and I *was* locked away, like a little bitch who couldn't be trusted on his own, because I *was* a little bitch who couldn't be trusted on his own. They sent me back to rehab for the obvious reasons, the drinking and the pills, but I knew they also sent me back because they just couldn't look at me anymore. I lost yet another six weeks to that bastard Vas.

39

Phoenix From the Fire, Or Just a Git Burned?

I WALKED OUT into the cold sunshine to meet my parents and blinked dramatically as though emerging from solitary confinement. I saw my dad roll his eyes without looking at me, while my mum chuckled nervously before hugging me tightly. It had been a grueling six weeks of rehab and DBT, which was unlike the cake-walk therapy I had gone through before. It was overseen by Miranda, who I had renamed Demanda, to her utter delight.

"That's not a compliment, Miranda," I scoffed shrilly, irritated with her ability to see right through me.

"You think you're the first one to call me that?" She laughed at me. "My mother wanted to change my birth certificate and my nanny refused to call me anything but. What else you got?"

I had pulled a face and wanted to throw myself on the floor like a toddler (again) but didn't. Instead I had given her my haughtiest expression and flounced out of the room, our relationship solidified.

My parents didn't say much in the car, my mum asked me how everything was, the food, the exercise, the groups, but studiously avoided the topic of porn and therapy. I answered honestly, and then changed the subject. We rode the rest of the way in silence, my dad had said literally four words to me. "Good to see you."

I'm not exaggerating when I say my dad didn't look at me for months, and my mother couldn't look at me without pain in her eyes. I suppose I can't blame their individual reactions; I mean none of the videos were titled, 'Mummy's little slut milks every drop, facial,' or 'Ronnie takes Mummy's monster cock deep. Bareback, EPIC cum shot!' Worst part is, I knew my dad knew why Vas called me 'Daddy's little slut,' but a teeny-tiny part of me didn't regret the moniker.

* * *

I begged to go back to school, but the term had already started and my parents did not trust me to be on my own. I spent the remaining month proving myself worthy, showing that I could follow a routine and stick to my landing. I meant it this time. Felicity was right, I *was* a Trumball, and *he* was nothing. He thought he could cast *me* aside? I had admirers and all kinds of lovers, practically banging down my door.

I was walking around, basically swaggering as I went from place to place, filling the time with meetings and yoga and sex, until I could get back to Oxford. That's how I failed to notice a black BMW lurking just off to my left. The cars I was counting that evening were blue, all shades in case you were wondering. I was on thirty (Christ, blue was a popular color), when I heard exactly two car doors slam and suddenly Olek was in front of me. I stopped short, startled but not worried, I told you, I knew all about his type.

"Oy," he said and glanced over my shoulder.

I looked, *oh fuck*, hadn't I learned my lesson about that? In this instance though, it was necessary, because Olek and his equally tattooed compadre, were not just messing around. All I had to defend myself with was my floppy yoga mat in a very poncy-looking carrying case, one that would never be mistaken for some sort of assault rifle holder.

I tried a nonchalant tone, and succeeded, if nonchalance sounded like a creaky garden gate. "Hey Olek," I said putting my hand in my pocket, searching for the pocket knife that I knew wasn't there and finding my phone instead.

"What the fuck do you think you're on about?" He asked in a cold voice.

I looked around, truly bewildered. "I don't know what you're talking about. I'm just coming back from yoga, is that a crime now?"

His face shifted. "Don't get sassy you little *fag*. You know exactly what I'm talking about. Vas is in jail and your petty, jealous ass put him there. So, you're going to drop the charges, tell everyone you lied or," he trailed off flexing his hands.

I frowned, *Holy shit my parents must've called the cops.* "I didn't say anything Olek, I honestly don't know what you're talking about. I swear."

He stepped closer, and I took a step back, encountering the broad chest behind me. I felt hands on my arms and instinctively writhed, panic flooding every cell of my body as I looked around the deserted street.

"You think I would believe a word out of your mouth?" He looked at my mouth then, and instead of it being sexual it was terrifying. I wondered in that moment just how many people Olek had killed.

I swallowed and looked at his feet. "I never lied. You said it yourself, there was no way I was seventeen, and Vas knew that," I said quietly. "He tried to kill me, with your help, your pills," I held his gaze. "You want to go down too? Vas will do just fine in prison, he likes fucking dudes. But you?" I shrugged, and because he thought I was nothing, just a skinny twink, I had the element of surprise. I brought the heel of my trainer up into the crotch of the guy behind me with all my might and felt him collapse, and then punched Olek right in the windpipe, just like I learned and practiced in rehab. *Oh yeah,* they had classes for women who had been victims, and I took all that shit, because what else did I have to do in captivity? And then I ran and fucking ran, like Vas' tigers were after me, because they were. I screamed "Fire! Fire!" as I ran dodging through back roads, back alleys, and people came, it really fucking worked. I would have laughed triumphantly if I wasn't so terrified.

I got home and told my parents everything that had happened. I had to, I came slamming into the house like the hounds of Baskerville were on me, and asked them point blank what was going on.

Turned out, Felicity had reported Vas. She had had enough of his shit, and his effect on me, and my parents supported her. She had enough evidence on her own that I didn't need to get involved, but because of Olek's intimidation, they now wanted to take it a step further. I hesitated, I didn't know why I still felt protective of Vas. I knew I had hopes of us getting back together, and I also knew that was delusional. It was so hard for me to let him go, even when I knew he had cut me free, used me and cut me down without a backwards glance like I was *The Giving Tree.* I would have let him sit and rest his bones on my stump, I was that naïve. Finally, with Miranda, and Madonna, in my head, I played the recording I had made on my phone of that night's events, and the other ones I had made.

I recorded things from time to time, out of boredom, and then for self-preservation, never knowing if they'd be useful. So, when Vas attacked me for lying about my age, the first thing I did after he smacked me in the living room, was reach for my phone in my pocket and swipe into the camera. I always kept it in video mode, it was habit. When I huddled in the corner of his bedroom I caught every blow, every kick, every head slam, on camera and audio. He said a lot of horrible things, most of which I could use against him, everything else, I had edited out later. When he was done, and I had crawled to the bed, I slipped my phone under the pillow when he was getting me the pills. After I nearly died, and regained consciousness I recorded the conversation that he and Olek had about the whole thing. Then I videoed me pissing blood in his toilet. It might not be admissible in court, but it was damning enough to anyone who saw it.

My parents stood listening and watching with shock, and my mum sobbed. Hearing and seeing those recordings again in the presence of my parents, made me realize how truly horrible Vas was. He had manipulated me from day one, and how I, *of all people*, could have missed that made me so angry that I sobbed too, and crumpled in my mum's arms, and then nearly fainted when I felt my dad come up behind me and hug us both.

40

The End?

MY DAD PULLED OUT all the stops to be sure Vas was nailed to the wall, and that my name was kept out of everything. Olek and his goon were charged with witness intimidation and served time, not as much time as Vas, but enough to know that if they ever tried anything again, they'd go away for even longer, and Vas wasn't worth it to them. I was on pins and needles throughout the whole proceeding, and his sentencing. I never had to testify, and was never named as an accuser (the evidence spoke for itself), and I was a protected minor. It's amazing what they can find forensically on the internet. The time stamp of when he deleted the videos, and the videos that were posted after without showing my face proved that he knew what he was doing was illegal and yet he continued to make me film. In the first few videos my bruises were still visible, peeking out from underneath my shirt, and damning.

I felt peculiar about the whole thing, to be honest. The thought of Vas in prison, and because of me, gave me such anxiety, and filled me with such chaos it sent me back to rehab (another six-weeks I lost because of him). I couldn't believe we had gone from being so in love, to being a victim and an offender, both locked away. Things got even worse in my life because that was when I lost Dee. She had been there for so much of it, so supportive, so steadfast, but she had her own life, she had school, had found love (and he hated me), and just didn't want the burden, or the taint of me anymore. There was no fight, no drama, just her ghosting me, and while at the time I didn't understand, because I still needed her so much, looking back, I couldn't blame her. I was a mess, and so needy and self-absorbed I was just impossible to be around. I was so lucky that my family didn't feel the same way, because so many people lost their families when things got this dark, and that's not helpful for anyone in recovery.

* * *

After my third stint in rehab, I was *really* ready to get back to school. I had missed two terms, Michaelmas, and Hilary, but was able to swoop in for the final, Trinity, term by special dispensation. I rented an Airbnb indefinitely, and spent my free time looking for housing for the summer and roommates for the fall. I studied hard, it was always something I was good at, and I found two great roommates who had a recent vacancy because their other flatmate got pregnant (whoopsie) and had to move out, so I moved in right away and it was perfect.

In many ways it was so much better and easier to be away from my family, because my mum had a full plate and I needed to stop being so fucking needy. She still had two kids at home and Felicity was finishing up at Cambridge, dating some guy everyone was certain she would marry (he came from good stock and had royal blood, albeit quite watered down). David was applying to uni, and George was a handful with all his activities and social life. Besides, I now had two captive audience members at my disposal. My new flatmates, Gertie (who I loved immediately) and Kayla (who was really great but more reserved), were finishing up their first year, and were really supportive and not at all judgey about the porn. They took my side, naturally, and said I had done the right thing holding Vas accountable for his actions, which made me feel so much better. They helped me stay focused and on-track, and, most importantly, entertained.

One of our favorite pastimes was looking for men to objectify and rate when we were out and about (conscientiously avoiding establishments that served alcohol, of course). We started with a simple, and already established grading system with ten being the highest. We based our scores on face, body, and eyes, but then naturally became far more specific and complicated over time, with points and comparisons. We each had our biases, and I mostly kept mine to myself.

"If he's got a great face, and a great body but he's short, then he can't be higher than a five," Kayla said, taking a bite of her burger.

"Everyone's the same height horizontally," Gertie grinned, "and I'm short so height isn't a deal breaker. I think bad teeth or a bad body can't be above a five."

"People can lose weight and go to the gym, teeth can be fixed, but not height, I think the ruling stands, sorry Gertie," I shrugged. "I think age is a deal-breaker, can't be higher than a five if he's over forty, unless he has money, in which case he could go as high as a seven, nine if he's got money *and* a title," I added with a grin.

"Agreed," they said in unison.

Most of our conversations were just that important and everything that I needed in between classes, studying, yoga, and meetings, which I went to at least twice a day first thing in the morning and last thing at night usually. I stayed in touch with T., as well as Demanda, having twice-weekly calls with both of them in the first few months, and then only weekly, or as needed with T., as I gained back my inner-strength.

My time wasn't filled with only wholesome activities (haven't you been paying attention?). I found two guys that I bounced back and forth between, neither of whom knew about the other of course. One was older and rich (a nine who should have been a five), and we fucked in his country estate, and the other was at uni, and had a buff body (a solid seven). I still wasn't ready, or technically allowed, to date, but I absolutely couldn't go without a lot of sex (sorry, not sorry). All of those ingredients helped me finish school, only slightly behind my original graduating class. I finished after Hilary term, and stayed through June to graduate with Gertie and Kayla.

My older lover, who I met in a drunken haze at a gay club back in London, took me away for a few weeks in April, after Easter. He knew about the porn (that's why he approached me at the club) and about the rehabs, and didn't care, but he didn't broadcast our relationship either, which was just fine with me. He was at least twenty-five years older, and while he was attractive, it was really his money that made him so. I never introduced him to Gertie, or Kayla, I never even told them his name, just referred to him as Lord Boomer (he hated when I called him that, insisted he was Gen X, but honestly anyone who came of age without a mobile, was a 'boomer' to me).

Lord Boomer took me to his estates in France and Italy, and posh hotels in Vienna and Prague. I found meetings everywhere we stayed and went religiously morning and night. Lord Boomer was very supportive, he didn't drink around me, and in return I blew him and his mind. We went sight-seeing, ate fantastic food, and had long conversations in between all the sex, but we weren't glued to each other's sides. He had long, boring meetings about his estate management that he had to attend, and I lounged by the pool in my tiny swimsuit or wandered the cities, trying to find and lose myself.

By the end of the trip, Lord Boomer was hooked, and I was questioning my motivation. I had caught his eye because of my youth (he liked them young) and the porn, but I held his attention with my brains, and my charm, and my pedigree. He wanted to extend the vacation but I was eager to get back to my routine, and to be honest, I was a little bored, his flattery was getting tedious. I knew he had been shocked to find out I was posh, and where I grew up, but I didn't need to hear about it as though it were a new discovery every day.

I begged off the extension and we flew back to London, parting ways at the airport, Lord Boomer's eyes on my back as I wheeled my Louis Vuitton suitcase to the taxi stand. I spent the night in Kensington, my mother eager to hear about the trip she thought I took with Gertie, and then left in the morning on the train (after a meeting of course). I couldn't wait to get back to my flat and plan my future. If only I had factored Lord Boomer into those plans, then I wouldn't have been so blindsided later.

* * *

After graduation, Kayla moved back to Cornwall, to work for a marketing firm or something, and Gertie and I moved in together back in London. Gertie was my new Dee, but even better. She really got me, and she had experience with addiction and recovery because her mother was an alcoholic (fifteen years sober, like a badass) so Gertie had been through Al-Anon, AA, and all the family programs. She was a godsend who favored dark nail polish and changed her hair color regularly. She was beautiful like Billie Eilish, smart and funny like Tina Fey, and loyal like Lassie, and we loved each other fiercely. Everything was amazing and we lived happily ever after, the fairy and his queen.

The end.

PART THREE

BUTTERFLY

$$41$$

You're Still Here? (I Suppose, Unlike Ferris Bueller, I Do Have More to Say)

I LOOKED UP from my computer at the sound of a footstep in the doorway. My beautiful husband was standing there, in a shaft of sunlight that made him look like he had a halo. I smiled. I told you before that my husband was a saint, but he wasn't always.

"What is it Marcus?" I asked softly.

"We've got dinner with the Golds in an hour," he said in his smooth, deep voice. "I figured you needed a time check."

"Thank you darling. I'm just finishing up some edits."

He smiled and turned to leave.

"Wait," I stood and stretched, "come here."

He stepped into my waiting arms and I kissed his neck, breathing in his faint cologne, his heady scent. "You look like a bloody angel," I ran my hands over his soft, grey-flecked hair. "I swear there was a halo here just a minute ago."

He chuckled, a low rumble I felt against my lips. "You're the angel. Really, you haven't aged a day since we married," he pulled back to look at me. "And you've always had the face of an angel." His lips touched mine and I was lost, as usual.

✳ ✳ ✳

I suppose you're waiting for the story. I should just gloss it over really, this is the story of me and Vas, not me and my bully, my savior, my soulmate. But then again, I suppose Marcus deserves his character arc, his story of redemption, just as much as I do. So, in order to tell the story of Marcus, and me, I need to go back to the beginning, fill in all the gaps.

I told you about Marcus and his gang of thugs, what they did to me, what he prevented them from doing to me, but that was really only half of it, *obviously*. That day, when Marcus came upon the gang of thugs from my old school beating on me, he stopped them, but only because he thought they were being excessive, no one needed to hold me, I was like forty kilos. He stayed after they left and looked me over, something behind his eyes I didn't understand. I was year nine, like thirteen or something, and he didn't understand it either, apparently.

The next time we crossed paths he was lower sixth and I was a new year ten, just transferred to the school to be with Dee, and to get away from the bullies at the all-boys school I had been going to. I laid eyes on him the first week, as I was making my way around, learning the hallways, and the hierarchies. He was at the athlete table in the middle of the lunch room holding court, large and gorgeous, surrounded like he always was with a mixture of girls and boys. He had his arm around a pretty blonde as he sat back and listened to one of his jesters tell a story. I remembered such an unusual feeling coming over me looking at him, like terror and awe mixed with a healthy dash of desire. He was friends with the brutish of brutes and yet he alone had the power to control them, and that was heady. I knew then that I needed to simultaneously stay out of their line of vision *and* stay in his good graces. I hugged that cafeteria wall and tried to become one with it until I found the safety of Dee's orbit.

That autumn term was peaceful, only a moderate amount of harassment from the goons, and nothing physical so I felt pretty, pretty, pretty, *pretty* good. I should have known that it wouldn't last. One day, early in the spring term I was walking home, counting cars, red ones that day, I don't know why I remembered that but anyway, I was counting cars and thinking of Harry Styles. I must've swished or flounced or waved my hand as I was singing in my head because the next thing I knew, insults were being hurled my way from behind me.

"Look guys, it's the queerest of folks," a voice called. I figured out later it was Gareth, he always liked to get the first insult in.

"Eddie Izzard called, he wants his gay back," another voice said.

I kept walking, wishing I could vanish.

"Hey faggot, we're talking to you," Marcus called.

I shuddered a breath and searched for an adult. I looked back, and that was when I first realized you should *never* do that.

"Oh guys, see, you weren't using his name," Marcus said with a laugh. "Yeah fag, hey, the gay bar's that way."

I ground my teeth at that and kept walking, every step bringing me closer to safety.

I heard running footsteps and my backpack was grabbed, nearly pulling me over backwards. Gareth had me by my backpack like it was a harness, swinging me around, I nearly whimpered but caught myself, thank god.

"I think he's headed home for his knee pads and glitter eyeshadow Marcus," Gareth sneered, his breath stinking like the onions from that day's lunch.

"Let me go," I said. "I've done nothing to you," I looked at Marcus who appeared in my line of vision. I implored him with my eyes to remember saving me before, and while it seemingly didn't register then, because they continued to harass me, the next time we crossed paths, he was far more receptive to my pleas.

They eventually let me go, and I went home shaken and faked a stomachache, not wanting to go to school the next day. My mum made me chicken soup and rubbed my back while I watched the telly. I think she knew that I wasn't sick, but never said a word.

The next week, I ran into Marcus on my way home. He was alone, and (weirdly, I thought at the time), seemingly waiting for me, sitting on the wall of someone's front step. My heart thudded its way into my throat and choked me. I wished I had been paying attention, if I had seen him before he'd seen me then I could have turned and gone a different way. As it was, I was trapped, he was between me and my house.

"Hey fag," he said jumping down, as though he were calling me mate.

"I'm not a fag," I said quietly. "I don't know why you pick on me, I'm nobody. I'm just trying to mind my own business."

Marcus raised his eyebrows and looked around. I studied him then. He was perfection. Dark haired, blue-eyed, perfect body, the tight body of a rugby star, which, as I said, he was. "You don't mind your eyes," he said looking back at me from under his lids.

I pulled up, and my heart fluttered at the tone in his not-yet-deep voice. I couldn't tell if it was angry or heated. "I'm not doing anything with my eyes," I said defensively.

He slow blinked at me and ran his tongue around the inside of his mouth.

In the time it took him to contemplate my response, my mind raced for solutions to my dilemma. "Thank you for helping for me last year, when those guys were beating me up," I said and bit my lip. It was a gamble to be sure, but there was still that something behind his eyes.

He looked away. "I don't know what you're talking about," he said completely unconvincingly.

"Well, thank you anyway, I would repay the favor," I said nonchalantly and held my breath.

His eyes came back to mine like a whip, and then he narrowed them. "What?"

"I mean I could help you with your homework, or do it for you, or," I answered in a rush with a shrug.

"I don't need help with my homework from a year ten," he said and turned away.

He left me then, holding my breath, rooted to my spot. I watched him, his perfect confident stride, his magnificent ass. No wonder he was the envy of the entire school. I told you I fawned over Liam Dougherty, who was cute in a boring, blonde way, but it was only because Marcus forbade me from looking at him in school after the next time we met.

42

Life Brings You to Your Knees

LOOKING BACK, it was a complete set-up, but at the time I was frightened by them as usual. I was like a hundred and sixty-two centimeters to their hundred and eighty-seven, and they out-weighed me by *so* many stones. I didn't even try to run, just focused on not shitting my pants, so that I wouldn't be known as doo-doo boy, or shitty fag, or whatever unimaginative slur they would have come up with. It was Gareth and Hector and Frank and they sang some song (I'm sorry I don't remember, it was out of tune and horrible so I'm doing you a favor really). Marcus appeared a few minutes or a few hours in, it felt like an eternity and I was so busy shrinking into myself that I couldn't be bothered with keeping track of time.

"Guys, lay off," Marcus said, tapping Gareth on the shoulder. The guys immediately straightened in the presence of their leader. "He's probably late for ballet."

They laughed like he was the king of comedy. It took all my willpower to not roll my eyes.

"You think he's got his leotard on under his clothes, or will he have to go home and change?" Frank or Hector said, I told you, I couldn't tell those cretins apart.

"We should check," Gareth said with a sneer, reaching for me.

I stepped back, suddenly truly frightened at the prospect of being stripped bare.

"Guys, I said leave him be," Marcus held up his hand. "You seriously don't want to be accused of a hate crime, banned from sports. Go on, we've got rugby in an hour, stay focused, see you on the pitch," he commanded and they listened, leaving Marcus standing next to me.

He watched them go, the tip of his tongue between his parted teeth, before looking back at me. "Shall we cut through the park?" He asked, but it wasn't a question.

I nodded dumbly. I kept trying to fall back, but not only wouldn't he let me, there was something in me that wanted to see what he had in mind.

We followed the path through the park and then with a glance all around, Marcus strayed, crossing the grass to a large, dense clump of rhododendrons. I followed with a frown, but let the realization wash over me.

He turned to face me once we were deep inside the bush, in a small clearing, hidden from view. "Well, I'm ready for your thank you."

I stood frozen. Just because I suspected what he was planning, didn't mean I was prepared for the bluntness of his demand. My hands hung numbly by my sides and I opened and closed my mouth repeatedly like a fish out of water. "What?" I squeaked.

He made a sound, like a laugh but more throaty, full of need. He looked at my mouth and then down at his belt.

I let out my breath in a whoosh. "But, I don't know," I swallowed again, "how."

Marcus smiled gently at me as he undid his belt above his bulge. "Just don't use your teeth."

I weighed my options, shrugged off my backpack, and knelt down. I performed with gusto, and he came like a firehose. I didn't know what else to do so I swallowed, and it tasted like heaven.

"You tell anyone about this and you're a dead man," he said breathlessly as he looked at me with hooded eyes. "Don't even look at me in school."

"I won't, I swear," I said earnestly, and meant every word. I never told a soul, not even Dee. "Please don't let them bully me," I added quietly, coming to my feet.

He zipped his pants and looked away. "They won't ever touch you again, but I can't promise no more teasing."

"Okay," I breathed, happy for whatever I could get.

* * *

We met there on a semi-regular basis during the school year, sometimes after he and his thugs would harass me, sometimes after I found a note in my locker. I practiced my tongue exercises with joy, discovering that they had a more pleasing outcome, because he loved it and I loved the taste of him. I loved going down on him, hidden in those bushes, our bushes. I was on my knees but I was the one with all the power, the one who made him come so hard his knees buckled.

Marcus had a rotation of girls, but settled on one after a few weeks with me. I found out later it was because she didn't ask questions, and fucked him however he wanted. I couldn't help but feel jealous after a time, I mean, I knew he was using me, but the way he reacted to my mouth, the way he kept after me, kept seeking me out, made me imagine there was something more. At the time I had no idea the conflict that was raging inside him, I just thought all jocks fucked around and didn't talk about it. A blowjob is a blowjob who cares whose mouth it is, doesn't mean you're gay. I was so wrong, and later, when Marcus told me everything, I understood just how risky his being with me was.

One day, after nearly a year of meeting in the bushes (weather permitting of course), the note in my locker had an address, but nothing else. I remember furrowing my brow and looking around before pulling out my phone and Googling it. It wasn't far from school or the park and I crumpled the paper and flushed it, like I did with all the others. I went there after school. It was a big townhouse like mine, but not fancy, his parents were less flashy than my dad. He made me go around back, and don't worry I rolled my eyes at that, but out of his line of sight, I wasn't daft.

I took off my backpack and stood looking at him in his kitchen. He stared at me like a deer in the headlights before breaking from his trance and nodding to the hallway, grabbing two sodas from the fridge on his way. I followed him to his room, which was plain but sporty, and adorned with rugby posters and some such. I never got a chance to really look because he grabbed me and kissed me, taking the breath from my body. It was the first time I had felt his lips anywhere on my person, and I nearly collapsed.

"You fucking tell anyone that you were here and I will cut you," he breathed against my lips.

"I would never Marcus, I promise. I've not said a word," I said urgently, kissing him again, my arms coming up around his neck, feeling a tingle raging through my body as my cock got harder than it had ever been. I didn't know what he had planned, but I would have let him cut me just to find out.

He stripped my uniform off as fast as I stripped his, and I felt his eyes on my body briefly before he pressed me back onto his bed. He used a mixture of spit and lotion, trying to wedge his large cock into my tiny asshole, whilst I spread as wide as possible, and relaxed like I was doing yoga to help fit him, until finally, he made it all the way in. I gasped and then moaned as he moved, the sensation was so indescribable and so pleasurable I couldn't help myself. It was over in a flash for us both. As soon as he began pounding into me, squeezing my ass with his strong hands, and making those blissful noises I lost myself. "Oh god, Marcus, I'm gonna come," I cried stroking myself and then shuddered euphorically as I felt him come too. He collapsed against my back, kissing my neck as he thrust a few more times against my ass, milking those last drops of come from his body.

I'm sorry if you thought I was virgin when I was with Vas, but I wasn't and I had to keep Marcus' secret. I knew then, well, my body knew then if my brain didn't, that I loved him. It was wrong because of how he treated me in public, but he was my first, and he was as confused about love then as I was.

He held me to him, his heart pounding, his cock eventually slipping out of my ass. I didn't know what to say, if anything, I could only breathe. I felt his hand on my hair and then he drew away.

"You should go," he said quietly, pulling on his underwear.

"Where's the bathroom?" I asked, sitting up carefully, uncertain about how to hold come in my ass, how to get rid of said come, and how to do any of it with any semblance of dignity.

"Across the hall," he nodded toward the door.

I picked up my underwear and left the room. Cleaning up wasn't as difficult as I imagined and after staring at myself in the mirror with a small smile, searching for signs of change, I was back in his room a few minutes later. He was fully dressed in jeans and a Trinity sweatshirt, sitting on the side of his bed and so heartbreakingly beautiful in that moment I lost my breath, until he stood and spoke that was.

"You have to go, I mean it," he said, his eyes weird.

"I'm leaving, don't worry," I frowned and picked up my pants.

"I'm not fucking worried. There's no reason to be, you're gonna keep your bloody mouth shut," Marcus said in a cool voice.

I felt tears behind my eyes as my throat swelled. Christ, he had just taken my virginity and there he was treating me like a disease he couldn't wait to be rid of. I dressed hurriedly, not because he wanted me out of there, but so that I could escape without blubbering embarrassingly.

I left out the back, at his insistence, and cried in our bushes in the park. Just the ugliest cry ever, nose running, red eyes, sobbing burning hot tears. I didn't eat that night, and I ignored his notes in my locker as fervently as I ignored him in the cafeteria and the halls. I hardened my heart to him, and it was easy, because I had met Vas and had my first kiss with him the weekend after Marcus' dickhead behavior.

I wasn't moping anymore, I left for school each day with perfect hair, perfect clothes, and the tiniest bit of lip gloss stolen from Felicity on my lips, just to make them extra, but not obviously so. I felt Marcus' eyes on me the few times our paths crossed and reveled in it, let him come to understand the error of his ways. Miss me and my beautiful mouth. The last note Marcus left in my locker simply said:

WTF

I looked at it for a long while, trying to figure out just how out of touch with reality this fucking rugby star was before writing:

Go fuck yourself

below it and stuffing it in his locker after math class.

He left me alone forever after that.

Just kidding. He and his thugs were on my ass immediately after school. I had to pretend to be scared. It took all my effort, and channeling Blanche Devereaux just to keep from rolling my eyes and kicking Marcus in the balls.

"What's your hurry gay boy?" Gareth called from behind me. "Is there a La Cage aux Folles Marathon on the telly?"

"Or Ru Paul's Drag Race that you want to study for tips?" One of the other shitheads said. For straight guys they knew an awful lot of gay stuff.

Marcus was silent, stalking me like a predator while his thugs tried to draw me out into the open. I ignored them, I did all the things that the director of a play would instruct me to do in that scenario until, as orchestrated by said director, the thugs dispersed and Marcus followed me into the park.

"What's your problem?" Marcus asked me after steering me into our bushes.

I wanted to scream. He had been with legions of girls, tons of experience with romance, how could he be so clueless as to not understand what he did to me was heartless? I frowned and reached into my pocket, fingering my phone.

"Nothing," I shrugged nonchalantly.

He narrowed his eyes. "Why you been ignoring me?"

"I've been busy," I said innocently, and trailed my finger down the front of his shirt. "Sorry?"

He flashed me a half smile, and something like relief flickered in his eyes. "Okay, I'll let you make it up to me." He unzipped his pants.

I dropped my phone on the ground between my legs as I fell to my knees, after pressing record of course. That was where I learned to record certain things, and hang on to them for a rainy day. At that point I knew exactly where Marcus' eyes went when I put my mouth on him (the top of my head, my eyes when I looked up at him, and around the bushes to be sure we weren't happened upon). I sucked his balls, I fingered his ass and I got all his moans and soft cries of my name on video and audio, before clicking it off just after he came and pocketing it discreetly. I wasn't sure if I'd ever need to use it, and as the weeks went by between Vas' kiss and finally hearing from him for my birthday, I didn't think I ever would.

Marcus wanting me when Vas was ignoring me was exactly what my ego needed, so I continued to meet Marcus in the bushes, and he even let me kiss him there, our tongues sliding across each other, before pushing my head down. He never knew I filmed us, until I sent him a clip after he broke my rib. I had to. I was with Vas, and needed Marcus to back the fuck off. It worked for the most part. He only forced me to the bushes one more time after that: when Vas was staying at my house that July. I was angry he tackled me and took my food, but I missed him needing me, so I went willingly to the bushes.

—————

43

—————

Here Comes
Your Twentieth
Nervous Breakdown

"HE BROKE YOUR RIB! He tackled you!" The masses cried aghast. "How could you forgive him?"

Easy. Three rounds of drug and alcohol rehab, DBT, and the famous twelve-step program forced me to. And he was profoundly apologetic, but don't worry, I didn't forgive him right away.

After the porn, after the downward spirals (so many downward spirals), after the rehabs, I was home for a short break before returning to finish my last year of university. I was in my term-break-groove of waking in the morning, having coffee, going to an AA meeting, doing yoga, showering, going out for more coffee, coming home to study, dinner, going to another yoga class, going to another AA meeting, and then coming home and going to bed with a big cup of chamomile tea. Occasionally there was an added step of some hot sex with a guy I met around the way, or with Lord Boomer who I was keeping at arm's length (and pulling away from), but otherwise I never varied the routine. I did this whenever I was home, and had held myself together for nearly a year. I wasn't thinking about drinking, or using, or Vas, and everyone was finally relaxing around me. I was in the happiest bubble and I never wanted it to end.

It was on my way back from the safety of the coffee shop, step five in my routine of the day, that I bumped into Marcus. Cue the bubble bursting. I gasped and dropped my cup, it fell and splattered all up my bare legs, scalding me, but I didn't feel it from the scalding I felt on my heart. He was stunning, his face matured, if not a little gaunt, with a manly five o'clock shadow bruising his jaw, his eyes so bright in his tan face.

"Shit! You okay?" Marcus cried reflexively.

I looked anywhere but at his face, feeling my entire body blush. It had been about a year since he belittled me about the porn, told me I was disgusting. All the ugly things he said to me reverberating in my brain like a chorus.

"I'm fine," I made to push past him.

"Robin," he said, touching my arm hesitantly.

Something in his voice made me pause. I hated him in that moment for it. It sounded like pity, it felt like he knew everything about me, how weak I had been, my multiple stints in rehab, and thought I was a failure, a disgusting, pathetic, failure.

"I'm sorry," he winced and exhaled audibly. "For literally everything."

I stared at his feet and then shook my head with a frown, I couldn't with anything he had to say or do in that moment, and I fled. I ran and ran until my lungs felt as though they would burst. I eventually arrived at home after an AA meeting, my routine disrupted, my entire system disrupted. I wanted a drink so badly. My mum must have sensed it, and took me to the museum, knowing how I loved to lose myself in the paintings. It worked, I was good again, I did yoga and then had dinner, and another AA meeting, and on the way home I stopped at a gay bar, not to drink, but for muscles and meaningless sex; Troye Sivan singing his song in my head the whole time.

It was hot, and he was, a Stud, whatever. I felt whole, went home and to bed, everything fine until I woke at three, in a cold sweat. I remember standing in front of the window of my room thinking, *I can't do this.* One day at a time? What kind of fucking bullshit mantra is that to someone who's only twenty-one? I wanted to die, everything felt so overwhelming and futile. Vas was rotting in prison because of me, Dee had ditched me, and Gertie hadn't yet fully replaced her, and I was just flouncing around without meaning. I was seriously adrift and I broke, *again*. I should've called Miranda, but I snuck downstairs instead and drank half a bottle of vodka, feeling like shit the whole time. Fuck you Vas. Fuck you god. Fuck you Marcus.

My dad found me sprawled in my underwear on his Persian carpet in the morning.

"Robin," he said sympathetically, but I detected a note of exasperation. "What happened?"

I sat up, my mouth fuzzy, my head pounding, and rubbed my eyes. "I don't know Dad. I wish," I trailed off and stood, because fuck if I knew what I wished at that moment. I mean, I guess I wished for everything and nothing.

After that, my dad locked up his booze and watched me like a hawk. I felt like a criminal. I assured them that it was just a slip up, I didn't need rehab (again) I just needed my school routine, my safe surroundings in Oxford. I had to leave and I was happy to say goodbye to everyone but my mum.

"Robby, darling, please reconsider. I don't think you're ready," she pleaded. "Does Miranda know what happened? You've already checked on the AA meetings? I really don't want to worry about you all the way out there."

"I'll be fine Mum," I lied, knowing I was far from fine, but that I wasn't likely to fall completely off the wagon. "I've already made my meeting schedule, and Miranda and T. are both available twenty-four seven though I won't need them. I'll be too busy with school," I smiled. "I want to finish my degree, I want to move on with my life, believe me. I managed perfectly last year, I will be fine, this was just a blip."

My mum looked away with a sigh. "You have to call me every day, promise," she said emphatically. "I mean it, and I want to see you regularly, even if it's just to do your laundry."

I smiled. "I'll call you, and you can come do my laundry whenever you want."

44

Blast From
the Past

I ALREADY TOLD YOU about school, about Gertie and Kayla, so I don't need to recap, besides you're still waiting to hear more about Marcus.

After I graduated the following year, I began really putting my life on the right track. Gertie and I moved in together into a decent-sized flat, with a balcony and a roof deck, in Chelsea and became even more inseparable, she was a rock for me and my sobriety. We formed a close-knit group with a mixture of her friends, my friends, work friends, and people we met around town. For the next two years we took cooking classes, went on day trips, overnight trips, and went to concerts, we were two peas in a pod but not attached at the hip, so it was perfect. She dated while I kept my eyes open. I dated a guy when we first moved there but for some reason I just couldn't connect, so went back to rotating among a couple of guys when the urge was too overwhelming to ignore (I had cut Lord Boomer loose, he was getting too serious and I didn't want to end up a nursemaid). It felt like limbo or purgatory (I'm being dramatic again, but you get my drift).

No one recognized me anymore, *thank god*, it had been five years. Porn memory is apparently quite short-term, and believe me I wasn't complaining about that. I was holding steady at a hundred and eighty-three centimeters and sixty-eight kilos, still had the wavy blonde hair and grey-blue eyes. I had filled out, wasn't a *real* twink anymore, and was drawing admiring glances from all the genders. I reveled in the attention, flirting outrageously but never making the connection with anyone that I so desperately craved. I didn't know what was missing, until I found it.

"Can you get oat milk while you're out?" Gertie called from the kitchen as she heard me pick up my keys. "Oh, and a few apples and a packet of crisps please," her green and blonde-haired head appeared around the doorframe with an impish smile.

"Will do," I replied returning the smile and taking a reusable grocery bag off the hook next to the door. It was Saturday in May, two years after graduation, and I was headed to yoga with my mat slung over my shoulder in its special, poncy bag.

"You look gorgeous in that color," she straightened and looked up at me; she was so short without her heels and I loved kissing the top of her head when she was barefoot. "Really makes your eyes more blue than grey." She swept her eyes over my bright blue sweatshirt and black shorts. "Your legs look really sexy too," she waggled her eyebrows. "Very muscly."

"That's why I love you," I kissed her nose. "You know exactly what to say when I'm feeling low."

"Are you glum?" She asked worriedly and looked at her watch. "There's a meeting somewhere, let me look at the schedule, I can go with you," she made to turn to the kitchen drawer.

"No, not that kind of glum," I stopped her. "It's been ages, and Miranda really helped with all that. No, I'm just missing having a bloke. All the guys in London are so blah. We should go to Spain!" I said, the thought suddenly occurring to me and giving me the jolt I needed. The guys in Spain were so hot, and dark and *Spanish*. I thought of the guy with the dragon tattoo and wondered if I still had his number.

Gertie made an excited sound and jumped on her toes. "We should!"

"I'll call my dad when I get back. Maybe next weekend he'll let us use the house," I turned and left with a spring in my step.

I lost myself in the ritual of yoga positions, gliding smoothly through them from years of practice. The instructors always admired my form, telling me I was built for it, and they weren't wrong. Yoga had transformed my body into lean muscle, and my mind into a mostly calm place. I let them touch me now, if they needed to correct my form, which almost never happened. I left as quietly as I came, I was never one to linger and chat with classmates and their muted voices followed me out of the studio.

Whole Foods was around the corner, and I walked in the automatic door, picking up a basket as I strode through with Gertie's shopping list in my head. I was in the health and beauty aisle, with a full basket, sniffing a bottle of shampoo when I heard my name. I managed to snap the lid shut before the bottle slipped from my fingers and bounced on the floor.

"Robin, wait," Marcus commanded as I turned to leave after looking at him. I felt exposed again, and awful, and something else. "Please."

I looked back at him and felt my stomach flip. It had been almost three years or so, since he burned me (okay that's dramatic, the coffee burned me, but you get my meaning). He was even more beautiful, if that was possible. He had grown his hair, it was wavy and curled around the collar of his shirt like teasing fingers. Did I say he had blue eyes? Because now, like that New Order song, they were green, or grey. No, green, the most beautiful shade of green-blue-grey that anyone had ever seen. I waited for my voice to return, but was sure it had rolled away with the shampoo bottle.

"You look great," he said, with an uncertain smile. He was coming toward me slowly like the horse whisperer approaching a wild and skittish horse, and I felt like bolting. I didn't need a mirror to tell me he was lying; I was a sweaty mess and I ran my hand through my hair nervously, glad that I had a sweatshirt on so he couldn't see the shirt underneath sticking to my skin.

I glanced at his expensive-looking slip-on shoes for the space of a few breaths, and then at his linen pants as my gaze went up his body. My eyes lingered briefly on the front of those pants, the image of his perfect cock appearing unbidden in my mind, before I continued my journey up his torso to his face with a slight blush. He was pink too then, and for some reason that made me happy.

He looked away and then back at me. "Please let me take you to lunch, or for coffee. I have so much I want to say. *Need* to say," he continued in a rush as he sensed me pulling away. "Please Robin. I'm sorry for the things I said, for what I, did."

Goddamn it, I felt the tears welling up from wherever it was that they waited, ready to stride out and make a scene on my face like Vegas showgirls, whether I wanted them to or not. I didn't even know why I felt like crying, just that his voice lacked pity this time, instead it was full of remorse. I drew a shaky breath to calm myself and cleared the lump from my throat. "I have to get my groceries home. Perhaps another time," I answered, proud that I managed to sound mostly strong.

"Do you live nearby? I could walk you home."

"Marcus," I shifted on my feet, the basket getting heavy, "what do you want? To apologize? Fine, I accept your apology." I made to walk past him to the checkout.

He sidestepped and blocked my exit. "Robin. We both know it's not as simple as that, and I owe you an explanation. You've never left my mind," he added in a near whisper.

The butterflies flapped their wings in my stomach at his tone. *What could he possibly mean? He was thinking of me, all this time?* I searched his face for guile and found only sincerity, and maybe something else, but at the time, the last thing I wanted to feel about Marcus was hopeful.

"Fine. You can walk me home, tell me all about it on the way," I said in my haughtiest, most insulated voice.

"Great," he smiled.

I don't know why he smiled, I didn't say I was going to let him come up, or even do anything other than kick him in the pants once we reached my building. I paid for my items and Marcus took the bag, and my yoga mat, which I handed to him suspiciously, and followed me out of the store. It wasn't until we reached the corner that I realized that he hadn't purchased anything and asked him about it.

"I saw you on the sidewalk, I followed you in there," he said with a shy smile. "Took me twenty minutes to work up the nerve to speak to you."

I bit my lip at that. "Do you live around here?" I puzzled, wondering why I hadn't seen him before and not wanting to unpack why he needed nerve to speak to me.

"I just moved here from Mayfair. It was too stuffy over there."

He wasn't terribly wrong about that, though Mayfair bordered Soho and I loved Soho. "Well, it's not really any hipper over here, but welcome to the neighborhood," I said with a smile and began peppering him with questions about his life. He told me he was a solicitor working for one of the 'magic circle' firms, which didn't surprise me knowing his father was a partner there, that he had one flatmate, and that he still played rugby and football whenever he could. That last part reminded me of his thugs and my spirits fell. I really hated that part of my childhood, unsurprisingly. Being bullied can make you stronger, if you survive it, but no one ever says they liked it, or would recommend it for character development.

We turned onto my street as Marcus sensed the shift in my mood (he became so good at reading me). "I don't hang out with those guys anymore," he said quietly. "I see Hector here, and Gareth from time to time, but he's in Edinburgh."

I nodded and bit the inside of my cheek. "Well, this is me," I stopped in front of my four-story brick building, in the middle of the row of expensive looking brick buildings on the sunny-side of the street. It was posh, yes, but so was I, and I could afford it (with my parents' help). "Nice chatting with you Marcus. See you around, probably," I shrugged with as much nonchalance as I could muster while gesturing for my bags.

"Which floor?" He asked looking up.

"Top."

"I'll carry these up for you," he said, not as an offer.

"Marcus," I began, "you can't be serious. We're not friends."

Marcus winced. "I want to be," he said quietly, looking at me.

And so it began. I let him in, and hoped he wasn't a vampire. Gertie was instantly entranced, and furious with me that I gave her no notice, as if she would have put on a ball gown or something. I showed him around our flat, starting with the kitchen, skipping Gertie's room, and ending with him in the middle of my bedroom. His eyes flitted around like birds, looking everywhere but at the double bed.

"This is nice," he nodded. "Gertie seems nice. You met her at uni?"

"Yes, she and another girl were my flatmates for two years," I looked in my mirror and nearly fainted. "I need a shower," I said trying to keep the horror out of my voice and his eyes from my person. I ushered him out of my room and dashed into my small en-suite bathroom.

Marcus was sitting in the living room with Gertie when I came out. He stood and looked me over, that something behind his eyes. I had kept him waiting, but not on purpose, I really couldn't decide on what to wear and felt like a kid again. I don't know why I wanted to look good for him, besides he'd just seen me looking like a sweaty pig, and he was not there to do anything other than make reparations, but still, I couldn't help myself. I had finally decided on lightweight pants and a linen button-down with loafers. I styled my hair using product and my hair dryer, which I'm sure Gertie heard and snickered at, wanting to make the waves perfect and nonchalant, just like Troye Sivan's.

"What do you feel like eating?" He asked me with a smile.

I shrugged. "There's a sushi place around the corner, or we could do pizza. I'm not picky."

Gertie snorted and I glared at her.

Marcus looked at her with a smile and then back at me. "You lived on those meal replacement bars for the whole of my time in secondary. I began to believe he didn't eat real food," he grinned at Gertie conspiratorially and then back at me.

I felt my knees weaken at that smile. *Did he just say that he noticed what I ate every day?* I thought it was just me watching him, practically keeping a diary of what he consumed. He forbade me from looking at him, but he didn't say anything about his plate. Mondays he ate Sunday's leftover pot roast, Tuesdays were three sandwiches and a packet of crisps, Wednesdays was whatever the cafeteria was serving, and Thursdays and Fridays alternated between some sort of pasta dish or soup.

I blushed and looked away, afraid I was being transparent. "I've gotten a lot better since then."

"I was just teasing, Robby," he said gently, the familiar of my name rolling off his tongue and into my soul with a shiver. "We'll eat wherever you want. Let's go," he held his hand out to the door and looked at Gertie. "Nice to meet you."

"Likewise," she stood and smiled. I knew from her expression that she would want every last detail about Marcus when I returned.

We went for sushi; somehow raw fish was acceptable to my palate but not flan and the like. We split a bowl of noodles and an assortment of sushi. I kept finding Marcus' eyes on me, and wondered if he was thinking about the porn. I didn't dare allow myself to consider that he might have been thinking about us. It felt weird, being 'normal' with him, when we really never had much conversation before. He had always been so closed off, aloof, you might say if you were a writer of generic fiction. I waited, as patiently terrified as I had been when we were teens.

He put his chopsticks down and blew out a breath. "It's really good to see you Robin, and looking so well. Especially since every other time I had seen you I was doing or saying something horrible to you," he breathed. "And what you were going through," he trailed off. Oh god did I see tears? I suddenly felt as though I should be the one to make him feel better.

"It's okay Marcus," I said, wanting to pat his hand. "Bygones. Besides, you couldn't have known at the time how fucked up I was after Vas. It wasn't your fault."

"Bullshit," he said harshly. "I blame myself for you ever getting involved with that man," he said, his face anguished. "If I had just been able to treat you with the kindness and respect you deserved, then you would never have thought it was okay for him to mistreat you. *Use* you."

I sat back in the booth then. It felt like the oxygen was being sucked from the room and I almost began gasping, because he wasn't wrong.

"It took years of therapy for me to understand that, and so many other things about myself," Marcus continued and leaned forward. "I want a second chance Robin. You have every right to deny me one, but I hope you won't."

I don't know why I never had that breakthrough in therapy myself. Oh, I know, it was because I was so caught up in Vas and what he'd done, and that I'd still felt some need to protect Marcus, that I'd never even brought him up. I closed my eyes with the sudden weight of realization. I needed Miranda or T., or both, but more importantly I needed air, immediately. I got up and ran, the ringing in my ears so loud I couldn't hear him calling after me.

I ran all the way to Kensington and into the first bar I saw. I took out my phone and called T. who came immediately, god love him. I had ordered a vodka but didn't touch it. He paid for it and ushered me out. I tried to tell him why, but the words wouldn't come, I couldn't bring myself to speak Marcus' sins out loud. He asked for my phone so he could call Miranda and walked with me to her office.

"I'll wait for you," he said. "You've been so doing well, I'm so proud of you. I don't know what's going to come out in your session, but we should go to a meeting after."

I nodded. "Text me which one and I'll meet you there. I don't want to disrupt your day."

"Your sobriety is more important to me. I'll wait," he said and hugged me.

I hugged him tightly and sobbed.

45

Talk Me Down

I RESUMED MY DAILY MEETINGS and twice weekly therapy, where Miranda told me how proud she was of me for not drinking that vodka, discussing, in-depth, the skills that it took for me to have resisted, and reinforcing that my therapy was working. I stayed with my parents for the duration, hitching a ride to work with my dad (did I mention I worked for his company?). I was determined to get through this without rehab, and I had Miranda echoing that. We both agreed that this was just a blip and I had responded to the triggers with tremendous strength.

My mum fussed over me and I let her. I didn't realize how much I missed her rubbing my back while we watched telly or while I surfed my phone. She made all my favorite foods and did my laundry, telling me how proud she was that I was being strong and doing the right thing, and not asking anything about why. I hung out with George and helped him with his homework just like in the old days. He told me about his girlfriend and what he was interested in. God he was so young, it made me nostalgic and to be honest, it also made me cut my stay short.

Gertie had been beside herself with worry. I had only texted that I was okay, that I was with my parents trying to get my headspace clear and would catch her up when I was better.

She jumped on me when I came through with my small bag, covering my face with kisses. "Christ Robby! I'm so glad to see you!" She stood back and looked me over. "You look okay on the outside, how is it in there?" She tapped my forehead, and then followed me to my room.

"Much better, sorry for the scare," I smiled, pleased with her concern, and put my bag on my bed. "I didn't drink or anything," I added.

She sat and pulled me down next to her. "You're so strong Robby, you've come so far," she said soothingly. "Are you okay enough to tell me what happened? Marcus has been here nearly every day looking for you. I didn't tell him where you were, but he seemed so worried."

I winced and my heart thudded at that. I so wanted to tell her everything, like I had with Miranda, but unlike her, there's no way Gertie could remain impartial, and I needed her to like Marcus, because I had decided to. "Seeing Marcus," I began, "dredged up all kinds of old memories, of being bullied, and then of Vas. I had to see Miranda like two, three times a week, and I went to so many meetings I'm still sweating out the caffeine," I grinned.

"Oh darling," she said and hugged me. "I'm so sorry, but I'm so glad you did the right thing and that there's this great community of people who are always there for you. I hope you know that I'm part of that community as well. I love you Robin," she kissed my neck.

"I know that, and I treasure you," I squeezed her and pulled back to look at her. "I just needed to work through some shit before burdening you with me again. I don't want to lose you like I lost Dee," I said, my voice breaking on her name.

"You're not a burden, and I'll never abandon you," she said firmly and took my face in her hands. "I hope Dee realizes someday how big the hole in her life must be without you, because I was so lost these few weeks without you by my side."

The tears flooded down my face at that, and they flooded down hers as we gripped each other for what seemed like hours. Eventually, she pulled away, wiping her face on her shirt and then wiped mine with it and we laughed.

"I'm gonna make you your favorite noodles, with shrimp, and we're going to watch silly movies for the rest of the night. Unless you want to go to a meeting, in which case I can go with you," she smiled.

"Sounds amazing. I love you Gertie," I kissed her and stood. "I'm gonna make tea, would you like a cup?"

"Yes please," she followed me into the kitchen. I saw a scrap of blue paper with a phone number scribbled on it under the magnet on the fridge that said 'worry is like a rocking chair; it will give you something to do but it won't get you anywhere.'

Gertie followed my eyes. "Marcus left that for you. Do you want me to throw it away?" She asked hesitantly.

I shook my head and looked at my watch. I put the kettle on, set out the tea and mugs and took the paper with me into my bedroom. I closed the door and sat on the bed with my phone in one hand and the paper in the other. I turned on my Bluetooth speaker and put on *Breathe* by Telepopmusik, ran my thumb across the ink, and swiped into my phone.

"Hello this is Marcus," he answered in his smooth, deep voice, a voice that made my ear tingle.

"Hello Marcus," I said quietly.

"Robin," he recognized my voice instantly. "Jesus, how are you? I've been so worried. Gertie said she hadn't heard from you, I called all the hospitals," he trailed off. "I wanted to call your parents or go by but I didn't dare. Did you ever tell them about me?" He asked cautiously.

"No, Marcus. I never told *anyone* about you. Not even my therapist, until three weeks ago that is," I chuckled humorlessly and swallowed. "You made me promise, and for some reason I felt like I needed to keep that promise."

I heard Marcus exhale. "Can I see you?"

I closed my eyes, thinking of what Miranda said to me. "Sure, when?"

"Today, tonight, now. Whenever you have time," he said, relief in his voice.

"Come for dinner then, Gertie's making my favorite dish."

I felt his reluctance through the phone, I knew he wanted to be alone with me, to maybe crush me with more of his confessions, inadvertently of course, but I wanted a buffer, so I waited silently for his response.

"Okay, I'll see you in an hour." The line went dead.

I had my tea, took a shower, taking care again with my appearance, and sat with Gertie while she cooked. "If I asked you to leave after dinner, would that be okay?" I asked looking at the dregs of my tea. "Would you have a place to go?"

She stopped mincing the garlic and looked at me. "You think it's smart to be alone with him?"

"I won't know until he's here, which is why I'm asking 'if,'" I said holding her gaze. "I'm hoping the tools Miranda gave me will see me through, but please know that I won't ask you to leave if I have even an inkling of doubt, and I know where every meeting is between now and two AM, and after that there's my sponsor who said I can call him whenever. Don't worry love, I've thought of everything," I smiled gently, hoping that I truly had.

She returned the smile and exhaled. "Okay, sure I can go to Peter's or Lola's," she started mincing again and stopped. "Is Marcus gay?" She looked at me.

"No," I answered wryly. "He had a million girlfriends, he was the star athlete in secondary, mostly rugby, but that man could play anything and make it look easy."

Gertie made a sound of appreciation and resumed with the knife. The buzzer rang, causing me to jump with a small squeal.

Gertie threw her head back and laughed. "You sounded like a mouse!"

"Sod off," I got up and buzzed Marcus in, leaving the door ajar as I heard his footsteps on the stairs. He appeared from around the railing, looking gorgeous in jeans and a linen shirt, the sleeves cuffed, and his Tag Hauer watch gleaming in the light. He had a bottle of wine in one hand and bouquet of flowers in the other. He saw my eyes go to the bottle and suddenly stopped his face going white.

"Oh shit," he exclaimed, "I forgot, I'm so sorry. Force of habit."

I smiled, "It's okay, I can be around it, I'm not a fiend," I added with an edge.

"No, of course you're not, I didn't mean it like that," Marcus looked away. "Fuck, I keep stepping in it."

"Marcus, don't worry," I stressed, "come in," I stood aside as he walked through. I watched him kiss Gertie's cheek, so smoothly flirty, I wondered briefly just how much time they had spent together in the name of worry over me. She took the flowers and looked askance at the wine and then at me.

"Open it. You guys can have wine, people can drink in front of me, I don't care," I shrugged, and I meant it, wine was never my thing, and Gertie knew that.

Gertie handed Marcus the opener and he had the bottle open in seconds, pouring into the glasses I produced from the cabinet. Gertie put the flowers on the table set for three and clinked her glass to my club soda and his wine.

"Cheers," we said in near unison.

Marcus sat at the island talking with us as Gertie and I put the finishing touches on dinner.

"What do you do for work Gertie?" He asked, watching her. I wondered if he thought she was pretty.

"I'm an editor at a small publishing company. My focus is memoirs and chick-lit," She added the shrimp to the bowl of noodles and stirred.

"Oh, that sounds a whole a lot better than reading legal rulings and contracts all day," he smiled. "You publish anything I've heard of?"

"I doubt it." She laughed and brought the bowl to the table. "Dinner is served."

We ate and talked and laughed about nothing, pop culture mostly. What movies we'd seen, what music we liked, what books we had read. Gertie had us beat there, she read a book a night practically, staying on top of what was hot in literature. I discovered Marcus had the most incredible laugh, and I realized I never really heard him laugh before. I watched them, I could tell Gertie was enamored, and I didn't blame her, so was I. He was so much better looking than any guy I had ever been with, even Vas, who really did have a weak chin. Marcus was even better looking than he was ten years ago, one of those guys who just kept improving with age like fine wine, the kind of wine I could absolutely make my thing, and then I shook my head, *what a bloody idiot.* He and I did gay things, but looking at him, there was no way he was gay, it was just experimentation on his part.

Speaking of wine, he poured himself another glass and emptied the bottle into Gertie's. Sometimes it bothered me that I couldn't drink, because it looked like fun (in moderation), but after a few years with Marcus, I discovered that being happy and feeling secure was all I needed, and I stopped feeling like I was missing out.

"What's your favorite movie Robin," Marcus looked at me, interrupting my thoughts and continuing our discussion.

"*Call Me by Your Name*," I said holding his gaze. "I always thought there was something so real about that story, so much so I could get past Armie Hammer's flat delivery. Though maybe his performance was deliberate," I mused, "I mean his character chose to be hetero in the end so, naturally, lacked luster."

"Oh, come on Robby," Gertie chided, "Not all hetero guys are boring and flat," she laughed and looked at Marcus.

"I've never seen that one," he said looking at me, "I'll have to check it out."

"You probably won't like it, it's okay," I replied, "you don't need to watch it, it's not the only movie I loved. I also love *The Grand Budapest Hotel*, and anything by Wes Anderson."

"Oh, I loved that movie!" Marcus said with a laugh. "I got yelled at by some uptight German guy on a plane home from skiing for laughing too loud at that one. There was a baby crying two rows up but my laugh bugged him," Marcus shook his head with a grin, while I wanted to punch that German guy. The thought of someone wanting to stifle Marcus' beautiful laugh enraged me. I took another bite, suddenly overwhelmed by the emotions I was feeling.

We finished eating and I cleared the table as Marcus and Gertie finished their wine at my insistence. I loaded the dishwasher and left the pans soaking as Gertie came in with the empty wine glasses.

She rubbed my back and smiled at me. "You want me to go?"

I nodded and she left the kitchen with her phone.

She came out of her room with a bag on her shoulder, as Marcus and I were settling into the low-lit living room with tea. "I'm off to Lola's, call me if you need anything," she said. We stood and hugged her goodbye, listening to the door close behind her. We stood awkwardly looking at each other until I sat and Marcus followed suit.

"Well, I guess if there's anything else you want to say or talk about, now is as good a time as any. I can handle it, I won't run, I don't think," I added with a small smile.

Marcus looked nervous, and fidgeted with his teacup. "Well, first, how are you, really?" He asked looking at me.

"I'm fine," I smiled, "I wasn't for a few years, and really had to work at my sobriety and my mental health, but I graduated university near the top of my class, I have a great job, great friends. I hadn't needed meetings or regular therapy anymore, until you came along," I frowned and looked at my tea. "You blindsided me with your insight. Because the things you did to me, well, it never occurred to me that you could have been responsible for anything beyond secondary," I whispered and looked back at him. His face was fallen, and I paused. "I spent the last three weeks working through a lot of shit, and I'm not done yet, by any stretch of the imagination, but Marcus, I want you to know that you weren't responsible for everything, I had so much more going on than just you. I have to accept responsibility for my actions. No one put a gun to my head. I forgive you, and want you to walk through that door full of relief, knowing that." I gestured down the hall with my chin.

Marcus looked away and then scrubbed his face with both hands before nodding slowly and returning his gaze to mine. "Thank you. I am just so sorry, and I wish I had a time machine, and a therapist back then," he said with a twist to his mouth. He took a sip of tea and stood suddenly. He walked to the bookcase and picked up a heart-shaped rock I found on the beach in Barcelona, turning it over and over in his hand. "Therapy is so underrated, and such a dirty word to so many, including my family," he looked back at me. "Did you seek it out, or did someone make you go?"

"A little bit of both," I said wryly. "Mostly it was the bartenders who got sick of seeing me coming with my same shit every fucking day."

He winced at that. "They can only do so much," he said with a small laugh. "Therapists give you tools, proper outlets for pain, not just the means to avoid and numb."

"How about you then? Did you seek it out or?" I trailed off.

"I was told I had 'difficulty communicating' and 'anger issues,'" he put the rock down. "You repress enough and that shit's gonna blow like a pressure cooker. I was so unhappy, that's why I was so good at rugby, I mean I still got all my teeth," he flashed me a humorless smile. "No one could take me down. Except you," he added in a whisper, in fact it was so quiet I thought I heard him say 'Hugh' and assumed he was talking about someone he played rugby with. "I beat a guy up, *badly*, in Dublin. It was after I saw you and said those awful things to you, I didn't mean them Robin," he said earnestly. "They thought I attacked him randomly, but I did it because he was harassing a little guy for being gay," he exhaled in dismay. "I beat someone within an inch of his life for doing exactly what I, and all my mates, did to you for years. I felt like I was looking in a mirror, beating myself. Isn't that strange?"

I kept my mouth shut, figuring he wasn't looking for a response.

He picked up a picture of me and Gertie, with Lola, Peter, and some guy I slept with a few times. We all had our arms around each other, and I only kept the picture because it was so good of the four of us, and would have cropped the guy out if he'd been on the end.

"You seeing anyone?" He asked quietly, putting the picture down.

I was startled by the change of subject and shook my head. "No, not for ages. You?" I managed to eke out, not wanting him to say yes.

"No," he sighed and turned back to me. "I was really fucked up at Trinity. To be honest, I haven't been in a relationship since I last saw you, and before then it wasn't ever a real thing with anyone," he looked around the room. "I don't suppose you have anything else to drink? I'm sorry for asking," he made a face.

"You should learn to express your emotions and words without self-medicating," I said like a rehab counselor and stood with a gentle smile. "There's wine in the fridge. I told you, I'm not a freak about it usually, just when gorgeous ballers come around to upend my world." I turned to the kitchen when I felt Marcus' hand on my wrist. What happened next, happened in a flash and in slow motion. He pulled me to him as though we had been dancing and he had just spun me away before returning me to his arms. I felt like that picture of Princess Di dancing with John Travolta. He hugged me tightly, and my arms went around his waist. I heard his heart pounding wildly, or maybe it was mine, but being there in his arms felt so right, even as I wondered what the hell I was doing in them.

"Robby," was all he said and then he kissed me, his mouth, his lips on mine, and then on my neck and then back on my lips.

We kissed for what felt like hours, my lips raw from his stubble, as we denied ourselves progress, or rather he did, it seemed as though he was holding back. I put my shaky fingers on his buttons and began undoing them. I got to the last one and he stilled my hand.

"I just want to hold you tonight," he whispered. "Okay?"

I stepped back slightly, and part of my brain, the rational part, heard that as romantic as he meant it, but the irrational, louder, part of my brain took it as rejection, taking the shame of my past and putting it in his words. "Maybe you should just go. This is a bad idea, I mean, what the fuck are we even doing?" I said as I ran through the list of AA meetings in my head.

"No Robby, that's not what I meant at all," he took my face in his hands, willing me to look at him. "I want your naked skin against mine, to cherish you as I never allowed myself to do in the past."

I looked at his mouth, as though he were speaking a foreign language. Did he just say *cherish* me? I suddenly thought of Madonna and her mermen frolicking in the surf all while that one button on her dress did its damndest not to fly off from her gigantic, heaving bosom. That, presumably, steel-reinforced button deserved an award. I giggled, and then that giggle turned into full-on hysterical laughter, with me trying to explain between breaths what I found so funny, as Marcus looked at me worriedly. I wiped my eyes and gave up, grabbing his hand and leading him to my bedroom.

We undressed each other, Marcus stilling my hand as I reached for the waistband of his underwear. "No Robin, I mean it. I only want to hold you tonight," he said firmly and kissed away my complaints, running his hands down my back before turning me to the bed and laying down beside me.

It was nearly impossible to sleep, especially with his erection pressing against my ass cheek, but he wouldn't let me touch him. He kissed my neck, ran his fingers through my hair, and kept my arms pinned, until I gave up. My mind was racing with all kinds of thoughts (most of them horny), until I finally surrendered to the gloriousness of just being in his arms. Held and needed, *cherished*, I thought with a smile before falling asleep.

46

Bombers Fly
at Zero Feet

WE DIDN'T HAVE SEX, proper sex, for two more weeks, but we talked every day, and he took me to dinner twice the first week, kissing me passionately inside the vestibule of my building after each meal.

"Tell me about Trinity," I said over dinner the second night at a quiet and romantic restaurant with white tablecloths and candles.

He looked around the small dining room, which was quiet for a Thursday, and then back at me. "Trinity as school was fine, great, I did okay. Wasn't top of my class like some people," he winked at me, "but socially I felt a little lost. I was a big fish in a little pond in Kensington, and realized I was krill at Trinity. It was eye opening, and everything my bloody ego needed. I came home that first term, looking for you. I knew you found someone but I was hoping it had ended," he said and stared at me. "You always made me feel real, even though I hated myself after," he shook his head looking down at his plate. "That was on me, and never had to do with you, but of course I didn't have that insight then. You have no idea of how much I cared for you then do you?" He winced and put down his fork. "No, of course you don't, because I was a fucking asshole."

I sat back in my chair. *What?* "What?" I frowned. "I thought you were just using me because I was willing. Are you rewriting history?" I asked him with an edge to my voice. "You shredded my hat, wrote 'fag' on it. You *broke* my rib, you tackled me in the park," I shook my head. I wish I never asked him anything, my heart started racing with the memories and I looked at the bar behind his head.

"Robin, I'm sorry for all that, please, I'm not rewriting history, I'm telling you I know I was an asshole. I was fucked up and couldn't admit my feelings about anything to anyone, least of all you. I did all those things because I felt you slipping away from me, and I didn't know how to tell you how I felt. That you were with him," he blew out a breath, nearly extinguishing the candle on our table, "brought me to my knees. I was so mad I couldn't see straight. I blamed you for the way I felt, and that was wrong, so, so wrong. I saw you go into the hotel with him. That's why I let them hurt you, why I kicked you," he winced, "I followed you and I wish I hadn't for so many reasons, that I hurt you was the main one," he looked out the door of the restaurant. "When he punched me, I wished he had beaten me. Any pain was better than the pain I felt seeing you with your arms around him. Him letting you, in broad daylight, without a care in the world who saw," he wiped his hand over his face. "I'm sorry, I need the bathroom."

I watched him push away from the table and disappear. I stared at his wine and felt a thirst so powerful I almost fell out of my chair. I picked up the glass and my hand shook so much I nearly spilled the entire thing, before putting it back down untouched, only spilling a drop, instead of a crime-scene's worth of red on the tablecloth. He had dropped another couple of bombs on me, and I wasn't sure I could hold it together.

I watched him warily as he came back to the table, a tiny ringing in my ears. He sat down and looked at me just as warily.

"I'm sorry," he shook his head. "I hope we get to a point someday when I'm no longer apologizing all the time," he twisted his mouth.

"It's okay," I covered his hand with mine, taking a deep calming breath, channeling Miranda as best I could. "You and I have a more complicated history than most, but we're older now, with years of therapy under our belts, and as such we should be able to be honest with each other, and you're telling me things the fifteen-year-old in me is thrilled to hear. It's overwhelming, but good, I promise."

He furrowed his brow and swallowed. "I'm glad to hear that, but it is so hard reliving that seventeen and eighteen-year-old me. I hated myself then, and I hate looking back at that pathetic beast."

I laughed and picked up my fork. "Well I hate my seventeen through twenty-one-year-old self, so don't feel bad. We're not kids anymore, and thankfully, won't ever be again." I took a bite of my food.

He picked up his fork and took a bite of his chicken. "Good point," he said and smiled lightly. "I can't wait to kiss you later. You have the most beautiful, soft lips," he said looking at my mouth, "and I have so much lost time to make up for."

I licked my lip and took another bite of my dinner. I couldn't wait for Marcus to kiss me, though I couldn't help but wonder what he had in mind, where it was all going, and hoped he wasn't just working through his guilt.

47

What, What, What?

GERTIE WAS READING in the living room when I came home carrying my leftovers. I wasn't sure they were still any good after sitting on my lap for hours. Marcus and I had made out for what seemed like an eternity in his car, before I walked straight to a meeting after his taillights disappeared around the corner.

"Where have you been?" She asked with a smile and looked at the container in my hand. "Were you on a date?"

I had made sure Marcus was gone before she came back on Sunday telling her we had a real heart-to-heart and then he left, everything mended. She was so relieved, and then asked if that meant he'd be joining our friend group, a hopeful note in her voice. I had shrugged at the time, truly not knowing the answer to that, but now I felt as though could say more.

"Yes, as a matter of fact I was," I said and flounced theatrically into the kitchen to put my leftovers in the fridge.

Gertie's laugh followed me. "With whom?" She asked excitedly. "Where did you meet him? Please don't say Grindr."

I wrinkled my nose and went into the living room. "No, I would never, though I'm not sure if it's any worse than hooking up at a club," I added with a grin.

She laughed. "So, who is he?"

"Marcus," I bit my lip. "Turns out he is a tiny bit gay," I squealed and jumped.

Gertie's mouth dropped open. "No way! Oh my god, that man's a fucking dreamboat, and he's a solicitor. Christ what a catch," she shook her head, and stood. "I'm super jealous, but so happy for you. You deserve it for fuck's sake."

I hugged her tightly.

"When did all this happen? And how? Who made the first move? Tell me everything," she sprayed me with questions like a machine gun.

"I didn't tell you the whole truth about Saturday. After you left, he said he always liked me, and then he panicked and asked for more booze, and when I got up to get him some he pulled me into his arms and kissed me. Right there," I pointed to the spot behind the couch. "He spent the night, but we didn't have sex. We still haven't," I said with a wistful note. I wasn't sure when we would. He kept me at arm's length though I knew he wanted to too, so it wasn't from lack of desire.

"Wow," she breathed. "How do you sleep in the same bed and not do it?" She pondered looking around the room.

"With great difficulty," I said dramatically, "but I really can't kiss and tell with him. Sorry to leave you hanging, but I have always pined for that man, so I don't want to fuck it up, or jinx anything," I added earnestly.

She searched my face and grabbed my hand. "I don't want to either. I'm so happy for you. Now let's put on a movie and strategize him introducing me to his single friends."

48

The One with
All the Sex

MARCUS SPENT THE NIGHT Friday. Gertie went to see Kayla in Cornwall, so we had the place to ourselves. We ate curry takeaway, and then made out on the couch like teenagers; Marcus' lips buttery and spicy, his tongue tasting like garlic and heaven.

"I'm just gonna hold you again tonight Robby," he whispered against my lips. "I want to do this right with you this time."

My cock screamed in my underwear (I swear that's not an exaggeration), and I pulled back to look at him. His gorgeous, indescribable eyes were dark in the low light. "Doing me will be doing it right, I promise."

Marcus laughed lightly. "I won't be 'doing you' ever," he made a face, "but I do want to feel your smooth skin against mine again, so let's go to your room." He stood and pulled me to him for a brief kiss and then led me through the door.

I kissed him lingeringly as we undressed each other, Marcus letting me take off his underwear as he took off mine (that was promising), and then climbed under the covers. His body was beautiful, firm but not bulging with muscle, and he had a light dusting of chest hair over not-yet tan skin. I wanted him desperately and he wanted me just as badly, his erection was straining away from his body in search of me, but he wouldn't let me touch it, and for fuck's sake that's all I wanted to do. It was bigger than it was in secondary, which I couldn't believe possible (mine had grown too in case you were wondering), and utterly beautiful. He rolled me on my side and spooned himself around me, trapping my arms in front of me so I couldn't touch him just like before. His cock, pressed against my ass, was warm and as hard as an anvil. I wiggled, of course I wiggled, trying to get it between my cheeks, knowing if I got the tip pressed against my hole he would lose his willpower and fuck me like I wanted him to.

He made a quelling sound and ran his hand down my body and then around front as he kissed my neck. He touched me and I can't believe it was for the first time, after how many times I had touched him. He stroked me, and then he spit in his hand and stroked me some more, pressing himself rhythmically against my bottom as he did, until I came, and I came so hard, crying out his name, that I didn't notice right away that my ass cheek was wet and Marcus was breathing as heavy as I was. I turned my head to kiss him, and then reached for the tissues. It wasn't proper sex, but I felt satiated, and something else I'd never felt before.

"Now will you go to sleep?" He asked in a breathless, but sardonic voice.

I rolled to face him with a smile and put my arms around his neck, kissing him thoroughly. "Yes. For a little while anyway."

He kissed my neck with a chuckle and spooned his body around mine. I fell asleep wondering what he was thinking about.

I woke in the night, maybe it was the playlist ending, maybe it was traffic outside, or maybe it was because I felt like I was having a fever dream, and when I looked in the bed next to me I felt certain it was the latter. Marcus Willoughby, *rugby god* of secondary, was sleeping in bed next to me. I had to be dreaming. I touched him to be sure, and he was warm, and real, so I lifted the covers and snuck a peek at his cock. I made a small sound of delight when I saw it was half awake, and, while it could have been a trick of the very dim light, it seemed to be moving toward me, rolling itself awake to stare back at me with its one beautiful slit of an eye. I ducked under to join it, not wanting to wake Marcus with the cool air, and placed a gentle kiss on its head. It moved encouragingly, so I gave it a lick, and then well, you can just imagine what I did next, I'm certain I don't have to spell it out for you. What I will tell you is that he tasted as glorious as I remembered, and his moans were music to my ears.

"Jesus Robby, what time is it?" He panted when I emerged with a grin.

"Who cares, it's Saturday. Go back to sleep, I was just having a word with your little friend. He had quite a bit to say, which was surprising after what he said all over my ass earlier."

Marcus pressed his head back into the pillow and laughed. God how I loved that sound. I snuggled up next to him and listened to his heartbeat under my ear.

"You are so beautiful Robin. Your face, your body, your spirit. You're an angel," he said quietly, his voice a rumble under my ear.

He said that to me so many times over the years that I believed it, and I became one, or rather, I was one all along. I looked up at him and kissed his waiting mouth.

* * *

I went to Marcus' rugby match in the morning, and I have to say it felt weird to able to cheer him on openly, his eyes searching for mine after a big play or when he'd score, smiling broadly at me on my feet cheering madly. I had occasionally gone to his rugby and football matches in secondary and watched from a hidden spot, marveling at his body, feeling a thrill thinking about our secret. I would look at the throngs of students, see his girlfriend surrounded by her ladies-in-waiting, and wonder if he loved her mouth as much as he loved mine. *Clearly not*, I thought now, because I remembered when she would stand and cheer after he made a goal, he never searched for her in the stands, he looked for me in the shadows.

Marcus and I had dinner on Tuesday and Wednesday of the following week, him leaving me in my vestibule or kissing me in his fancy sports car, firm in his refusal to come up and spend the night. I was beginning to think we'd never have sex, that maybe there was something wrong with him, and he'd developed some kind of weird kink in only getting off, by not getting off. Thankfully, all my worries were assuaged after dinner on Friday, when Marcus spent the night and we made love. It was perfect, and tender, and passionate, and the best sex I had ever had. Marcus said so too, clutching me tightly to him, kissing my face, my neck, my chest.

"I knew it would be like this with you," he whispered. "I have so desperately wanted you since our first time, but in a way, I'm glad it never happened until now, because I know I would have just fucked it up."

I just breathed in his scent, and listened to his pulse under my ear. I felt so safe, so contented, I never wanted the night to end. I smoothed my fingers over his chest, the light dusting of hair coarse under my fingertips. He was so perfectly formed, and not in a way that required hours every day at the gym, it almost wasn't fair to the rest of the men in the world. "I was so mad at you after you took my virginity, I doubt I would have let you until now," I said in as light a tone as I could manage. I don't know why I felt the need to ruin the moment by picking at that scab, but in my defense, he brought it up.

He squeezed me as I rolled to his side. "It was my first time too, with a guy I mean, and I felt such love for you then and hated myself after for it," I felt him shake his head. "I was so angry at my weakness, *perceived* weakness," he clarified emphatically, "and so busy being angry in general that it was years before I could step outside of myself long enough to realize how *awfully* I had treated you. It's why I just wanted to hold you the past weekends," he kissed the side of my head. "I should have just held you again tonight, but of course I wanted you too badly."

I furrowed my brow. All the words he said after telling me that he loved me back then took minutes to reach my brain. *He loved me then?* I propped myself up on my elbow. "Would you please stop bombing me?" I left the bed and went into the bathroom.

"Robby wait," he called after me.

I let the water get really cold and splashed my face repeatedly to stave off the anxiety I felt gathering around my edges, and then filled the cup that was on the counter. What would I have done differently if I had known any of this back then? Would I have looked twice at Vas if I had known I had *Marcus'* love?

There was a light knock at the door before Marcus just opened it, standing there like Michelangelo's David, but with a bigger cock. (Sorry, I always noticed things like that).

"You okay?" He asked cautiously, taking in my dripping face, and looking at my cock. (Apparently, he always noticed things like that too).

"I will be," I grabbed the towel and swiped my face before kissing him. "Part of me wishes I knew all of this back then," I searched his face. "But, if you had ever been able to admit any of it to me, I know that it would have had to be a secret from everyone, and would have imploded, if we were lucky, and exploded horribly and publicly if we weren't." I put my arms around his neck. "I know we need to talk all this through, but maybe not right away. I need my footing with you, before I can have my world shaken."

He nodded with a small smile and pressed his body against mine.

✳ ✳ ✳

He ended up staying the weekend, neither of us ready to part. We talked about everything except us, sticking to the time period after secondary, after Vas. He told me he dated women, but fucked a few guys secretly during uni, always feeling awful and angry after. It wasn't until therapy that he could admit that he was bi, or maybe even just gay.

"They all looked like you, but of course didn't," he rolled me onto my back and kissed me so I couldn't complain, or leave, or do anything but let lust rule my brain. "You are the most beautiful man I have ever seen," he kissed his way down my fluttering stomach, breathing deeply through his nose as he reached where my bush should have been. Old habits die hard and I always liked it waxed and smooth. His mouth was magic, I mean he was so unbelievably good for a top, I couldn't believe my luck. He just kept getting better and better in my mind and then naturally, I began to worry. He felt so far away from me all of a sudden and I nudged him back up wanting his skin on mine. He covered my body with his and we kissed for days, or minutes, I lost track of all time and space as I always did when his lips touched mine.

* * *

We did it a million times, a million different ways over the next few weeks. I couldn't get enough of him, pouncing on him the minute he walked through the door after work, him barely able to put down his bag before returning my kisses with a smiling mouth. Sometimes Gertie was there and would say hello and just shake her head as we made our way past the living room and into my bedroom, Marcus kicking the door closed with his heel.

"I'm going to absolutely die if you don't put your fantastic cock inside me this instant," I said nearly every day.

"Can I get my pants off first?" Marcus would ask. "And maybe my shirt, because I do love the feeling of your smooth skin on mine."

"Christ, if you insist," I would respond with mock exasperated sigh.

Sometimes he used spit, because I couldn't wait, and sometimes he used lube. Both felt amazing, because it was only him that I was interested in, whatever the delivery method was, didn't matter.

Then we would lay there after and he would tell me about his day and listen to me about mine.

"I have to go to Belfast next week," he said quietly one night, tracing his finger on my bicep.

"Oh, when do you leave and will you be back by Friday?"

"I leave Sunday and return in two weeks, if I'm lucky."

I stopped rubbing his shin with my foot. "What?" I sat up on my elbow with a frown. My new routine was being disrupted and I didn't like it.

"Big project for my team and I'm still low man on the totem pole, and will be for years. You know my firm doesn't promote quickly. I have to go," he touched my face. "I'll call you every day," he paused. "You could come for the weekend," he suggested with a small smile.

"I've never been to Belfast," I said in a speculative voice.

His smile broadened. "Come then, I'll miss you desperately otherwise."

I kissed him as he ran his fingers through my hair. "I'll get my ticket tomorrow."

49

Belfast and Ballyhoo

THE WEEK DRAGGED, and I had to remember how to fill my nights. Marcus and I had only been dating for about a month, but it seemed like we always had been together so it took me a minute. He was working long days in Belfast, often not free to talk until after ten and he was so tired I felt bad keeping him up, so our conversations were brief. Gertie and I cuddled on the couch and watched the telly two of the nights. I did yoga and went to a meeting on the others until finally, I was getting off a plane in the mid-July "heat" of Belfast (if one considered 15°C hot) and into a taxi on Friday at five.

I went straight to the hotel and got a key to Marcus' room from the front desk. I took a quick shower after texting him I was there, and waited for him in the lobby with a bottle of water, dressed in mauve linen pants, a black cashmere t-shirt, and white trainers. I was in head-to-toe Burberry, an outfit I bought just for the trip, and I was feeling as good as I looked.

Marcus came through the glass doors with two men and a woman, and I stood with the biggest smile on my face because he looked so gorgeous in his suit, I was guessing it was an Alexander McQueen from the pagoda shoulder. I knew instantly from the look in his eye that he wished I had waited for him in the room. He had said he'd figured out in therapy that he was probably gay (he was definitely gay by the way) but apparently that hadn't crossed the divide into his day-to-day life. I wanted to sit back down and give him his privacy but his coworkers had already noticed me staring at him like he was the second coming. I dialed the smile way back and closed the distance between us, holding my hand out to him platonically.

"Marcus, hi. What a wonderful stroke of luck that we happened to be in town at the same time," I smiled. "It's been ages, so great to see you."

He relaxed and nearly laughed at my off-the-cuff story but his coworkers were instantly convinced. I mean, the look of naked hunger and joy I had on my face briefly, could easily have been mistaken for the happiness one expressed when one saw a long-lost friend. I didn't have a boner or anything, and I certainly wasn't as gay appearing as I was back in school, in fact, if I've not already mentioned it, I didn't lisp, or swish anymore.

He took my hand and squeezed as he shook it and introduced me. "Ruth, Ian, and Sean, this is Robin, he and I went to secondary together back in Kensington," he gestured to each of them and I shook their hands and we said our pleasantries.

"We're having a drink in the bar, join us," Ian said looking at Marcus and then me.

I smiled politely, and waited for Marcus to decline.

"Sounds great, join us Robin," Marcus answered looking at me. My spirits fell. While waiting for him for in the lobby, I thought we'd go to dinner, but then after seeing him all I wanted to do was go up to the room and fuck his brains out, and now he wanted me to sit and make nice while they all drank in front of me. I felt a flash of irritation at Marcus and, because I could be the pettiest person in the world when I felt put out, I looked at the two guys speculatively. They were unquestionably straight, so I looked at Ruth, a woman who looked like she took no prisoners, and then I looked at her ring finger, which was, unsurprisingly, bare. I gave her my winningest smile. Women, even battle-axed faced women such as Ruth, loved me.

I sat next to her, ordered a club soda and proceeded to charm the fucking pants off her. She didn't know what hit her. She had a hard candy shell, of course she did, she worked for a fucking nightmare of a men's-club law firm and probably had to claw her way to where she was, fighting off sexual harassment the whole bloody way. She didn't want to let me in, but she couldn't help herself. I had her laughing and ignoring the rest of the table like it was just the two of us in the whole damn bar. When she smiled, she was actually pretty but of course pretty didn't get you taken seriously.

I quickly found out her favorite TV shows (police procedurals and *Dexter*, hello dark passenger), which type of music she liked (publicly classical, privately the same awesome pop music I did) and whether she preferred mountains or beach (the mountains, Ruth was not a woman who would don a swimsuit).

"What brings you to Belfast?" She asked having a sip of her white wine.

I really wished I had given some thought to the answer before being asked, because I couldn't very well say it was for Marcus' amazing cock and at the moment it was all I could think of. I caught sight of an advertisement and looked back at her. "*Game of Thrones*, actually."

"Oh I loved that show! Who was your favorite character?"

Shit. I loved sci-fi but hated fantasy, and racked my brain from all the conversations about the show I was forced to endure. "Oh, Peter Dinklage," I answered, barely able to keep the sound of joy from my voice at remembering he was in it, and how I loved him based on how funny I thought his last name was. "He's an amazing actor. I loved him in *Death at a Funeral*," I added, meaning it, because after I discovered him and his hilarious last name, I watched nearly everything he'd been in.

"I loved that movie too! American one wasn't as good but loved that he was in both," she agreed happily.

"Same," I smiled and held up my glass, finishing my club soda as they ordered another round. Marcus pushed his chair back and looked around the table. "We've got a dinner reservation, enjoy the weekend," he smiled at them. "I'll see you all on Monday, bright and early."

I stood happily and shook Ian's and Sean's hands, and bowed over Ruth's like she was the queen. "Next time I'm in London we should go to the symphony," I said to her with a wink.

She beamed and I was certain she watched me follow Marcus out.

We stopped in the lobby and Marcus scanned his eyes over me. "You're something else, Robin Trumball."

"What?" I asked with pure innocence.

He laughed and walked out the door with me in tow.

We ate at some fucking restaurant, I don't remember, because I literally shoveled the food into my mouth and waited for the check.

"You really had Ruth's ear and undivided attention," Marcus said as he ate nearly as quickly as I did.

"She's lovely," I replied.

Marcus snorted. "She's the devil, and she's our boss."

I widened my eyes. "You're mean."

Marcus threw his head back and laughed. "She's like Meryl Streep from the *Devil Wears Prada* but, scarier."

"She's smart and funny, and while she has questionable taste in TV shows, I mean you should seriously worry whether she's plotting to murder someone, she has absolutely spot on taste in music. I liked her," I shrugged.

"Well, she liked you, I've literally never seen her smile," Marcus looked at me with wonder.

I produced a hotel key card between my two fingers. "She gave me this," I said with a devilish smile.

Marcus' mouth dropped open. "She did not!"

"Of course she didn't. It's to your room. When the fuck we leaving?" I widened my eyes and put my napkin on my plate like it was a gauntlet.

Marcus laughed huskily and looked for the waiter.

We had a week to make up for so, use your imagination. I woke up to room service wheeling in a cart and a shirtless Marcus tipping generously.

I wish I could say we didn't see Ian on our way out after breakfast, both of us glowing after some amazing morning sex, but I can't. It was so awkward that Marcus didn't even say hello and we just walked quickly out the door to the waiting rental car.

"I'm going to have to find a new job," Marcus said as he put the car into first and pulled away from the curb.

"Stop it. I'll just give Ruth a call on her private mobile and straighten everything out. I'll explain that I took advantage of you because I couldn't find her room, and then I'll sing her some Harry Styles and she'll promote you to VP or whatever the big-shot lawyers call themselves."

Marcus laughed and shook his head. "Just put the Giant's Causeway into the GPS and turn your pop music on."

I squeezed his leg, kissed his neck, and we were off on our tour of the Antrim Coast. God that country was beautiful, and we had an amazing weekend, took a thousand pictures, maybe even fucked in a nook way down a bluff with the ocean crashing all around us. Everything was perfect until Sunday night, when after a delicious dinner in the Cathedral Quarter, we stopped in a pub so Marcus could have a pint. I drank my club soda and we recapped the weekend in the way lovers do before parting. I had an early morning flight out on Monday with plans to go straight to work, but wished I didn't. I was aware of a guy staring at me from across the bar, but didn't pay any mind. I suppose if I read the room, I would have figured out this was a pub that leaned more gay than straight but I was too caught up in being a lover leaving his lover for a week.

"Is that guy looking at you?" Marcus eventually said, an undercurrent to his tone. I straightened and panicked in that way I did when the man I was with dialed his testosterone way up.

"No. Who? What?" I asked, my voice shrill, looking everywhere but at that man. I prayed it wasn't someone who knew me from porn, while also knowing that was exactly why he was looking at me.

The man got up and came toward us, carrying his drink, looking buzzed but not drunk, with shrewd eyes.

"Ronnie?" He said and then smiled when I blanched. "I knew it were you. You've grown but the eyes never change, do they?" he looked conspiratorially at Marcus who was tenser than a firing pin.

"I'm sorry, my name isn't Ronnie. You have me confused with someone else," I said, repeating what I said to anyone who though they recognized me. Luckily it hadn't happened in years, as I mentioned. I smoothed my hair nervously.

"Of course your name's not Ronnie, no one in porn uses their real name," he laughed and sipped his pint.

"Porn?" I scoffed. "Now you definitely have me confused with someone else."

"If it weren't the eyes, it was the smoothing of the hair. Everyone has a tell son," he winked.

I looked at Marcus who had gone white and was looking at me with the most awful expression. "Marcus," I said in a rush as he stood and without a backwards glance left the pub. The Vegas showgirls came as I stood, wanting to punch that man. "You dirty fucking cunt!" I spat as the tears flooded my eyes. "What did you hope to gain from approaching me? You think I was gonna sign your bloody cock?" I threw money down and ran futilely after Marcus who was nowhere in sight.

I went to the room but he wasn't there. Now the showgirls were flailing their legs wildly down my cheeks. I got out my phone and called him. It went to voice-mail and I sobbed. I wanted to go in search of him, but he could be anywhere in this foreign city. I looked around the room and thought of the bar downstairs. My bowels went loose and I rushed to the bathroom.

The more time that passed, the more panicked and thirstier I became. I tried the cold-water trick, I tried laying on the floor with my feet up the wall but nothing was working. I called T.

"Hey Robby, where are you?" He asked. Somehow, he knew, or maybe they trained them to say that.

"Belfast," I sobbed.

"You're okay, you're gonna be okay," he said calmly, "I'm looking up meetings, tell me five things you see right now."

I made a sound and took a breath, "Ugly hotel artwork, a flat screen TV, a telephone, the door to the hallway, and a dustbin with a plastic bag in it."

"Good, now tell me four things you can physically feel right now."

"The carpet, the phone in my hand, the crushing pain of shame, the burning in my heart," I moaned.

"Okay Robby, you're okay, I'm right here, in your ear, and there are a zillion meetings happening right now in Belfast," he said in his soothing voice. "Where are you so I can direct you to the closest one, regardless of the format, with all the friends you need right now."

I gave him the hotel name, and he gave me an address two blocks away, and stayed on the line with me the whole way, making sure I passed the phone to someone when I arrived, mumbling that it was my sponsor, so he knew I was at a meeting and not a bar. I sat down, turned off my phone and wiped my eyes. I stayed for the duration, listening to people who had it so much worse than me. Feeling both better and worse as I sat there. I stood, briefly, when there seemed to be no one else ready to.

"Hi, I'm Rob, I'm an alcoholic, twenty-two months sober."

"Hi Rob," everyone said.

"I'm just here for the weekend, leaving tomorrow," I took a breath. "I'm here with my boyfriend, but someone recognized me, from a dark time in my life, and my boyfriend panicked and left me in the restaurant. He wasn't back at the hotel and I just want to feel numb, because I think he can't," I shook my head unable to say the words as the tears streamed down my face. "He has a big job and he's here on work and I'm," I took a breath, and looked at the faces, some were sympathetic, and some were bored, but I didn't blame them to be honest, because I was a white, privileged fag, and not everyone was down with that. I looked at my feet and sat.

"Rob, you're not done, and it's a safe space, you can't leave burdened," a heavyset man with a kind and weathered face said from across the room.

I rubbed my hands on my legs and stood. "I did porn, when I was a teenager. My ex was twelve years older than me, and he made it seem okay, but I didn't know how it much it would ruin my life. I was a child," I took a deep, shuddering breath as I noticed I had everyone's attention. Porn, the *magic* word. "There's nothing wrong with porn, not the people who do it or the millions of people who watch it, but out in the open, it's a dirty word and dirty thing, and I just don't see how I can ever have a normal life with the man I love. I've been to rehab three times, I've stumbled more times than I can count, and I can't do this," I exhaled shaking my head, swallowing a sob.

Someone took my hand, and someone else took my other and squeezed.

"You can Rob," someone said. "You're here."

"Hang in there."

"Keep it simple."

"If you want what you've never had, you must do what you've never done."

I perked up at that one.

"You're never alone, god is with you always."

I nodded and listened to the words of encouragement coming from all around the room, feeling soothed, and knowing I would make it another day, and that's all I had to do.

It was near midnight when I made it back to the hotel, walked there by the large man with the kind face, whose name was J., and who stayed after to talk to me.

"Go straight to bed, and make your plane in the morning," he said shaking my hand. "You will feel right as rain when your feet are back in London, I promise, and you will call your sponsor to let him know you have arrived."

I hugged him. "Thank you. You have no idea how much better you've made me feel."

"To the contrary, I know exactly how I've made you feel, because I've been you. It gets better, trust me," he nodded with a soothing smile. "I've got my thirty-year chip, and you'll get yours too, hang in there."

I let myself into the room and pulled up at the sight of Marcus still dressed in his jeans and t-shirt. He stood from the chair as I came in.

"Robin," he breathed.

I leaned back against the door, his beautiful face so anguished I couldn't take another step. I was certain he was breaking up with me. I hated myself for my past, and I hated him for his weakness.

"I just came for my things," I said softly, stunned that I could even manage to speak.

He crossed the room then. "Forgive me. I should never have left you," he said with a wince. "I panicked, I was weak, and I failed you again. Are you okay?" He pulled me into his arms and I heard him sniff me.

I pushed him away. "I didn't drink. But you hit all my triggers." I walked past him to my suitcase. "Sometimes people recognize me, you think I like that?" I stopped with my back to him. "You think I like the reminder that my teen years were not only stolen from me but put on display for the whole world to see?" I turned to look at him and sighed and shook my head. "The worst part is, I let myself believe that *we* could have a future, that I could be happy."

"Robby," Marcus stepped to me, his eyes shining. "I'm sorry. I'm here on work, and when that man came, I was just unprepared for the recognition, and I only thought of myself. I'm begging you to forgive me. It's new for me," he pleaded with his eyes. "I called you the minute I stopped to think, but it went right to voicemail. I was so worried about you."

I listened to him, and part of me understood what he was saying, but the other part was screaming that he would never love me enough, that he would only think of himself like he always did, that there would always be a part of him that lived in fear. "I did porn, gay, fetish porn. I can't wave a magic wand and make that fact ever go away. If you're worried about work finding out, or your friends finding out, or your parents finding out, then we can't be together, because they will. I can't say if it'll be tomorrow, or next month, or next year, or ten years from now, but they will, and it will hurt, trust me," I sobbed then.

He pulled me into his arms and I sobbed ugly tears into his neck as he rubbed my back, his own eyes damp with unshed tears. After who knows how long, he helped me undress and put me under the covers. He undressed and turned out the lights and held me all night, until my alarm went off before dawn. I set it for that early before all that shit went down, hoping for morning sex before I had to leave but instead, I turned it off and made to get out of bed.

Marcus pulled me back to him and kissed my neck. "I love you Robin. I have *always* loved you, and I will never leave you again," he whispered and stroked my body.

We made love silently, well, not completely silently. There was a tremendous amount of moaning on both our parts, and at the very end, when I said, "Oh god Marcus, I'm gonna come," he said, "oh god Robby, yes," and then came with me.

50

Meet the Parents

I BOARDED THE PLANE with a contented smile, feeling hopeful again, Marcus and I exchanging declarations of love before I left him getting in the shower. I texted T. on my way to work letting him know all was good and thanking him for his help finding such a great meeting for me. He texted back saying he expected to see me later that night at our usual meeting.

After work I filled Gertie in, telling her everything, the highs and the lows of the weekend, she made all the appropriate responses, and forgave Marcus just like I did.

"You know Robby, it's completely understandable that he was caught off-guard by that guy. I don't agree with how he handled it, but he seems like someone with triggers of his own," she said with a questioning tone. "He's only human, and he owned his mistake, I think Marcus is a solid guy, and a keeper," she smiled and kissed my cheek. "I approve anyway. I think your parents will be the final judges."

"Oh, my parents," I said dramatically. "They don't think I have the greatest taste in men," I made a cringey face, thinking that if they only knew my history with Marcus that they would lock me away and never let me date again. I kissed her and left to meet T.

***

As it was, Marcus ended up meeting my parents sooner than I had planned. We were waiting for a table at a restaurant in Chelsea two months later when I heard my mum call my name.

I let go of Marcus' hand and turned to greet them with hugs and a kiss for her.

"Mum, Dad, this is Marcus Willoughby, Marcus these are my parents Gerald and Winnie," I stood back, quaking suddenly, as they shook hands.

"Willoughby," my dad said thoughtfully. "Are you from Kensington?"

"Yes. Robby and I went to secondary together," Marcus answered with a quick smile, looking at me for approval.

I saw my mum look at me, but I wouldn't let her catch my eye.

"I know your father, you played rugby, was it?" My dad said with a smile, and some other recognition in his eyes as he glanced ever so briefly at me, clearly pleased with Marcus' lineage.

"I did, and I do, but just pick up or club now," he added with a smile, sensing my dad's approval.

My dad looked between Marcus and me and then at my mum. "Should we get a table for four?" He trailed off.

The three of us nodded, Marcus making sure I nodded first. We were seated at a table in the middle of the dining room and settled in, my mother and I ordering Pellegrino, my dad a scotch and Marcus wine. My mum looked at Marcus and then at me and smiled but with a hint of concern, or perhaps apprehension, about his drink order but I smiled broadly.

"What do you do for work Marcus?" My dad asked as we looked at the menus and waited for our drinks.

"I'm a solicitor," he answered, and named his firm.

"Oh, fantastic, that's where your father is a partner, if I remember." My dad had a memory like a steel trap (if you didn't already guess), and yet pretended that he didn't. He looked at me. "You work with your father just like Robby here. I hope you see more of him than he does of me," he said congenially, as he if were constantly swanning around my desk looking to have lunch with me.

"He's upper and I'm still nose to the grindstone," Marcus looked at me. "I also travel and work long hours, sometimes I go weeks without seeing him." He looked between my parents as the drinks came. "Cheers, it's a pleasure to finally meet you."

We clinked glasses.

My mum looked between us. "Finally? Have you been seeing each other for a while?" She couldn't help herself.

Marcus looked at me and then back at her. "A few months, but I just meant more that I can't believe I never met you when we were in school," Marcus said awkwardly, spreading his hands.

"Marcus and I weren't friends in school, he was two years ahead, he's just being polite," I interjected. "You didn't even know I existed," I added with a flirtatious smile that made my dad uncomfortable.

"Where did you go to university?" My dad asked changing the subject.

"Trinity," Marcus replied, rubbing his knee against mine under the table.

My dad's eyebrows went up, Marcus was hitting all of my dad's marks as much as he hit all of mine. He really was perfect, and not a night went by that I didn't thank my lucky stars that he was mine.

"What law do you specialize in?"

"Real estate, all kinds, I haven't narrowed my focus yet, it is quite a broad field, but I'm leaning toward environmentally responsible development."

"Oh, that's marvelous," my mum declared. "We really need to take care of our planet, she's trying to shed us like a virus."

Marcus nodded at her with a sad smile. "You're absolutely right. If we don't do something about climate change, nothing else will matter, we'll all be dead."

"Marcus," I frowned. "Can we please talk about something else. You're going to give me an existential crisis."

He flashed a smile, he really was fortunate he still had all his teeth after years of rugby, and such beautiful teeth they were. "Of course, what would you rather talk about?" He knew that I honestly couldn't think about the fact that the world was definitely going to end, and it was too late for us to do anything about it because we were too busy wanting more of everything. Greed is most definitely not good, Mr. Gekko.

"Well, I'd love to keep talking about you, so why don't you tell them about the LLM you're considering?" I smiled proudly at my parents.

Marcus let out a little laugh. "That's staying on the topic of the environment though," he looked at my parents. "I'm currently researching programs at universities in the area, haven't started the application process, but I definitely want an advanced degree in environmental law."

"That's wonderful!" My mum exclaimed.

"Friends of ours, the Turners, their son did a master's in law at Oxford not too long ago," my dad added, looking at my mum.

"I think that was eight or ten years ago," my mum mused. "And he's a general counsel in Boston now, but I bet he'd be happy to talk to you if you had any questions about getting a masters in law at Oxford. Do you remember Oliver?" She asked looking at me.

I had a vague memory of a tall, gorgeous blonde about seven or eight years older than me. "A little," I shrugged.

"Thank you, I'm focused on staying in London," Marcus glanced briefly at me, "but if that changes or I can't find the right program I may take you up on that offer."

We ordered when the waiter came back and the rest of the meal my mum stared so happily at me and at Marcus. She was thrilled that my dad was so impressed with him, and I knew she could tell how in love we were, and how happy I was. I knew this because she ordered wine with dinner, and she hadn't had a drink around me since Vas and I split.

"You were really brilliant at dinner," I said and kissed Marcus when we were back at my flat. I couldn't keep my lips off him, and he definitely didn't mind that.

"I have to admit, I was really nervous, your dad has a terrifying reputation, but turned out to be quite nice and your mum is lovely."

I laughed. "My dad is not 'nice,' but he definitely liked you. What's not to love about you, you're perfect," I said undoing his belt and dropping to my knees. I freed him from his underwear and licked him. I felt his hands in my hair and took him deep, looking up at him after a moment hoping for a passionate exchange but saw an inscrutable expression on his face instead, before he pushed me away.

"I don't want it like that," he said and turned away to the window, zipping his pants.

"I'll do it the usual way then, don't zip up," I stood, worried at the change in mood, and put my arms around him. "What is it?"

He swallowed roughly. "I guess seeing your parents, talking about school, and then you on your knees," he shook his head. "Reminded me of when you filmed us." I loosened my arms. "That scared the shit out of me, and I was so pissed at you but knew I had no right to be. I eventually, mostly, forgot about it, until now."

"I'm sorry about that Marcus, I did that on impulse, I didn't think I'd ever need to send it to you."

He took my arms away and turned to look at me. "When I stumbled across your videos, and I don't want to talk about them," he said firmly and held up his hands, "I saw one called something like, '*rugby player dominates the water boy in the bushes,*' or some shit, I nearly fainted. I thought you had posted us, until I clicked on it of course," he looked away. "Seeing it from your point of view, the *storyline*," he paused looking back at me. "How is it that you don't hate me?"

I remembered that one. Actually, the title was '*Twink fan gobbles rugby star's MONSTER cock in the bushes, Epic facial!*' It was my idea and I filmed it exactly how I had filmed Marcus: from between my legs. Vas and I were in the bushes of a walled garden at an Airbnb that we had rented for the weekend in some countryside. The storyline was the rugby star (Vas, dressed in a rugby kit and boots) guided the naïve boy (me, dressed in a *very* pervy version of a school uniform) into the bushes and said 'I'm ready for your adoration,' and then pretty much followed the verbal exchange between me and Marcus that first time word for word.

I was mortified that Marcus had seen it, or any of my porn to be honest, but that one in particular, because in a way I was reliving, and reenacting, that day, and all the days with Marcus in those bushes. I did everything to Vas that I had done to Marcus and standing there, felt even dirtier for having done so in such a deliberate way, like I had violated our privacy or something.

"I'm sorry you saw that," I said quietly. "I didn't mean it in an angry way. I mean, I don't want you to think I made that as some sort of victim piece. I didn't hate you," I touched his arm. "I didn't know how to put in to words how I felt about you, because I didn't know how you felt about me."

"Well, you should fucking hate me. I know I hate me," he stepped around me. "I can't stay. I promise I'll call you," he strode to the door.

I knew exactly how he felt, the shame of things done in the past, feeling unworthy, oh, feeling *so* unworthy. For Marcus to feel that way, after things had been going so well for us shocked me and I ran for him. "NO!" I shouted and stopped the door from opening. "What's done is done. I told you we're not those kids anymore," I said earnestly. "And we didn't know what the fuck we were doing then. You hurt me, I hurt you, and we've grown. I love you, and I want to love you in *every* way possible, forever. So, you're going to stay and make love to me, or fuck the shit out of me, I want it all from you," I said, my voice husky. "And then tomorrow we're going to find a couple's counselor, something we should have done when we first got together," I pressed my body against his and kissed his reluctant lips, feeling him warm to my advances until he finally brought his arms up and opened his mouth to my tongue.

We undressed each other hurriedly. Marcus was like a fiend, pressing me back onto the bed, covering my body with his. He went down on me briefly, licking my asshole, and then fucked the shit out of me. It was as if he'd been holding back the whole time and finally had permission to express the passion he had for me, permission to do all the things he wanted to do to me, including ass-to-mouth, (yes, do me dirty), pulling my hair (yes, dominate me), and choking me (wasn't expecting that one, but okay). We were both covered in sweat, and come, and panted breathlessly in each other's arms until our heartbeats slowed.

"I love you Rob," he kissed me so gently. "Let's have a shower."

He left the bed without waiting for me and then soaped my body from head to toe when I joined him, smoothing his fingers between my ass cheeks, inflaming me before pulling his fingers away. It was as though he were anointing me and then baptizing me as he maneuvered me under the stream of the water, rinsing the soap and everything else away. I returned the favor, taking my time to wash him from head to toe, pushing his foreskin back as I stroked him with my soapy hand, then smoothed my fingers between his legs and his ass cheeks, watching his eyelids flutter as I did, before turning him under the stream of water.

We fell back into bed new men, and our relationship was solidified that night. We found a couple's therapist and we hashed out a lot of shit. I'm pretty sure that therapist was like 'this is way above my pay grade,' when we left that first session, but he didn't turn us away and I credit him for our longevity, because if not for him, Marcus and I would have been done for after he told his parents about us.

51

Meet the Roommate 2.0

I SQUEEZED MARCUS' KNEE as he navigated the narrow streets back to my flat after dinner in Kensington a few weeks later. "Why don't we stay at your place tonight? You must have off-street parking, and I've never been," I held my breath.

Marcus looked at me as we came to a stop at a red light. "I want to fuck you, and I want to be loud," he looked out the windshield as the light went from red and yellow to green, and his fancy sports car purred through the intersection. "I can't do that at my place."

I felt a thrill, because I wanted him to fuck me loudly. I did a mental happy dance, glad that we were on the same page, but why couldn't he do that in a place he paid top dollar for?

"Does your flatmate know you're gay?" I saw him wince at that, and winced myself in response. "Wait a minute Mr. Willoughby. Does your flatmate know about us? Does your flatmate know you suck dick and like anal?" I wasn't fucking around or mincing words. This wasn't secondary or college, this was *real* life and *real* love.

"Christ Robin, do you have to be so crass?" He asked harshly, turning on Queen's Gate.

"Christ Marcus, do you have to be so embarrassed?" I asked in an equally harsh tone. I didn't get it; he took me to dinners, held my hand, would put his arm around me in Soho, but I couldn't meet his flatmate? Who was this man he lived with? The Pope?

"Fine," Marcus nodded his head as he turned onto my street. "Next time. Tonight's too late, you don't have your things and I've already got my stuff at your place. Besides, all I can think about is your smooth white ass, and how much I want to bury myself in it."

I made a sound of delight because we were *so* on the same page. I grabbed his crotch and leaned across the console. "I can't wait to get home and ride you," I licked his neck and savored the taste.

Marcus chuckled throatily. "I can't wait. I love it when you ride me," he turned his head and kissed me briefly as he pulled into a parking space on the street. "Your lips, your eyes, your *perfect* body," he turned off the car and pulled me across the console to kiss me. "I would fuck you right here, right now, but I'm so glad I don't have to. Let's get inside."

I jumped out of the car and barely held the door to my building open for him as I raced in, his delicious laugh echoing behind me up the stairs.

Marcus left in the morning for rugby and I was having coffee at the table in front of the sunny balcony window when Gertie came out of her room. "Morning gorgeous," I smiled at her. "I like the pink," I said commenting on her new hair color.

"Thanks," she patted her head and went to the kitchen for coffee. She came back out with a mug and a bowl of cereal. "Do you guys sleep?" She asked as she sat down. "Do you care if anyone else in the flat, or the building for that matter, do?"

I snickered and made a face. "Sorry, were we loud?"

She looked at me with her are-you-kidding-me? face. "The two of you. It's really hard to tell which one of you is better in bed from the chorus of moaning and name screaming. Christ, I heard 'god' so much, made me wonder if he was in there too."

I laughed, pleased. "He's so fucking good in bed, I'm sorry. We'll keep it down, I thought you were gonna be out all night anyway, when did you get home?"

"Around eleven thirty, sounded like somewhere between act one and two. I fell asleep during the intermission, and then was awakened by act three sometime around dawn," she shook her head and shoveled cereal into her mouth. "Got back to sleep thankfully," she added chewing.

"Well, I'm hoping to go to Marcus', haven't seen his flat yet, so we'll give you a break," I patted her hand. "How are things with Peter?"

She made a sound and shrugged. "We had a fight. I dunno, we're so on and off, I think we should just be off. What about that friend of Marcus' I was chatting up at the pub? He was cute."

"Evan?" I asked as she nodded. "Yeah, he was cute. I can ask Marcus, we could go on a double date! I've never been on one of those," I added, already planning our double wedding in my head. I wondered if Gertie and I should have matching outfits, or color coordinate, I thought we should at least for the photos. Or maybe, Marcus and I would be in matching suits, Gertie might end up with a giant dress and upstage me at my own wedding. Maybe not a double wedding then.

"Earth to Robby," Gertie snapped her fingers. "What were you just thinking about? I know it wasn't something pervy about Marcus, because *that* face is quite distinctive," she wrinkled her nose.

"Nothing," I said and stood, anxious to look at suits online, but just for fun, I'm not *that* delusional (usually). "I'll ask him about it tonight."

✳✳✳

Turns out I didn't see Marcus that night, or the next four; I was beginning to forget what he looked like, and told him as much when we spoke.

Marcus laughed. "You're absurd Robin. Let's have dinner tomorrow, I'm away this weekend."

"What?" *Why was I just hearing about that?* "Since when?"

"I'm sure I told you," Marcus said nonchalantly. "My cousin is getting married in Edinburgh, but I'll be back Sunday night."

I was sure he hadn't told me. "When did you get the invitation?"

"I dunno, like a month ago."

"You didn't get a plus one?" I asked quietly.

He made a soft sound. "No, but Robby, babe, I couldn't bring you. Please understand."

I winced at that. "You haven't told your roommate, you haven't told your parents, you haven't told your coworkers. Does anyone know about us? *Will* anyone ever know about us?"

"It's different for me, Robby, I've told you that. Neither of my parents are very accepting of the alternative lifestyle. I have to ease them into it, and bringing you to a wedding with my whole family is the opposite of easing them in," he said calmly. "I'm gonna tell them, I promise. I love you."

"And your roommate?" I couldn't think about the wedding at that moment. I *so* wanted to be on his arm, dressed to the nines, him showing me off proudly, as proudly as I would be if my cousin was getting married. I would have *demanded* a plus one.

"I'm telling him tonight," he said sounding like he wanted to do anything but, "so you can stay over after dinner tomorrow."

It made me want to put on a dress for dinner, maybe some fucking glitter. Okay, I wouldn't do that, but I was totally wearing a thong. "Where are you taking me? I hope somewhere in Soho. It's been four days and I want to grope you without judgement."

He chuckled, and I felt it in my groin, *god I missed him.* "How about tapas, I know you love Spanish food, or there's French, you decide."

"Copita's, I'll meet you there. Good night Marcus." I pressed end and looked out the window.

* * *

Marcus had clearly stopped at home to shower and shave after work because he looked and smelled amazing and I jumped on him, sniffing his neck before kissing him and pulling back to stare at him. He smiled at me, his arms around my slim waist, and then let go to pull out my chair. We sat at a table outside, it was warm for October (hello climate change) and they had propane heaters set up to turn on as the night cooled. I put my small Louis Vuitton crossbody bag on the back of my chair and sat as Marcus folded his tall frame into the wooden chair across from me.

"You look beautiful, did you do something different with your hair?" He asked and picked up the menu.

"I got highlights, Gertie wanted me to go pink, like her, but I declined," I replied with a smile and ran my hand through my hair.

"You'd look good in any color," he winked at me and looked up at the waiter.

He had several sangrias and we split nearly a dozen dishes. Seemed like he never wanted the night to end, and I didn't either, but I really wanted to get him naked.

I raised my eyebrows when he ordered another sangria. "You're going to have a wicked headache from all that sugar," I warned.

"I'll be fine," he shrugged.

I sighed. "So, tell me about the wedding. Which cousin?" I asked, figuring we were going to be there a while.

"My cousin Betty, her dad is my mom's older brother," Marcus said finishing the shrimp. "She's marrying some Scotsman, they met at St. Andrews."

"How old is she?"

"Few years older than me, I think twenty-eight. Her younger brother Jules and I are close, they grew up in West Brompton."

I looked away as the waiter brought him his sangria. "Where's the wedding?"

"Melville Castle, it's somewhere outside the city I guess," he shrugged and took a sip.

"Is it like a hotel now? Is everyone staying there?" I took a sip of my coke.

"I think so," he looked at me. "I'm staying with Gareth," he added and looked at his drink.

My stomach clenched at that. It was weird that they were still friends, and I wondered what that meant for us. How could he ever tell Gareth he was with *me?* The doom cloud began to roll in, and I felt its rain pelt my heart. I wanted to ask, but it was too soon, I'm not that big of an idiot. Part of me wanted to walk away from this relationship, as unscathed as possible, and the other part of me wanted him to turn me inside out and stomp all over my heart, because I was already in too deep.

"Well, should be a nice weekend, beautiful time of year to get away, have a wedding," I smiled and finished my soda. "Maybe I'll go away too."

Marcus looked amused, which kind of irritated me. "Where would you go?"

"Not Edinburgh, don't worry," I said with an edge.

His face shifted, and he finished his sangria.

I flagged the waiter for the check and paid cash, waving for Marcus to put his wallet away. "I picked the place, you can pick the next one."

I got my bag and we took a taxi back to his place. We pulled up in front of a big, beautiful, brick building with its own courtyard not far from the Thames, and I followed him in and up to his flat on the third floor. He turned to face me at the doorway, with his key in his hand and kissed me, pressing his tongue (which tasted like sangria) gently into my mouth. He left me quite breathless as he broke the kiss and unlocked the door.

His flat was almost the same size as mine, with a smaller balcony and a larger dining area. It was fairly tidy, and there was a large TV in the living room with an Xbox in the cabinet underneath. I had a quick, dizzying flashback to Vas and Olek and caught myself with my shoulder on the wall as his roommate stood from the couch, with his controller in one hand. He wasn't tattooed or Ukrainian, thank god, in fact he was quite plain and not at all dangerous looking.

"Rob this is Harry, Harry this is my friend Rob," Marcus said taking a breath.

I wanted to glare and scoff at him, friend? but held my tongue. "Nice to meet you Harry," I shook his hand as we smiled at each other, and then nodded at the screen. "Is this Halo 3?"

Harry shook my hand and looked at me with surprise. "Yeah, you play?"

"I've played them all, I fucking love Halo," I shrugged. I was suddenly torn between fucking Marcus' brains out and impressing his roommate. "Can I join you?" I saw Marcus look at his watch. I fought the urge to smile, someone was eager to fuck my brains out. Well, maybe he should've introduced me as his boyfriend (harrumph).

I took off my bag and joined Harry on the couch. He handed me the second controller, I logged in and we were off. *Bye Marcus!*

Marcus got himself a beer and watched for a while, then he got his phone out and surfed that for a while, and then he up and left the room. Harry and I were kicking ass and having a blast doing it. He was even better than Olek and much friendlier.

"So, you and Marcus went to secondary together?" he asked dodging bullets on the screen.

I looked at him without turning my head. "Yeah, he was a few years ahead. What else did he say?"

"Just that you reconnected and probably were going to spend the night, needed a place to crash," he looked at his watch then. "Oh, crap it's getting late, you probably want the couch. We should wrap up."

I logged out and stood with a stretch, wanting to scream at Marcus. "No worries about the couch, I'm sleeping in Marcus' room. Great game," I smiled and picked up my bag and left the room, feeling his bewildered eyes on me.

Marcus was in his underwear and a t-shirt on his laptop in bed and looked up as I came in.

"Is it okay if I sleep in here, or should I make up a bed on the couch?" I asked with my most irritated tone and face.

Marcus closed his laptop and stood. "I don't know, do you want the couch or Harry's room?" He asked with an equally irritated tone and face.

"Well, I'm just a friend making friends," I said haughtily and put my bag down on the dresser and kicked off my shoes. I stripped off my shirt and faced him. "Are you going to be on top of the covers, or shall I?" I asked and undid my belt. "Don't want Harry to get the wrong idea."

Marcus watched me undress, his eyes dark and fathomless in the low light. I stepped out of my pants and turned my back to him before bending over to pick them up, straightening my shoes while I was bent in half. I smiled when I felt Marcus' hands on my bare cheeks (I knew he'd love the thong). I rolled my body up as Marcus' hands came around my front and smoothed over my skin up and down my body, giving me goosebumps.

"You touch all your friends this way?" I whispered and turned in his arms. "Am I going to have to worry about you and Gareth?"

"Robin don't be absurd," he murmured against the side of my head, "I only touch you this way. I've missed you and you've kept me waiting for hours." I felt his tongue on my neck.

I ran my fingers through his soft hair. "I would have fucked you twice by now if you had just introduced me properly," I shook my head and stepped back raising my eyebrows.

Marcus held my gaze challengingly and then went to the door. "Harry," he called into the dark apartment, his eyes locked on mine. Harry responded from the direction of his bedroom on the other side of the living room. "Rob is my boyfriend. Good night."

"Oh, okay. Good night." I heard Harry respond before Marcus shut the door.

"Happy?" He raised his eyebrows.

"Extremely!" I beamed and pulled him to the bed.

Marcus woke me with morning sex and then kissed me lingeringly before I left for work.

"I'm going to miss you," he said between kisses, "But I'll be back Sunday night and would love to take you to dinner Monday."

"If you're not back too late, come spend the night Sunday," I said and picked up my bag.

"It's gonna be a busy weekend, but I'll let you know. I love you."

"I love you too," I kissed him and left the flat.

52

The Earl and Countess of Knightsbridge

GERTIE AND I went to a dinner party at Lola and Kevin's on Friday. There were seven of us and we played stupid games until the wee hours laughing until our sides hurt. I had planned on bringing Marcus, wanting to introduce him to everyone now that we'd been together nearly four months. I wondered how Marcus would have fit in as Gertie and I made our way home, and decided that while Marcus was reserved, and more serious than the people I usually surrounded myself with, he would have had a blast.

On Sunday I walked to my mother's parents' house in Knightsbridge, a large four-story mansion facing Hyde Park (poshest of the posh). Their butler let me in as always. No, his name wasn't Carson, it was Gil, but he was as imposing and had been with them forever. I was in a double-breasted Balmain suit, because I always wore a suit, or my ever-faithful Burberry, when I visited them. Not because they required it, but because my gram always fawned over me when I did, and they knew about the porn, so every impression had to be an impeccable one with them.

They were far too well-bred to ever mention it, other than remarking on that 'unfortunate incident' as if it were a one-time thing and gone from the planet forever because they had willed it to be. In a way it *had* been wiped from the planet, every trace of it gone from the internet, aside from the people who had downloaded it. My father, or the Earl (as I called my grandfather), had used connections to get the top brass at every website to remove everything as if it had never existed. Ah, money, and power, and white privilege, the ultimate trifecta.

"Gram!" I exclaimed as Gil led me upstairs into her sitting room, a sparkling clean room that hadn't changed in probably fifty years, maybe more. "My word, you look stunning." And she did, in a vintage tweed Chanel suit I'd seen her wear countless times. She looked like I imagined Princess Diana would have in her late sixties if she hadn't been taken from us at such a young age. She wore her grey-blonde hair in a perfectly blown-out bob, and smiled as she stood to hug me. I kissed both her soft cheeks (just like my mum's perfect cheeks), and joined her on the sofa for tea.

"You are looking quite handsome Robin, if not a little flashy," she said sweeping her eyes over my suit and highlighted hair.

"I needed a new suit, and I like being a blonde. My hair is darkening with age," I added with a sigh.

"Your grandfather has a closet full of suits, next time you need a new one come over and I'll call the tailor."

"Gram, I'm too young and gay for tweed just yet," I laughed.

"Nonsense, there's nothing gayer than tweed and a silk ascot these days," she grinned mischievously. "And you would look magnificent in it just like he did when he was your age, wearing his grandfather's suits."

I smiled at the thought. My grandfather was an exceptionally handsome man, and she was always telling me how much I looked like him when he was my age. "Speaking of the Earl, where is he?" I asked looking around.

"He's down in the library with Uncle James, they're going over the books and such, he'll be done shortly," she waved her hand.

I straightened. "Uncle James is here?" I hadn't seen him in nearly two years, for obvious reasons, well, obvious to me, maybe not to you. He was a colossal snob, even more so than my father, and I was just too messy to associate with. I was guessing he would be happy to go his whole life without ever laying eyes on me again.

"Yes, but he isn't staying," she picked up her tea cup and took a sip as I harrumphed. "He's quite busy, that's the only reason he can't stay," she patted my knee. "He hopes we can all have dinner sometime soon, Theo and Oscar will both be home for the holidays in December, perhaps we'll have Christmas Eve here."

Theo was two years older than Felicity, and just like his father, whereas Oscar was a year younger than I and we followed each other on Instagram and the like.

He and I had talked about the porn, and he was cool about it, I mean, he never laid into me like Theo did. God, you would have thought I used Theo's name and likeness and filmed on Buckingham lawn the way he carried on about the shame I brought to him and to our family. I didn't care if I never laid eyes on him for the rest of my life. Problem was, he was the future Earl, after his father, and could make my life difficult if he chose to someday.

I looked at my Grandmother, and with all the bearing bestowed upon me from my esteemed ancestors on both sides I said, "I would like that very much," and then got out my phone. "In the meantime, before Grandfather comes, I have to show you my new beau."

She put her teacup down and put on her reading glasses with flourish as I swiped into my phone and showed her the picture I took of Marcus at dinner in Belfast in his Alexander McQueen suit, and then ones of us on the Antrim Coast that another tourist had taken, our hair being swept by the wind, Marcus so gorgeous standing in a sunbeam, and finally one Gertie had taken of us holding hands on our roof deck.

"He's quite handsome," she said and took her glasses off. "What's his name? What does he do?"

"Marcus Willoughby," god I loved saying his name, "and he's a solicitor. His focus is real estate law, wants to specialize in environmentally responsible and sustainable development, and is going back for his masters," I said proudly, adding the name of his firm and that his father was a partner there.

"Wow," she said impressed, "he sounds like quite a catch. Where'd he grow up? Where'd he go to university?"

"Kensington. Trinity," I replied and pretended to sweep my hair off my shoulder.

She laughed. "I can't wait to meet him, bring him around for tea."

"I will, if he doesn't faint dead away at the invitation," I added with a grin. My ears perked up at the sound of voices coming from the foyer downstairs, and I jumped to my feet.

"Robin," my grandmother chastised as I strode to the open door and down the stairs.

The Earl and his successor were standing in the foyer saying their goodbyes.

"Uncle James," I called as I came forward, "delightful to see you, and you're looking so well."

Discomfort flitted across his patrician features, but his upbringing forbade him from ignoring my outstretched hand. He shook it with all the enthusiasm of someone who thought I had just had it up some guy's ass.

"Robin," he said and gave me a thin-lipped smile.

I turned and hugged my grandfather, who had no problem touching me. "Grandfather, you somehow manage to look younger and more stylish every time

I see you." Gram definitely wasn't exaggerating when she said he had a closet full of suits, and each one of them undoubtedly handmade. He was always perfectly dressed; he was currently in a navy pinstripe suit, and he was one of those old-school types who changed outfits twice a day, sometimes more in the country. He was straight out of a movie, like central casting for a Duke, not just an Earl. He was tall and had full lips like mine, though they had flattened with age, and blue eyes that were grey like a stormy sea, just like mine. In fact, I was the one grandchild who looked the most like him, and maybe that's also why my uncle had a chip on his shoulder about me.

He smiled broadly and slapped my shoulder. "Robby, so glad you could come early, gives us a chance to catch up before the rest of your family arrives," he looked at my uncle. "Next time I hope you and Evelyn can join us."

James nodded and shook his father's hand. "Well, I'm late for the club. Father, Robin," he said and turned to the door, which Gil opened for him.

We watched him go, and then my grandfather put his arm on my shoulder and steered me into the blue drawing room as my grandmother swept down the stairs as though she were Scarlet O'Hara.

"Now tell me about this new 'app' that your father tells me you're working on."

I was so happy when I left Knightsbridge, as I always was, catching a ride home with my parents, that I wasn't too crushed when Marcus texted that he was exhausted and would see me the following night. Gertie and I cuddled on the couch and watched some fluffy rom-com I forget the name of, but it was about a girl, who meets a guy, but then the nerdy guy at work wins her over and they live happily ever after. I wondered if they'd ever make one about the bully who makes the little femboy polish his knob in the shrubbery, all the while calling him names and such in public, and the little femboy goes along because he doesn't know how to say no, but maybe that's because he doesn't want to. And then, after years of being horrible, and both making bad decisions, they fall in love. Would anyone believe in that romance? Should anyone? Especially the ones in it. Or were they doomed?

I fell asleep and dreamt of twisted branches, gripping hands, and soft earth beneath my knees. And of angels, and judgement, and darkness.

53

Wedding (Story) Crashers

"HOW WAS SCOTLAND?" I asked Marcus on Monday, kissing him before we took our seats at a table in the corner of the pub near my flat. It was late, and he'd come straight from work, his laptop in a bag next to him and his jaw dark with a weekend's worth of whiskers.

Marcus looked around as he sat. "I don't remember too much of the weekend. Gareth got me drunk the minute I landed, almost missed the rehearsal dinner," he shrugged. "My sisters gave me a fuck ton of grief. I don't know why, it was just a dinner."

"Some people take weddings very seriously," I answered and perused the menu.

"Weddings are boring, the receptions can be fun, hers was. They had a band and then a DJ, and an open bar, so a lot people were quite drunk."

The waiter came and took our order, returning promptly with Marcus' pint and my club soda with lime.

"Did you dance?" I asked, watching him sip his IPA.

"Yeah, I suppose I did."

"Were there a lot of single people there?" I asked, my jealousy peeking out from behind the same curtain the showgirls used.

He shrugged and looked away. "She's only twenty-seven, half the wedding was single. The other half was family."

I wondered how many of those single women draped themselves all over him, how many of them he kissed drunkenly. I was working myself up and needed to rein myself in. "Were there any single gay men there?" Whoopsie, it slipped out, so much for reining myself in.

"I have no idea," Marcus frowned.

"Please Marcus, I happen to know if there were any, they would have been all over you like Border Force on an illegal. So, were there?" I raised my eyebrows. I could see he was weighing his answer and the longer he took the shorter my fuse became. *What the fuck was taking him so long?*

"I was with Gareth, being a 'bro,' if there were any interested parties they steered clear. But Robby, even if they hadn't I would have told them I was seeing someone, just like I did with the women," he said finally.

Again, I stopped listening after he said the first part. *He took Gareth to the wedding?* The rest of the words fell around me like snow and I gathered them together like a snowball and hurled it at him. "*Gareth* was there? You did get a plus one, you bastard!" I scoffed and nearly stood, but the waiter appeared with our food.

He looked between us, put our plates down, and nearly ran from the table.

"Robby," Marcus said in a quelling tone.

"Don't *Robby* me," I furrowed my brow. I was jealous, and crushed, and the shame was coming back. I couldn't tell if I was being rational or not. On the one hand it had only been four months, but on the other we'd known each other for more than a decade, and we were in love, hot and heavy, ass-to-mouth committed, and he wouldn't bring me as a plus one to a romantic wedding in gorgeous Scotland. I was really beginning to have my doubts about his heart. "You took a mouth-breather to your cousin's wedding, instead of the man you supposedly love," I held up my hand as he began to speak. "I get that you didn't want to tell your family about us there, or for fuck's sake anywhere apparently, but you took another man! How is that different? I'm not such a twat that I don't know how to behave like a bro. And, I could've dry humped a horny bridesmaid on the dance floor to really sell it."

Marcus looked away and worked his jaw from side to side. "I'm sorry Robby," he looked back at me. "I took Gareth because he would have been pissed if I came to Edinburgh without seeing him, and because I can keep my hands off him. I don't look at him and imagine him naked under me, or over me. I don't smell him and want to kiss his neck or run my fingers through his hair. I don't watch him dancing and get hard. Robby, I need to tell my family slowly, and if I had taken you, I'd have been dry humping you on the dance floor," he paused and held my gaze. "There are two things you can never do at a wedding: wear white, and upstage the bride," he sat back in his chair.

My cock went ping in my pants. Christ, I *was* being irrational, and if I didn't stop it, I'd drive him away with my insanity. "Well, when you put it that way," I trailed off, feeling contrite but haughty, because I didn't know any of that. I fake swept my hair. "I suppose I can forgive you. I don't want to do any of those things to Gareth either. Safe choice," I raised my glass and dug into my dinner.

"Gram wants you to come to tea," I said, between kisses later as we were laying in his bed, the moonlight coming in between the slats of his wooden blinds and covering us in blurry stripes.

"The Countess?" Marcus said reverently. "What about the Earl? Do I have time to fake my own death?" He jerked lightly with a laugh as I poked him in his side.

"I didn't mention you to the Earl, there weren't a moment to. Gram and I were gossiping over tea. I showed her pictures, she thinks you're dreamy, and I agree," I swooned back on the pillow and squealed as he tickled me.

"Shh, you'll wake Harry," Marcus chided. "When is tea?"

I shrugged. "She didn't specify. Perhaps you'll get a hand-delivered, cream-colored invitation written in calligraphy, with her livery-clad footman instructed to wait for your reply. Her crested carriage out front, double greys stomping and snorting in the cold."

"What kind of fantasy world is in there?" Marcus asked with a grin, tapping my forehead. "I'd love to get lost inside."

I wrapped my arms around his neck and kissed him soundly. "Careful, if I let you in, I'll never let you leave. Can't have you telling my secrets to the world."

"I wouldn't breathe a word. How could I when you kept mine?" He promised and looked at me earnestly, his soul shining in his eyes like a gift.

I kissed him, and took what he gave me.

54

Summons to (Wenham) Court

MY GRANDMOTHER CALLED ME in the middle of November, whilst I was sitting at my desk going bleary-eyed looking at the blondes, brunettes, and redheads.

"Hello Countess of Wenham," I crowed happily, "to what do I owe this incredible honor?"

Her laughter came down the phone line like faeries playing in a meadow. "Robby darling, I'm dying of thirst over here, when are you and your gentleman friend coming for tea?"

I wondered briefly if my gram knew about the double entendre of thirst, but dismissed it, no way. "Oh, forgive me, I didn't want to impose so didn't make a plan, but we are at your beck and call. When would you like us to join you?"

"Sunday. Come for tea at four, and then he can join us for dinner," she replied, then blew a kiss and hung up.

I smiled and did a happy dance in my chair, because Marcus had already won my parents over. I texted him and spent the rest of the afternoon thinking about what I was going to wear, what Marcus was going to wear, and how beautiful we were going to look sitting next to each other in that grand dining room.

* * *

Marcus was so nervous, but looked so handsome, I nearly fainted. He was in a Brioni suit, just like James Bond, gorgeous but not flashy. He had a large bouquet of flowers in one hand and a bottle of Krug Grande Cuvee in the other. I wanted to unzip his fly and worship at the altar of perfection, but managed to restrain myself.

Gil let us in with his usual lack of fanfare, and Marcus looked around, in the way he always did. We were led into the west drawing room, it was mid-sized compared to the other two drawing rooms, and housed several impressive paintings and objects d'art. I kept the shock off my face at my grandmother's attire as she stood from the ornate settee. She was wearing a gown (I kid you not), and she looked magnificent. It was taffeta (darling), and probably mid-century, all that was missing was a tiara, which I knew she had several of, but this was tea, not dinner at the palace. She took my kisses and looked over the gifts Marcus brought before gesturing to Gil to take them, and then let Marcus bow over her hand. She looked at the top of his head as he did so and then at me with a mischievous twinkle in her eye.

Marcus performed beautifully, he charmed her in his quiet and reserved way, answering her questions, complimenting her in subtle and roundabout ways, just as she liked from strangers, you couldn't come on too strong with her, she could see right through insincerity. I could see that she was wowed, as was I. The doors opened and the Earl strode through, in tails. My god, was this an episode of *Downton Abbey?* I narrowed my eyes at them both as Marcus stood immediately and shook my grandfather's hand with a 'pleasure to meet you Lord Wenham.'

We made our way through the connecting door into the blue drawing room, Marcus widening his eyes at me and then at the artwork in the giant, formal receiving room. This was the massive and imposing drawing room they used to impress visitors and for holidays. My grandfather introduced him to the ancestors in the room, some stacked one above the other in gilded frames, while I sidled up to my grandmother.

"Are you trying to frighten him away?" I asked out of the side of my mouth. "Because I nearly fled. You look more royal than the bloody queen," I swept my eyes over her. "Is that your mother's gown?"

She giggled (goddamn it). "No, it was his mother's," she nodded at the Earl.

I shook my head and put my arm around her. "God you're wicked, I don't deserve you."

"Does he know?" She asked quietly as we watched them.

"That you're wicked?" I replied looking at her with an amused face. "If he didn't before, he does now."

She laughed. "No, I mean about the," she dropped her voice to a whisper so quiet she basically mouthed the words, "unfortunate incident."

I made a sound of understanding and nodded. "Yes, he does, he knew about it, I didn't tell him," I clarified and looked at Marcus.

She leaned into me, and looked at Marcus coming back toward us. "He's quite the specimen. I'm glad he knows, so it's not something hanging over you."

"I know, me too. I love him, god help me."

We had tea, and little crumpets. Marcus and the Earl discussed land management, and sustainability, and Marcus' work, until Gil led my parents in, with all my siblings and Felicity's boyfriend in tow, even David graced us with his presence. He was only a few neighborhoods over at King's College, but he hardly ever showed his face around. Introductions were made, and Felicity swept her eyes over Marcus a few times before settling them back on her boyfriend. Elliott was rather plain, but kept himself in nice shape, played polo and came from money as old as ours, so he was nothing to sneeze at (however, I would kick him out of bed for eating crackers). Drinks were poured, appetizers were passed and then we made our way into the dining room.

The dining room was bigger than my flat and adorned with massive paintings of landscapes, and antique furniture. I noticed two footmen (dressed in livery for fuck's sake), one on either side of the table holding chairs for the ladies, and caught my grandmother's eye, raising my eyebrows, and she looked away with an expression the Dowager of Grantham would have envied.

Marcus was seated to my grandfather's right at the long dining table that was actually one of three that could be set together end to end, seating up to thirty. The other two tables were unadorned at the opposite ends of the room. I saw Marcus' flowers on the table, divided among two large vases, the flowers that had previously graced the table had been put on the mantle over the giant marble fireplace. I smiled to myself and listened to the chatter around me, hoping that Marcus had noticed too. I felt Marcus' knee against mine from time to time, and I knew he was nervous, because he wasn't drinking, his wine glass hadn't been filled since the first course. The footman took it, and everyone else's, away to replace it with a red for dinner.

I watched him surreptitiously as he conversed with the Earl and Elliott, and felt my heart flutter at how well he was handling himself, and how handsome he looked doing it. I smiled at my mum across the table, feeling warm under her happy gaze, and then looked at my grandmother at the other end of the table. She was watching David and Felicity with a small frown so I followed her eyes. David was saying something quietly to Felicity while glancing at Marcus. I looked at my plate, wondering what they could be discussing, until realization dawned and I felt a cold pit in my stomach. I tried to catch David's eye but then saw my grandmother looking at me. I smiled and held up my glass to her, but she was suspicious. Shit. I figured David told Felicity about Marcus, and I could kick myself for ever having slipped back in Spain.

Only David and Dee knew that it was Marcus and them knocking me down that day, but nobody knew about the rib (well, maybe Vas, but he was in prison). George said something to me about something and broke my worry, but not really.

"Isn't he the guy who took your phone in the park? And shoved you?" George asked quietly, looking past me at Marcus, so much in the way he had looked around me at Vas all those years ago, that I lost my breath. Christ, everyone was remembering and if I wasn't careful there was going to be a scene.

I swallowed and laughed. "He was just kidding around then, you know how guys are in school," I shrugged nonchalantly.

George hummed and frowned as though he didn't believe me but wasn't interested in pressing the issue. "Is he your boyfriend?"

I nodded with a happy smile. "Are you still seeing the same girl?" I asked changing the subject.

"No, I've got a new one," he shrugged, "you can't let them linger too long at my age, they get notions," he waved his hand as though he were forty and not fifteen.

After dessert we went to the Chinese drawing room (I told you the house was gigantic, there were like thirty rooms), which was decorated in art and such from the Far East (yes, the Ming vases were real). I stood next to Marcus and touched his hand with my finger. "We should go," I said quietly.

He gave me a half-smile. "You tired, or?" He tilted his head and quirked his eyebrow.

"No, I'm worried," I glanced at my sister.

He straightened. "What do you mean?"

I leaned in close, sniffing him briefly as though it would be the last time I did. "David and George remember who you are, but David knows you were the one who knocked me down and scuffed my chin, which was nothing," I put my hand on his arm for emphasis. "But he told Felicity, who loves stirring up trouble. I'll do damage control if you give me space."

Marcus blanched and looked at Felicity who was watching us. He flashed her a small smile and took my hand, squeezing it gently before walking to my dad to begin saying goodbye.

Felicity made a beeline for me the minute Marcus left my side. "Hey Robby," she smiled haughtily. "So," she trailed off.

"Hey Feliss, you look great, Elliott looks great, how are things in Mayfair?"

"Grand, thanks for asking," she took a sip of her wine. "What the fuck is the matter with you?" She hissed with a frown. "We grew up in the same house, same parents, same rules, and yet you are *completely* mental when it comes to men," she looked around the room. "There are like billions of men in the world, millions of them gay, and yet you pick a pedophile and a bloody bully. He's the guy who tormented you all through secondary isn't he? You came home covered in blood," she frowned.

"You have it all wrong Feliss, he's the guy who kept everyone from bullying me," I replied calmly.

"That's not what David said," she scoffed.

"David misunderstood, he was like twelve," I scoffed. "Marcus always liked me, and I always liked him, he protected me," I looked at Marcus talking to my parents. "Stop trying to find something wrong with him. He's perfect, and he loves me. I appreciate your concern, but Vas was my only big mistake, and after what I've been through, Marcus is my reward."

She followed my eyes, and then looked at David. All of a sudden, my grandmother appeared at my side, like a ninja and I jumped slightly.

"How you managed to keep all that taffeta silent is a miracle Countess," I said and grinned, trying to cover my nervousness. "What are you skulking about for?"

"What are you two talking about?" She looked between the two of us. "What was that at dinner?"

"You're not gossiping are you milady?" I raised my eyebrows.

Felicity elbowed me. "Robin," she hissed.

Felicity could never see past our grandmother's age, her title, or her bearing, and as such she never spent any time with her, but I listened to all her stories, loved looking at her photo albums and hearing about her youth. When I looked at my grandmother, I saw the teenager and young woman she once was, I saw the mischief in her eyes, it was still there. So, I could speak freely with her and she loved it.

"Not gossiping, I'm showing concern," she linked her arm through mine. "Is there something worrisome about your young beau? I mean, someone that beautiful, and successful, must have some glaring flaw."

"Is that so?" I said pensively. "What's yours then?"

Her face broke into a broad smile and she squeezed my arm with a chuckle. "You are far too clever, I've told your mother that all along."

Felicity looked torn between rolling her eyes and seething with jealousy. "Robby's dating his bully, he used to beat him up."

Gram frowned and looked between Felicity, Marcus, and me.

I sighed dramatically and patted my grandmother's hand. "There's been a big misunderstanding. Marcus was the star rugby player, as I told you, and some of his teammates were bullies, but Marcus always stood up for me, and made them stop. One time they caught me when he wasn't around and knocked me down, cut my chin," I looked at Marcus who was watching me out of the corner of his eye. "Marcus found out, and it *never* happened again," I said truthfully and smiled back at my gram and at Felicity. "He always liked me, but couldn't say then, because well, *obviously*," I shrugged with a secret laugh.

"Well that's terribly romantic," the Countess said and unlinked her arm with one last squeeze. "He's your champion, and you're together after all these years."

Felicity looked at me with one last suspicious glance, but even she couldn't poke holes in the story, not with David's youthful second-hand knowledge as her intel. She tried another tack. "Does he know about you and the Chav?"

I looked at Gram. "Yes, he does," I shrugged, "he doesn't care. Be happy for me Feliss."

"I am," she said defensively. "I just don't want you to get hurt."

"That's sweet," I said, only a little sarcastically. I turned to my gram, "Marcus and I have to get going, he's got to be at work early," I hugged her and kissed her cheeks, and then gave Felicity a brief hug.

Marcus and I said goodbye to everyone else and got in his car. He looked at me after pulling away from the curb. "Well?"

"It's all sorted, I told Gram your friends bullied me, and you came to my rescue," I squeezed his leg. "And then years later, you came to my rescue again. She adores you, and I love you Marcus Willoughby."

He covered my hand with his after shifting gears. "And I love you Robin Trumball."

55

The Lotus Eater

THE NEXT FEW MONTHS I was living the dream. I was in love, I was successful at work (the app launched and was a huge hit), and my social life was at an all-time high. Marcus had met all my friends and blended right in, played our silly games and actually enjoyed himself. He touched me freely in front of them, unlike how he kept himself mostly apart from me when we were with his friends. We spent so many hours talking and discovering just how much we had in common, though we were vastly different in personality. He was so smart, and so loving, our chemistry was unlike anything I'd ever experienced or believed possible. I thought what I had with Vas I would never find again, and then Marcus completely blew my expectations out of the water.

Vas and I had sexual chemistry (honestly, because I was horny teenager), but had little else in common. He was a gym-head, hated museums, and we came from two (or too) different worlds. Whereas Marcus grew up with as big a silver spoon in his mouth as I did. He was connected to the peerage: his father's second, or maybe it was third, cousin was titled (a Marquess no less), and his mother's family was above reproach. I hadn't had the opportunity to drag Marcus to a museum (hello, when we weren't eating or socializing, we were fucking, no time for art), but I was itching to do so because he said he loved them.

I don't mean to sound as if it were all eating, laughing, and fucking though, Marcus had his sports that I had to share him with. I loved watching him play rugby and football, he was so good and so fast in both, but I worried over every tackle and every hit in rugby, in a way I never did in secondary. I wanted to wrap him in bubble wrap and far preferred football where he played center or wing, and there was no tackling whatsoever.

At either sport I would cheer myself hoarse in the stands or the sideline, depending on which pitch he played, and he always let me hug him after. I didn't mind the sweat, I loved his scent and pressing my face against his sweaty neck. He never kissed me or let me kiss him, but I'm guessing his teammates suspected, he would occasionally let his arm linger around my waist for a few moments (which I loved) as we chatted with some of them.

The only downside, as our courtship progressed, was that I wasn't seeing Marcus as much as I'd have liked, but I suppose I was just being needy. He worked super long hours and traveled a lot, visiting clients, real estate developments, and countless government buildings. He had made time for me in the early days, like all courting beaus, but as we solidified he shifted his priorities back to his career. I kept working normal hours, following my routine, spending time with friends, and whenever Marcus was free, I made time for him, he was my priority. I was so happy just eating the fruit, ignoring the realities, ignoring the elephant in the room, that I nearly let Marcus go.

* * *

I was down to just a couple of AA meetings a week, mostly to support the newcomers, and to hit the Big Book, and twelve-step meetings as refreshers. The holidays were upon us and while I could be around people who drank in controlled settings (dinner with the Earl and family for example), it was a struggle for me or any alcoholic, to function in the season of making merry. Marcus was very understanding and didn't drink excessively around me, but was likely getting bombed everywhere else, I didn't care. I did, however, care that I wasn't invited to any of his holiday parties that season, including his office holiday party, though I invited him to all mine. He had a viable excuse, I supposed, wanting to keep his private life and work life separate, and I didn't really want to go to his office party (those things were so boring), but I didn't like the feeling of why I was being excluded. I couldn't help but feel that if I were a woman he would've brought me.

Ian had never said anything to Marcus about that morning in the hotel, but Marcus perceived a bit of a shift in his attitude, which I assured him was his imagination, though it was impossible to prove either way, which just enraged me.

Straight people had it so easy, and were so oblivious to just how easy they had it that sometimes I *really* hated them. I would even go as far as saying that straight privilege was worse than white privilege. The fact that Ian, or anyone else at his company or in the world, felt as though it were their business to judge someone for who they loved, really made me want to unfurl my wings and burn the masses like the dragon in that *Game of Thrones* episode that everyone hated (I told you I never watched the show, or that episode, but my god, everyone talked about it so much I felt like I had).

The week before Christmas I found an LGBTQ AA meeting in Soho to deal with that very problem. I needed solidarity. Usually I avoided those meetings, because there was always a 'thirteenth stepper' looking for new meat. Those people existed in every meeting, gay or straight, and their cover was that they wanted to offer guidance and 'be there for you' but what they really wanted was to get into your pants. I never talked about the porn in *those* meetings, well, not since the first one I went to in the beginning as a newbie. I was literally swarmed after the burning desire at that one, and none of them were hot (sorry).

"Hi my name is Rob, I'm an alcoholic, two years sober," I stood midway through the meeting.

A chorus of welcomes and congratulatory applause followed.

"I'm struggling with frustration right now. I'm at a point in my life where I've mostly accepted my past, and my failures, and I'm deeply in love," I smiled, "but, my boyfriend is taking his time coming out of the closet, and I can't tell if I'm being unreasonable wanting to meet his family, which makes me doubt myself, which then makes me want to drink," I looked around at the nodding faces. "The fact that he is scared to tell anybody in his life that he's gay, makes me angry at the world, and straight privilege specifically, and that makes me want a dragon." I got some puzzled looks at that. "*Game of Thrones?*" I raised my eyebrows, looking around.

A chorus of understanding filled the room.

"Anyone know where I can get one?" I added with a grin and sat.

"Hang in there."

"If you find a dragon let me know," someone called from across the room.

"Think of the solution, not the problem."

"Everyone is struggling with something, he needs your help not your anger."

"If you find a path with no obstacles, it likely leads nowhere."

I felt comforted by the responses, as empty as some of them were, they gave me something to focus on other than my doubts.

After the burning desire a few people approached me, sharing their own stories of coming out, or dating people in the closet. I loved hearing coming out stories, everyone's was so different even though we all said the same words: 'I'm gay.' The settings, the responses, the burden after, were all so varied and fascinating. Unfortunately, none of the stories of dating people in the closet had a happy ending, and everyone who stopped to talk to me about that, said I should cut my losses; that it was like dating a married person who swore they would divorce their spouse, but never did.

I hoped they were wrong as I deflected a few advances and made my way to my Uber. My phone buzzed. "Hi Mum," I answered with a smile.

"Hello lovey, oh, are you outside?" She asked as a gust of wind muffled my phone.

"Yup, just leaving a meeting."

"Oh good. I'm calling to see if it's only you coming to Knightsbridge for Christmas Eve, Gram wanted to know if Marcus was joining," she trailed off.

I opened the back door of the Uber and confirmed the driver's name before getting in. "Yes Mum, it's just me, we're not doing families this year, Marcus has something that night," I didn't have the heart to tell her his family still didn't know about us.

"Please tell him he'll be missed, and I looked forward to seeing you in Knightsbridge on the twenty-fourth at five o'clock sharp."

"Actually, I'll see you at home on the twenty-third, I have presents for under the tree," I blew her a kiss and put my phone away. It was grey outside, and I watched the cars and the people as we drove past, wondering where they were all going, what meaning their lives had, why they got out of bed in the morning. I thought about Marcus, and his parents. Why was he hesitating? The niggling of doubt started to worm its way to the front of my brain. *Was he ashamed of me?* What if he was waiting because he didn't think we had any staying power? 'No sense in telling my family or rocking the boat for nothing, if we weren't meant to be,' I imagined him thinking. I couldn't conceive of any other reason for the hesitation, and I honestly didn't know what to do about it.

I wanted to meet with Miranda, but what I really thought should be happening was that Marcus should reach out to his therapist. I knew he hadn't seen her since we'd been together. I was definitely going to bring it up again the next time I saw him, but not as an ultimatum or anything truly ghastly, people who did that were the worst. No, I was going to speak with him about telling his family, and suggest that he speak with his therapist, or our couple's therapist if he needed help doing so. Trouble was, the next time I saw him he wasn't alone.

56

Mean Boys Reunited (and It Feels So Not Good)

IT WAS THE NIGHT before Christmas Eve, I had gone to my parents' house and stayed for dinner and a chat, because Marcus was working late and I wouldn't be seeing him. We had plans to see each other for brunch, where I was going to make a full spread of food and then spend the rest of the day ravishing him until I had to leave for Knightsbridge.

It was dark when I left, of course it was, the sun hid her face from the cold as early as she could in December, she did it every year and I didn't blame her, I just wanted to snuggle in bed too. I had my collar up to the cold, just like in the movies, as I made my way to The Tube when I saw a group of four guys walking into the pub across the way. There was nothing remarkable about them, only that I had a sudden, clear flashback to the gang of four who used to torment me. The guys who just disappeared from view were older, and bigger, but I knew unmistakably it was them.

My feet crossed the street of their own accord and I stopped just before being able to see in the window, to collect myself. Marcus was working, it couldn't be him, it could be them, but with someone else. Gareth, Hector and Frank all grew up somewhere in Kensington, I never knew where they lived, but was guessing they were all home for the holidays and met up for a couple of pints. I shivered there in the cold, not wanting to know, but unable to look away, and I stepped into the doorway wondering how premeditated their night out was.

I went in, and I promise that when I did I had no idea what I was going to do. Marcus was a free man, he could go out with whomever he wanted, he wasn't even required to tell me, but that he lied and said he was working late, really got under my skin. He could hang out with all the douchey people he wanted (not really though), but I expected honesty. Christ, that was the backbone of the Big Book, the whole fucking Program, and I'd never lied to him (yet anyway).

I sat at the bar, and looked at them at their table against the wall, frothy pints delivered on a black tray by a saucy waitress. She stopped to flirt, of course, Marcus had his back to me but her eyes were locked on him. Hector, or maybe it was Frank, said something that they all laughed at, including the waitress but the laugh didn't reach her eyes. I wanted to hug her and warn her that he was just getting started, and he wouldn't be getting any funnier.

I flagged the bartender over. "I'll have a water, but please put it in one of those glasses you reserve for double-shots, and do you have a pen?" He filled a small glass with water from the dispenser and handed me a sharpie.

I scrawled two words in large letters on a bar napkin and folded it inside another bar napkin. I heard their laughter from across the room as I pulled out my wallet and slapped a ten-pound note on the bar. One of them (Frank or Hector) caught my eye briefly but then continued on without real recognition. It looked as though I reminded him of someone but he couldn't be bothered to remember who. I saw the waitress headed past me to the table beyond.

"Excuse me," I touched her arm gently. "Could you give this to the dark-haired guy with his back to me, the good-looking one, not the oaf next to him," I clarified as I handed her the folded wad of napkins and a ten-pound note.

"Sure," she shrugged with a broad smile and pocketed the money.

I watched as she took the order for the table behind me and then walked to Marcus' table. She handed him the napkins and said something while nodding at me. They all turned to look and I raised my glass and tossed back the water like it was vodka and stood while Marcus read what I wrote in all capitals.

HEY FAG.

I stayed long enough to see his face go white and then I left. Fuck him.

I was nearly to the corner when I heard him shout my name. I stopped and turned, my haughtiest expression on my face, it was so hard to hold it, but I did.

"Robin," he said futilely when he reached me.

"Marcus," I replied, holding his guilty gaze.

"My god, I'm sorry, what can I do? Should you call T., or Miranda maybe? I could go to a meeting with you." His face was panicked. "Shit," he looked away. "You've been so good," he trailed off.

"It was water," I said calmly and his eyes whipped back to mine. "But I wished it were vodka. What the fuck Marcus?"

He frowned, but with a look of relief. "They're in town for the holidays, they called me," he trailed off with a shrug. "Are you fucking following me?"

I dropped my jaw and turned my head holding his gaze. "I was walking to The Tube from my parents' when I saw a gang of *thugs* go into the pub. Had a bloody flashback to be honest," I said harshly, the emotions coming up. "What are we even doing Marcus?" I shook my head as if I had just woken up. "Go back to your mates. I mean it. It was grand, but there's no way we could ever have a future. Seriously. Us?!" I laughed bitterly. "What are they even saying in there?

"Go back, I forgive you, I absolve you, and I will be *perfectly* fine. You're not all that, Mr. Willoughby," I added, knowing that he was, in fact, all that.

"Robin, I'm sorry, I should have told you, please," he grabbed my arm as I started to turn away, "don't leave me."

I furrowed my brow and looked away. *Don't leave him* in *general, or don't leave him tonight?* I was guessing he meant in general because there was no way he was going to ask me to join them. I looked back at him. God, he was so beautiful, I didn't want to let him go, but I had to. I leaned forward and kissed him lightly. "Don't you ever say I just walked away, because I'm gonna fucking run. Happy Christmas Marcus." I turned, and I fucking ran.

I went back to my parents' and spent the night in my old room. They were surprised but happy to have me. I woke to the smell of my mum's Christmas Eve casserole and French toast, exactly what I was going to make Marcus, and I couldn't help the tears. I showered and went to the kitchen. I let my mum fuss over me, sitting back as she poured me coffee, put syrup on my French toast, and then joined me while I ate. My dad came in and sat across from me, chatting about everything and nothing.

I knew my brothers wouldn't be up for hours, so after breakfast I went to a meeting. I listened to everyone's struggles with the holidays and it made me feel better, I wasn't fragile anymore. As I sat there I realized that all I needed, truly, was closure with Marcus. He had the upper hand in our youth, I didn't understand him, or us, back then, but then we had our months, we had our declarations, and while he couldn't admit to anyone in his life, except Harry, that he was gay, he had to me, he bared his heart and soul to me. I called that even, and in such a way that I wasn't truly harmed. That is not to say that my heart wasn't wounded, it was, and gravely, but I also knew that I would be fine, because I was a Wenham.

57

Miracle on Hyde Park (Street)

INITIALLY, I COULDN'T DECIDE between tails or the tweed suit that my grandmother insisted last month that I pick out and have altered to fit me, but in the end, I went with the tweed. She was right, it was very gay and it looked amazing on me, and even better, my uncle frowned when he saw me in it.

We had drinks in the blue drawing room, which, like the rest of the house, was decorated to the nines as usual for the holiday, all the Christmas heirlooms and ornaments brought out and on display. There was a giant tree in the corner, and smaller but still large ones in the foyer, the west drawing room, and in the dining room, and garlands on the bannisters and mantels. Candles and lights were everywhere and it was beautiful and every distraction I needed. I was so desperate for a drink I was even considering sherry. The fact that I had left Marcus, and then had to face Uncle James and Theo was too much, I wanted something to take the edge off, but of course I could never stop at the edge. I thought about going to a meeting.

My grandmother caught my eye and came to me. She was dressed in another taffeta gown, this one was a deep ruby red, and she had her emeralds on; I wanted to fall at her feet and said as much.

"Oh, dear Robin, not in that suit, that was your grandfather's, grandfather's, and he would never have swooned over a woman," she grinned with a twinkle in her eye and sipped her drink, "not in public anyway."

"Then there was never a beauty like you in his lifetime, and I pity him for that," I bowed over her hand.

She beamed at me. You might think I was just pandering, but I meant every word. She *was* a beauty, and I *would* fall at her feet. She was just like my mum, and my mum walked on water, she learned how from Gram.

I caught Felicity's glare from across the room where she was standing with Elliott and shrugged, then looked at Theo who was also glaring at me but for different reasons. He wasn't bad looking, he looked like his father, tall, brown-haired, blue-eyed, straight nose, blah, blah, blah, but he would never be gorgeous, or interesting looking. He was like Prince William, but with hair, (sorry Your Highness).

Theo shook my hand when they arrived, but then turned his icy shoulder, as his nicer, more relaxed brother, Oscar, embraced me. I spent my time chatting with everyone, including Felicity, Elliott, and my aunt Evelyn, who, even before the porn, was hard to like, and was feeling pretty proud of myself for not sneaking a drink. Oscar and I took turns making each other laugh, to the annoyance of Theo, but to be honest, that's why we were doing it.

We were about fifteen minutes from being led to the dining room by a footman when Gil appeared in the large doorway and announced Marcus, only he said it like the way they used to back in the day, 'the honorable Marcus Willoughby' and I heard trumpets. Okay, none of that happened (Marcus doesn't get a title, he isn't a member of the peerage), but it may as well have from the response in the room. There was a brief hush that came over everyone, but not a horrified one, and Gram, who looked like she had been expecting him, immediately stepped forward to greet him as he came toward her, magnificent in a Brioni tuxedo. I swear it was like James Bond greeting the Queen. He bowed over her hand and kissed both her cheeks as she pulled him forward, and then he shook hands around the room starting with the Earl, who introduced him to my uncle and his family, and kissed my mum, and Felicity, on both cheeks, until finally coming to me. He looked me in my (haughty) eyes, and shook my hand, squeezing tightly as he smiled. I raised my eyebrows and gave him a cool smile in return, but was thrilled to my toes. A footman brought him a glass of champagne and conversation resumed.

I could tell he didn't want to leave my side but he made for Theo (whom I had told him all about), and forced him to engage. It didn't take long at all for Theo to warm up, they had a lot in common, and Marcus knew how to be a man's man in all the ways I didn't. Turns out, Marcus and Theo knew many of the same people, as Theo worked in banking, private equity to be specific. His biggest client was the Earl, of course, but he had other deep pockets he managed, and many of them did business with Marcus' firm.

"I thought you said he wasn't able to make it?" My mum said as she appeared at my side.

"He clearly changed his plans," I shrugged. "I broke up with him last night, and I'm guessing he's seen the error of his ways."

"What?" She pulled up and looked at Marcus and then back at me worriedly.

"It's complicated, but rest assured I love him with all my heart, and if he's here, that can only mean he's willing to do what it takes," I placated her, knowing I couldn't go into the full story there in the drawing room, and looked at my grandmother as she joined us. "You little sneak," I shook my head at her, "you didn't look surprised to see him."

"He called me earlier today to inquire whether his invitation still stood, and then asked me to keep it a secret," she grinned. "I love intrigue, you know that."

"Yes, I do, you minx," I looked around the room as if in thought. "That's a word that's woefully underutilized, especially when it comes to you." I kissed her cheek as she laughed.

My mum just looked at us both and shook her head. "The two of you."

A footman appeared to announce that dinner was served, and everyone filed out the door and across the foyer to the dining room.

I stopped Marcus, and waited for everyone to leave. "What are you doing here? I dumped you last night."

"I know," he returned my gaze. "I tried to call and text, and can only assume that you blocked me. I had no choice but to come. You didn't give me a chance to say anything before you turned and fled, and I have things to say, that can't wait."

I made a sound like 'is that so?'

"Yes, you little brat," Marcus grinned and took my hand. "I'm sorry for going out with them and not telling you, and I'm sorry for going out with them period."

"Marcus, I wouldn't dream of dictating to you who you can and cannot be friends with, but I also can't help but remember what they did to me, what you did to me with them, nor can I discern whether they did it of their own accord or at your behest. Seeing you with them brought it all back, and made me question everything," I frowned. "I simply can't see how we can be, how we can have a future. I forgave you because we were more, but I cannot forgive them."

Marcus searched my face, and looked away. "I told them," he said quietly and looked back at me. "I was going to anyway, I swear, but they were quite bewildered when I ran after you."

I exhaled quietly. "What? What did they say?"

"Frank nearly fainted, Gareth refused to believe me, and Hector said he always suspected," Marcus twisted his mouth. "Hector was the only one who never said anything to you. He's a psychologist now."

"I could never tell him apart from Frank, but that's interesting. I never thought any of them knew what an emotion was," I was still reeling from the news that he told them; I wished I could have been a fly on the wall. "What happened next?"

"The food came, there was a stunned silence, and then we ate, everyone looking at me like I had three heads," he looked at our hands. "Frank asked if I took it up the ass, I told him no. That seemed to make him feel better, as if there's something wrong with it. God he's such a homophobe," he looked at me. "I don't know what his problem is, I absolutely love that you take it up the ass," he grinned and kissed me.

I laughed. "Christ Marcus, you're so crass," I scolded mockingly. "You can fill me in later, we better go into dinner," I put my arms around his neck and kissed him as his arms came around my waist. "My uncle probably thinks we're fucking and filming in here."

He let me lead him to the dining room and, with a brief squeeze, I released his hand outside the door. We took our seats as the footmen made their way around the table counter-clockwise from my uncle's seat next to the Earl.

"I was showing him the hidden figures in the Caravaggio," I said to my grandmother and looked at my mother with a smile. She gave me a relieved smile in return and turned her attention to the soup being served from her left.

I watched Marcus work his magic on Evelyn, and then on Felicity while I chatted with Elliott and Oscar. I couldn't believe he told Gareth and them, I couldn't believe he was sitting there in the dining room among my family, just six months in, and it was as though he'd been there all along. He was such an old soul, I got that sense back in school too, like he was older than everyone else, and I wondered if he ever truly let loose back then. I wondered if he'd let me paint his toenails. I couldn't help but smile at that random thought, and the image of him naked with red toes, no maybe blue, a bright, electric blue, and I'd kiss each toe.

"What the fuck are you thinking about?" Oscar asked from my left. "You have the most ridiculous expression on your face."

"Painting my boyfriend's toenails," I whispered with a laugh.

Oscar looked at Marcus. "You can't be serious. He'd let you?"

Marcus felt our eyes and looked inquisitively at me.

"No, he'd never," I lied, I knew he'd let me. "Are you seeing anyone?" I asked changing the subject.

"Nah, and it's just as well, I've taken a new job, I'm moving in the new year." He shrugged and took a bite of food.

"Is that right? Where you off to?"

"I took a job in biotech in Manchester," he said happily, "you should come visit, I'll be missing home."

My stomach clenched at the thought of ever going back to Manchester. At the thought of my favorite cousin living there. I took a deep breath, and forced a smile. "Manchester's a great city, lots to do, you'll love it," I swallowed.

"You've been?"

"Sure, who hasn't?" I turned my attention to my plate. "Best football team in the UK, if not the planet," I laughed stiffly, but he didn't notice.

"You got that right!" Oscar said enthusiastically.

In truth I hadn't watched a United game since Vas left me, and the thought of anything to do with Manchester was still upsetting. I needed to change the subject. "Are you going skiing this year?"

I listened as he told me about his past trip and his upcoming one with some of his college chums and looked around the table, suddenly ready for dessert and getting the fuck out of there.

"Happy Christmas Robin," Marcus murmured against my lips once we were back at my empty flat, Gertie was home to Hampstead for the holiday. We left the Earl's just after nine, Marcus driving his fancy car through the cold and nearly empty streets. I returned his kiss and began stripping his tuxedo from his body, until he was fully, and gloriously bare, his muscles shaded beautifully in the low light. "Happy Christmas Marcus, I love you."

"And I love you, especially in this fantastic tweed suit. God you look amazing, was it your grandfather's?"

I grinned against his lips. "Yes, shall we leave it on?"

"Absolutely," Marcus replied and steered me to the couch, bending me over the back.

58

The Truth Will Set You Free

I DIDN'T PRESSURE MARCUS about telling anyone else. I had hoped that by telling Gareth and them, and seeing that their reaction wasn't to have him drawn and quartered, would bring him to his own reckoning with his family, but the weeks stretched as we passed the New Year without him bringing it up.

After Christmas Eve with my family, and that amazing night that followed, Marcus began spending the night more frequently, and when he wasn't at my place, I was staying at his. I wasn't sure why we hadn't made a habit of it sooner but perhaps it was because of our flatmates, and the fact that we were both people unaccustomed, or wary in my case, of living with a lover. As much as I wanted Marcus in bed beside me every night, I was reluctant to make it official because of what had happened with Vas, and Marcus' reluctance was likely from worry about his family.

Gertie wasn't bothered by Marcus being there four nights out of seven, and she had begun seeing Evan, one of Marcus' football buddies, and he spent the night when I wasn't there and sometimes when I was with Marcus. The four of us had such fun together, and went on a lot of double dates to my great delight. Harry was equally chill about us being there two or three nights a week, and while he didn't have a steady girlfriend, other than the Xbox, he was on Tinder, and also went out with friends so we weren't always invading each other's space. Those days were so grand that I was able to ignore, for the most part, that Marcus still hadn't taken me home as his boyfriend.

* * *

It was late-February, and I was waiting for the water to boil, an Earl Grey teabag in my favorite giant mug that said '*blow me I'm hot*' (actually it was Marcus' mug, I gave it to him for Christmas), when Harry came into the kitchen and looked at me with a smile.

"Is there enough water for me?" He asked and went to the cabinet and pulled out a plain, boring mug with no saying at all.

"Always," I replied, looking him over in his jeans and striped jumper. "You have big plans today?" Usually Harry was in his sweats and on the couch Saturday morning.

"I have brunch with some friends in Hammersmith," he looked at me in my sweats and Burberry t-shirt. "How about you?"

"Laundry, and then Marcus' football match." The kettle dinged and I poured for us both. "I think Marcus said he's got dinner with his parents but I don't think that includes me," I shrugged.

Harry looked away. "It was shocking to find out about him, and you," Harry looked back at me, and lifted his hands slightly. "I don't care, of course, and you guys are like really happy and good together, and you kick ass at Halo, so that's even better," he grinned. "I've only met his parents a few times, but I don't get the sense that they're welcoming. I know he's gonna tell them, and that he's sick with worry about it, so, if I'm allowed to offer advice, I'd say let him do it in his own time."

I nodded. "I know, I'm not pressuring him, and I won't, but just for a minute, put yourself in my shoes. Let's say you were dating a girl, a white girl with a snobby family, and she never brought you home, even though you were practically living together," I held his gaze. "Would you feel like she was ashamed of you, or perhaps she didn't think you were marriage material so it didn't matter anyway, or even worse, that bringing you home would force her to choose between family and love, and she delayed because she knew she would always choose family."

Harry looked down at his tea. "I have been in that situation," he said quietly and looked at me. "I was in love with a Pakistani girl, we lived together in secret after uni and when she finally brought me home, because I pushed her to, it was a bloody shit show. Her father railed against her dating an Indian, and within a few weeks we crumbled and she moved out. Broke my fucking heart," he sipped his tea and shook his head. "I see both sides now, and all I can say is I'm sorry for you both. I hope, and bet, Marcus is stronger than Fatima was." He finished his tea and put the mug in the dishwasher. "Well, on that cheerful note, I'm off," he smiled, picked up his keys from the dish by the door and left.

Turns out it was dinner with Marcus' sisters and I was invited. We met at The Jam, a funky restaurant where you had to climb a ladder to your table. It was busy of course, but Marcus had made a reservation. We were seated at one of the upper booths near the window, Marcus holding my hand while we waited for his sisters to arrive.

"Are you telling them tonight? Is that why we're here?" I asked as we waited for his drink and my club soda.

Marcus nodded and took a deep breath. "Just going to rip off the band-aid and then ask them not to say anything to the family until after I tell my parents," he looked down at the door. "There they are."

He climbed down the stair/ladder without waiting for me. I followed, and stood behind him as he hugged his sister Emma first, she was my age and was in school with us, and then Kate who was a year older than David. He stepped back and introduced me.

Emma had a flair of recognition in her eyes and a polite smile. "Nice to see you again Robin, you look great." She was always nice even though we never said more than four words to each other in school, at least she didn't bully me.

I had never spoken with Kate, and shook her hand firmly. "You might have known my brother David in secondary," I said as we took our seats up in the booth. "He was a year behind you."

"Oh right, star footballer, he dated a friend of mine," she smiled. "Where's he at uni?"

"King's College, studying politics or economics, I can't remember."

They ordered cocktails and Marcus got some appetizers for the table. I was nervous as fuck and wished I had asked Marcus at what time during the meal he was planning on dropping the bomb.

"So, I don't recall you two being friends in school," Emma said lightly after their drinks arrived and we toasted. She looked at us sitting side by side with a curious expression. I knew she knew I was gay, I told you I lisped and swished back then.

Marcus took a large swallow of his drink and glanced at me. "We weren't, not really," he shrugged. "He lives in my neighborhood and we bumped into each other over the summer. I'm not the dickhead I used to be."

"He's not," I agreed with a smile.

Marcus ordered another cocktail and we all ordered food as the appetizers came. I asked for another club soda as his sisters switched to a bottle of white.

"How many glasses?" The waiter looked around at us.

"Just two," Marcus replied without looking at me. I saw his sisters exchange a glance.

"I don't drink," I said simply. "Two years sober last September. Yay me," I said in a quiet cheering voice.

"Good for you," Kate said with a smile. "I have a few friends who don't drink, their skin is amazing, as is yours."

I beamed happily, my skin *was* amazing. "Thank you."

We continued to make small talk, me sneaking glances at Marcus, who had switched to beer, and was on his second. I seriously began to worry about him making it down the stairs from the table, but maybe that was part of his plan. Get really drunk, tell his sisters, and then plummet to his death so he never had to spill the tea to his parents. I was nearly finished with my pizza and Marcus still hadn't said a word.

I took a deep breath. "So, how's the love life? You two seeing anyone?" I looked at Emma first.

"I'm seeing a guy I used to work with, wanted to wait until we didn't work together before dating him, shitting where you eat and all," she laughed.

I laughed and nodded, before looking at Kate expectantly.

"I just broke up with a guy from my biology class, it's been a tad awkward," she looked at Emma with a shrug. "Totally shat where I ate."

"That is awkward, but you're only nineteen, you'll both move along," I shrugged.

"He's my professor," Kate replied with a furrowed brow and took a sip of her wine.

"What?" Marcus said sternly as he and I both stared at her aghast.

She burst out laughing. "I'm kidding! God that were priceless," she high-fived a laughing Emma.

Kate put her wine down. "How about you boys? You guys seeing anyone?"

I felt Marcus tense next to me, as I smiled at her. "I am. He's bloody gorgeous, so fucking smart, and I love the shit out him," I reached for my phone. "Do you want to see a picture?" I asked as they nodded. I began swiping, "I think I might even have one of him shirtless in here."

Emma wasn't shocked, and Kate looked slightly taken aback that I said 'he' not 'she,' but they both leaned forward eagerly.

Marcus put his hand on mine and made me lower my phone. He swallowed and looked at his sisters. "I'm gay," he exhaled, "and Robby is my boyfriend. Please, don't indulge him, he's incorrigible," he looked back at me with a soft look.

I beamed at him and then looked at Emma and Kate, who were watching us with uncertainty. I suppose on the heels of Kate's joke that maybe they thought we were kidding as well, but the doubt didn't linger, especially with Marcus putting his arm on the back of the booth behind me.

"Do Mum and Dad know?" Emma frowned, but with concern not disgust. "And, uh, I'm not sure what to say, is it congratulations? Is it thanks for telling us? I really don't know what to say," Emma talked over herself.

"No, they don't know," Marcus answered quickly. "I will tell them, and ask that you keep this to yourselves until I do. This is something they need to hear from me," he looked at them both with such an aching look on his face. "I told you first, because I'm hoping I can count on you to be on my side. This wasn't easy for me," he glanced again at me, and I squeezed his leg. "And it will be even harder with Dad. And Mum."

"Congratulations is appropriate, because this is nearly killing your brother to admit," I smiled at Emma. "I'm holding his leg so he doesn't roll over the side," I raised my eyebrows at Marcus.

Marcus laughed then, a little bit of relief, a little bit of hysteria, and a lot nervous. I implored both his sisters with my eyes, and they reached across the table to grip Marcus' hands.

"I love you Marcus," Kate said, "thank you for telling us, and I couldn't give a shit who you love, as long as they treat you well and love you in return," she looked pointedly at me. "And it sounds like Robby not only does, but also knows how lucky he is to have you."

"I'm luckiest man in the world," I said earnestly with a grin, meaning every word.

We hugged tightly on the sidewalk after dinner, each pair going in different directions. Marcus loved me extra thoroughly when we got back to my flat, but I sensed the turmoil buried deep, the worry about his parents, and I did the best I could to make him feel better.

59

Meet the Fuckers

OH MY GOD, I discovered why Marcus thought my dad was a nice guy. Turns out, his dad was a fucking douche. He didn't tell them about us while I was there (I think he took one look at his father's face and chickened out), only said that we were friends who'd reconnected. Mr. Hoity-Toity Willoughby (I was never allowed to call him by his first name, which was Edward, by the way) already knew about the porn, but we didn't know that until he laid eyes on me. After a brief, stunned, glance at me when I came through the door, he wouldn't look at me for the rest of the night. Turns out he was one of the high rolling lawyers my dad contacted about the case with Vas. Apparently, I have him to thank for the judge (a close personal friend of his) having thrown the book at Vas, who was a first-time offender and, while I was a child, I wasn't a *child*, so the courts would have normally gone easier on him, but thanks to Sir Hoity-Toity (oh, did I forget to mention his title? Sorry, my grandfather is an Earl so 'Sir' is like, hardly worth mentioning), Vas got the full sentence with no potential for early release.

Sitting there at dinner, in the massive dining room of their large, but understated, townhome, I channeled my inner Dowager Countess of Grantham. My manners were impeccable, and above reproach. I spent my childhood going to my grandparents' where I was schooled in every etiquette known to man *and* the ones known only to the aristocracy. I was my father's son when I wanted to be and porn or no porn, the Willoughby's were not above me. I couldn't allow myself to think they were, otherwise I would have crumbled, and I was done doing that. I looked at Marcus across the table, and just wanted to make him proud and happy, so I laid the charm on thick with his mum, and treated his father like my dad treated everyone, like they were lucky to be in his presence. I was determined to make a good impression with both of them, because the next time I went to Marcus' parents would be when he acknowledged us, I would make sure of that.

Marcus held the door of his car for me after dinner and then folded his tall body behind the wheel and looked at me as he pushed the start button. "What?" He asked as he buckled his seatbelt.

"Your dad's a dick, but I think I like him," I said with a shrug of my shoulders and my eyebrows.

Marcus laughed roughly and put his car in gear and pulled away from the curb.

"He will never love me, but I'll get him to look at me," I said with a smile.

∗ ∗ ∗

Marcus didn't wait long to tell his parents the real reason for bringing me home, and while I wasn't there for the disclosure, I was there for the clean-up. He didn't warn me, just showed up at my flat (I had given him a key of course) mid-week looking shell-shocked. I didn't know what was wrong at first honestly, I checked him for stab wounds before clutching him to me. "Are you okay Marcus?"

He held me tightly and nodded. "I heard from all the law schools I applied to," he said against my neck.

I worried he'd been rejected from them all. "Oh babe, you can apply again next year, maybe they had too many applicants, maybe you need help with your resume," I soothed.

He laughed then and pulled back. "I got into them all Robin," he scoffed, "with scholarships, save for one."

"Well, that's fantastic!" I kissed him. "Of course you did. I didn't doubt you, you're just looking quite peaked. Why the fuck do you look like someone killed your dog?"

Marcus stepped out of my arms and went to the fridge where he had an open bottle of red wine. He poured the rest of the bottle into the mug that said 'You're my favorite thing to do,' with two stick figures doing it doggie style. Marcus had given it to me for Christmas, and he was lucky it was clean in the cupboard since I used it every day for tea.

I made a small sound at the quantity, and felt worry in the pit of my stomach. I poured myself a glass of water and watched him, trying to channel Miranda, but only hearing a broken Robin.

He drank half the mug in one swallow. I took his hand and led him quietly to my bedroom, knowing that intimacy, the soothing calming space of just being, was what he needed, and I thanked Miranda for that too. It doesn't work on everyone, I couldn't have done this with Vas to save us (there was nothing to save), but with Marcus, I knew he needed it as much as I did. We stripped down, got into bed, and I held him as he finished his wine and waited for the truth.

"I told my parents," he said in an exhale, his voice a rumble under my ear.

I laid quietly in my spot under his arm. I had so many questions, but he felt so . . . precarious, in that moment, I didn't want to alter anything. The moments passed like sheets on a clothes line, blowing in the breeze.

"It was awful," he said finally and sobbed.

Oh god, I had never heard Marcus cry, and I just clutched him to me, my whole being undone. This man, this steadfast lawyer, rugby player, afraid-of-nothing-man, was sobbing in my arms and I vacillated between not knowing what to do, and wanting to stab his father in the heart. I wondered what he said to Marcus.

I rolled on my side and pulled him against me, running my hands up and down his back, swallowing my own tears. Eventually he stopped and wiped his eyes, his body still pressed against mine. He kissed my neck, and then my lips, and I was lost.

When I woke in the morning he was gone, and I panicked thinking about Harry and his Pakistani girlfriend. I checked my phone and there was nothing. I sent him a quick text telling him I loved him and that I hoped to see him later, but I heard nothing from him for two days. I went to work and straight to two different meetings in town, both days, and was on my way home to watch a movie with Gertie, my purple-haired rock, when Marcus texted that he was at my place. I ran the rest of the way home.

I calmly entered my flat, with all the nonchalance I could summon, tossing my keys into the bowl on the table by the door. Gertie was nowhere to be seen and Marcus was standing on the balcony having a cigarette in the cold.

He turned when I opened the door, his cheeks pink, his jaw dark with whiskers.

"That's new," I remarked, nodding at the cigarette in his hand, hoping it wasn't something he was going to make a habit of.

He looked at his hand, and then put the cigarette to his lips. The tip flared bright orange as he drew and then he ground it out on the brick. "I smoked a bit at Trinity, just when I was stressed," he said exhaling the smoke.

"What's going on?"

He picked up his (my) mug, which was steaming, and took a sip. "I took the last two days off from work, drove to the middle of nowhere, kicked a ball against a wall," he looked at me. "Drank in some pub from the fifteen hundred's or something, maybe older. There's so much history, tradition, everywhere you look in England, bogging everything, and everyone, down." He blew out a breath that steamed in the cold. "I stayed the night in a tiny room over that pub. It felt like a coffin, I could barely breathe. I opened the window, which helped, but then I fucking froze," he shook his head. "I came back today and went to the bank to apply for a loan."

I frowned at the image and then at the last part. "A loan for what?"

"Law school."

"But you said you got scholarships, and your parents or your savings will cover the cost of living, no?" I puzzled.

He winced at the mention of his parents. "I got scholarships everywhere but one school, and that's the one I want to go to, I *need* to go to."

"How much is it? Can't be more than twenty thousand quid, I can help with that," I said with a smile.

"It's more like a hundred thousand US, with living expenses."

"What?" I looked away thinking. *Why the fuck did he just quote me in dollars?* "What are you talking about?"

"I'm going to America Rob," he looked at my chest, not able to meet my eye.

"What? You applied to school in America? How? Why?" My stomach clenched, and I felt like my face was going disappear into a giant frown-wrinkle. The outer edges of my mind were pounding in on my psyche, like a drumbeat.

"I did it on a whim Robin. We have offices in New York, and there's a partner there who comes to London from time to time, he specializes in environmental law," Marcus put the mug on the table. "He's on the advisory board at Boston College Law School, and said it's the best environmental law program on the east coast. He encouraged me to apply, he vouched for me. So, I did, not thinking I would ever follow through," he shook his head. "It's Boston, I didn't want to go any farther from you," he forced my gaze. "It's only for a year, and I can come see you on holidays, you could come visit me."

We were outside so I couldn't have been struggling for oxygen, but god help me, I was. I felt like if I didn't move I would collapse, so I went inside.

"Robin," Marcus said, closing the balcony door behind him. "Please, this is my future, I have to go. I have to leave. I'm not doing this to hurt you or us," he said earnestly. "My parents have cut me loose. I have to make my way, and rise above. I have to prove to my dad that I can do this on my own," Marcus pointed at the floor mindlessly for emphasis. "I want to beg you to come with me, I *need* you Robby, but this isn't moving to Oxford, or Cambridge, this is a whole other country. Fucking America. And I wouldn't dream of expecting you to uproot your life, your routine, your meetings, everything, just to indulge me for a year."

My mind was racing, the chaos was coming back and I just wanted to be able to think straight. I took a deep breath, checking my surroundings, weighing Marcus' words. I was only twenty-three, I had a great (cushy) job working for my dad, I had family, I had a posh flat, but the best part of my life was Marcus, and he was leaving. What was honestly tethering me there, other than Gertie, or my family?

I crossed the space between Marcus and I and hugged him, smelling his neck. "I've never been to Boston," I said quietly.

I felt Marcus melt into me, and breathe deeply through his nose. "Will you be a tourist, or a temporary resident?" He asked, his voice barely above a whisper.

"I'm gonna be your roommate, your lover, your income stream," I pulled back and kissed him gently.

He made the most delectable and indescribable sound, like need, and disbelief, and relief all combined into one, and steered me to my bedroom.

60

Withdrawal from the Bank of Wenham

I SMILED AT GIL as he let me into the mansion on Hyde Park. I was in the tweed, with a cream-colored silk scarf tied as an ascot around my neck. I took extra care with my appearance, my hair styled and tamed in the wavy manner that mimicked what I had seen in the scrapbooks of the Earl at my age.

I knew my grandmother didn't just hang around the house all day, up in her sitting room, awaiting visitors, but she had that gift of royalty that made you believe as if she did, without a care in the world. She was dressed in a Stella McCartney pantsuit, and on any other day I would have called her out on it, but today was too precious.

"Did I catch you just coming back from a fashion show?" *Whoopsie.* I know I said I wouldn't tease her but, one, she loved it, and two, she deserved it for looking so fashionable.

She looked down at her outfit after taking my kisses on her cheeks. "This old thing?" She shrugged. "It was sent to me."

I chuckled and sat next to her on the couch. We made the usual small talk, and then the conversation turned quickly to Marcus and life in general.

"How are things with Marcus?" She asked me as she sipped her tea.

"We're fantastic," I smiled. "He is everything and more than I could ever have hoped for Gram, and that he loves me just as much, is mind-boggling."

"He's lucky to have you Robin," she said firmly and patted my cheek. "And he's a good man, holds his own on the spot. I looked up his lineage," she shrugged nonchalantly, "he comes from very good stock indeed."

I nodded slowly and let my smile fall. "If only his family were as accepting and well-bred as mine," I frowned. "He came out to his parents, and told them about us, and they, well, it didn't go well."

My grandmother looked around the room and then back at me with a furrowed brow. "Why didn't it go well? Because he's gay, or because, something to do with you?"

I didn't have the answer to that question, because Marcus still wouldn't tell me what happened. I shrugged. "I don't know, but either way, Marcus is leaving. You know he's going for his master's in law, well, he's decided on a program in *America*," I said dramatically.

My grandmother straightened (that was encouraging). "What do you mean, he's leaving?"

"He got into all the schools he applied to, naturally, but the one he wants to go to, the one he said he *needs* to go to, is in Boston. Not only that, but it's the only one he didn't receive a scholarship for," I sighed. "His parents won't help, he said they've cut him loose," my eyes welled at that (I still wanted to stab his father).

"What kind of parent won't help pay for their child's education if they have the means to?" She looked out the window and then waved her hand. "No mind. The real question Robin is what are you going to do while he's all the way across the pond?" She looked back at me. "How many years will he be gone?"

"It's a year, and I'm going with him," I held her shocked gaze. "I've already reached out to a family friend who is general counsel for a billion-dollar cyber-security company in Boston, and am meeting with him in a week when he's here for Easter. I'm praying he'll hire me for a year, they do a lot of other things now, in addition to security. Marcus can't work while he's there, he's taking out a loan to cover his tuition and living expenses which the school calculates to be about eighty-six thousand pounds, but we're not going to live in a studio apartment and eat packaged noodles for a year, so I'm going to take care of him. We'll need my income to live *properly*."

My grandmother stood and went to the window that overlooked Hyde Park. "How long have you been together?"

I wondered how much to tell her, how to convey just how deep our connection was.

"Nine months, but Gram, he was my first, I was his," I added softly.

She turned her head sharply. "In secondary?"

I nodded solemnly. "No one knows," I said earnestly. "We had a secret relationship, it wasn't healthy for either of us, but we've loved each other since then, and we're so healthy now," I added with a smile.

She stared at a spot over my shoulder, lost in thought. She blinked and held out her hand. "Come with me."

I followed her down the stairs and into the Earl's sanctuary, after a knock of course. The library was massive and lined with bookcases and artwork. His desk was at one end, in front of double doors that led out into the back garden.

"Robin, how wonderful to see you," my grandfather stood and crossed the room for a hug. "That suit looks better on you than it ever did on me."

"Stop it Henry, he's the spitting image of you at that age, and you looked this marvelous in it. It's why I married you," she added with a twinkle in her eye. "Robin's here because he needs our help."

I started to contradict her (not really) but she stopped me. "Marcus has been cut off by his parents for his relationship with Robby, for being in love," she pursed her lips. "He's going all the way to America for law school, and I don't blame him for wanting to get away, but he hasn't got the money to attend. Robin is going with him, to support him financially, but he's going to need his tuition paid. *We're* going to pay it."

"Gram," I said, my mouth hanging open, I truly didn't expect the full amount.

She ignored me and held up her hand. "It's only," she paused to look at me, "how much for tuition?"

"Around fifty-two thousand pounds."

She looked back at my grandfather. He was never one to tell her no, so he shrugged and said, "consider it done."

I hugged him, nearly knocking him over, and then hugged my grandmother. "I don't deserve you," I said and the showgirls came, as if on cue.

I took Marcus to Bob Bob Ricards in Soho, for the champagne; I wished we could split a bottle of the Krug '96, but I just watched him have his Dom Perignon '10 by the glass.

"What are we doing here?" He asked me after kissing me hello. He'd come straight from work again and had his laptop on the blue leather booth next to him.

"My parents love this place for special occasions, and I have some great news," I smiled and held up my club soda that the waiter had poured into a champagne flute for me. "You don't need a loan, and I'm certain I can get a job at that cyber-security company."

"You don't have the job yet, and fall tuition needs to be paid by August. You have twenty-five thousand quid laying around?" He furrowed his brow.

"No, but the Countess does, and she wants to pay," I smiled.

Marcus frowned. That wasn't the look I was hoping for. "What are you talking about? You went and asked for them to pay for my school?"

"No, not exactly," I swallowed. "She offered, when I told her our plans. Marcus, she really likes you, she was *very* upset about your parents. Family is everything to her, and she loves me most of all," I flashed a smile.

"I can't take their money Robin. That wouldn't be me doing it on my own. She doesn't even know me, Christ we've only been together nine months, how can she want to do this?" He shook his head.

"She loves me, *and* I told her that we were each other's firsts," I added softly. "She's a hopeless romantic."

Marcus sat back in the booth. "Fuck's sake Robin, you've taken something incredibly awkward, and made it so I can never face them again. I can't take their money and that's final," he finished his champagne in two swallows.

"Marcus, you're being ridiculous. Put aside your fucking pride, and stop being such a prude. I didn't draw her a diagram or say anything more than what I just said to you," I scoffed. "Think of it as a loan then, and the payment is you have to have sex with me at least three times a day for the whole of school," I shrugged and sipped my drink. "No, starting now, I mean," I corrected myself and waggled my eyebrows.

"I already do that," Marcus said and pulled a face.

"So, repayment will be a cake walk." I pushed the 'press for champagne' button on the wall and waited for our server. "Let's hurry up and eat so you can get working on your first installment."

Marcus held my gaze with an inscrutable expression. I hoped he wasn't thinking of ways out of it with me. "You are something else Robin Trumball."

61

Working Boy

I MET WITH OLIVER TURNER, the family friend, general counsel of the global cyber-security, high-tech company SharkFinn, based out of Boston. I told you I had a vague memory of a hot blonde, but I couldn't have understated his beauty more if I tried. I felt like I was interviewing with Charlie Hunnam but like, even more appealing. He had some serious magnetism about him, and I'm not into blondes, as a general rule. We had a great chat, he was incredibly charming (not more than me though), and I was very frank with him. I told him about the porn, emphasizing my youth and naiveté, trusting someone I shouldn't have, etc., I figured it might come out in a background check with them, despite the scrubbing, and I wanted to be as transparent as possible. I also knew that the Earl would be writing to him, as well as several other top people I worked with, and some professors from Oxford, so it would be a tiny spot on an otherwise perfect resume.

We reminisced about Oxford; he was there for undergrad and grad school, and then he told me what it was like in Boston, said I was going to love it, and that Boston College Law School, and the Boston College main campus, weren't actually in Boston, but in a suburb, the suburb he lived in, with his husband. Yup, he was gay too, I nearly did a little dance there in the restaurant, and then speculated (to myself of course), whether he was a top, a bottom, or a flipper.

He didn't make any promises to me, naturally, about the job, but said he would speak with his CTO and his CPO, and his R2-D2, and see if there were any openings. He did warn me that they paid far more for their talent than any of their competitors and as such had very low turn-over. I already knew that because I had done my research, and told him I would keep my fingers crossed, and praised his company profusely *and* specifically, so that he knew I had done my research. I gave him my resume and he looked it over briefly, making impressed sounds as he read.

"I use this app," he said and looked at me with his eyebrows raised. "You designed it?"

"I did, I use it too, that's why I designed it, I needed it," I smiled pleased to hear he used my little clothing app.

He folded my resume and put it in the inside pocket of his beautifully tailored Tom Ford suit. "There's a fairly new apartment building down the street from me, right on the train, and your boyfriend could walk to the Law School. There are markets, and restaurants and everything you would need right there. I think some of the units come furnished, but don't quote me. I dropped out of paying attention once the plans were approved," he added with a smile. Oh god, I felt that smile all the way to my toes. Marcus had nothing to worry about, Oliver wasn't my type, but I always appreciated beauty when I saw it. I wondered what his husband looked like, and whether they were as an attractive couple as Marcus and I were. "I mean, I'm guessing you don't know anything about the area?"

"Thank you, we don't, and any suggestions are appreciated. I'll definitely check it out," I said as he stood, and I stood with him, watching him run his eyes over me.

"I like your suit, but I can't place the designer," he said as he shook my hand.

I looked down at the grey pinstripe suit I was wearing. "It was the Earl's, my grandfather I mean, and I think it might have been his father's," I gave a little shrug. "It came from somewhere on Saville Row," I chuckled. "Thank you so much for your time Oliver, I know how busy you are, I really appreciate it."

"Call me Ollie, and it was a pleasure to see you again. I'll be in touch."

We walked to the door and a driver leapt out of the black Range Rover idling at the curb, opening the back door for him. "Tell your parents I said 'hi,'" Ollie flashed a smile and disappeared into the car.

God he was smooth and so posh while I wanted to jump in the air and kick my heels together, but I didn't, instead I turned and walked back toward my office. I texted Marcus and couldn't wait to see him.

62

The Wonder Years

I GOT THE JOB, not a surprise to me, shouldn't have been to you either. We rented an apartment in the building down the street from Ollie. I usually took the train, but occasionally Ollie would offer to pick me up in his fancy electric Maserati. He'd plug it in next to the boss' unbelievably sexy Aston Martin (I took a picture of it for Marcus and he swooned, said it was a super leggy or something), and we'd take the elevator up, me stopping on the fourth floor, and Ollie going all the way to the top. The offices took up an entire glass building in the Seaport, the most beautiful location, with the most beautiful views you could imagine, not from my cube of course, but it was heaven working there.

Marcus and I loved Boston so much, we stayed. It was so freeing, for him especially, to be where no one knew us, and we could just be gay, not that we swanned around singing about it, because it's still a straight world, but there was no one we needed to hide from either. Ollie told me about Provincetown, a gay oasis on the tip of Cape Cod (it's the fist of the Cape really, and I giggled at the appropriateness of its location) and Marcus and I spent a week or two every summer there. It was only a short ferry ride from Boston, so we would go for weekends as well whenever we could until early November.

We were so busy, Marcus was at school or studying twenty-four seven, and I supported him one hundred percent, knowing how important it was for him to do well. I helped him, editing his work, keeping him organized and in a routine, while I worked long hours, proving myself at SharkFinn. He graduated, top of his class, because he worked his bloody ass off, and he did it for so many reasons. For the Earl and Countess, for me, and for his dad (who I still wanted to stab through the heart every time I saw Marcus look forlorn). Everyone (except his parents) flew in for his graduation. His sisters, my parents, my grandparents, Gertie and Evan, Gareth and Hector (I nearly fainted) and Harry. We rented out a restaurant in West Newton known for its cocktails and amazing food, and everyone raved about it. Ollie's parents happened to be in town visiting, and we invited them as well, to see my parents. Ollie put in a brief appearance, and chatted up Marcus, congratulating him on his new job with Kirk and Sweeney, one of the oldest, and most premier, law firms. They had bonded over a mutual love of football, and Ollie had invited Marcus to join his team shortly after we moved there, the two of them taking over any pitch they played on (god they were a sight to see, moving in sync, but that's for a different story).

* * *

After graduation, we bought a place in the city, Ollie advised us on the best neighborhoods in Boston, and we ended up on Marlborough Street, exactly where Ollie himself had begun, and where he still had a place. I might have preferred the South End, but I knew, from living in London, that your neighborhood meant everything so we rejoiced about finding a flat in one of the toniest and oldest of moneyed neighborhoods, and quickly found our favorite spots for everything within walking distance.

We went back to London for visits, me more frequently than Marcus, as he felt as though he had nothing really to go home for, and caught up with our friends. We went to Felicity's wedding, Gertie and Evan's wedding, Kevin and Lola's wedding, watched all our friends get married really, even Gareth. I tried my best not to show that it bugged me that we weren't, but maybe not really, because a year after we bought our flat, two years after our arrival in America, Marcus proposed to me on a beach in Provincetown. I was wearing tight, silver short-shorts, a black, thin-strapped, cropped tank-top, and Marcus' initials strung on a leather strap around my neck. I looked very gay, but we were in the gayest place on the planet and I felt Miami sexy, without the drugs.

The sun was setting behind us as we walked hand in hand on the beach, me sober and Marcus buzzed from his cocktails at dinner. He (fake) stumbled and I went to catch him when all of a sudden he turned on one knee and produced a ring from his pocket. It was an intricately carved band, with channel-set sapphires and diamonds all the way around, and was the most beautiful ring I had ever seen. He said he got the idea from Ollie's engagement ring, which was a plain band, channel set with just sapphires. The Vegas showgirls came dancing down my face and I covered my mouth as someone appeared off to our left and began taking pictures. I wiped my eyes furiously, and preened briefly for Marcus' paparazzi.

"You little sneak," I cried as he put the ring on my finger. "I love you!" I wrapped my arms around his neck when he stood, and peppered his face and lips with kisses.

He cupped my ass in his large hands and returned my kisses, pulling me up against him. I felt him wave his hand at the photographer and the camera stopped clicking away. "I love you Robin. You have been there for me in every way possible, and I can't imagine my life without you. I can't wait to be your husband," he murmured against my lips, running his hands over the bare skin of my lower back. I would have said something in return, but I was lost in his kisses.

✳ ✳ ✳

We had a modest-sized wedding back in England, and by modest, I mean only a hundred and fifty people. We wore matching linen suits, his was blue and mine was white. We invited his parents, and while they initially declined, they did actually show up. I couldn't believe how old Sir Hoity-Toity looked, and his mother would have too if not for the injections and hair dye. They stood with Marcus' sisters, but I felt their eyes on us, especially with the Earl and Countess fawning over us happily. My grandmother looped her arm through Marcus' and stood with him like he was her beau as he spoke with my family and other guests, including Ollie's parents David and Maggie Turner. The Earl had his arm on Marcus' shoulder from time to time, and it took me a minute to realize they were doing it on purpose, for us, and for Marcus' parents, and I felt the showgirls peeking out from backstage.

The wedding and the reception took place at my grandparents' estate in Buckinghamshire, on a beautiful summer day. I always wanted to be a June bride, and we married just before my twenty-sixth birthday, in the most spectacular of settings. Marcus was blown away, as was I, at the way the estate and grounds had been transformed. The house was massive and built in the eighteen hundred's, in maybe a neo-renaissance style, maybe baroque, I knew as much about architecture as I did sports cars. It was brick, and had towers, and four floors above ground and was set on like a million acres, or a thousand, or a hundred, I didn't know exactly, but everything was manicured, and lit, and festooned, and alive with merriment. I was so high on happiness, I didn't even miss having a glass of the Krug '96 (my favorite vintage) that everyone was so happy to enjoy, and not even Sir Hoity-Toity could bring me down.

Marcus' parents made up with him, I saw him talking to them and wiping his eyes after dinner. I know they tried to pay my grandparents back for his education but the Earl was having none of it, politely of course, he was the Earl after all. They were treated impeccably; my parents spoke with them, my grandparents, as I said, and the rest of my family chatted briefly, but I was shocked when his mother appeared at my side while Marcus was off with Gareth and the guys.

"Hello Robin," she said, her voice quavering ever so slightly. Her dark hair was up in an elaborate chignon and her blue summer dress skimmed her slim frame.

"Hello Jane," I replied with a smile. "I'm so glad you and Edward could join us," I said with only the tiniest bit of sarcasm.

She looked away. "It was a beautiful ceremony, beautiful setting," she gestured around nervously with her hand and then looked back at me. "You and Marcus looked, look, very handsome," she took a breath. "How's he been? How's America?"

I fought the urge to laugh, it had been three fucking years. "He's amazing. He's poised to make partner, we have a beautiful flat in the city, and we're so happy, I love him. I would never abandon him, for any reason," I added pointedly, I couldn't help myself. How the fuck she could stand there and act like Marcus had been the one to shut her out.

She winced (good). "I love my son," she said vehemently. "We obviously wanted more for him," she looked away and then back at me with hard eyes. "You can't fault us for that. I wonder what his life would have been like if he'd never met you."

I frowned, what in the actual fuck was she accusing me of? "I'm sorry?"

"You set your sights on him back in secondary, even before that," she said, something hidden in her tone. I waited. "The little victim, with the angel face, who needed rescuing. Always happened to be in his path, beguiling him. You had him so confused, his writing was tormented," she paused.

"You're not serious?" I scoffed. "I didn't make Marcus gay, your god did that. I'm just the lucky bloke he loves," I smiled congenially.

"You're so charming, aren't you?" She looked at the grass, and then back at me, before turning on her heel.

I felt shell-shocked and short of oxygen, and searched the crowd for Marcus, or Gertie, my eyes finding Hector instead. He had grown a beard, and I knew that Frank wasn't invited, he couldn't deal with Marcus being gay, so didn't have to think too hard about who he was as he came over.

"Everything okay?" He asked, in his therapist voice.

I laughed lightly. "Of course, it's my wedding day, marrying the man of my dreams," I shrugged dramatically. "Why wouldn't I be okay?"

"Because his mother, who he hasn't spoken with in nearly three years, said something to you, and I'm guessing it weren't all that friendly."

"Hector, where was all this insight in secondary?" I asked him with a frown. "I appreciate who you are now, but you did fuck all for me back then. Have you found a cure for misplaced testosterone? A cure for homophobic parents?" I sighed and stalked away, needing the bathroom.

I never said a word to Marcus, and his relationship with his parents at least existed again. We went back to Boston and lived in marital bliss, Marcus still making his law school 'loan payments' to me, not getting credit for any payments over three per day, (he had missed several payments during school and I was a proper bank). He worked hard trying to gain a partner position, and I worked hard, my year-long contract had turned into a permanent position because I was full of ideas and had the means to execute them. SharkFinn loved that, and I had the number two in the company's ear, not just because of the family connection, but also because he and Marcus played football nearly every weekend, and Ollie loved Marcus.

63

Little Earthquakes

I SHOULD HAVE BEEN WARY of all our good fortune, but it just became such second nature. I was promoted to Lead Developer, Marcus made Partner, we moved to a full brownstone on the sunny side of Marlborough Street, which had cost a fortune, but the Countess insisted on helping us. She said it was because she was so proud of all we had accomplished, and overcome, but I knew it was because she wanted to come visit and have her own floor, which she did, without a single complaint from Marcus (of course not, he loved her and she loved him). My grandparents would come and stay for weeks, we'd hardly see them, they took to Boston, and New England in general, just like I had, and they had time and money, and were using it wisely (in my opinion).

Marcus and I had our stupid fights, of course we did, I told you I was petty, but Marcus had the patience of a saint with me, and we always made up, and made up vigorously. Sometimes Marcus accused me of manufacturing problems just so we could have make-up sex, and I would get so angry at him when he did (but only because the make-up sex would be *that* much extra). I was a strong proponent of keeping things spicy, it was in my marrow. Marcus loved it, and especially loved it when he would strip me after a fight and find me in a thong, or mesh undies, or a colorful jock strap, ready for his apology, or punishment.

He understood me. I told you, he was an old soul who could see beyond the minutia in a way I never could. He supported me as much as I did him, even accompanying me to a meeting from time to time, though he *hated* them. He never said a word, in fact Marcus was the very definition of the strong silent type. I was the only one he opened up to, and even then, not very often, but I knew him through and through, he didn't need to say much, I could read him as well as he could read me. Honestly, his love was so all-encompassing and intangible and yet at times, I felt as though I could gather it to me and put it in my pocket to run my fingers over like a treasure, and treasure it, I did.

***

Six years into America, ten years after we'd last spoken, Dee requested to follow me on Instagram. I had a private account and people had to wait to be let in (unlike my long ago deleted Finsta which anyone could follow). I remember seeing the notification when I was at work and sitting in a near trance for hours. I hadn't thought about her since my wedding when I had contemplated inviting her, but didn't know where she lived, and figured, she ghosted me, if she wanted back in, she would have to reach out to me, and here she was, reaching out.

I scanned her profile; she looked the same but thinner, and it looked like she was with someone, though I couldn't tell if she was married or just dating. I accepted her follow request, but didn't request to follow her back right away, I wanted to see what she wanted first. She liked a bunch of my posts, including my wedding ones (of course she did, Marcus and I looked amazing) and the honeymoon ones on Mykonos, where Marcus looked like a god in his tight, square-legged trunks.

I told Marcus about it as we were getting ready for bed and he looked at me with his eyebrows raised. "What does she want after all this time?"

I shrugged. "Maybe she misses me, has seen the error of her ways."

"Okay," Marcus said and disappeared into the bathroom.

I frowned at his back, at his nonchalance. Didn't he understand the magnitude of the whole thing? "Marcus, I haven't heard from her in nearly ten years, all I get is 'okay?'" I felt a fight coming on, and it wasn't *entirely* manufactured, this time. I'm not sure if it's actually possible to hear people roll their eyes, but I swear to god, I heard him roll his in the bathroom. I raced to the doorway to catch him. He was brushing his teeth at the sink in his underwear.

He looked at me, the electric toothbrush buzzing away in his mouth. "What?" He asked in a possibly irritated tone.

I widened my eyes and then narrowed them, looking him over. "You seriously don't think this is a big deal?"

He shrugged and spat into the sink, rinsing his toothbrush before turning it off. "I guess. But I wouldn't read too much into it until you hear from her, personally," his eyes scanned my body and it's language. "Am I gripping your arms and throwing you on the bed exasperatedly, or touching you softly and begging for your forgiveness tonight?" He raised his eyebrows and waited with the tip of his tongue peeking out between his teeth.

I picked up my toothbrush as I tried to decide. Honestly, a little of both would be nice, but I couldn't give in so soon, it felt like he was mocking me. "Why don't you tell me about work, since you don't seem to want to take me or my conversation seriously."

"Robin," he smiled, "I do think it's shocking, and we won't know why until she reaches out to you. My advice is to keep her at arm's length, she is likely as different a person now as you are, and I can only imagine what she thinks of us," he shook his head. "Did she comment on any of our wedding or honeymoon photos?"

I spat and rinsed my toothbrush. "She liked them all, and the videos, and your graduation. She must've gone through the whole six years of us in America and perhaps even further back. But no comments, and I won't follow her back until I hear from her," I added, crossing my arms over my chest and resting back against the sink.

"I'm sorry for not taking it more seriously Robin," he stroked my arm, and I tensed slightly, not quite ready for the soft apology, but liking what he was saying, he should take me more seriously. "I should never treat you as though you turn every little thing into a dramatic event. For example, that time you wrote a scathing, two-page email to that friend of yours, ripping her for returning the gift you gave her," Marcus said against my neck, "was a perfectly reasonable response. As you explained, very thoroughly to me, you were completely justified."

My mouth dropped open and I stepped back with a frown. *Why was he bringing that up?* "I was justified. That was the third gift I had given her over the years that she opened and then handed back to me!"

"She said she had it already, and wanted to spare you the expense," Marcus shrugged. "Maybe a short note, or a phone call would've have sufficed."

Did I see something behind his eyes? *Was he taking her side?* "That is just not done!" I felt myself getting riled up again. "There is gift etiquette and she violated it. If you have something already, you politely accept it and then re-gift it to someone else, or return it, or donate it, or fucking throw it away. You don't hand it back and say 'no thank you,'" I gaped at him with my mouth open. "She was clearly raised by animals and I'm glad I'm no longer her friend."

I made to flounce angrily past Marcus when he grabbed my arms and kissed me firmly on the lips as he steered me into the bedroom. I barely had time to register that this was the exasperated sex scenario and that he'd purposefully riled me up just so he could throw me on the bed, before he did just that. He rolled me over, pulled my shorts down exposing my bare ass, just the elastic of my blue jock-strap around my waist and under my cheeks, and spanked me.

If I were to give that night a title, it would have been *'Sexy, pouty blonde gets punished by MONSTER cock twice, cums instantly! Cream-pie AND facial.'*

64

Lucy, I'm Home

I SLUNG MY LOUIS VUITTON crossbody bag over my head as I stepped out of the cab and smoothed my hair nervously. Dee had eventually instant messaged me, and we struck up a brief exchange, which was surreal and filled me with all kinds of feelings. She asked when I would be in London again and we made a plan to meet up in early March, when Marcus and I were in town for his mother's birthday (always an awkward experience). I wished I had brought him or Gertie, as I stood outside the Ritz in Soho. Dee knew how much I loved Soho, and the Ritz specifically, and I smiled as I made my way through the lobby. I scanned the bar and didn't see a shining blonde head but I did see the hostess who was looking at me inquisitively, her eyes sweeping my Burberry outfit with appreciation. I wanted to wow with a suit, but instead opted for something youthful, in remembrance of our teenage years together.

"I'm meeting someone, Dee?" I said to the hostess.

She smiled and said, 'follow me,' leading me to a booth in the corner, with tall sides. Instead of seeing a beautiful, and, formerly chubby, blonde, I was face to face with a dark-haired Ukrainian with snarling tigers on his arm and an inscrutable expression on his face.

"Hello Robby," Vas said, his eyes scanning my body, his smile full of sin but not sex.

I held my shock, and at first, nearly ran because I thought I saw a teardrop tattoo next to his eye, but it was just a shadow. He looked older than ten years should have worn him, and the look he gave me snatched my breath and shifted my shoulder but not for the same reason it had all those years ago. The hostess left us and all my instincts screamed that I should follow her, but Vas reached out and seized my wrist.

"Sit down Robin, we have a lot to discuss," he said in a cold voice that bent my knees, and I joined him.

"Why would you do that?" cried the masses. "He's going to kill you!"

I knew he wouldn't kill me, the look in his eye screamed that he would never go back to prison, and they would never not think he had something to do with my disappearance or murder. There was bottle of gangster champagne chilling on ice and two glasses filled with bubbly. He raised his glass and looked at mine and then at me.

"I don't drink. You made me an alcoholic," I said calmly.

"And you made me a sex offender, so drink that fucking champagne. You're paying for it, might as well enjoy it," he said forcefully in his medium-deep voice.

Well, he had me there, so I picked up the glass, dumped the contents into the ice bucket, and poured myself a new glass, checking for residue and wiping it out with my napkin first. I was born at night, but not last fucking night.

He watched me carefully, his mouth a thin line. "You were always smarter than you led on. Took me ten years," he shrugged and downed his glass with a hard expression. He poured himself more while I watched him. He was still handsome, weak chin and all. His body seemed bigger, and I couldn't tell if that was because of his prison workouts, or if it had been so long that I had forgotten him.

"Vas, I didn't turn you in, I don't know who did. Could have been the school, could have been Dee, she was there to pick up my pieces," I winced and looked away. "I loved you," I breathed and looked back at him. "You left me," I added softly.

He held my gaze, and I never looked away. "And you felt scorned, so you turned me in."

"I swear, I didn't," I watched the champagne bubbles dance up the inside of the glass. "Why did you leave me? We might still be together," I waved my hand, not meaning it.

He laughed harshly. "You're so full of shit. You were always full of shit. Everything was an act with you, and you were such a spoiled fucking brat," his eyes swept over me. "Still are, I'm guessing."

The indignation welled up inside me, *how dare he?* "I did everything for you, fuck you. What is it you want, Vasyl?"

"I want those ten years back that you stole from me. I want you to suffer, you and your bully husband," Vas said with an evil grin. "That stumped me for a while, and then I figured it out," he shrugged, "you two were fucking all along, I should've known from the snap he sent me."

"You stole years from me and you ruined so much in my life. You set me up, used me. I was nothing but a source of income for you, and your panic was real when you found out I wasn't eighteen. You should probably have cut your losses then, but you were too greedy," I spat and watched him bristle. "Marcus loves me, I love him, and it's *real*. He treats me like a king, and he certainly never beat me until I peed blood," I said harshly and held his gaze. "He also knows there's nowhere but down from me. Something you learned the hard way. I can't imagine you think that slag twink was worth it. How fast did he drop you?"

His face hardened, and I worried briefly that I took it too far. I glanced at the bar and what I saw reassured me. I looked back at Vas who had followed my gaze.

"Is he wit you?" He asked in a low voice, gesturing to the burly guy watching us, so burly and attentive he couldn't be anything but hired security.

I smiled. "I knew you weren't Dee," I stood and put two hundred quid on the table. "Bye Vasyl."

I never said a word to Marcus about Vas, and he never asked about Dee because I never told him I was meeting 'her.' I suffered through his mother's birthday dinner, exchanging the briefest of pleasantries with her and Sir Hoity-Toity, before devoting the rest of the night to fawning over Marcus and gossiping with his sisters. We went back to Boston and resumed our perfect routine, for a little while anyway.

65

A Marquess Abroad

IT WAS A FOGGY DAY in Boston, somewhere between winter and spring, that doldrum period when many people want to slit their wrists and aren't blamed at all for the thought. It had been nearly four years since I saw Vas, and I was on my computer in my home office, a big room with giant windows, doing research, looking for ideas, and answers, when Marcus came to the doorway looking like he was bleeding out. I straightened and then stood, my belly filled with worry.

"What is it Marcus?"

"My dad just called, his cousin died," Marcus said and then frowned.

I relaxed slightly, and then looked around wondering at the weight of the news. I knew Marcus wasn't very close with his extended family, only his cousins Betty and Jules and their spouses had been at our wedding. "I'm sorry to hear that darling. Will we be going back for the funeral?" I asked, already mentally picking out my mourning wardrobe.

"Yes, of course," he looked at me. "He died without heirs."

I raised my eyebrows wondering at how much of a queen his father's cousin was. "Oh, did he have a will? Were you close? Do you think he left you his candelabras and tiaras?"

Marcus laughed lightly. "No, I don't think he mentioned me specifically at all, but he did leave me something, inadvertently," Marcus paused and stepped into the room. "His fucking title."

Oh, *that* cousin. "Holy shit Marcus!" I looked around in wonder with a flutter in my stomach. "Does that make me Marchioness?" I asked sweeping my imaginary hair from my shoulders. "And you Marquess Marcus?" I bent over in a fit of laughter.

"It doesn't make either of us anything yet you ninny," Marcus laughed and put his arms around me. "My dad is the successor, but I am freaking out. All jokes aside Robin, this changes everything."

He said it gravely, and I remember at the time only thinking of myself, and that maybe he meant we'd have to move back to England or join the House of Lords, but it was much worse.

* * *

We went back to London for the Marquess of Brougham's funeral, for the reading of the will, for the paperwork, and government bullshit. Everyone who's anyone in the aristocracy (or as they say on *Bridgerton* 'the ton'), including the royal family, and the Earl and Countess of Wenham, was at the funeral. My aunt and uncle were there as well, along with Theo, and I tried not to look as excited as I felt about being among the center of attention, people looking at the mourning family, and at me and Marcus specifically, the gay-married, someday-to-be Marquess. He stood between me and his parents, as a buffer, and his sisters stood on my other side. I held Marcus' hand in the pew at the Abbey, but he wouldn't hold my hand as we walked out behind the casket. I didn't let it bother me because I knew all eyes were on us.

I met the Countess' eye with a secret glance as we exited the pew, and then scanned the crowd of mourners. I pulled up at the sight of Vas, standing in a suit at the back, watching me. I looked again for the Countess, and saw she had already followed my eye. I wasn't sure what he was doing there but it couldn't be anything good and I felt a powerful thirst at being caught off guard. I looked at Marcus and, luckily, he hadn't noticed. I was desperate for his hand, but clenched my fists instead. Fortunately, everything after the funeral was private and for family only, so I relaxed and kept close to Marcus' side.

Marcus' father avoided me as usual, at the funeral and after, and his mother was cool, but his sisters embraced me tightly. We had become quite close over the years, I visited them when I was in the UK, they visited us in Boston, and they loved me. When Emma had her first baby, she sent me a t-shirt with a rainbow on it that said 'GUNCLE, noun: *An uncle, only more fabulous, See also: Fun, good looking*' (Marcus didn't get one). You better believe I wore that shirt every time we went home for a gathering, including that trip.

Marcus had to have meeting after meeting with stuffy people and his father, while I caught up with Gertie, and her baby, and saw my parents, brothers, and Felicity and her babies. Went to a meeting with T., which was fantastic, but most importantly I spent time with the Countess. We always stayed with the Earl and Countess when we were in town, the house was massive as I said, and we had our own dedicated suite of rooms. We were guests who could come and go as we pleased, but Gil always let us in, and guarded her and the Earl's private space carefully. He led me into her sitting room, where she was waiting dressed in a Chanel pantsuit, magnificent, and full of mischievous light.

"Soon I'll be bowing to you, Marchioness," she said with a laugh as I bowed over her hand and then hugged her tightly.

"That's if I grant you an audience," I said haughtily, "awfully presumptuous of you Countess," I looked around wildly with wide eyes.

She kissed my cheek again with a laugh and had me sit next to her on the couch. We had tea and looked at Instagram, and caught up about life, and how stressful everything was with the title, but that Marcus was grateful for my support through it all.

"Once the paperwork is signed and sorted, and the dust has settled, everything will go back to normal, except you'll have estates to manage," she beamed, "some truly grand estates I know, and you'll be so good at it. I always thought you were born to the wrong child, you should be Earl. But here the universe did one better," she kissed me with a wink and hugged me tightly. "You are as lucky with Marcus as I am with the Earl, but they are even luckier to have us. I love you, Robin."

"I love you Gram, and I am the luckiest of all, to have you and Marcus, and the Earl," I shrugged, feeling overwhelmed. "My cup runneth over."

She looked at her watch and stood. "Come downstairs to the drawing room." She didn't wait for me as she left.

I followed her into the Blue Drawing Room, and nearly fainted at the sight of Vas, sitting on one of the settees near the massive fireplace, a bone china tea set in front of him. He stood as we came in, dressed in the same suit I'd seen him in at the funeral, his hand tattoo sticking incongruously out of the sleeve. I swallowed and wondered at what my grandmother was on about.

"Hello Mr. Boiko," she said in her haughty but cordial voice. "I'm the Countess of Wenham, I believe you know my grandson Robin."

He flashed me a smug look as he held out his hand to my grandmother. "It's an honor to meet you, My Lady."

She took his hand with her fingers and gestured with her other hand. "Please, sit." She looked at me and then back at Vas. "How's the tea? Would you care for something stronger?"

I was still trying to catch my breath and watched her carefully, god she was so poised, so regal, I was in awe, to be honest. I sat in the Louis XIV chair (yes, it was real) next to the settee and looked at Vas warily.

She poured him more tea at his request before sitting in the other Louis XIV chair opposite mine. She looked at me. "Would you like some tea Robin?"

I looked at the teapot, and back at her. "No thank you. You and I had three cups each upstairs," I smiled and then looked at Vas. "Put your phone on the table."

He looked sharply at me and then reached inside his coat. He put his phone face up and shook his head with a humorless laugh. "Yours too, Robby. You're the one who records everything."

I shrugged and put my phone on the table next to me. I had no need to record anything at the Countess'.

"Nice place," Vas said to my grandmother, picking up his tea cup, which looked absurdly small in his massive tattooed hand. "These all former Earls and Countesses?" He gestured with his free hand before taking a swallow of tea.

My grandmother smiled. "Of course they are. Our title goes back to the fifteenth century, when Earl was the highest title after Prince. This is but a small sampling of our *great* ancestors," she looked at me with a soft expression and then looked back at Vas. "We've survived wars, famine, uprisings, upstarts, and schemers. Our cream always rises to the top."

Vas looked at me and put down his empty teacup. I wondered if his blood had frozen in his veins, because if I were him, mine would have.

"The only schemer in this room is Robby," he gestured with his thumb. "Did Robby ever tell you about us?"

My grandmother looked at me. "Did you, darling?"

I nodded. "Yes Grandmother, I told you we dated, briefly, between secondary and Oxford."

Vas laughed harshly. "Your grandson and I dated for three years and he had me sent to prison. I find it odd that he never introduced me to you and your husband," he paused, dropping his 'h's' as he was clearly riled. "It took captivity for me to realize what a devil he really is, and I wonder how his husband's family would feel about the truth," Vas sat back in the sofa.

My grandmother frowned and then pressed the button on the floor with the toe of her Roger Vivier pumps. Gil appeared immediately. "Something stronger Gil, please," she smiled at him. Gil nodded his head slightly and a footman returned a moment later with a crystal decanter filled with red wine on a silver tray with two glasses, setting it down on the mahogany sideboard under the Caravaggio.

He poured wine into the glasses and put one in front of Vas and one in my grandmother's hand, before closing the door behind him.

"What is the truth, Mr. Boiko?" She asked with a tilt of her head, taking a sip of her wine.

And then Vas proceeded to make a lot of outlandish claims: that I was the one who left him (what in the actual fuck?), that I lied about my age and was the one who posted the videos when I was seventeen (excuse me?), that I faked rehab (yes, I loved it so much I went three times just for fun), and that I married my bully for retribution (some sort of long game of chess) and for his title.

My grandmother sat and listened politely, looking at me from time to time. "Mr. Boiko," she sighed. "These are outrageous and incredibly farfetched claims, dreamt up by someone with far too much time on his hands. I know they're outrageous because if Robin wanted that title, he could have gotten it straight from the Marquess himself, who was as gay as the day is long, not that I expect you to have known that." She took a gloriously haughty breath through her nose. "Now, is that all? Because I'm afraid I've a very busy evening ahead of me."

"I can't work, I'm a registered sex offender," he glared at me. "They didn't take all my videos; I wonder how your husband and his family would like them?"

"Are you blackmailing me?" I asked, narrowing my eyes. "Marcus and his family already know; his father was the lawyer my family consulted."

Vas looked like he wasn't expecting that detail, but recovered quickly. "That was before he was made Marquess, and his son the heir. There is no way the royal family would tolerate a porn star in their ranks."

"The Windsors have greater things to worry about, and the House of Lords always circle around their own, something else I don't expect you to know," my grandmother interrupted. "You do anything with those, films, and I will crush you like a bug," she stood. "No one would ever have anything other than sympathy for Robin. My grandson was a child, you were a *man*, twelve years older. You exploited him, you profited off him, you tried to ruin him, by my accounting you nearly killed him twice, and now you're trying to extort money from him?"

"Vasyl, please don't cry poor, the porn you're making more than pays the bills I'm sure," I said with my eyebrows raised.

"You watching my porn?" He asked with a smirk.

"No," I scoffed, "you've seen my husband. He's more man than you'll ever be, and he knows all the ways to love me. It was just a guess, and of course I was right." I pulled a face.

Vas narrowed his eyes at me and turned to my grandmother. "He stole ten years from me, what are ten years' worth to you, Victoria?" He said her name derisively, and I couldn't believe he called her by her first name, I don't even think the Earl did that.

She looked at him, and he didn't know her body language like I did, because otherwise he would have jumped out the nearest window. "I'm not a criminal Mr. Boiko, and even if I were, our lives are not comparable." She pressed the button on the floor. Gil arrived a moment later and Vas stood, pocketing his phone. "Good day," she said coolly.

Vas looked between me and my grandmother and then at Gil, who was older, but didn't take shit from anyone. "Good bye," he said in a tone that meant anything but, and let Gil usher him out.

"That man," she turned her gaze to mine and shook her head. "I remember the lust and poor decision making of youth," she sighed. "He ever contacts you, or the Willoughbys, you had better let me know, but I'm hoping we never hear from him again."

I stood and hugged her. "You were magnificent, and I'm sorry you had to be. I am filled with regret over that man."

She patted my back and pulled out of my arms. "You are not the first Wenham to have a black mark on your pedigree, but as I told that man, we've lasted six centuries, we know how to erase the smudges," she looked at me as we heard raised voices from the beyond the closed door. I met her gaze and hurriedly flung the door open to see Gil and the footman trying to calm a very angry pair of men, ones who for all the world looked like the tigers on Vas' arm. Marcus had Vas up against the wall, his forearm pressed against Vas' throat, an exact flip of what happened all those years ago, and Vas had the front of Marcus' suit in his fists. "Marcus!" I cried. He and Vas both turned their heads to look at me. "Let him go, he was just leaving."

Marcus stepped back but didn't relax, as Vas let him go. He looked frightening and magnificent, towering over Vas. They were both breathing heavy as Gil opened the front door behind them.

"Mr. Boiko," my grandmother said calmly, and gestured to the door. "I'm sure you don't want a police escort."

Vas looked between all of us, his eyes lingering on me before turning his gaze back to Marcus. "You're an idiot, and you're going to find that out the hard way like I did," he pushed past Gil and strode down the steps.

Marcus watched him leave as Gil closed the door and then turned to look at me. His face was a storm cloud and I took an involuntary step back. I felt my grandmother's hand on my arm.

"Join us in the drawing room," she said to Marcus before turning to the footman. "Please clear the tea and glasses."

Marcus followed us angrily into the blue drawing room and waited, pacing, as the footman cleared everything but the wine decanter away. As soon as the door was closed Marcus turned to me. "What the hell was he doing here?"

"I invited him." Marcus' eyes went to the Countess like a whip. "He was at the Marquess' funeral. I'm certain you didn't notice him, such was your grief and familial duty, but I saw him, and I know how to handle people like Mr. Boiko," she looked at me and then back at Marcus. "You have to nip them in the bud."

Marcus exhaled and looked at me.

66

The Madness
of the Marquess

MARCUS AND I went out to dinner, Marcus eager to leave and drink. We spoke in hushed tones in the back of the cab, I filled him in on what happened, including Vas' preposterous claims, and then his threats.

Marcus looked out the window. "He better not try to contact my dad," he said and then shut the conversation down.

Marcus was distracted and evasive over dinner, and I just assumed that it was because of Vas and all the rigamarole around the succession, and I was right, in part. I was distracted with thoughts of my own so didn't press until after Marcus' second cocktail. Turns out that while the Marquess was a *queen*, he was on the verge of getting married to a woman, for heirs presumably, and had had a heart attack. He was only in his late fifties and the, much younger, fiancée was being a bit of a sticky wicket, trying to claim something. I don't blame her for grasping at straws but there was no way around the fact that she wasn't entitled to anything. I remembered her eyeing Marcus after the funeral, and I did everything but pee on the man to make sure she knew she was barking up the wrong tree.

"What is it?" I asked, over dessert, knowing that it was more than just the fiancée and Vas that was troubling him.

Marcus brought his eyes to mine. "My father is hale and hearty, and will hold the title for many years, thankfully. But, my parents want the title to stay in our branch. This is a title that has been passed back and forth in my family more times than a ball in a rugby match, because of no direct descendants or only girls," he waved his hand, looked at his plate and took a breath. "They want me to divorce you and marry a woman," he said in a rush, looking up at my stunned face. "I was told I need to procreate, and need more than just an heir and a spare."

I was rendered speechless (shocking I know), and was suddenly certain I had misheard him. "What? Who said this?" I asked, narrowing my eyes.

"Both my parents, and the solicitor managing the title transfer," Marcus answered looking away.

Oh my god, you have to be fucking kidding me, I thought. "Marcus, it's the twenty-first century. If you want kids, we can hire a womb," I felt the oxygen fleeing the room. "I would love to raise your children, *our* children," I added emphatically, thinking I wanted to do anything but. Kids were noisy, and needy, and expensive. Oh Christ, I didn't want kids, but so help me god, I would never let Marcus know that.

He looked back at me. "It's just unprecedented," he spread his hands. "My parents are adamant and I don't know what to do. Tradition is smothering me," he finished his third cocktail.

I saw the anguish in his face, and knew he was struggling. I didn't want to add to it. "This is fucking bullshit, but I love you Marcus, and I know this is so much bigger than the both of us. I will love you *forever,* and I don't want to stand between you and your dynasty, or what your parents want, as much as it breaks my heart," my voice caught. "I think by now you know I've only ever wanted to please you, from day *one.* This is family duty, you have to do what you see fit. I just want to be absolutely clear that it will be clean break, *forever.* I won't cause a scene, but I won't be your side piece." I licked my lips as the showgirls began warming their legs up backstage.

Marcus winced, perhaps truly realizing what he would be giving up, what his parents were asking of him. He flagged the waiter for the check.

We went back to Wenham House, Gil letting us in, and it was awkward in our suite. Marcus maybe lost in his thoughts, me maybe wanting to be petty, but the two of us realizing the gravity of everything, and who knew how it would come out in the light of day. We undressed, got into bed, and reached for each other with desperation.

I got Marcus to admit the next morning that it wasn't just him being gay, that it was me, and Vas, and our scandal, that caused his parents to insist that we divorce. I wondered how much of that was just his parents finally seeing a way between us, and how much was based on people on the outside knowing about me and Vas, or god forbid, that Vas had already gone to the Willoughbys. I told Marcus that I didn't want to stand in the way of his succession while at the same time planned on paying Sir Hoity-Toity a visit.

67

I See Dead People

I LOOKED AT Sir Edward Willoughby's secretary, excuse me, assistant (labels are so fucking ridiculous, constantly trading one for another), and took a breath. "Hi. Robin Willoughby (I loved saying that almost as much as I loved saying Marcus' full name), nice to meet you. Please let Edward know his son-in-law is here to see him," I said in my most charming voice, with my most charming smile.

"Of course," his secretary said, trying not to sound flustered as she picked up the phone. I was guessing she didn't know Marcus was gay, or married. "Your son-in-law Robin, is here to see you," she listened briefly before hanging up and gestured to his closed office door.

I strode through in my latest acquisition from the Earl's closet, a glorious, navy blue, Saville Row three-piece suit, channeling the Countess. "Hello, sir," I smiled and held out my hand (he was always so insistent that I call him 'Sir Edward,' that I couldn't help but use it the American way).

Marcus' father came around his desk to meet me, and shook my hand warily, his teeth clenched.

I looked around his spacious office and then back at him with a smile. "How are you, Edward?"

He frowned, maybe at my use of his given name, maybe at my presence. Who knew? Who cared?

"I'm fine," he answered in a voice that indicated he was anything but. "What are you doing here?"

I laughed lightly, *how could he not know?* "I'm here because you're dictating some truly abhorrent shit to your son, and I'm wondering at your audacity."

"I don't know what you're talking about," he shrugged. "He's going to be a Marquess and, not only does he need offspring, but he needs them bred the proper way," Edward scoffed and scanned his eyes over me.

I laughed. "He breeds me proper *every* night, and while I can't birth the babies, he can make them, and you, of all people, won't dictate to us just how Marcus' heirs are begotten."

Sir Hoity-Toity looked away then.

"Edward," I said calmly as I pulled my phone from my pocket. "I haven't made a big deal about how shittily you've treated Marcus the past twelve years, I haven't said boo at all, even though we both know why," I swiped into my photos and held up my phone, smiling when he blanched. "You will back the fuck off with your demands, and Marcus and I will produce as many heirs as you want. Or so help me god, you will be sorry." I turned on my heel and strode out.

I know I told you we didn't know Marcus' dad knew about the porn, but I lied. I was the one who recommended my dad reach out to him, I knew how connected he was. I met with Sir Hoity-Toity all those years ago, to tell my side of the story, and I guess you could say, the apple really never falls far from the tree.

I immediately began looking at surrogate websites, and for houses in the suburbs, on my laptop when I got back to Wenham House. I wasn't sure if we'd be moving back to London, or raising our family in Boston, so I looked in both places. I knew I could work for SharkFinn in Europe, or honestly just retire, become a housewife, raise our boys (of course we'd have boys), with a nanny, and make Marcus dinner every night. I'd probably need a whole new wardrobe for this radical life change, definitely some new tennis whites and of course, slutty bedroom attire. I was having just that fantasy when Marcus came through our suite door.

I stood happily and kissed him. "How was your day?"

"Exhausting," his arms came up around me. "I need a hug and, maybe something more, if you can wait for dinner," he trailed off.

I smiled against his neck. "I will always choose sex with you over food you ninny."

$$68$$

Stepford Wife

WE WENT BACK to Boston, and resumed our normal lives, well, as best we could. I knew Marcus was still mulling things over. He'd thrown everything away to be with me, but it never mattered before. I knew he was someone who was determined, and faithful, and solid, in a way I could never be, and that frightened me. His shoulders sagged under the sudden weight of tradition and expectation and that's when the grey hairs appeared, oh, and the cigarettes. He never smoked around me, but he came home on more than one occasion smelling disgusting. I kissed him those nights with my nose wrinkled.

I did everything for him, all the things he loved, but with nonchalance, I am not an idiot, I didn't need to seem desperate, he was the one who was going to lose out if he dumped me. I didn't wait for us to have children to go out and buy myself some really slutty undergarments, and some fun toys, all of which made Marcus' eyes go buggy and his cock go ping. I sent him to work several mornings a week bleary-eyed, but with a huge smile on his face.

I interviewed a slew of surrogacy agencies in Rhode Island (the laws were better) and Massachusetts, and once we settled on one, they began finding us matches. Marcus came to one meeting with a potential host body (I know I'm not supposed to call her that) but she wasn't a good fit and Marcus got discouraged. I wasn't discouraged but I really resented my anatomy during the whole process because I should be the one providing my husband with a baby (not that I'd ever do such a disgusting thing if I were actually a woman), and I hated being at the mercy of a stranger.

It didn't matter what she looked like, she wasn't providing any genetic material, but what did matter was the connection, because we would be in each other's lives for nearly a year, possibly more if the embryos didn't take the first time. I didn't worry at all about that, I knew Marcus' embryos would be strong and determined, just like he was. My one requirement was that she have a sense of humor, and unfortunately, a surprising number of these women didn't. I knew we'd find one eventually, so I turned my focus to other things while the agency kept looking.

Now that we were going to have a family, we had so much more to consider. We needed the best schools, a big yard, a swanky neighborhood, an attached garage, and fabulous neighbors. I looked for real estate in all the 'W' towns: Weston, Wellesley, Wayland, and then at the better towns, like Newton, and . . . Newton. I found several in our old law school neighborhood, near Ollie's house, two of which were right around the corner from him.

One night after work, after weeks of Marcus' nonchalance on the subject, I pressed him to care. "Marcus, you said it yourself, your father is hale and hearty, and there's no need for us to uproot ourselves now and move back across the pond. You're doing so well at the firm and I want to start our family," I said, and stopped dicing the garlic. I ran my eyes over him in his t-shirt and shorts. "In fact, we should really get started on that tonight," I added suggestively, waggling my eyebrows. He breathed out a laugh and went to the fridge for a beer.

I had been so good the last few months, not picking a fight, not being petty (mostly), but that little fucking laugh undid me. "What the fuck Marcus?" I put down the knife. "You're so vague it's like you're not even here most days, transparent like a bloody ghost in the movies."

He straightened and popped the cap off the bottle on the opener mounted on the doorframe of the pantry. He took a swig, looked at me and then walked out of the room. I picked my jaw up off the floor, stopped my head from spinning on my neck, and looked around the kitchen, thinking. I scraped the dinner I was prepping, chicken and all, into the trash and loaded the dishwasher. *Fuck you Mr. Willoughby.* I had been doing too much, and now, I was going to take a break. I picked up my phone and went out the back door, calling my American Gertie on the way to the Oak Bar.

I had a club soda, but told the bartender to pretend like she was adding vodka to it, because I was feeling petty (but not thirstily so), and listened to Holly talk about her (shitty) husband, and work, and what our other friends were up to. It was everything I needed, and we stayed out past ten, both of us ignoring our husbands' texts, though we did have to pose for a selfie for Rich; he was such a jealous prick, he didn't trust that she was out with me.

We kissed and I walked home, the night was a perfect, early summer night, and yet I was beginning to feel morose. My birthday was around the corner, I was turning thirty-four, not a milestone but I felt bereft, suddenly. If Marcus did leave me, if he chose the path his parents wanted, what would I do? Would I stay in America? I was a dual citizen now, I could, but would I want to stay, or would I want to be back in London, with my roots, Gertie, and the Countess and Earl? Could I avoid Marcus in the circles we ran in? Could I stand to see him with a *woman* on his arm? I stopped and gasped for air. Fuck's sake, why was the outdoors so short of oxygen? I had to sit on a doorstep and put my head between my knees. Could he be happy with a woman, or would he find some man to replace me on the side? I took a deep breath, and gathered myself, pushing that thought firmly away. No one he could find would be better than me, and I stood, sweeping my imaginary hair off my shoulders as I continued home. I felt better but there was a small part of my brain that said maybe I wouldn't find better either.

I let myself in the front door and found Marcus waiting for me on the couch in the downstairs living room. I liked to call it the beige drawing room, but Marcus always rolled his eyes when I did, saying they didn't have drawing rooms in America, and there were no ancestors on the walls or history to the room.

"Where have you been?" Marcus asked quietly as he stood, his voice worried.

"I was with Holly," I put my keys in the bowl in the foyer. "You seemed like you needed space. You seem like you *need* space," I said emphasizing the word. "I understand the pressure you're under, and I've done my best to make sure you aren't feeling any pressure from me. Are your parents still pushing you?" I whispered, worried maybe his father had alluded to something.

He hung his head and shook it. "No," he said softly. "All the pressure I feel is coming from the inside," he looked back up at me. "I'm *nobody*," he winced, "I was just a man loving a man. I don't want to be a trailblazer, I don't have it in me."

My heart broke, and I shook my head at him. "You're not. Lord Mountbatten, a literal relative of the Queen, blazed that trail more than fifteen years ago, and there have been three gay marriages in the nobility since then, two have had children," I took his hand. "People around you are making this bigger than it should be. I told you I can't wave a magic wand and erase my past, but I was a child, and I think if it ever came out on the larger stage, people would see that."

Marcus held my gaze and then pulled me to him. "It was just so easy before."

I didn't know what to say, so I just hugged him, tightly.

69

The Gronk
on the Cape

I SURPRISED MARCUS with a weekend in P-town, renting our favorite cottage near town and the beach. We walked hand in hand, and arm in arm under the warm sun and just let everything fall away in our favorite spot in America.

"Ollie keeps telling me we need to see Chatham, says there's a great main street, shops and restaurants," I said on our way back to the cottage after lunch. "We should go for a stroll, and then he said to have dinner at the Impudent Oyster and drinks at the Squire."

"Dinner spot sounds right up your alley darling," Marcus grinned and squeezed me to him, kissing the side of my head.

"I think you're the one being impudent at the moment," I elbowed him playfully and then wrapped my arms around his waist. "But I love you anyway."

He sighed and kept his arm around me, kissing the top of my head as I rested it against his shoulder. I never wanted the moment to end.

We stopped at Lighthouse Beach and took some pictures, and then shopped on Main Street, ending at Gustare's, which Ollie recommended for their oils and vinegars. The selection was amazing and I picked up a few flavors to try. We put our shopping bags in the car and had dinner, which wasn't impudent at all, but quite delicious, and then walked across the street to the Squire, an absolute dive bar, covered in license plates, and Marcus loved it. We sat at the double-sided bar in the middle of the room and ordered. It was dim and crowded and several women stared at us, or Marcus really, though he would say they stared at me, we were both each other's number-one fans.

The bar filled up as Marcus ordered another pint and soon we were surrounded by and chatting with a group of women in their mid-to-late thirties. I willed at least one of them to notice our matching wedding bands, but Marcus was enjoying the attention so I eventually kept my hand in my lap and off his person.

"Our friend Dierdre will be here any minute, she's just driving up from Dennis, but she's from England too," one of the brunettes said and turned to the door as it opened.

Suddenly the sound and the people around me disappeared and my stomach bottomed out. Dee met my eyes and stopped walking, like she'd seen a ghost. I watched someone push past her, jostling her shoulder and breaking her trance (to be fair she had stopped in the middle of the only clear path around the bar). She looked the same, but thinner, all the so-called baby fat was gone from her face, and her blonde hair clearly had assistance like mine. I stood and Marcus followed my eyes, stiffening in his seat and looking back at me.

"Robby," she said, her eyes wide as she reached me.

"Oh my god, you two know each other?" The brunette said as Dee and I hugged.

It was awkward, but I nearly melted from the comfort her arms and bosom still gave me. I felt the showgirls' headdresses tickling my lashes and swallowed roughly as I stepped back. "Dee, what a surprise!" I looked at Marcus who had stood.

"Robby! So good to see you," Dee followed my eye and did a double take. "Marcus?" She looked back at me with a face full of shock. I nodded with a smile. She turned to him and shook his outstretched hand. She looked so small next to him, they all did, he was a hundred and ninety-two centimeters after all.

"Hello Dee," he smiled, "you're looking well."

"Are you two friends then?" She puzzled. "Wow I really am out of the loop."

"We're married," he said quietly, looking around at Dee's friends and then at me with an inscrutable expression.

"To each other?" She gasped.

Marcus nodded. "Aren't you two friends on Instagram?" He looked between us with a frown.

And there it was, that was the question in his eye and I wish it had never occurred to him, but he was nearly as smart as I, and his attention to detail was incredible, it's why he was such a good lawyer.

Dee was shaking her head and looked at me. "No."

Now they were both looking at me, so I looked at the brunette. "What a small world!" I marveled with a broad smile. "How do you all know Dee?" I studiously avoided Marcus' eye, as they answered me. They all lived in the same neighborhood in Natick, and had kids the same ages. Dee had two kids, five and seven, I couldn't believe it. She had married an American, not Chad or the fish guy, but some other guy, though they had recently divorced. I felt bad for her at that revelation.

"Don't be," she patted my arm when I said as much, "he was a cheater, and I'm so much happier now."

Marcus bought them all a drink and ordered me another club soda. A high-top table behind us opened up and her three friends moved to sit down leaving us to catch up. Marcus gave Dee his barstool and stood watching me.

"You're still sober then," she said softly, "I'm so proud of you."

"Thanks. I was only messy for a little while," I said, trying to keep the edge out of my voice.

"I'm really sorry about that, Robin," she touched my arm, and held my gaze. "I think about you all the time, and I have been meaning to track you down, I just felt so guilty and have been busy with my kids and my divorce, and managing custody and co-parenting," she trailed off and looked at Marcus. "So, you two are *married*? How the fuck did that happen?"

"It's a long story," I wrinkled my nose and chuckled lightly. "But we've been together twelve years and married nine." I smiled at Marcus, taking his hand briefly.

"Wow," she breathed. "Well, you both look amazing, really. I can't believe you're here," she shook her head and blinked as though she were trying to wake up. "Are you on holiday?"

"No, we live in Boston," Marcus answered. "I came for my masters at BC Law, and we never left," he shrugged.

"Holy shit! You live here? For how long?" She looked between us with her mouth open.

"Eleven years, he's at Kirk & Sweeney and I work at SharkFinn. We live on Marlborough Street," I smiled. "But we're starting a family and moving to the suburbs, Newton hopefully."

"We're *talking* about moving, we haven't done anything yet on either front," Marcus corrected and winked at me. Oh, thank god, he wasn't mad, maybe he'd forgotten about Instagram (ha, right).

"Wow! Kids? The burbs? Are you adopting?" She looked between us.

"No, surrogate, we're working with an agency on finding one, but it's been so hard, and quite discouraging," I twisted my mouth.

She made a sympathetic sound. "I'm sorry to hear that. My god, we have so much to catch up on! Are you staying in Chatham?"

"No, we rent in P-town, we only came on the recommendation of a friend," I looked around nodding. "It's a nice town." My eyes stopped on her friends talking quietly amongst themselves and looking at me strangely. They quickly looked away and I turned to Dee. "Why are your friends looking at me like that?" I asked softly, narrowing my eyes as my stomach clenched. I watched Marcus turn his head and then look back at me with dismay.

She looked at them and then back at me with a blush. "I'm so sorry Robin. I only told one of them, and I never thought I'd see you again, shit. I wasn't gossiping I swear. I was missing you, and I was drunk and it was ages ago, I can't believe she remembered to be honest."

After all these years, it still cut, and freshly because of all the time that had passed. At least none of them had seen it for themselves, but I still felt the shame and blushed. I saw Marcus signaling for the check, ever protective of me. I looked back at Dee who was watching me guiltily and I didn't want to ease her mind. I felt violated but of course I couldn't blame her, it was a juicy story, and we weren't friends. Maybe we still weren't. I felt my haughtiness gather around my edges. "Marcus is going to be a Marquess. I did marry rich and titled," I said quietly and smiled, leaving the unspoken part unspoken (where was your titled husband Dee? Or your husband at all). I stood as Marcus put money on the bar. 'Wonderful to see you again," I kissed her cheek, and smiled at her friends. "Enjoy your girls' weekend."

"Robby, I'm sorry," she pleaded, her eyes filling.

I shrugged one shoulder. "Bye." I held myself together and led Marcus out the door. "Do you want me to drive?" I asked when we got away from the crowded sidewalk.

"No, I think you're too upset, and I'm fine to drive," Marcus took my hand and squeezed.

I squeezed in return and then pulled away. "Not sure if Chatham is the kind of place you can do that. Look at all the Lily Pulitzer and Vineyard Vines," I gestured around, swallowing roughly, because I needed his hand, I needed his hug, and I was feeling like we were too far from safety.

We were near the main parking lot behind all the shops and Marcus pulled me to him. There were people around but not like the crowds on the street. "I don't care. My husband is upset."

I cried against his neck as he rubbed my back and he held me until I pulled away after several moments. I wiped my eyes and he kissed me briefly. "I love you Robby, we'll be back to the cottage soon." He held open the door to his fancy electric Maserati (same as Ollie's, but carbon grey).

We rode in silence as Marcus followed the GPS back to Route Six. Once we got on the highway though, Marcus looked at me and then back at the road. "If it weren't Dee on Instagram, who was it? And why didn't you ask her about it? You seemed like you knew."

Shit. "It was Vas," I said quietly, still wondering how much I should divulge.

"What?" He shouted and looked at me.

"I figured it out quick enough, and blocked him."

"Jesus Christ Robin. You never told me," he scowled angrily.

"I didn't want you to worry, and nothing came of it. I'm not stupid."

"No, you're not, but you're secretive as hell," he added. "That was four years ago, and when I asked you about it, you lied. You said some shit about her liking posts from time to time."

"I said that initially because it was true, he was liking the posts before I blocked him, and the last time you asked I said I thought she had dropped off. Don't make it sound as though I was stringing you along about it for years," I scoffed. "I didn't want to think about him, and I didn't want him between us again. Please let's not fight, I love you and I need you," I smoothed the hair over his ear and buried my fingers in the waves.

He glanced at me and ran his eyes down my body, putting his hand on my knee before looking back at the road. He turned the radio up on the steering wheel and we rode the rest of the way listening to my playlist.

$$70$$

Egg Hunting

I NARROWED MY SEARCH down to two egg donors once we were back in Boston, one, a recent graduate of Boston University with crushing student debt, and one looking to pay for graduate school at Harvard (neither girl qualified for need-based aid, sucks to be middle class in America, you're literally fucked by everyone). Both had impeccable medical histories, both were 'identified donors' (that is to say not anonymous), and both were pretty, as far as women go. I held up their pictures for Marcus while he was watching the Rugby Championship. "Which one would you fuck?"

He looked between the two of them and then up at me. "Seriously Rob?" He asked suspiciously and scanned my body. "What is this? We angry fucking tonight? What do you have on under those track pants?"

I looked away. I was going to have to switch up my game with his expectancies, maybe get some proper, knee-length knickers like from the eighteenth-century to wear under my pants, really teach him a lesson about mocking me. I looked back at him. "No, I mean it. These are the eggs. You're at a bar, and *straight*, and these two are sitting at the end, which one makes your little friend go *ping*?" I waggled my eyebrows and raised the pictures up and down like I was Lady Justice.

Marcus slow blinked at me and then shifted his gaze between the pictures like he was Jerry Lewis in the *King of Comedy* looking at the cue cards. "That one," he said without indicating either one.

I frowned and looked between the two and back at him. "Which one? Come on Marcus, I'm being serious." I had to lock my knees to keep from stomping my foot.

"The blonde," he said with a sigh. "And for fuck's sake, if you don't know that by now, then you're not as smart as I thought you were."

I grinned happily and bent to kiss him before flouncing out of the room. I felt like a matchmaker for Marcus' sperm and this woman's eggs, and it was going to be a match made in heaven. All that was left was the surrogate company finding us a womb.

71

(Out of Left) Field of Dreams

MY SECRETARY (she let me call her that) buzzed me. "There's a Dierdre Wallis here to see you," she said expectantly.

Shit. I really didn't want to see her. Marcus and I had been over and over it since that weekend, and decided we had gone this long without her in my life, and could be fine without her for the rest of it. I had more than replaced her, but I couldn't say no, she knew I was there, I had picked up the phone. I had a glass door to my office but my desk was positioned such that I could see my secretary but anyone on the outside would have to step to the door and peer in.

"You can send her in. Thank you, Kathy," I hung up the phone and stood, buttoning my suit coat. Ollie and the boss always wore suits, the tech team wasn't required too, but I did, I was my grandfather's grandson.

Dee came through dressed in capris, wedge heels and a brightly patterned shirt, she looked very fashionable and pretty. I kissed her cheeks and watched as she looked around my big office lined with industry awards, and photos of Marcus and me and my family, including, of course, the Countess and Earl. I now had views of the water, was on one of the top floors, and was pretty fucking proud of my space and how far I'd come in the company.

"Wow, you're like a hot-shot, nice office," she smiled and looked at me shyly.

"Thank you. Please sit," I gestured to the chair in front of me (not the couch against the wall, I didn't want her to stay), and leaned my hip against the desk and raised my eyebrows in expectation.

She laughed nervously. "This is so weird, and surreal, and awkward. We were best friends, and now you're like a complete stranger. Doesn't that make you feel odd too?"

It did make me feel quite peculiar, but I just shrugged. "I survived two over-doses, countless relapses, and incredible shame and heartache, but I had a fantastic support system that helped me rebuild my life. Of course I'm not the same person. That Robin was weak, and frivolous, and forgot who he was. Now I have Marcus, the love of my life, and I'll never forget who I am."

"And I am so happy for you Robby," she leaned forward earnestly. "I'm so sorry about telling Krystal about you, and them gossiping at the bar. I feel awful and I set them all straight, and chastised them for upsetting you. Seeing you again, made me so happy, I wish our reunion hadn't been tainted," she paused. "Can I have a second chance? Please? You're here, I'm here, we're like a half hour apart, I miss you."

Part of me couldn't resist her pleas, I wanted her in my life again too, but the other part of me remembered that she left me at my lowest. Yes, I was messy, but I pulled myself together, something she never bothered to stick around to see. Was she just a fair-weather friend? Could I trust her again? I took a breath. "I don't know Dee. I mean, I'm not, not going to be your friend, but I'm not actively looking for new friends, and I certainly don't want to be around your friends. I've closed the door on that part of my life, and I don't need their judging eyes and such. And I certainly don't need to explain anything to anyone, or want to relive it to fulfill anyone else's curiosity." I crossed my arms.

"I completely understand Robin, and I'm not asking for you to be friends with them, I'm asking for you to be friends with me, and I'm not a new friend," she said softly. "I was wrong to abandon you, I just wasn't equipped to help you when we were young, and I felt like a failure. I want to make it up to you. We had such fun together, come on, I know the silly Robby is still in there. Let me see your toes," she raised her eyebrows in challenge.

I couldn't help the grin, they *were* painted, a deep purple.

"I knew it!" She stood.

"Marcus' are painted too," I said with a laugh, feeling like a kid again.

"No way!"

"He indulges me. He loves me like I've never been loved before," I shook my head, "I'm the luckiest boy in the world."

She beamed at me. "You have no idea how happy I am for you Robby," her eyes were shining. "I'm dying to hear the story of you two, and I promise I will keep it to myself like I did with all our other conversations and secrets. I swear, the shit with Vas was the only thing I ever said." She took my hand, and squeezed it. "You know me Robby, I want the best for you, and I've spent the last few weeks thinking about a lot of shit, and talking to a lot people about my thoughts," she held my gaze, and it made me uncomfortable initially. "You were my best friend, and I still feel our connection, even though you might not, and," she held up her hand to stop me, "I want to prove to you how much I love you and how dedicated I am to wanting back in your life. I'll be your surrogate, if you'll have me," she shrugged.

I felt the air sucked from the room, I'm not kidding. Marcus would tease me, maybe you would too, but I felt that shit. I frowned and gasped lightly (I think, but it might have been quite audible). My hands gripped the edge of my desk and I closed my eyes, certain I misheard her. "What?" I opened my eyes and chuckled nervously.

"I mean it Robby," she breathed and touched my chest lightly before pulling her hand back at my flinch. "I loved being pregnant. I'm healthy, unmarried, and I owe you so much," she forced my gaze. "You gave me confidence when I was so low, everyone razzing me for being fat, even my sister, I would have hated myself," she shook her head. "If not for you, who knows," she shrugged. "It's nothing for me to give you a child."

Believe me, I was absolutely speechless. So many things were racing through my head, and I couldn't believe what I was hearing. "Dee," I managed to choke out, "you don't know what you're saying or committing to. You don't know anything about Marcus and me now, how complicated it is, and most importantly, you can't know that we're looking for someone to be just a host body for our child. We don't want connections, Christ, we don't want messy," I scoffed. "Marcus and I have had our absolute fill of messy. We want someone who will birth his babies and walk away into the sunset."

She stared at me, and then, if you can believe it, she threw my words back in my face, words she had never heard me utter. "I am offering you a gift Robin Trumball *Willoughby*, and you're handing it back with a 'no thank you?'" She stared at me with her mouth open. "How rude."

I gasped, *how dare she?* This was not the same thing at all. "It's not a 'no thank you,'" I straightened with a frown. "It's a 'do you understand what you are offering?' It's a human life, not a fucking insta-pot."

"Robin, of course I know what I'm offering," she scoffed and made that face that was so quintessentially Dee in secondary, "I told you I spoke with people. I consulted with a lawyer, I spoke with my ex, I asked my gay friends," she shrugged. "I'm not offering this lightly, or ignorantly. And I don't expect anything from you, aside from covering my expenses of course. I know what surrogacy is, but I would hope that I could have a presence in the child's life, your life, is all."

I took some deep breaths. "I have to talk to Marcus, it's his heirs we need, he has to agree. Thank you, for offering, I do mean that. It is huge, and I understand that. Marcus may still want to use donor eggs, to keep a separation, would you be willing to do that?"

She looked away and then back at me. "I'd really prefer to use my own, and I promise I won't insert myself into your lives, and I won't keep it or them, because I already have two of my own, and it's so hard. Even though my ex is a great dad, I'm a single mom for most of the time," she sighed. "I didn't marry wealthy or titled, I caught your unspoken words, you little shit," she said twisting her mouth and smacking me lightly on the arm with a soft look.

I looked at her, and while I saw her, I also saw the seventeen-year-old her, and all her younger iterations and Christ, the showgirls started queuing up. "Well, your child, if it's a boy, would be a *Marquess* someday, and that's almost nearly the same thing," I said gently and held her gaze with a smile. "Let's go to lunch, Lola's is amazing, you're going to love it," I said and held the door for her. "Cancel my three o'clock Kathy," I said as I passed her desk.

We had lunch and once I let go of my reservations, I was transported back to her bedroom, my bedroom and all our secret confessional sessions. It really was like no time had passed, and we slipped back into our ridiculous, but lovable, selves. She had me laughing and I had her rolling in her chair about what we had done, and then all the things she had missed out on. I told her about Marcus and me, I had to, she was offering to have his babies, I had to be honest. She wasn't horrified, god love her, and in fact she said it all made sense, not that she had the insight that Hector had, but she could see how it all played out.

"I wish you had told me all this then," she looked at me and took a bite of her salad. "But I get it, that would have been a huge secret to get out. How are his friends now?"

I shrugged. "I only know about the ones who bullied me with him, I don't know about Liam and them. Where are they now anyway?" I asked with a laugh. "And who cares?"

I called Marcus the minute I left Dee, and broke the amazing news, letting him know of her thoroughness in looking into it.

There was a long pause, I hated when he did that and I couldn't see his face. "Holy shit. That would save us a lot, but also bring so many complications. Robin, I thought we decided to keep her at arm's length?"

"I know we did, but she was really apologetic, and wanted a second chance. Reminded me of someone else who was really apologetic and who I gave a second chance to, and I've never regretted one second of it," I said meaningfully.

He chuckled lightly. "Touché," he paused again. "Complication aside, I don't know Robin. I still haven't told my parents, this is a really big thing," he trailed off.

"We don't need their permission," I stopped walking and looked around. "They want heirs and we're giving them heirs. Are you still considering their demands?" I frowned.

"No, of course not," he said reassuringly, "Though Robin, I'm wondering, are you going to stay home and raise them?" He asked in a skeptical tone.

I frowned, even though I had already written my letter of resignation (a draft only), and had Ollie sponsor me for membership at the Tennis and Racquet Club on Boylston Street. "Why do you assume I would stay home, you could retire."

Marcus laughed out loud, and I narrowed my eyes. "Your membership to the tennis club was approved, I got the letter *and* the bill, and every time I turn around you've got a new outfit perfect for a ladies' luncheon. I promise you won't have time for any of that if we've got children running around."

"That's what nannies are for," I scoffed.

Marcus sighed. "I don't want to have this conversation on the phone. I'll see you at home, love you," he hung up.

I looked at my recent call list and pressed the third most recent call.

"Darling Robin," the Countess called happily down the line, "how are things in your gorgeous city? Are you two pregnant yet?"

I laughed. "Lonely without you, and no not yet, but are you sitting down?" I asked happily and kept walking down Exeter Street.

"Yes, why?" She asked.

"Marcus and I bumped into my friend Dee a month or so ago, do you remember her?"

"Of course I do, darling. How is she?"

"She's great, a divorced mom of two, and lives about thirty minutes from Boston, if you can believe it. She married an *American*," I paused as my grandmother made a sound like she was wrinkling her nose. "Thing is, she felt awful for abandoning me and has offered to be our surrogate, to make it up to me."

"What?" She asked incredulously. "That's incredible. Does she realize what's she offering?"

"Yes, she said she's contacted a lawyer, spoken with her ex, probably her therapist," I sighed. "She loved being pregnant, and would be thrilled to have a child of hers go on to be a Marquess."

"Well, she's no dummy, it would be a high honor, I love being the mother of a future Earl, and being married to one of course. We really are an exclusive little club," she chuckled.

"I agree, I love my Marquess-to-be. Speaking of my love, I just have to convince him it's a good idea. We're going to talk it all through tonight, I just wanted you to be the first to know. I'll keep you posted My Lady. I'm home now, gotta run. I love you Gram," I blew a kiss and listened to her do the same.

Marcus came home to one of his favorite meals: shrimp with tomatoes and feta, jasmine rice, and green beans with garlic. I watched him eat as I took small bites, hoping he was as excited as I was about Dee's gift.

"Well? We could have babies on the way within two months, and with a known entity," I said watching his face carefully.

Marcus put his fork down. "I know Robby, it's exciting, but it's also potentially disastrous. There's a reason why people use a surrogate with someone else's eggs. A host body for the spawn, as you're so offensively fond of saying."

I felt slight umbrage at that. It was a completely factual description, and made me think of one of our favorite movies (*Aliens*) whenever I said it, how dare he mock me? "But this is Dee, and she doesn't want any more children, she's got her hands full with the two she's raising nearly on her own. She has great genes, and your children with her will be beautiful," I smiled and took his hand. "I wonder if the clinic will let me hold her head in my lap while they inseminate her, you know, like *Handmaid's Tale.*"

Marcus threw his head back and laughed, still one of my all-time favorite sounds (the other was his moan). "You're absolutely absurd Robin Willoughby, and I love you to pieces," he pushed his chair back and patted his lap. I sat astride him and buried my fingers in his hair. "I'll have a contract lawyer start the paperwork, and you and I can get started on baby-making tonight."

I kissed him deeply and then looked in his eyes. "Brilliant plan. You can pretend my mouth is the cup. Practice makes perfect."

72

Murder
She Wrote

I WAS AT WORK, reviewing the finishing touches on my latest app, glad I had a team of MIT grads under me who did the heavy lifting, when my mobile buzzed on my desk. I smiled and answered "My Lady!" I crowed happily.

"Hello Robin," the Countess replied with a smile in her voice. "How are things in your beautiful city?"

"Grand, but everyone keeps asking about you. It's getting embarrassing really."

She laughed. "We'll be visiting soon, I can't wait to go back to your Cape Cod, but that's not why I'm calling," she paused. "I just saw that Vasyl Boiko died."

I felt the room disappear around me, like in those movies where the camera zooms rapidly in on the character. "What? How?" I exclaimed.

"He was murdered," she replied, and maybe she said something more but I dropped my phone and when I bent down to pick it up I hit my head on the desk. I was so disoriented and out of body I couldn't feel my extremities. I returned to the conversation, but who knows what I said. I hung up and immediately laid on the floor and put my legs up the wall. I'm not sure how long I laid there, but my direct report found me and asked if I was okay.

"I'm not," I said and looked at his knees, "but if you'll help me to my feet, I should be okay, eventually."

He gave me his hand and pulled me up. I swayed briefly, and he steadied me. "I'm alright. The app looks good, send it to Krish for final approval, I'm leaving."

I went straight to Ocean Prime and ordered a double vodka neat, shaken over ice first. I looked out the window and then down at the glass, and I drank that bitch. She burned my throat the whole way down and then warmed my belly like a heater in an ice fishing hut. I ordered another one, and another, and then lost track of time. I felt someone at my elbow, and wanted to shrivel up into a speck when I met Ollie's eye (I should say eyes, there were like four of them, and I had to shut one of mine to make his face stop shifting). I heard him talk to the bartender and then pay my tab before he turned his gorgeous face back to me.

"Come on Rob. Marcus called me. I'm bringing you home, we can talk about it on the way," he took my arm and kept me upright. I could have kissed him for his care, and I'm sorry to say, I (definitely) might have tried. He was a great sport about it, especially when I poured my heart out to him in the car. I told him about Vas, about sending him to prison, about Vas trying to blackmail me, and he was surprisingly non-judgmental, in fact it seemed like he completely understood.

He parked behind my brownstone and walked me in. I looked at him with my one eye and then around my kitchen. "You didn't have to come in. What are you doing?" I slurred and swayed.

"Marcus is on his way back from New York City and asked me to stay with you until he got home," he looked around and strode to the electric kettle on the counter. He busied himself making tea, I snickered when he laughed at Marcus' mug as he took it from the cabinet.

"I gave that to him our first Christmas together," and for some reason, saying that made the Vegas showgirls stride onto my face in full regalia. I felt their head-dresses tickle my lashes as their legs kick their way down my face and Ollie, god love him, just came and hugged me. He steered me to the bathroom, and encouraged me to throw up. Which I did, after making sure he left the room.

After that I don't remember much, it was like a fever dream. I swear there was some other man with Ollie, and they spoke to each other in hushed tones. I knew it was a fever dream because the guy looked like Chris Hemsworth when he played Thor, and I'm sure Ollie knows a lot of celebrities, but there was no way he had Thor over to my house. No way Chris Hemsworth (wearing a t-shirt that said 'I'm Here About the Blow Job') touched my forehead and filled me with warmth, calming my mind such that the next thing I remember was Marcus sitting next to me on our bed, where I stayed for the rest of the week.

***

The Countess told me about Vas' death after his funeral, not that I could or would have attended anyway, for *so* many reasons, but I wished I had known the minute he died. Apparently, he treated his new twink about as well as he'd treated me, but the new twink had a stronger backbone than I had at that age, and had stabbed him, repeatedly (like *a lot*, according to the news reports) in self-defense. I felt so out of sorts and followed the story obsessively, to the point where Marcus was getting annoyed, and perhaps that's truly why he told me to write my story down, as a distraction. Vas was awful to me and used me, but we had some really great times too, and I felt a strange sort of sadness that took me a while to shake.

Marcus was a saint as I said, and so supportive, he gave me space to write in my free time. I didn't sleep longer than three hours for months, such was my obsession with getting my story onto the page. We resumed our routine, Marcus ever vigilant because of me falling ass-over-teakettle off the wagon, though I really had no desire to drink at all.

I insisted that he and Dee get started on making the babies; life was fragile and, while I wasn't worried that someone would murder Marcus, I knew anything could happen at any time. I accompanied him to the clinic, and assisted with the sperm harvesting, making sure they had plenty of happily created specimens to work with. If the doctors were bothered by the saliva, they never said. I liked to think of it as my DNA contribution to the babies.

I apologized to Ollie for trying to kiss him, and blushed a deep scarlet for weeks whenever I saw him until he grabbed my face and kissed me (not sexually, his husband would kill him), and told me to shut up about it. I asked him about Thor and he just shook his head and laughed.

"Of course he was there, all the Avengers were. I'm only human, and you needed superheroes," he said and squeezed my shoulder. "You're gonna be fine."

And he was right, I was fine, for more than a year.

73

Birth of Words
(and Babies)

DEE HAD GOTTEN PREGNANT right away (I told you Marcus' sperm was strong and determined), both embryos she had been implanted with took, (the remaining embryos were kept on ice, for later) and we were over the moon, all three of us, perhaps Dee most of all (she was having Marcus, *rugby-god-of-secondary*, Willoughby's babies, so of course she was). She and I were able to spend a lot of time together during the pregnancy, because she didn't have her kids full time, and could come stay with us in the city. She marveled over our brownstone (of course she did, it was fucking magnificent), and took over one of the guest rooms on the floor above the Countess and Earl's.

Dee accompanied me to some of Marcus' football games, occasionally bringing her children, cheering and marveling over him right alongside me, as though she were married to him too. She marveled over Ollie as well, of course.

"He grew up in Kensington? And married an American, just like me," she mused one day as we watched them weaving around defensemen in unison like synchronized swimmers.

"Well, not just like you," I clarified with a teasing tone, "he married a gorgeous fucking billionaire. You think Ollie is hot, you should see his husband."

She looked around the sidelines of the field. "Is he here?"

"No, he hardly ever comes," I shrugged. "He likes to pretend he's straight, no one knows about them really, so don't tell your gossipy friends." I rolled my eyes.

She shoved me lightly. "I won't say a word, I promise."

Marcus came running by then and gave me a brief smile, running his eyes over Dee's big belly, before turning his focus back to the ball between his feet. I always felt a tiny thrill when he looked at me mid-game, knowing that it broke his concentration but he couldn't help himself. I looked away with a smile and glanced at Dee's belly, making a sound of alarm, causing her to turn her head sharply.

"Help, I can't move, I'm stuck in some sort of gravitational pull or orbit around this small moon!" I exclaimed, miming as though I was trying to get away.

"Robin Trumball, you're an ass," Dee said with a laugh and began chasing me.

"Wait a minute, that's no moon, that's a space station," I cried, "and it's headed right for me. Save yourselves!" I laughed as I ran past her kids.

✳ ✳ ✳

My grandparents came to visit us, once before the babies were born, and once after, when the babies were a week old, fawning over Dee for the beautiful twins she gave us. Dee was living with us for two weeks after they were born, breastfeeding them, and helping us figure out how to be parents. After which we got a night nurse and a nanny to help me when Marcus went back to work. I took paternity leave from SharkFinn (they had the best fucking benefits), while I wrote my story down, and decided whether I would go back to work at all.

On their second visit, the Countess brought a package with her, and gave it to Dee after dinner, while Wade and Wendy were sleeping. Dee opened the beautiful, hand-painted wrapping paper carefully and then oohed and ahhed over the intricately carved box inside. She opened it and gasped, to the Countess' delight.

"Oh, My Lady," she shook her head and looked up at my gram, "this is, too much, it's exquisite." She lifted out a diamond and emerald necklace with a teardrop-shaped emerald pendant the size of a quarter, surrounded by small diamonds, and looked at me with something like terror in her eyes. I smiled reassuringly as the Countess spoke.

"When I had my babies, the Earl gave me push presents," she winked at my grandfather, "and you deserve a grand one for what you have done for Robin, and Marcus, and his title. This one isn't from the Earl's collection, those belong to Robin's Uncle James, but this was a special gift from the Queen, god rest her soul, to my mother, who had been her lady-in-waiting. She gave it to her for her years of service, when she left to have me," my grandmother smiled.

"Oh my god! I will cherish it and wear it at every opportunity, maybe even just in the tub," she said softly and put it on, hugging the Countess.

I looked at Marcus and willed him to realize that I needed a push present too, but he just rolled his eyes at me. We were interrupted (the first of many times over the coming years) by tiny cries coming from the video monitor and I scurried off with Dee to feed our little bunnies.

* * *

The following months were busy with writing and edits, and feedings and walks, and collecting 'loan payments,' which had dwindled to one a day if I was lucky because of exhaustion. Marcus' parents came to visit (they did not stay with us), and couldn't help but moon over the twins (they were beautiful, of course), and our brownstone. My parents came (they did stay with us) and also mooned over the babies, my mother extended her stay an extra week, to help, but mostly because she was so in love with them.

I finished my memoir in less than six months, sent it around to a few agents, and fuck's sake, there was a bidding war. Who knew how interesting my story of porn, and bullying (don't worry, I didn't tell Marcus' secret), and addiction, and love, and redemption would be? I picked my agent and let her manage the bidding war among publishers. I got a six-figure advance because one of Marcus' cohorts at Kirk and Sweeney negotiated a brilliant deal for me, one with a potential for a TV series.

Marcus was worried initially about the demands on an author, the publicity and appearances, especially with our twins who were so busy and exhausting, but I reassured him that I could limit my appearances and book signings (but not my wardrobe of course). He and I settled into a perfect routine that made my heart sing (especially once the twins slept in longer increments), and kept me busy. I was focused on the design of the book cover, and approving marketing ideas, and scheduling studio time to read my book for the audio version, so busy, in fact, that I forgot to think things through.

74

Worlds Collide

WHEN THE TWINS were a year old, Marcus and I, and Annie the nanny (yes, I hired her almost solely for the fun I had saying that), flew to the UK and then Europe for a summer vacation, and to see the estates that would someday be ours. Annie, a recent college grad with a bachelors in education and crippling student debt, couldn't keep her mouth from dropping open at each stop on the trip. We stayed with the Countess and Earl first, before flying a private jet to the South of France, to the Marquess of Brougham's (now Lord Hoity-Toity) manor house in Cannes, and then flew (private again) to Tuscany, to the vineyard estate in Impruneta, with views of Chianti and Florence.

The manor house had ten bedrooms, a pool and a huge fountain in the circle driveway that I let Wade and Wendy splash around in, to the horror of the staff, who watched me suspiciously. We didn't stay in the master bedroom (excuse me, *primary bedroom*, again with the label nonsense), because that was technically his parents', but the suite we stayed in was just as grand, with a huge balcony and sweeping views of the countryside and the ocean in the distance. It was heady and fantastic, and made Marcus horny, to my great delight.

"I can't believe all of this is to be ours," he murmured against my neck.

I had just been imagining myself as Madonna on the balcony in *Evita* when he appeared behind me. I turned in his arms and pressed myself against him. "It is like a dream," I agreed and swept my tongue into his mouth as he gripped my bottom tightly. "We should totally fuck out here after everyone goes to bed."

Marcus chuckled, the sound vibrating in his chest. "I love you Robin Willoughby."

* * *

Italy was even more beautiful. The massive three-story house was cream-colored stucco with a terracotta roof, and had twelve bedrooms, an expansive stone patio, and a large infinity pool surrounded by fragrant flowers and marble statues. We took the large suite overlooking the hill of grapevines (no balcony sadly), and Annie had the bedroom next to the twins overlooking the pool. The Marquess, Clark Fordham, had recently had the entire villa redone, including the pool, before his untimely death, and everything gleamed and sparkled, and was pristine.

Some of the statues, of naked men mostly, were new too, glowing white among the grey ones. There was a scandalous one of two naked men, one young and smooth, one older and bearded, in an embrace, and while it seemed passionate upon first glance, the more you looked at it, the more it seemed sad, anguished really.

"He looks a bit like you," Marcus said as he floated on an innertube next to me, following my eye.

I glanced at Marcus and back at the statue. The older man was gripping the young man tightly, his face soft and yearning, and the young man, while he had his arms around him, was looking away, at something you could only imagine to be, more interesting. "Don't be absurd. He's got a beard and is far too muscly, he looks like you," I grinned and splashed him lightly.

"I meant the younger one, and don't splash me unless you want to go under," he raised his eyebrows in challenge.

"Marcus," I warned, and glanced at the shallow end of the pool where Annie was watching over the twins and out of earshot. "I don't think you'd be pleased with the consequences." I pulled a face.

He flashed me a broad smile. "If I thought for a second that you could follow through on that threat, I might be worried. However, in *that* swimsuit," he scanned his eyes over my nearly naked body and lingered on my tiny trunks, "something tells me, your splash was an invitation to wind up over my knee later," he said in a low voice and quirked his eyebrow, the tip of his tongue between his parted teeth in that way that indicated he was thinking of sex.

I felt my cock go ping and gave him a look before swishing my hand to turn my float. I *definitely* wanted to end up over his knee later, but couldn't give in so soon. His throaty laugh followed me to the shallow end.

* * *

My ass cheeks tingled under his gaze the following morning as I left the bed. I was taking the twins in to town while he met with the vintner and staff of the estate. He had had similar meetings back in France, doing the estate oversight for Lord Hoity-Toity who had his hands full managing the rest of the assets. It was truly staggering just how much came with the title, and I knew we likely wouldn't see each other until dinner time.

"I love you, My Lord," I said saucily before leaving the room.

"I love you, My Lady," he called with a laugh.

Gino, the chauffeur, dropped Annie and me with the twins at the edge of town, getting the stroller out of the back while I unbuckled Wade and Annie unbuckled Wendy from their car seats. I know I told you I didn't want kids, and I so didn't at the time, but I couldn't imagine my life without them. I loved them so much; Wade looking like Marcus more and more each day, and Wendy so beautiful and blonde with an infectious smile. Marcus teased that my DNA *had* got in and that Wendy was mine in looks but that Wade had my personality, which always infuriated me (mostly because it was true), but he did it on purpose, with a glint in his eye, his hand ready for a spank.

We traversed the town, eating lunch at a café, watching the twins playing in the square, and picking up some souvenirs from a tiny shop that had postcards and trinkets on a table out front. Wade wanted a ball with the Azzurri team logo on it, but I knew Marcus would throw it away (with a tirade), so steered Wade in a different direction.

I called Gino back, and the twins promptly fell asleep on the ride home. Annie and I put them in their cribs when we got to the villa, and parted ways in the hallway. It was hot, but not oppressively so, and I floated in the pool for a bit, then changed and went to the conservatory with my laptop. About an hour later I heard a step in the hall. I looked up from my computer as Marcus came through the door, with a strange expression on his face, one I wasn't familiar with. He had a couple of picture frames in his left hand.

"What is it?" I asked, keeping the apprehension out of my voice as best I could as I closed my laptop and stood cautiously.

"I'm not sure. You tell me," he said, his voice weird as he held out the frames.

I took them from him and my mouth went dry. The top one was a picture of me, young me, stretched out on a chaise in a tiny speedo, next to the pool that was just beyond the window behind me, shading my eyes as I looked at the camera. I lifted the frame to look at the one beneath, my hand shaking ever so slightly, and saw another picture of me, wearing a t-shirt that had a little rainbow heart on it, and pink Burberry shorts, my head on Lord Boomer's shoulder, his arm holding me tightly against him, the sun setting over the hills behind us. A fellow tourist had taken that one when we stopped at the wall outside our dinner spot. I couldn't believe how young I looked, and how truly plain Lord Boomer was with his brown eyes and trim beard.

He had sent me this same picture, in the same silver, beaded frame, after our vacation together. I kept it for a little while, and then threw it, and all the letters he had written me, away when Marcus and I started dating; I should've known he'd have one printed and framed for himself, not that I could have done anything about it. I couldn't have tossed *every* room at both estates searching for any evidence of our relationship (though I had searched both primary suites in the wee hours).

I swallowed, trying to free my voice as my mind raced. "Where did you find these?"

His face went from unfamiliar to clouded with anger. "You're not answering me, but I was looking for some documents that the winery needed. Those," he nodded at my hand, "were in the bottom drawer of Clark's desk."

"Marcus, it's nothing. It was ages ago," I said with as much nonchalance as I could muster and put the frames on the table and walked toward him in hopes of distracting him with one of my famous blow jobs.

"No Robin," he stepped back, (god, I was really going to need to switch up my game, I told you he became excellent at reading me), and ran his hand over his face and looked at me. The silence became heavier with each breath. "You're so secretive. You've lied to me, and I let it go, because I love you," he said holding my gaze. "I have *always* loved you. You have done, and been, everything for and to me."

"And I love you, you are my life!" I cried earnestly, interrupting him. I felt the reckoning, and looked around for St. Michael.

"I can't believe you were fucking the Marquess. Here!" He gestured angrily with his hand. "Where else did you fuck him? Christ! You've been acting like you knew *nothing* about the man. His funeral, any mention of him ever, you played so dumb," he shook his head and looked around. "I knew the staff were looking at you funny. In France, here." I didn't like the way *he* was looking at me. He looked out the window and his eyes stopped searching. "That is you." I didn't need to follow his gaze to know that he was looking at the statue of Clark and me, the expression on the young man's face the same as the one on mine in the picture. "You weren't just fucking him, were you? You had a *relationship*." His eyes came back to mine like a whip.

I shook my head, slowly at first and then more vehemently. "No Marcus, it was just a fling."

"Not to him it wasn't! Obviously," he sneered. "How long?"

Shit. I didn't want to answer that, because although it truly wasn't a relationship, it had gone on (more off actually than on), for nearly three years. "I only saw him occasionally."

"How long Robin?" He pressed.

I figured I needed to be honest, if he caught me in another lie, we were doomed. "Two and a half years," I whispered and then gasped at Marcus' face. "But Marcus, I swear, it meant nothing. And you and I weren't together. It ended way before you came back to me."

Marcus frowned and looked out the window. He took a step back and I vacillated between worry and irritation. "I can't believe this," he said shaking his head and looking around the room. "I knew you had secrets, but this?" He turned on his heel and strode out.

"Marcus!" I cried, running after him. No way I was going to let him mull this over unattended. "Stop. You're making a mountain out of a molehill. I never said anything because it wasn't worth mentioning, and then when he died, it felt weird to bring it up, so I just let it be. I didn't intentionally keep it from you." *Please just let this slide Marcus,* I said with my eyes.

"Would Clark think this was a mountain, or a molehill?" He frowned incredulously. "He's got your pictures framed, he had a fucking statue made! And you're like, 'oh, it were just a fling,'" he scoffed. "You're either lying to me, *again*, or you are just so fucking heartless," he paused. "And he was my cousin. A distant one, but you had to have known who he was." I looked away. In school, everyone knew who was connected to, or in, 'the ton,' (believe me, we lorded that shit over everyone, *literally*). "Oh my god," he murmured dreadfully.

I shifted my gaze back to him at that, and saw some realization in his eyes. "NO!" I reached for him, and pulled him to me as he struggled to get away. "Marcus, whatever you're thinking, NO."

Marcus looked like he wanted to believe me, but his brain wouldn't let him. He turned and continued walking away.

"Marcus! I'm sorry. Please." I grabbed his arm and searched his face as he turned to look at me like he'd never seen me before. "God, this is exactly why you shouldn't snoop in people's things! You will always find something to question or make you feel disappointed, and you could've gone your whole life not knowing and been fine."

"This is not nothing Rob!" Marcus shouted and shook his head. "This is not finding a vibrator in your mother's side table, or a smutty text, and I wasn't *snooping*, I was looking for something important." He took a breath and narrowed his eyes as he looked me over. "He was more than twice your age, and not at all your type. I heard your comment to Dee at the Squire. You two have some kind of pact about marrying rich and titled?"

"No," I scoffed shrilly. "That was just something dumb we used to say." He looked at me skeptically and I felt the showgirls straightening their headdresses, ready for the big show. I took a deep breath and everything I could never tell Marcus (or truly admit to myself) about Lord Boomer came out. "You're right, I knew who he was. I was lost, and angry, and I suppose I wanted to get back at you for what you did to me when we were kids. I didn't tell you because I was ashamed of my motivation, especially after you came back to me and explained everything. I can't help how he felt about me, I never did anything to make him believe I ever felt anything for him," I paused. "I love you, and I'm begging you to let it go."

He shook his head slowly, and looked at my feet. "I just don't," he paused, "You're an angel, my angel. The lies, the omissions," he trailed off as he looked at me.

"I *am* an angel," I said earnestly, and felt a crumbling inside me, along with something else, like a memory. I felt him pulling away and knew the tighter I gripped, the faster he would go, so I stopped. "But so was Lucifer. And he was *so* misunderstood," I turned and walked away, my wings threatening to unfurl. St. Michael was dead (RIP Mr. Boiko) and I thought my troubles were dead with him. I had to gain sovereignty over my realm, calm over the chaos that was building again. I had to make Marcus understand that it had no bearing on our relationship; I couldn't let Lord Boomer be the thing that broke us.

I heard the twins fussing as I climbed the stairs and detoured to their room, waving Annie away. I got Wade first, he was more demanding and would fuss loudly if he was made to wait in his wet diaper. I gave Wendy her pacifier as I passed her crib and she smiled as she took it in her mouth. I changed Wade's diaper and put him on the floor with a toy while I changed Wendy, who burbled and chatted happily as I did.

"Let's go have a snack, my little bunnies," I said, scooping Wade up and carrying them both to the kitchen where the chef and her assistant were prepping food for dinner. They looked at me with something behind their eyes. The assistant was new, but the chef wasn't and must've filled him in. Staff were paid to keep their mouths shut, but they still fucking judged you. I had searched Lord Boomer's suites in the wee hours to hide from Marcus, not from *them*. I would never mistakenly converse with any of them, and so ignored them haughtily as I put the twins in their chairs and asked for food.

I looked out the side window as I waited for them to bustle and serve, and saw Marcus getting into the back of the Marquess' Mercedes, and my heart lurched. I hoped he'd be back for dinner, but he wasn't.

* * *

I left the twins with Annie and strode purposefully to the Marquess' study, a massive, sparsely furnished, book-lined room that had a desk, two fancy modern chairs, and a wall of six black and white photographs of two men that Lord Boomer had told me were from some mega-talented photographer in New York. I remember staring at those pictures nearly two decades ago, transfixed by the complexity of how the images were layered, by hand (pre-photoshop), over background images of silver laurel leaves and such. In the first picture, one man was buttoned up in a tuxedo, and the other man was naked except for a top hat, and each subsequent photo had the clothed man in various states of undress, the two men posed differently in each one, until the final one when they were standing naked, their bodies muscled and glorious, but angled in such a way as to obscure any full nudity. I had been mesmerized and marveled over the incredible sexiness of the covert sexuality in them.

I shook my head to focus and crossed the room to the desk, sitting in the leather chair with a determined sigh, and opened the bottom drawer. There was a small stone elephant, a stack of empty file folders, and a salt shaker (that was weird). I pushed everything aside, and around, and found underneath it all, an envelope. I pulled it out slowly, feeling as though I was discovering King Tut's tomb but encased in nitroglycerin, ready to blow at the slightest jolt. I recognized my handwriting on the front (who wouldn't recognize their own scrawl?), and couldn't believe he kept it, but was so thankful he had. I pulled it out and unfolded the single piece of paper inside.

Hey Boomer,

I got your letter. Had to take it all the way to Bletchley Park, as I had done with your other letters, to have someone decipher for it for me, well, not actually Bletchley, but I'm pretty sure some of the residents of the nursing home I went to once worked there. A lovely old lady, whose name-tag said 'I'm Dorothy, but please call me Dottie,' read it to me. Don't worry, she was in the memory-care unit and forgot all about me and your letter 5 minutes after she read it. Seriously LB, if you don't want anyone else to read your dirty words, you shouldn't write them in cursive. You know my generation can't read that shite.

Anyhoo, I thought a lot about what you said the last time I saw you, and hope you thought as much about what I had to say in response (mostly because I don't want to have to write it all down longhand. Honestly, I have NO idea why you choose to write letters, my hand is cramping already). It reminds me of when you told me how you had to write all your papers in school by hand, which then reminds me of how much older you are. SIGH.

You're a great guy, and we had a bit of fun, but my answer is still no. You have so much to offer, are truly genuine, and will make some man very, VERY happy, but that man isn't me. I don't love you. I wish I could, for your sake, because I REALLY hate hurting you.

I could never marry you. You said you wished I was a gold digger, but I know you didn't mean it, you shouldn't mean it. You will find someone who will be head over heels for you, I promise.

As you guessed, in your letter, I did block you on my phone, and I beg you to move on, forget about me. I tease you but you're not THAT old, and you have many, many years ahead of you. Don't live in the past.

All my best, Rob.

I put the letter down and took a breath. Well, not many, many years apparently (poor LB), but this was the proof I needed to show Marcus, and I said a silent prayer of thanks to Clark, folded the letter back in the envelope, and left the room.

———

75

———

(Our Love) Don't Throw it All Away

I DELAYED DINNER as long as possible, before Annie and I sat with the twins on the patio. She and I chatted, but I never truly conversed with her either, and I certainly never discussed anything other than the twins with her. I kept my phone close, and the alcohol far as I waited for any sign of Marcus. Annie and I bathed the twins and put them to bed with a few books and a song that I let her sing, my mind elsewhere.

I was feeling thirsty and looked up meetings after my own shower as I waited, certain that Marcus had decided I had gone a bridge too far, when the bedroom door suddenly opened. I stood from where I was laying on the floor with my legs up the wall. "Marcus," I said in a stunned voice, my stomach fluttering like Ariana Grande was in there whipping her ponytail around. My eyes scanned his body hungrily as though he'd been gone for days not just hours.

He leaned back against the door and his eyes scanned me with equal hunger and an inscrutable expression. The silence became unbearable and I walked quickly to the side table.

"Marcus, I swear, there was no subterfuge, there was no deep secret I was hiding. I truly didn't know how to tell you." I held the letter out to him. "If I wanted the title, I could've had it without the wait, and you would've been bowing and scraping to me for the past fifteen years, *believe me*," I added dramatically, putting my chin in the air.

He took the letter and with a brief glance at my face, unfolded it and scanned the page. I saw his mouth twitch with amusement briefly as he read it, until he got the end, when his face grew serious. He checked the date stamp on the envelope and then looked at me from under hooded lids, his eyes scanning my body again (of course he scanned my body, I was in my underwear after all, and the only thing he loved more than the sight of that, was the sight of me fully naked).

He dropped the letter and sighed. "You are the most beautiful angel, and I imagine Lucifer was too. Perhaps his bad rap was just jealousy in the heavens," he took my hand, and it tingled in his grasp. "God help me Robin, but I can't live without you," he shook his head with a small frown and then kissed me, his tongue sweeping sensuously around mine.

I savored his mouth (even though it tasted like beer and cigarettes), and pressed my body against his as every nerve ending came alive with his touch. I pulled back and searched his face. "Where have you been?"

"I had Gino drive me to a pub, or whatever they call them here," he waved his hand, "where I had several pints, and then I kicked a ball against a wall." Marcus exhaled. "I needed space Robby, and it was excruciating for so many reasons." He looked away, and I saw his eyes shining. "I love you, like a straight-up crazy person. You could be a serial murderer and I would still love you," he said with a wry grin as he brought his eyes back to mine. "I forgave you, even before I read that," he pointed at the discarded letter. "That was before us, and I understand why you kept it from me, though I wish you hadn't.

"Robby, you're in my DNA. I can't hardly function without you. In secondary you consumed my every thought; you were the light I looked forward to every day, despite the darkness I felt because I was young and dumb. I forbade you from looking at me, but I didn't keep that rule for myself," he chuckled lightly. "At uni, and after, I was so lost and astray without you, until I found you again, and it was like being reunited with the missing half of my body. I don't fault you for your motivation with Clark, or what did you call him? *Boomer?*" He shook his head with a laugh. "I can't be jealous of a dead man, jealous of a relationship that happened before us, especially if doing so costs me you," Marcus sighed. "I love you, Robin. Be my Lucifer, not my angel of doom, and I will love you forever," he said burying his fingers in my hair.

"I love you, Marcus. I have never loved anyone, and will never love anyone the way I love you," I said vehemently as my wings unfurled, and I kissed that gorgeous man, my husband, until the world disappeared around us.

ACKNOWLEDGMENTS

I HAVE SO MANY to thank, it truly takes a village. Especially as an American woman writing about a young, gay man growing up in London. . . .

First and foremost, a special thanks to Randy, who I've known since we were thirteen. She laid on her couch every Sunday (sometimes her husband would sit in, so thanks to Jack as well), listening to the hot-off-the-press installments, laughing out loud, interrupting me when something particularly moved her, and lying to me about how great my British accent was. She also helped with the Dialectical Behavior Therapy (oh, did I forget to mention that she's is a social worker specializing in DBT? Sorry). Any mistakes about DBT are mine.

Thanks to John, who was a 'new' friend when I asked him to be my first reader. It took me a few weeks to work up the nerve to ask if he'd read it, and then I almost threw up after I hit send. He finished the book in two days (my ego did a little happy dance at that), gave me terrific notes, and our relationship was solidified. We had many, many, great lunch dates discussing this book and other important things, like the prostate, Doris Day parking spaces, and how lucky our husbands are.

Thanks to Jeremy, who I've known since we were ten. He is hands down the funniest person I know, and making him laugh feels like winning an Oscar. His guidance with grammar, the aristocracy, and plot devices was invaluable. We had hours-long zoom calls (because that bastard abandoned me for the west coast years ago) reviewing the manuscript chapter-by-chapter, and brainstorming the ending, which he helped me change completely in the eleventh hour.

Thanks to Igoe, another friend from back in the day, who read this (so-not-his-genre) book, and loved it. He was one of my biggest champions, and texted me at all hours with many exclamation points about the things he loved in the book, to my heart's great delight.

Thanks to Josh, who read the manuscript with the original ending and gave me specific and detailed notes which were so useful in my decision to change it. He also buoyed my confidence by assuring me (as a young gay man himself) that Robby's voice was authentic and believable. It took four years for our stars to align, but better late than never!

Thanks to my youngest son, who helped me with all the video game stuff, and really listened, without mocking me, as I obsessed about the story on our many car rides (I love you forever and ever and always).

Thanks to Lydia, for her help with all things UK: British school terms, slang, uniforms, etc. Her guidance was invaluable, and any mistakes are mine (or Google's).

Thanks to Suz, for all her guidance with rehab and AA, and of course the great conversations and laughs. Any mistake about AA, are mine.

Thanks to Bryan, who was my work husband until he moved offices (I called him that behind his back because I'm not sure he'd agree). He was a great sounding board for some of my most outrageous plot ideas, and I'm certain he thought my book sounded insane at times. I miss him and think of him every time I use the dish scrubber he left behind.

Thanks to Carol, a dear family friend who read it, despite my best efforts to convince her not to, and had many interesting things to say about Robby, and Vas, and Marcus the bully. She asked me how I decided to write this story, and then just stared at me while I explained the evolution of it. She has decades of experience working with victims of sexual violence and really helped me with Robby.

Thanks to my life-long friend Sigi for doing the cover art. She took my vision and translated it into a masterpiece (believe me, if you had seen the sketches I sent her to work with, you would agree she is a miracle worker). She stepped in to save the day when my first artist bowed out due to the subject matter (I don't blame him) and I couldn't be more thrilled with the result.

Special thanks to my dear friend Bob, who hasn't actually read the book, and might never read it (when I told him it was a narration style similar to Holden Caufield, he said "I despise Holden Caufield. I *hated* that book."). He then told me I should stick to writing what I know (just like Tolkien the hobbit, or Rice the vampire, I suppose). He helped with the subject matter because no topic is off-limits with him, which is my *favorite* trait in a person. He and I had lengthy conversations about porn, gay sex, and throwing hot dogs in hallways. I love you babe, and I hope you like the book.

Super-duper thanks to Thibault, my silver sister, who, after listening to me read part of the story to her, and Edie and Hally (thanks to them too btw) on our girls' weekend in Maine, declared I should self-publish and that she would do my marketing. I sent her the manuscript, and when she finished, she was even more enthusiastic about helping me. You would not be reading this book if not for her utter and complete belief in my little story.

Finally, an extra, extra special thanks to my husband, the *saint*. He gave me space to write, kept our boys from bugging me too much when I was on a roll, and encouraged me every step of the way. He listened to me read, was a sounding board for ideas, and never complained when I'd be up in the middle of the night, typing away on my laptop next to him like a fiend when I couldn't sleep. I truly couldn't have written this book without him (please don't tell him I said any of this, he'll be insufferable). There is more than a little of us in Robby and his husband's relationship, and I'm the luckiest girl in the world (though he's pretty fucking lucky too).

www.ingramcontent.com/pod-product-compliance
Lightning Source LLC
Chambersburg PA
CBHW021208310726
48971CB00006B/1494